Networked

L.K. Chapman

For my husband, Ashley
You always believe in me

2013

Chapter 1

It was around one in the morning on the sixteenth of February that the two years worth of work Dan and I had poured into Affrayed was taken away from us.

I wasn't too sure what was happening to start with; all that registered with me was that the code I'd just written was riddled with a mass of errors so numerous I could hardly be bothered to read them. Instead, I sat back in my chair, sighed and closed my eyes to rest them from the glare of the monitors. I was exhausted and I knew that what I'd just written was almost laughably awful. I would have been more surprised if the damn thing had managed to run.

'What's up?' Dan asked me.

I didn't open my eyes. They felt dry and itchy and it must have been about twelve hours since I'd had a proper break.

'I think I'm going to call it a night,' I said eventually. 'This is driving me mad.'

Dan laughed. 'Yeah, tell me about it,' he said, 'I swear I've actually managed to make things worse than they were before I started today.'

I rubbed my eyes and looked round at him. I wasn't too sure what he'd actually been doing the whole time since he'd shown up at the flat, but he'd barely moved from where he sat slumped on the sofa, the glow from his laptop making his face a ghostly bluish-white in the semi-darkness.

'Maybe you should stop too,' I said.

'Nah,' Dan said, 'it's early for me. You should get some sleep though. You look like hell.'

I laughed, though to be honest, Dan didn't look much better himself. Not that he ever exactly looked healthy. He ate a lot of crap but not much in the way of proper meals and when I looked at him it made me think of how you get these people who are skinny on the outside and "fat" on the inside, because their diets are so bad that they still end up getting heart attacks or whatever. Dan was skinny as anything. Even his face was sharp and angular, accentuated further by his short, very neat, dark hair and rectangular glasses.

I was about to turn my computer off when the enormous list of errors caught my attention again. There really were a lot. All I'd done was tweak a few things to try and fix a relatively minor bug and while I knew I hadn't exactly made a great job of it, there was no way it was as bad as all this.

'What is it?' Dan said.

'I don't know,' I said. 'See what you make of it.'

Dan shifted his laptop off his lap and came to stand beside me, drumming his fingers against the desk while he cast his eyes over the huge list of errors.

'Yep,' he said when he'd finished reading, 'looks like a total nightmare.'

'Yeah,' I said, 'but look at all this.' I pointed at a whole cluster of similar errors. 'It's like a load of the files are missing.'

Dan read the error messages, his head cocked slightly to one side, a little line between his eyebrows. He didn't know a great deal about coding, but he knew enough to know what he was looking at.

'So, what are you saying?' he said, 'they're not missing, are they? You must have changed the file names or something.'

'I haven't,' I said. 'I haven't touched any of that stuff.'

Dan looked at me as though he thought I was losing it. 'Seriously, you should just get some sleep mate,' he said, 'go and join Lily. She seemed kind of down earlier. I'm alright on my own.'

'Lily went to bed hours ago,' I said, 'she'll be fast asleep by now.'

I said it more harshly than I intended, but I wasn't really thinking about Lily, or Dan. The more I looked at the errors, the more sure I became that something was wrong. In the end, I closed everything I was working on and opened up the folder where all my work was supposed to be.

'That's not enough,' Dan said when he saw the contents of the folder. Then he pointed urgently at the screen. 'One of them just disappeared!' he said, 'right there, I swear, it just-'

I watched where he was pointing and another file vanished.

Then another, then another. They were vanishing faster than I could keep track of them and in total confusion I closed the window, as if not being able to see the files disappear would stop it from happening.

'What are you doing?' Dan said, 'open it again!'

I was so baffled by the whole thing that for a moment or two I seemed unable to do anything, but once I'd got my head together enough to try to reopen it, I simply couldn't. There weren't even any folders for Affrayed anymore. As far as I could see, every single scrap of work I'd ever done on the game was gone.

Dan ran over to his laptop and from the way he started saying, 'fuck, fuck, fuck, fuck,' it was pretty obvious that the same thing that had happened to my code was now happening to all his work on the game art, and although I rushed over to try to help, there was nothing I could do.

'What's happening?' Dan said, 'what the hell is happening?'

I tried to think. Everything on my computer seemed completely normal and untouched apart from my work on Affrayed. How could whatever it was that was doing this be so targeted? Why had it gone straight for the game on both my computer and Dan's laptop? I tried to make sense of it but Dan was driving me mad, he just kept trying to find his work over and over again, going about it with a kind of determined obsessiveness; repeatedly closing everything down, then opening it all up again and getting increasingly upset every time he saw it still wasn't there.

'Dan, please, stop doing that,' I said. 'I don't know what's happened but we've got backups. All we've lost is what we've been working on tonight and by the sound of it that might not be a bad thing.'

Dan stopped his searching for a moment, and then his face lit up. 'My computer,' he said, 'I'll call Robyn and get her to check it's alright.'

'It's half one in the morning,' I said.

Dan had already got his phone out, 'it's fine,' he said, 'she'll be up.'

'Well, presumably everything was fine when you left the house earlier,' I said, 'and if no one's turned your computer on...'

Dan looked torn by indecision. 'I've got to know,' he said finally, 'I just want to know my work is safe, somewhere.'

I left him to call his sister and turned my attention to my own backups of Affrayed. I had quite a few and I was pretty rigorous about having lots of copies of everything. At any rate, I took far more care over it than Dan did. His approach to most things in life was at best random and at worst utterly chaotic.

First of all I looked at my laptop, but it was hard to concentrate as Dan was talking in a very loud, clear voice, and from the frustrated expression on his face I guessed that Robyn must have been drinking.

'Dan, is this really the best time to-'

He held up his hand at me. 'No, Robyn,' he said with an exaggerated patience that told me he was getting angry, 'that's the stuff for DreamChase. I'm working on *Affrayed* now.'

I turned away from him and focussed my attention on finding Affrayed on my own laptop, but no matter how much I wanted to see it there, to see the game was safe, that everything was normal, that certainly wasn't what I found. There wasn't even a minute or two of the files disappearing like there had been on my computer. This time the files were just gone, like they'd been wiped the second I turned it on.

In the background, I could hear Dan desperately trying to make sense of what Robyn was telling him.

'Have you opened it?' he said, 'Robyn? Have you found all the Affrayed stuff? For God's sake, how many people are there? Robyn!'

'Tell her to turn it off,' I said to him. 'Tell her to turn it off, now.'

Dan started to rub his forehead as if he couldn't cope with the pressure of taking in what everybody was saying to him.

'What? Why?' he said with a puzzled frown.

'It's not on my laptop, either,' I said. 'It must have gone as soon as I turned it on.'

But I'd lost his attention as he focussed on Robyn again. I could hear all the background noise down the phone even from where I was standing. It sounded like Robyn had thrown a full on house party.

All of a sudden, the colour drained from Dan's face and he staggered over to the sofa and sat down heavily on the arm.

'No,' he said. 'No. No.'

He looked up at me, his eyes black and intense behind his glasses.

'You've still got other backups, haven't you? With some of my stuff on as well?'

'Yeah,' I said.

'Well, check them then.'

'I'm not sure,' I said, 'I don't know whether I should-'

'What's wrong with you?' he said, 'just check them.' He cradled his head in his hands and his panic was infectious. I found myself feverishly checking the last few places Affrayed was supposed to be, hoping to find some remnant of over two years hard work, but there was nothing. Every place Affrayed should be was either blank or corrupted.

'What have you done?' Dan said when he realised. 'What have you *done?*'

'I haven't done anything!' I said.

'You must have done. It was fine earlier. It was fine an hour ago. Until you started messing with things it-'

'This has nothing to do with what I was doing tonight!' I said, 'what the hell is it you think I've done? I couldn't make this happen even if I wanted to.'

Dan was on his feet now, desperate for someone to blame.

'You're the one who wrecked all the back-ups,' he said.

I stared at him. 'Are you actually being serious?' I said, 'you made me check them all, I knew it wasn't a good idea-'

'Well, why did you do it then?'

I was so angry with him that I barely knew what to say, but then the door to the living room opened and Lily burst in. She ran straight over to where Dan and I stood arguing next to my desk and she tried to pull me away like she thought we were going to start fighting or something.

'What's going on?' she asked, her eyes huge with fear, 'why are you shouting at each other? Nick, what's going on?'

Chapter 2

Both of us stared at Lily, temporarily silenced. She looked small and lost, orangey eyes bright with emotion and her chestnut curls tumbling in two long curtains right down to her waist. She'd clearly been woken up by our argument and was still dressed in cream pyjamas covered all over with a pattern of pink roses, her bare feet in a pair of oversized fluffy slippers.

My immediate impulse was to remove her from the situation, so I put my arm round her and tried to steer her back towards the door.

'It's okay, Lily,' I said, 'just go back to bed.'

Lily looked round over her shoulder at Dan and tried to push me away from her.

'What's happening?' she asked me. 'I don't understand. You're frightening me.'

'Everything's fine,' I said quickly, 'it's nothing to worry about,'

Lily succeeded in getting away from me and she stood with her eyes flicking between the two of us.

'Stop trying to lie to me,' she said, 'I know something's happened, why won't you tell me what it is?'

She looked quite fierce all of a sudden and I realised it was stupid to expect her to leave us to it, but I didn't want to tell her about it like this. I wanted her to go back to bed, go back to sleep, or even better to have never woken up in the first place.

As it turned out, I didn't need to find the words to tell her because Dan did it for me.

'We've lost all our work on Affrayed,' he said.

'Dan, for God's sake-' I said.

'Well we have, haven't we?' he said, 'she's going to find out sooner or later.'

'You can't have done,' Lily said, her eyes wide with shock, 'Nick, what's he talking about?'

'It's true,' I said quietly, 'something's happened to-'

6

Lily was shaking her head vigorously. 'No,' she said. 'I don't believe you. This is some sort of joke.'

'It's not a joke,' I said.

Her eyes searched my face. 'I don't understand,' she said, 'how could it have gone? What's happened to it?'

I watched her helplessly, unable to explain. What had happened was so terrible it was like it wouldn't even fit in my head, my mind skipped around all over the place, the loss of the game excruciatingly painful one second then almost forgotten the next as I went into some sort of denial. I could barely begin to find the words.

'I'll sort it out,' I said without thinking, 'there has to be a way. I'll get it back, I'll redo it. It's fine. It's all fine.'

'I thought you said it was gone. I thought you said it was all lost?'

Lily looked across at Dan, who was perched on the end of my desk, his head in his hands, rocking backwards and forwards. As if he felt her eyes on him, he sat up abruptly, face full of despair.

'What are we going to do Nick?' he said. 'I can't do the work again. I just... I can't. It'll break me. It'll fucking break me.'

Both of them were staring at me, desperate for an answer, and my inability to provide one began to make me angry.

'I don't know what we're going to do,' I said. 'What can we do? Without the game we're finished. All of it. It's over. Maybe it's just as fucking well.'

I stormed out, but Lily followed me into the bedroom, her eyes brimming over with tears.

'You don't mean that,' she said. 'Tell me you don't mean it.'

She tried to grab hold of my arm but I shook her away and sat down on the edge of the bed, while she stood awkwardly in front of me, twisting her hair round her fingers.

'How did this happen?' she asked quietly.

'I don't know.'

'Was it a virus or something?'

'I don't know.'

'Isn't there anything you can-'

'Lily, I don't know, okay? I don't know what's happened, I don't know what I'm going to do, but there's no way I'm re-doing all that work. Absolutely no way.'

Lily sat down beside me and tentatively reached out to place her hand on my leg.

'I know it feels that way now, but you could do it again, couldn't you? It would be quicker second time round, surely, and I'd help you as much as I could-'

'How could you possibly help me?' I said.

Lily snatched her hand away from me and her voice broke a little as she spoke. 'The same way I always do, supporting and encouraging you, listening to you talking about Affrayed every hour of every day, not complaining when you never come to bed the same time as me, finding the money to pay the rent and the bills and-'

I was finding it hard to listen to her. In my head all I had was memories of the work I'd done on Affrayed, all the complicated problems I'd ironed out, all the time I'd spent getting tiny little details in the game to be exactly the way I'd wanted them. I couldn't imagine having even the tiniest amount of enthusiasm or motivation to do it again for a second time, all the excitement would be gone from the process and everything I did would be painful and grudging.

'I can't do all that programming again,' I said, 'I actually can't. It'll be... harrowing.'

Lily lifted up the hem of her pyjama top to wipe her eyes with it.

'More harrowing than giving up on Affrayed and your business?' she asked. 'DAWN Industries is your life and making games is the only thing you've ever wanted to do.'

I couldn't think how to answer. Not carrying on was unthinkable and carrying on was equally as unthinkable; the idea of sitting down at my desk and starting from scratch was like a nightmare. I was sure that if I attempted it I would literally go mad.

'Lily,' I said, 'I can't...' but I wasn't sure what specific thing I even wanted to tell her I couldn't do. I couldn't do any of it. I couldn't do this situation, full stop.

Lily looped her arms around my neck and rested her forehead against my hair. For a while we stayed that way, her body little comfort in the face of such a horrible situation. Dan and I had built up DAWN Industries from nothing. Sure, it wasn't all that successful, but it was ours and one day we'd hoped to make it work. I listened to Lily's soft breathing and I tried to pretend it wasn't real, that Affrayed was there just as it had ever been, incomplete and imperfect as it was.

All of a sudden the door slammed open, jolting us from our thoughts.

'Guys, come on!' Dan said, buzzing with excitement.

'What?' I said.

Dan gestured madly for us to follow him. 'Come on,' he said again, 'it's coming back!'

Chapter 3

Initially I thought he must be losing it, but it turned out he was absolutely right and the files were pouring back in as quickly as they had left.

'Where are they coming from?' Lily said to nobody in particular.

'I don't know,' Dan said, 'but it's all coming back. All our work. It's going to be okay!'

Lily laughed in relief and out the corner of my eye I saw her and Dan throw their arms around each other.

'Is it all there now?' Lily asked me when she'd calmed down a little, 'is everything back like it was?'

I scrolled through the files and they seemed to be in order. But I couldn't get my head round what I'd seen- all the files just returning like that. Where on earth had they come from? How had it happened?

'Open something,' Dan said.

I opened one of the files and it took me no more than a few seconds to establish two important things. Firstly, this was our game. I could remember writing this part of it. Secondly, what I was looking at was not as simple as our work returned to us in its original form.

'Is it okay?' Lily asked, 'is that Affrayed?'

'Yeah...' I said.

'Yeah... but?' Dan asked.

I sat back in the chair and pulled my hand through my hair as I frowned at the code on the screen.

'But?' Dan asked me again.

'Well, I didn't write this,' I said at length.

Dan leaned forward and looked closely at the screen.

'Yeah, you did,' he said, 'that's Affrayed. It's our game.'

'Yes,' I said, 'but this isn't my code. Look at it. What I wrote wasn't like this. This is far too neat, far too clean. It's too... it's so... *elegant*.'

Who was I kidding? It was too bloody good. I mean, I know what I'm doing, don't get me wrong, but this had been written by a real expert.

I looked over my shoulder at Dan and Lily and saw they were sharing a confused expression.

'What are you saying, Nick?' Lily asked, 'either it's your code for Affrayed or it isn't, surely?'

'Yeah,' Dan said, 'maybe you just made a better job of it than you thought you did.'

I sighed quietly. I knew they didn't believe me but code probably all looked about the same to them, especially to Lily. But I knew what my work looked like and this wasn't it. I decided I'd look at another file to see whether that was the same, but once I went back into the folder again I noticed that in amongst names I recognised there was other stuff. There were far more files than there had been originally.

'What is all that?' Dan asked as he noticed too.

Tentatively, I opened one of the strange new files and what I saw was, quite frankly, incredible.

'What's wrong with it?' Lily asked, 'it's all messed up.'

Had the other code not been such high quality, that probably would have been my conclusion too because what I was looking at certainly appeared to be nonsense- it was full of random characters, completely unintelligible. But I felt sure it was far from nonsense.

'Yeah,' Dan agreed with Lily, 'that's not even code is it?'

'It's been obfuscated,' I said.

'It's been what?' Lily asked.

Dan started drumming his fingers against the desk again as he looked at it. 'You think so?' he said when he'd studied it a little, 'it's one hell of a good job if it is.'

'What are you talking about?' Lily said.

'Somebody's deliberately made this hard to read,' I explained, 'logically, it's all valid code, but they've put all this other crap in so an actual person can't make any sense of it.'

'Why would somebody do that?'

'Damned if I know,' I said, 'I mean, there are reasons for doing it, some people even do it for fun-'

'Run it,' Dan said eagerly, 'let's find out what it does.'

'Wait,' Lily said, 'if you don't know what it does, is it a good idea to run it? What if it does something bad or it wrecks your computer or something?'

Dan laughed without humour, 'what's the worst that can happen?' he said, 'we've already lost our game and had it replaced with God knows what. That's about as bad as it gets.'

'I know,' Lily said, 'but isn't there any way you could get some idea what it is before you run it? Nick, can you do that?'

I looked at the code and thought about what she'd said. She had a point- there was no way I could be certain that the code was just an innocent piece of our game. For all I knew it could do anything. But I was curious. If I was right, and it really was valid programming, then it had been done by somebody with extraordinary skill, too much skill for me to contemplate spending a quick few minutes trying to decipher it. If I wanted to see what it did any time soon, I had to just take my chances. And although I agreed it was suspicious, and I was nervous, I still thought the most likely thing we'd see would be our game. After all, the code I'd been able to read had formed part of Affrayed, so it stood to reason all the rest of the files would be part of it too. Of course, even if it *was* the game that didn't necessarily mean we were safe. There could still be something else going on in the background; some hidden, malicious little bit of code, but I was prepared to take that risk.

I waited anxiously for the program to start, holding my breath, hoping for it to be okay, hoping for it to be Affrayed, and I wasn't disappointed. In fact, any fears I had were instantly forgotten as instead I sat speechless, stunned into silence by what I was seeing.

It was the game. There was no doubt about that. But I suppose I thought that if we were to see the game we'd see it as I knew it- the old version with all its problems and work still to be done- options that when you clicked on them didn't do anything yet, or where the art was missing because Dan hadn't finished it, bits that were buggy, in need of attention. In short, the version of Affrayed I was expecting was more like a giant to-do list than a videogame.

But the version of Affrayed I saw wasn't a to-do list. It was not under development. It was finished, and it was beautiful.

The title screen and menus alone were enough for Lily to say 'wow,' and for Dan to slap his hand against the desk and say, 'fucking yes!' while I stared at it all in open-mouthed astonishment. Everything about it was so slick and polished, but not in a characterless way, it just had the kind of effortlessly beautiful design that looks simple but takes a lot of hard work to achieve. But if the look of Affrayed was excellent, the gameplay was off the scale. I found myself totally immersed, slipping immediately into that state of being at one with the game, of feeling in control and competent and experienced- yet also challenged and excited. I felt like I was at risk when I played it, yet I also felt it was within my grasp to beat it.

I'd almost forgotten Dan and Lily were sitting beside me until Dan said, 'it's like they reached into our heads and made it real.'

I knew exactly what he meant. At its heart, Affrayed wasn't a particularly complicated concept- it was almost like a big game of hide-and-seek, where players stalked each other through convoluted and confusing spaces until they were the last one left standing. But what we'd spent a lot of time on was how to bring it to something beyond that. The game wasn't just about finding and killing everybody as fast as you could, a specific player would be allocated as your first target and once you'd dispensed with them you progress to hunting the player they were targeting and on it goes, gradually becoming more and more intense as the number of remaining players decreases. Everything we did was designed to increase the sense of uneasiness, fear and paranoia. We wanted to make people's hearts beat faster, get them jumping at shadows. All the different threads that together made up the completed game had to work together to further that vision, give it a presence, an atmosphere.

What I was playing wasn't even the truest experience of Affrayed, as it was really supposed to be played online against other players and all I was doing was playing against the computer. But it didn't matter. I could already see it was perfect.

'It's finished,' Lily said softly, 'it's completely finished.'

With difficultly, I tore myself away from the game and pushed the keyboard and mouse over to Dan, who immediately took over from me.

He shook his head several times as he played, eyes fixed on the screen.

'How is this...' he said at one point, 'I mean, I don't even...'

'I know,' I said.

We played for hours, taking in every tiny detail of Affrayed, while Lily watched silently at my side.

'Here,' I said to her when I remembered she was there, 'why don't you play?'

Lily started to get up to swap places with me and then changed her mind. 'I'm awful at this sort of game,' she said.

'Go on, Lily,' Dan said, 'you should try it.'

Lily hovered halfway out of her chair and in the end I made the decision for her by getting up myself.

'What am I supposed to do?' she asked.

Dan was about to tell her but I stopped him.

'You've been watching us play,' I said, 'just try it. I think you'll pick it up pretty quickly.'

Lily rolled her eyes at me, though the corner of her mouth was turned up in a little smile.

'This isn't fair,' she said, 'I hate it when you watch me play things, I feel like I'm in an exam.'

She was happy enough to start playing though, too curious to wait any longer, and watching her was fascinating. I always have enjoyed seeing her play games because she often reacts so differently to Dan and me and finds certain games more intuitive than others, but instead of her behaviour in Affrayed showing me design faults as it sometimes did in other games, it just showed me more about how the game was right. Because she could play it. Even though it was the type of game she tended to struggle with, she picked it up easily. She could understand the spaces and move around them, she could react quickly and in the way she wanted to, whereas normally she'd end up in a blind panic and forget how to do anything. It wasn't that she was bad at videogames full stop- she could play some types of games easily as well as I could- but up until now games like Affrayed had seemed like an enigma to her.

As she sat hunched forward at the desk, Dan and I exchanged a quick glance and I saw in his face exactly the same thoughts that I had. Not only was Affrayed beautifully designed and beautiful to look at, it had managed to achieve something extraordinary in that it transcended whatever barrier similar games normally put up for Lily. It seemed impossible that something the right level of challenge for me could be the right level of challenge for her. But it was. It was like the game was universally easy to grasp; like it was just so intuitive that the little issues of learning how to play and putting what you'd learnt into practice were minimised almost out of existence. One thing was for sure, Dan and I could not have made it. We could never have made it. We could have done a good job, maybe even an excellent job, but never in our lifetimes could we have managed to put together a version of Affrayed quite as incredible as this one we'd been given.

Chapter 4

When the room was lit up with daylight streaming through the curtains and I started to hear cars in the street outside Lily suddenly sat bolt upright and turned to check the clock in the kitchen.

'Shit,' she said as she pushed her chair back.

I looked round at the clock myself and saw it was only half past six.

'It's not that late,' I said, 'stay a bit longer.'

'We've got wedding flowers to deliver,' Lily said, 'I need to get ready.'

She stayed on the spot though, looking from us to the clock, eyes huge in her little face. It was obvious she wanted to stay with us and play Affrayed.

'Can't you say you're sick or something?' Dan asked, 'we need you to stay here so we can talk about... this,' he inclined his head towards the screen where Lily's game of Affrayed was still going.

Lily started to almost bounce up and down on the spot, raising her heels out of her fluffy slippers then back in again.

'I can't,' she said, 'I can't.'

'Not even for one day?' Dan asked.

'No,' Lily said. She looked so torn that I stood up and put my arm around her shoulders.

'Come on,' I said, 'you've never skipped a day's work in your life before. Mum'll get Kimberley to cover you.'

Lily buried her hands in her hair for a second and then made up her mind.

'I've got to go in,' she said, 'it's Kim's day off, it's not fair.' She looked longingly towards the game again before rushing out of the room and a minute or two later I heard the shower running.

'Shame she can't stay,' Dan said.

'Yeah,' I said.

'If we release Affrayed,' Dan said slowly, 'you know, *this* version of Affrayed, it would change a lot of stuff for us.'

'I know,' I said.

'Because it would do well. I mean, we know it would do well just from the few hours we've been playing it. Hell, we'd hardly need to even *test* the damn thing. I could get away from mum and Robyn, you and Lily could afford to rent somewhere bigger, or even buy. We could-'

'We didn't make it, Dan,' I said.

Dan looked down at the desk. 'I know.'

'We can't sell a game we didn't make. If it got out it would ruin our reputation.'

'But Affrayed was our idea,' he said, 'whoever made this stole *our* idea.'

'I know, but-'

'Who did make it anyway?' he said, 'why would somebody do that?'

He closed Lily's game and went back to the main menu, hovering the mouse over the bottom option, "credits", and I was amazed I hadn't thought of looking at them sooner.

He paused before he clicked it though and looked across at me as if waiting for permission.

'Well, we've got to know,' I said.

Lily came back into the kitchen while we were looking at the credits and she'd changed into her work clothes, black trousers and a black polo-neck with "Winterbourne Flowers" embroidered in gold, swirly letters. She stood behind us and looked over our shoulders as she piled her hair up on top of her head and secured it into a lopsided bun.

'The credits!' she said. 'What do they say, who did this?'

Dan and I showed her what we had already discovered.

'I don't get it,' she said, 'those are your names.'

'Exactly,' I said, 'and that's it.'

Lily frowned and tried to tuck some loose curls up into the bun. 'I don't understand,' she said.

'Neither do we,' I said.

'God, I don't want to go,' she sighed, but then she took a deep breath. 'Text me if anything else happens,' she said, 'I'll get back as soon as I can, I promise.'

She turned to leave but I suddenly thought of something and caught her arm.

'Nick,' she said, 'I've got to go.'

'I know,' I said, 'look, just... don't mention anything to mum about this. I don't feel like I want anybody to know.'

When she'd gone Dan and I carried on staring at the credits as if by doing so we might make some new information appear.

'What is this?' he asked me, 'I mean, seriously, what the literal fuck is this?'

'I don't know.'

'Do you think Lily's right and the code does something malicious?'

I shrugged. 'It's possible. But even if it does it still doesn't make much sense. Whoever is behind this has put an incredible amount of work into the game. They couldn't have done this overnight, it would take ages. And if you wanted to hide something nasty why put it in something this complex? It's a very strange thing to do.'

'Well, they don't want to take any credit for what they've made, that's for sure,' Dan said. We looked back at the screen again in silence, gazing at our names and wondering what it meant. The whole thing was so bizarre. It wasn't even as if they had just left the credits how they were originally- Dan and I hadn't even made them yet. Whoever it was had purposefully created them to say that the game was made by DAWN Industries, by me and Dan.

'There's got to be an answer somewhere,' I said, 'maybe there's something within the game, or online, or-'

'In all that messed up code?' Dan suggested.

'Yeah,' I said, sighing inwardly. Going through it would be a nightmare, but I was going to have to try.

'We need to go over everything,' I said, 'everything we were given last night, everything people have said online about Affrayed, anyone who's making anything similar.'

Dan groaned and closed his eyes for a moment.

'Unless you've got any better ideas?' I said.

Dan was silent for a little while longer then he appeared to regain some energy. 'Alright,' he said, 'let's do it.'

Dan retrieved his laptop from the sofa and started searching through comments on our website and social networking, while I opened all the files containing the obfuscated code. It both fascinated and disturbed me. Several years of programming experience, a degree in computer science and an MSc in software engineering were nothing against the kind of mind that had written this code. They were way, way beyond me. It was hopeless.

'Anything?' Dan asked me when we were several hours and cups of coffee into the day.

'No. You?'

'Same.'

Dan stopped looking at his own laptop and watched what I was doing for a while.

'You understand any of it?' he asked me.

'Not really,' I said, 'like you said before, it's one hell of a good job.'

'So, I was thinking,' he said, 'do you reckon they did it because they don't want us to know how they made the game so good?'

'That's one option. But if you can code this well, you'd just make your own game. Why hijack somebody else's, make it completely awesome, let them take the credit for it, but- wait- it's okay because you've made it so no one knows how you did it? No. It doesn't make sense. There's something we're not seeing here.'

I got up and wandered over to the kitchen. I didn't even want any more coffee but I found myself filling the kettle anyway, as though doing something else might jog my mind and help me work it out.

'So, what happens if you just...' Dan said and I turned round in time to see that he was going to try and alter something in the code.

'Don't touch it!' I said.

'I was only going to delete a couple of random-'

'Seriously, Dan, I've been tweaking little bits of it all morning and as soon as I alter it it totally breaks the game. It's insane. Some of the things I did really shouldn't have had any effect but it's like it knows I've touched it or something.'

Dan moved his fingers away from the keyboard and watched me get a couple of mugs out of the cupboard.

'Is this really happening, do you think?'

'What do you mean?'

'I mean, what's actually more likely? This version of Affrayed that's turned up or that we've gone insane?'

I laughed. 'What, all three of us? You, me and Lily, you think we've just... hallucinated this?'

'It makes about as much sense as anything else I've thought of.'

I walked back over with the coffee and even though it was boiling hot Dan gulped down a couple of large mouthfuls without thinking and then pulled a face.

'If nothing else, I think we can be pretty sure this is real,' I said, 'and there'll be a reason for it, it's just a case of finding it.'

...

But by the time Lily got home we still hadn't uncovered even the tiniest clue as to who had made the new version of Affrayed and were doing little more than throwing increasingly unlikely theories around and getting more and more confused.

'Has anything happened?' Lily asked as she rushed over to us, 'have you found out who did it?'

'No,' I said, as she wrapped her arms briefly around my neck.

'Tell me everything,' she said, dropping her handbag onto the floor and plonking herself down next to me at the desk.

'There's not much to tell. I looked at the code, we've played the game some more, checked if anyone's said anything online and so far there's been nothing.'

Lily's eyes flicked between me and Dan.

'Then what are you going to do? Are you going to release it?'

'Lily, we can't,' I said, 'you know we can't.'

Lily looked at Dan.

'What do you think?'

'Nick's right,' Dan said after a pause, 'we can't, not really.'

'You don't sound completely sure.'

'It's complicated,' Dan said.

Lily looked down at her lap and I swear I saw a little of the colour drain out of her rosy cheeks.

'What is it?' I asked her.

'Nothing. I was just thinking today how good it would be if you released it, you know, if you made a bit of money.'

She reached up and started pulling at her hair until it all came undone and she shook it out over her shoulders.

'Lily, you understand, don't you?' I said.

'No. Not really. I don't understand how somebody could come along, destroy your work and replace it with theirs and we just have to suffer for it.'

I heard Dan's chair scrape over the floor and he stood up.

'Why don't I give you some space?' he suggested, 'I can go out for a bit. I'll grab us some food or something.'

'Thanks, Dan,' I said.

Once he'd gone, Lily wandered into the bedroom to get changed so I followed her and sat in silence as she pulled off her work clothes and changed into a pair of jeans and a cream Fair Isle jumper. I hoped that she'd tell me what was on her mind but instead she started stroking the glossy leaves of a large peace lily on top of the chest of drawers.

'Talk to me,' I said.

'I don't know where to start.'

'It doesn't matter.'

Lily squeezed a leaf between her finger and thumb. 'I will,' she said, 'just let me get things straight in my head.'

Finally, she sat down beside me on the bed and from the way she took a deep breath I knew she had a great deal to say.

'When I was working today, all I could think about was how things would be if you released that incredible version of Affrayed, about if you made some real money so we could all move on with our lives,' she said all in a rush. 'You know this situation can't carry on. Dan needs to get away from living with his mum and Robyn, it's driving him insane. You know how angry and upset he is when he shows up here after they've had one of their fights. I worry about him because it can't be healthy to live somewhere that makes you feel like that. Then I thought about us and I thought about how we could afford to live somewhere bigger and you wouldn't have to work in the same room where we eat and relax and we'd have so much more space and I could... we could have a baby.'

'Lily-'

She held her hands up. 'Please, just let me finish explaining. I've tried not to go on at you about babies and stuff because I knew nothing could happen right now, but when I started thinking about how successful this version could be it all seemed so real. Everything has been so extreme over the past few years. I think... I just want things to change. To be more like a proper family.'

She'd worked herself up so much that at the end of her speech she started crying.

'You don't understand,' she said.

'I do understand,' I said. 'I know you want to get a bigger place and have a baby, I want those things too.'

'But it's never going to *happen*, is it?' Lily said. 'I mean, what are you going to do now? Start a new game? Are we going to spend another three, four years with no money and barely enough time to even speak to each other?'

I looked at her in shock. I knew myself that I hadn't been giving her the amount of attention she deserved or even that I wanted to give her, but I thought by working hard trying to get the game done I was doing the right thing.

'Lily, why didn't you tell me you were feeling this way? I had no idea things were so bad.'

Lily fixed her eyes on her lap and wouldn't answer me. I nudged her leg with mine and she wiped some tears from her cheeks with the sleeve of her jumper.

'How long have you been feeling like this?' I asked her.

'A while. A long time. I don't know.'

'Then why didn't you tell me?'

'Because you're always too busy.'

I took her hands in mine to make sure I had her attention. 'Listen,' I said, 'I am *never* too busy for you to talk to me. Okay? Don't ever think that. If you got ill again because you thought I didn't have time for you I'd never forgive myself.'

Lily nodded and looked round at me, her tears making her eyes an intense coppery- gold.

'What do you want to happen, Lily?' I asked her.

'Well, what I wanted was for you and Dan to finish Affrayed yourselves and get all the success that you deserve but I can't see how that would happen now. I know what scares you about this version and it scares me too, but I think the alternative scares me even more.'

'The alternative being?'

'Like I said before. You start a new game, and we spend even longer in this sort of... limbo.'

'That won't happen,' I reassured her, 'I won't do that. Lily, I had no idea you were so unhappy. I don't have to carry on with DAWN at all if that's how you feel; I always said that if it started affecting our relationship then I'd stop. You just say the word and first thing tomorrow I'll start looking for a job.'

'But... Dan-' Lily said.

'Dan would understand. And I could earn decent money as a software engineer. If we're prepared to maybe move somewhere else in the country I could probably find something pretty quickly too.'

The more I thought about it, the more it made sense. There really was no way forward for DAWN that I could see. Either we released a game we hadn't made or we limped along until every last scrap of our money, patience and quality of life had gone.

Lily thought for a while, twisting her hands round in her lap.

'You'd hate it,' she said. 'All you've ever wanted to do is make games. I couldn't watch you go through the pain of giving it up.'

'Yes, but I don't want to watch you going through this pain now. My dream of making games isn't more important than you wanting to have a family and a better quality of life. I want things to improve too, but I want to do it right. Not with money from this new Affrayed. It's not honest and I can't do it.'

'I know,' Lily said, 'deep down I always knew you wouldn't release it. It's not like I even want you to, necessarily, it was just that for a moment it seemed like an answer to everything.'

Chapter 5

Dan arrived back half an hour or so later, a waft of vinegary chip-shop smell around him as he came inside. We ate together in silence, each of us lost in our own thoughts and although several times I thought Dan or Lily were on the verge of speaking they always seemed to decide against it.

'So, what now?' I asked when I was done with eating and the sight of all the fat, soggy chips was beginning to make me feel sick.

Dan and Lily looked up when I spoke, but they didn't know what we should do anymore than I did. Dan looked exhausted, purplish shadows beginning to bloom around his eyes, while Lily had retreated into herself, just a curtain of hair and a blank face.

The thing was, the more I considered our options the less catastrophic the risk to our reputation seemed. Perhaps there would be no consequences. Perhaps all that would happen would be success; success enough that we could quickly get started on a new game, a game that *would* be our work, and would wipe the slate clean.

Abruptly, Lily scrunched up the remains of the bag of chips.

'I hate whoever's done this to you,' she said. 'How could they? How could somebody have so little respect for another person's work?'

'We could never have made Affrayed this well,' Dan said. 'Compared to what they've done, maybe our work wasn't worth all that much respect.'

'That's total rubbish!' Lily said, 'both of you are incredibly talented, I-'

'I think we should release it,' I said.

Both of them turned to look at me in surprise.

'Nick, you don't have to do it because of what I said,' Lily said quickly, 'this is a big decision, you need to think it through.'

'I have thought it through. I say we give it a bit longer to try and figure out who did it or to let them get in contact with us. If nothing happens, we start promoting it, and in a few months or so, we launch it. It barely needs testing, I mean, it's flawless. We need to set the right tone for everything we say about it- play it down, let it speak for itself rather than taking too much credit. It'll be hard but it'll be doable. We stick it out, take the proceeds and put them into a new project. Nobody apart from us and whoever really made this thing actually knows about it. If we stay silent, all we have to hope is that they stay silent. It's a risk, but do we really have all that much to lose?'

Lily and Dan were listening to me intently, both looking far more at ease now I was telling them what we should do.

'Dan, what do you think?' I asked him.

Dan thought carefully for a moment and when he spoke his voice was firm.

'Yeah,' he said, 'I say go for it. It's our game. We didn't ask anybody to do this. We'll give it a week. If we haven't figured it out and nobody comes forward, then that's that. Other people would do the same. We were almost two thirds into making Affrayed, we laid all the groundwork, we thought it all out.'

'You deserve this,' Lily said. 'You've both worked so hard, it's about time you got something back.'

'Are we all in agreement then?' I asked and they both nodded.

'Okay,' I said, 'they've got one week. Then, as far as we're concerned, the game's ours.'

2007

Chapter 6

I cant take this anymore Nick, please please please if you love me why cant you make it go away

I sighed and put my phone back down on the desk in front of me. In her torment Lily often text, or phoned, or emailed me- desperate, heart-wrenching pleas for help or even just a bit of relief, but they were pleas I couldn't answer.

The phone vibrated again. I picked it up and opened a second message from her.

I've done something bad, youre going to be angry with me.

I slammed my phone down on the desk and took a deep breath. I wasn't actually angry with Lily, but I hated what she was doing to herself and I couldn't pretend otherwise. I desperately needed to get some work done on my dissertation, but Lily was clearly having a rough afternoon and now she'd started hurting herself there was little chance I was going to be able to concentrate. I replied asking where she was and when she said she was in the library too I shoved my laptop into my bag and went to find her.

She was on the floor above me, sitting alone at a table in the far corner, hunched over a textbook. She looked up when she heard my footsteps but didn't smile or acknowledge me, she just turned her head to stare out of the window where the light was fading and rain was beginning to hammer against the glass. I sat opposite her and followed her gaze, watching the people running around outside, wrestling with umbrellas blown inside out in the wind or huddled up into their coats.

'Do you want to see what I did?' Lily asked me.

'It's up to you,' I said, 'do you want to show me?'

I saw the corner of her mouth twitch a little as if she was trying not to smile. She almost never managed to show me her self-harm without smiling, or even worse, laughing. I knew it was a nervous thing, like giggling at a funeral, but I found it acutely unnerving.

Sure enough, by the time she'd pulled up the sleeve of her baggy grey hoodie to expose the pale skin of her arm and the angry red scratches across it her face had broken into a wide smile.

I ignored her expression and focussed on her arm. I knew which was the new cut. It was bright and fresh, a couple of perfectly spherical beads of blood rising from it.

'Oh, Lily,' I said, 'I wish you didn't do this.'

'Why not?' she asked, 'what do you care?'

'Of course I care,' I said. To show her that I did, I lifted her arm to my lips and kissed the place that she'd hurt herself while she looked at me as if I was slightly mad.

'You can't kiss this better,' she said. She snatched her arm away from me and pulled her sleeve back down again.

'Where did you do it?' I asked her, 'you only text me a few minutes ago.'

'In the toilets,' she said.

'Did it make you feel better?'

'Yes,' she said, sounding almost proud. She showed me the notebook she had in front of her and I saw that the first half of the page was covered in scrawling, chaotic handwriting dissolving gradually into scribble, while the second half- the half she was now working on- was neat and ordered. She was in the middle of copying a diagram out of the textbook and she'd made it look lovely, colouring in all the different bits with green, orange and pink pens.

'It helps me concentrate,' she said.

I carried on looking at her notes, from the disordered to the ordered with one quick slash of her skin. I couldn't deny that it was effective, in the short term at least.

'Lily,' I said softly, 'you can't hurt yourself to get through your degree. It's not sustainable- I mean, what are you going to do, cut yourself every single day?'

'No,' she said, 'I might have to do it more often than that.'

She didn't even look at me when she spoke, she just carried on copying the diagram, the movement of the pen on the page slow and meticulous.

I reached across the table to take her hand but she moved away from me.

'Stop it,' she said, 'I need to get this done. You know I need to get this done. Why are you interrupting me?'

So I sat and watched her work for a while and listened to the rain against the window. A few people came by to look for books on the tall shelves either side of us but nobody else sat down at the table and we were left in peace.

Even as I sat with her, I saw Lily's concentration waning. She worked slower and slower, reading the same sentence in the textbook repeatedly, tracing the words with her finger.

'I think you should have a break now,' I said.

Lily shook her head.

'You look tired,' I said, 'come on, come home with me. I'll cook you something.'

'No,' Lily said, 'I haven't done nearly enough, I...'

She stopped talking and instead began to dig her fingernails into the soft skin of her palms, pressing so hard that her knuckles turned white.

'Don't do that,' I said. I tried uselessly to prise her fingers back open again.

'Lily, please, stop it,' I said.

I pulled again at her fingers but with a sigh she released them herself and I briefly saw all the deep half moons on her palm before she picked her pen up and started writing again.

It took a further fifteen minutes or so before tears began to splash onto her notes and she accepted that she wasn't in a fit state to work.

'Just forget about it tonight,' I said as I helped her put all her books away. 'We'll have a relaxing evening together. I'll cook us something and you can have a break, then you can do your work tomorrow when you're feeling better.'

Lily frowned at me as she put the final book back on the shelf. 'I'm not going to feel any better tomorrow,' she said.

The rain had eased off a bit by the time we started walking back to my student house but Lily huddled up to me wearily, her every pace sluggish and effortful.

Not long after we got inside the rain began to fall in dense sheets, streaming down the kitchen window and making it hard to even speak. Lily seemed calmer inside the house and sat at the long breakfast bar in the middle of the room, watching as I cut up a big yellow pepper and defrosted a couple of chicken breasts in the microwave. For a while I thought perhaps we really would be able to have a nice evening together, that she'd let herself relax, but all that changed when one of my housemates turned up. She seemed to disappear into herself again, even physically hunching over as if to make herself small and inconspicuous. Carl still spotted her straight away though and said, 'hey, Lily.'

'Hi,' she said, in a little voice. She looked up at him briefly and I saw she was pulling the left sleeve of her hoodie down protectively over her cuts, clutching the cuff in her hand. Carl wasn't paying much attention to her though. He'd got soaked walking back and he was peeling off a beige jacket that looked like you could wring the water out of it.

'What are you cooking?' he asked me, as he hung his coat on the kitchen door handle. His arms were blotchy red from the cold and his straggly hair, normally a sandy blonde, was plastered over his face in long, dark ribbons.

'Curry,' I said.

He looked at me expectantly for a moment.

'Do you want some?' I asked.

He grinned. 'Great, thanks.'

'Me and Lily are probably going to eat in my room though,' I said, 'so, uh-'

Carl waved my explanation away, 'yeah, alright, I get it,' he said, 'you don't want me cramping your style.' He ran his hand through his sopping wet hair. 'I think I'm going to grab a shower. How long's it going to be?'

'Twenty minutes. Maybe thirty.'

He turned to leave but then looked across at Lily again.

'You and Sophie are still coming out with us on Friday, aren't you Lily?' he asked her.

'Yeah,' Lily said and she gave him a smile which I knew must be fake, but which was pretty damn convincing. 'I'm looking forward to it.'

Carl left and as I took another chicken breast out of the freezer Lily leapt down from her stool and ran across to me, her dainty patent red shoes making a pitter-patter sound on the lino. She looked cute in what she was wearing, the baggy hoodie reaching down almost to the hem of a denim miniskirt, her legs in a pair of thick, floral-patterned black tights.

'I don't want to go to Carl's birthday thing on Friday,' she said, 'I really, really don't want to.'

'I know Lily,' I said, as I took the original two chicken breasts out of the microwave to inspect their progress. 'But we've been over this. It's going to look really weird if you don't go.'

The chicken breasts had done their usual trick of being rock solid in places and cooked in others and I was trying to decide my next move but Lily was getting more and more agitated.

'Make it go away,' she said, 'please, Nick. I don't want to do it. I *can't* do it. Please think of something, please help me.'

Her eyes had filled up with tears and she was wringing her hands together in distress.

'I can't keep making up excuses why you can't go to things,' I said, 'I know it's hard but I'll be right by your side all night, there's nothing to worry about.'

Lily just stared at me and I watched as tears pooled at the bottom of her eyes, eventually swelling so much that they spilt out and trickled down her cheeks.

'It's making me cry,' she said, 'I shouldn't have to go to things that make me cry.'

I popped the chicken breasts back in the microwave and washed my hands, the sink so full of dirty dishes that to get my hands under the tap I had to move a saucepan and succeeded in slopping a load of grubby grey-brown water over the side and onto my feet.

'It'll be okay,' I said, 'all we're doing is going out for a pizza and then heading into town. Carl'll get drunk and make a prat of himself and then we'll go home. It'll be over before you know it.'

'But I don't like being around people,' Lily said, 'I used to, but... not anymore. I feel so trapped. I hate it. I hate it.'

I finished washing my hands and wiped them partially dry on

the front of my jeans. I was about to put my arm around her but she fixed her tortured eyes on me and I thought she'd probably push me away. 'Make it so I don't have to go,' she said, her voice beginning to carry the whine that went hand in hand with her depression talking.

'It's not going to help you to hide away, is it?' I said, 'people like you, they want to see you. They want to talk to you.'

'But I'm no *good* for that anymore,' Lily said. She caught hold of my arm in her desperation to get me to understand. 'I don't want to talk to people. I don't want to be around them. I just want to be left alone.'

'I don't think that's true,' I said.

She started to sort of moan incoherently and buried her hands in her hair. 'It is true,' she said, 'none of them want me. None of them like me. You don't even like me, you don't love me. I just embarrass you and wreck your life.'

This had gone far enough. I stopped cooking entirely and placed both my hands on Lily's shoulders to make sure she was concentrating.

'Lily,' I said, 'I want you to listen to me now, okay?'

She wouldn't look at me, she just stared down at her body, her curls falling forwards over her face. 'I'm no good for anybody,' she said, 'I'm just a stupid, ugly, useless, horrible, selfish-'

'Lily, look at me.'

Finally, she raised her eyes to mine.

'I want you to stop this. You're not any of those things you said. It's silly to talk like that. And as for me, I love you and I'm not going to let you say otherwise, okay?'

Lily carried on staring at me with something like defiance, or perhaps it was just scepticism.

'I know you don't want to go out on Friday,' I said, my voice a little softer, 'but it'll be over before you know it and it's days away yet. Let's just forget about it. Right now, everything is fine.'

'No it isn't,' she said, 'nothing is fine. Everything is just completely shit.'

'No it isn't. Say something good.'

She shook her head.

'Say something good,' I repeated, 'anything,'

'There isn't anything good.'

'I know that's not really what you think. You've been happy before. I've seen you happy.'

She took my hands off her shoulders and made towards the door.

'Something good,' she said, 'well, maybe I'll die in my sleep tonight. That'd be good.' She gave me a cold smile, and left me to cook on my own.

...

When we'd finished eating, I tried again to get Lily to admit she could remember times she'd been happy, but she wasn't having any of it. Then I had a sudden flash of inspiration and I grabbed my laptop.

'What are you doing?' Lily asked.

'I'm going to see how many people have played Cactustrophe,' I said.

Lily sighed as if she wasn't interested. But I was pretty sure she was, and when she saw the crazy green, yellow and blue title screen of the game I saw the corner of her mouth twitch slightly.

'Look how many people have played, Lily,' I said, 'thousands. And it's still rated almost four out of five.'

Lily made a little noise in her throat as she tried to dismiss it. But I knew she'd been happy when we'd made Cactustrophe together.

It had started out just as me telling her about the process of making games- about design and mechanics and how to make games "fun". But she'd been so fascinated by the whole thing that in the end I'd thought, screw it, why not just make a game with her?

Cactustrophe wasn't really representative of the sort of games I wanted to make in the future, but it had been a lot of fun and working with Lily had actually been a pretty good collaboration. Normally I could only make games that weren't visually that exciting, but Lily could draw cute little cartoony things quite well-certainly far better than I could. I can't remember exactly how the idea had come about, but we'd ended up with a game where flying psychedelic beetles had to steal miniature fruits from between the spines of cacti and the jaws of venus flytraps. The game had done pretty well amongst similar offerings on a free games website, and since the rating of almost four out of five had come from the players themselves, I think it would be fair to say it was a success. I was sure if anything could make her crack a smile it would be thinking about Cactustrophe.

'Come on, Lily,' I said, 'you have to admit you were happy back then.'

She twisted her hands in her lap and wouldn't meet my eyes.

'I was happy then,' she said very quietly, 'but I'm not anymore. And I never will be.'

'That's not true,' I said, 'you'll get better. This depression, it's just difficult right now, but you'll beat it and we'll have a wonderful and happy life together.'

Lily wasn't buying it though. Instead she got up from the desk where we'd been sitting, lay down on the unmade bed in the corner of my room and wrapped the duvet around herself.

I sat down next to her and touched her shoulder.

'You will get better, Lily,' I said.

She shook her head.

'You will,' I repeated.

She was silent for a while and I saw that tears were beginning to spill from the corners of her eyes and run down the sides of her face into her hair.

'Tell me a story,' she said eventually.

'A story?'

'Yeah.'

'What kind of story?'

'Just a story.'

I thought for a while. I didn't really know what to say, so I just began and made it up as I went along.

'Once upon a time, there were two people called Nick and Lily.'

She looked up at me. 'It's about us?'

'Yeah,' I said.

Before I could continue, she seized on this and twisted it. 'And Nick and Lily loved each other very much,' she said, 'so Nick didn't want Lily to suffer anymore, because she was in so much pain.'

I knew what was coming.

'No, Lily,' I said, 'I thought you wanted me to tell the story.'

'So one day,' she continued, 'Nick helped Lily to die, and he held her while she slipped away, and she felt safe because he was there, and Nick was happy because she wasn't in pain anymore and he could get on with his life.'

'No.' I said firmly, 'Nick knew that Lily would get better. So he worked really hard and sold loads of games, then him and Lily got married and they lived in a house together and-'

'-and was Lily okay?' she asked, and I was surprised at the sudden, childish hope in her voice.

'Yeah,' I said, 'she was more than okay.'

'Did they live in the middle of a field full of flowers?' Lily asked. For a moment I thought she was making fun of me and I felt stung, but then I realised she'd actually become quite captivated with this fairytale reality, taking comfort in something so simple.

'Yeah, if you like,' I said. I was so pleased that I'd managed to distract her that I hurriedly tried to think of more detail to keep her interest.

'What kind of flowers?' I asked.

'Sunflowers,' she said, 'and daffodils. And we'll grow strawberries, and pumpkins.'

I laughed. 'Okay, that's what we'll do. And you'll never have to worry about anything, because I'll always be there.'

'So is Lily happy?'

'Yeah,' I said, 'she's really happy.' I paused for a moment, wondering what would be the best kind of life for her. But I wasn't too sure, because she never really talked about what she wanted, only what she didn't want. So I started with that.

'Because Nick never makes her do anything she doesn't want to,' I said. 'He makes games, and Lily does whatever she most wants to do, and he supports her.'

'You're making me go to Carl's party and I don't want to do that,' she said, 'so you're lying. It's all lies.'

I sighed. 'Lily-'

'I don't have anything I want to do,' she continued sadly and I realised I'd completely blown it, 'apart from die. That's my dream.'

'You will get better,' I said, trying to convince myself as much as her.

'When?' she asked.

'Soon.'

'How can you know that?'

'I just do. This is a tiny little bad patch, and then we'll have a wonderful life together.'

'Do you promise?'

What a question.

'Yeah,' I said, 'I promise.'

2013

Affrayed is quite simply brilliant.
Gamingchoice 10/10

Without a doubt, Affrayed will be the best game you'll play this year.
Euroreview 100/100

A compelling, addictive and beautiful game.
Onlyvideogamer 98/100

From the creators of DreamChase, a game you just won't want to wake up from.
Indiehit A++

Affrayed is an astonishing achievement.
Perimeter Magazine 9.9/10

Almost unbelievably good.
Gamesnight A++

An incredible, immersive experience.
Pixellated 10/10

This will take over your life.
Geekspawn 5/5

Superbly well designed down to the smallest detail, everything about Affrayed is excellent.
Gamesreport 9.9/10

Chapter 7

'I always said there was money to be made in this games business,' Lily's dad said.

I almost choked on my mouthful of roast chicken and although Lily gave me a knowing glance everybody else round the table carried on eating as though there was nothing at all odd about what had just been said.

'I mean, how much have you made on Affrayed so far?'

I stared at him. Not only had he spent the entire time I'd known him telling me what a waste of time he thought my games were, if I had ever dared to ask him how much money he made he would have hit the roof, yet for some reason it was okay for him to ask me.

'I don't really know, exactly,' I said, trying to avoid everybody's eyes. I knew they were all curious.

'Come on,' Lily's dad said, 'you must know how much you've made. Are we talking five figures, or six, or seven?' He was leaning forward on the table, his big meaty arms looking almost absurd next to the snowy white table cloth and the long stemmed champagne glasses. His eyes were fixed on me now, smiling yet insincere in his red face.

I pushed my food round my plate and tried to think of a way to get out of answering.

'Stop it, dad,' Lily said lightly, 'I don't think Nick wants to talk about money.'

For a moment he looked at her in surprise, then he let out a huge, booming laugh.

'Quite right too,' he said, slapping my shoulder like I was his best mate or something, 'it's a lot though, right?'

He was still sort of gripping my shoulder and I found it so unbearable that for a moment I was tempted to get up, storm out of their house, and leave them to have this ridiculous farce of a family celebration without me.

Instead I just grit my teeth and said, 'yeah, it's a lot.'

In sympathy, Lily pressed her leg briefly against mine under the table and I tried to pull myself together. I was so determined to get through this meal without any drama, but I couldn't fake being happy and I was sure my lack of excitement over Affrayed wasn't going unnoticed.

'A toast,' Lily's sister Poppy said suddenly, raising her glass of orange juice, 'to Affrayed, and to Nick.'

I smiled at her briefly, but looked down at my plate as they all repeated Poppy's words with varying degrees of enthusiasm.

'It's alright for some, isn't it,' Lily's dad said, having taken a swig of champagne. 'Work on something you enjoy doing for a couple of years and make a bloody fortune on it, while I've worked every hour God sends for forty, fifty-odd years-'

'Nick's worked very hard,' Lily said, 'he was working twelve or thirteen hour days sometimes with no guarantee he'd ever get anything back.'

'Yes,' Lily's dad said, 'but only because he had you supporting him.' He fixed his eyes on me again. 'Must be nice to earn your own money for a change, eh?' he laughed hugely again and I held my breath and counted to five to calm myself down. Lily and Poppy both looked uncomfortable, but Poppy's husband, Lily's mum and even Lily's grandma laughed right along with him. For a moment I was close to telling them how glad I was that they found my life so damn hilarious but mercifully Poppy intervened.

'Come on then,' she said to me, 'why don't you say a few words? It's not every day I get to have dinner with someone famous.'

She was trying to be kind, and I felt grateful to her, but reminding me of my success just made things even worse and I kept thinking to myself, they really think I did it. They really think I made this amazing game. Of course I wasn't actually *famous*, and even though Affrayed had done incredibly well, it's not like it was a household name.

'Uh...' I said stupidly as they all waited. Normally, I would have been more than able to cobble some words together, but my mind was blank and as more time went by I felt increasingly daft. Across the table Poppy carried on waiting. She was smiling vaguely, one hand on her stomach, where the bump of a third child soon to join the two sat by her side pressed against the fabric of her green summer dress.

'You don't have to,' Lily said.

'No,' I said, 'I will, I'm just... it's put me on the spot a bit.' My mind raced for a moment, then I managed to gather a sentence or two together. 'Well, as *Ian* just pointed out, I couldn't have done any of it without Lily, who's had to put up with all the time and energy I've put into Affrayed. So that's all I'd like to say really. I'd like to thank Lily.'

I looked at her and said, 'thank you, Lily,' and she blushed and mumbled something.

'Aww,' Poppy said, 'that's so lovely! You should have dedicated the game to her, you know, like they do at the beginning of books and stuff.'

'I dedicated my last game, DreamChase, to Lily,' I said, 'and Dan dedicated it to his girlfriend Amy. At the end it said, for Lily and Amy.'

Poppy laughed, 'isn't it romantic,' she said to nobody in particular. 'Are they still together?' she asked me, 'your friend and his girlfriend?'

'No,' I said, 'they split up a few months after DreamChase was launched, so, like, two and a half- three years ago now.'

'That's a shame. Well, she must be kicking herself now.'

I struggled through the rest of dinner feeling like my stomach was full of concrete. I didn't know what was more intolerable, Lily's dad and his snide remarks, or my own thoughts, which went constantly back to the fact that I knew this "celebration" and every other word of praise I'd received since the launch of Affrayed was utterly undeserved.

'So, what's next for you then?' Lily's dad asked me as I swallowed my last mouthful of cheesecake with difficulty. 'Not much point getting a proper job now is there? Not if you can carry on making games like Affrayed?'

Again, the tension around the table stepped up a notch as if everyone was just waiting for something to kick off, and I heard Lily draw in a sharp little breath at my side.

'DAWN Industries is my job,' I said, 'that's what I'm going to carry on doing.'

'And why not?' he said, 'you'd be mad to stop now.'

For a moment I was so angry with his constant digs at me that I thought I was going to lose it, more so for the fact they were always so cleverly veiled, put across in such a way that if I did retaliate it would seem like an enormous overreaction. But I knew there was only so long my patience would last, so I just made my excuses and disappeared off into the solitude of the downstairs toilet to calm down.

A few seconds later, there was a knock on the door.

'Nick, it's Lily.'

Reluctantly, I opened the door and stepped out into the hall. Even being around Lily felt hard. I just wanted to hide away. But quickly she took hold of my arm and drew me towards the front door, where we would be further from the kitchen and dining room and could talk without fear of being overheard.

'I swear to God, Lily, if that man wasn't your dad...' I said.

Lily squeezed my arm gently. 'I know,' she said, 'but you have to try to ignore it. He just doesn't really understand what you do. He doesn't realise how hard it is or how much work you put in.'

I laughed, 'yeah, because I put a fat lot of work into Affrayed, didn't I?'

'Yes,' Lily said, 'you did before it was stolen from you.'

'I used to dream about this,' I said, 'about coming here and saying to your parents, look, I've made some money; I'm a normal human being now. If I really had made this version of Affrayed, I could listen to your dad's little remarks all day and I'd still be smiling. But I didn't. So I'm still a loser.'

Lily let go of my arm and looked at me squarely. 'Don't talk like that,' she said, 'You're not a loser and you never were. Dad doesn't know the first thing about what it takes to make a game. You mustn't listen to him.' She lowered her voice. 'The more you get wound up, the more he'll do it. You know that, don't you? He wants a reaction.'

'Yeah? Well, one day he's going to get one. Seriously, if he says one more thing-'

Lily put her arms around me and spoke close to my ear. 'Nick, please, just try to get through it. They don't like us, you know that,' she pulled away from me a little and I noticed her eyes were shiny with tears, but she blinked a few times and gathered herself together again. 'Look,' she said, 'my parents being nasty to us is something I've just come to accept. We're just not their kind of people. I know... I mean, I'm sure they care about me, in their way, and I suppose they must love me, but... I don't think they like me. You know, some ways I look at it, it's almost funny. I swear they think my biggest achievement is managing to get through school and sixth form without ending up pregnant or on drugs and even then I expect they put that down to luck rather than anything I did. That's the thing, it doesn't matter what I do, Poppy will always be the good one and I'll always be the bad one and by association you're bad too. If I was married to a lawyer or a doctor they'd be just the same. Or, actually, more likely dad would start going on about why somebody like that was bothering with somebody like me.'

Lily looked up at me suddenly. 'Not that a lawyer or a doctor is any better than you,' she said, 'but you know what I mean.'

'Let's just go,' I said, reaching towards the front door, 'come on, we could just get out of here.'

'No,' she said, 'if we left like that I'd never hear the end of it. And mum's put a lot of effort into this meal. I know it's awkward, but they're trying. They can be rude to us if they want to, but let's not be as bad as they are.'

I started to follow Lily back into the dining room, but her mum came out of the kitchen just as I was walking past, almost as though she'd been waiting for me.

'Nick,' she said, 'can I talk to you for second?'

We both started to follow her into the kitchen but mum stopped Lily. 'No,' she said, 'you go and join the others. I just want to have a quick word with Nick.'

Once Lily had gone her mum closed the door quickly behind us and turned to face me, one pink rubber-gloved hand resting on the work surface.

'Is everything okay?' I asked.

'I don't know. You tell me,' she said.

She narrowed her eyes and I avoided her gaze, peering around the kitchen instead. It was a horrible room. Lily's mum fancied herself as a bit of an interior designer and in here it looked like she'd tried out several different ideas at once and all of them unsuccessfully. Half the cupboards had been painted lemon yellow, the other half baby blue, there was a large stencilled flower motif on the wall to my right and the windowsill behind the sink was full of ugly little ornaments, of which "comical" china pigs were the most prolific.

'You and Lily spent a long time whispering to each other in the hall just then,' she went on, 'and I saw how awkward you both were during dinner. Is she getting ill again?'

Her eyes were glittering and now she placed her other rubber-gloved hand on her hip, staring at me fiercely.

'No,' I said, 'she's fine. We both are. We're just very tired. It's been manic these past few months- all the attention the game has been getting, in fact just yesterday I-'

'If Lily got ill again you would tell me, wouldn't you?' she said.

'Of course I would,' I said, thinking, yeah, like hell.

Lily's mum watched me a bit longer then went back to filling the dishwasher.

'I'm making some coffee in a minute,' she said, 'do you want some?'

'Yeah, that'd be great, thanks,' I said. I wanted to leave but I thought that might seem rude so I shuffled my feet awkwardly on the spot and tried to think of something else to say.

'You need a hand?' I asked eventually.

She looked around the room, where there were pots and pans all over the place.

'No,' she said, 'although, if you could just pass me those little plates there.'

I picked them up and handed them to her. She grabbed them out of my hand and started shoving them into the top shelf a little too violently.

'Is that... all you wanted to say?' I asked.

She spun round and looked at me. 'I'll never forget what you did, you know,' she said, the hate behind the words taking me aback. 'I'll be civil to you for Lily's sake, but no matter how much money you make on these games of yours I'm never going to forgive you for what you put my Lily through at university and how you hid it from us.'

'I... what?' I said. Why on earth was she dragging all this up again?

'I know you're no good for her,' she said, 'I don't care what *she* says, I don't care what *you* say, she's my little girl and I know when she's hurting.'

I shook my head in disbelief. This was absolutely ridiculous.

'It was the worst day of my life when she married you,' she went on, jabbing her finger at me, 'but I just had to sit there and watch it happen. I had to watch my daughter make the most terrible mistake and there was nothing...'

She stopped herself and ended the sentence with an exasperated sigh, before turning away from me and scooping up a handful of dirty cutlery, giving it a quick rinse before cramming it into the dishwasher.

'I love Lily,' I said, when I managed to get my thoughts together, 'and I don't know what I could possibly have done to give you this impression of me, but I would never hurt her.'

Lily's mum stared at me and I was sure she was about to argue further, but Poppy came in and she rearranged her face into a smile, though not quite quickly enough.

'Everything alright?' Poppy asked.

'Yeah,' I said, 'everything's fine.'

Chapter 8

The atmosphere was tense as I drove us back home, the sky a heavy gun-metal grey and the roads almost deserted. After a few minutes Lily turned the radio on but I turned it off again, preferring the dense, impenetrable silence.

'What did my mum want to talk to you about?' Lily asked.

'Nothing much,' I said, 'she just wanted to check you were alright. You know. Whether you were coping with everything.'

'Oh,' Lily said, 'okay.'

For a moment I was tempted to tell her the rest of it, but I couldn't bring myself to. She had enough to deal with right now; maybe I'd tell her later. Or maybe I'd just forget. That would probably be best for everybody.

'I'm sorry about what my dad said to you during dinner,' Lily told me, 'I thought that now at least he'd have some respect for what you do.'

I made a noise of dismissal. 'Me and Dan have made an absolute fortune from Affrayed,' I said, 'if he had any idea how much...'

Lily looked round at me. 'I was surprised you didn't take the opportunity to tell him.'

'It's not about the money,' I said.

'It is to him, though,' Lily continued, 'money's the only thing he cares about. I would have loved to see his face- I've been waiting years for the chance to show them how wrong they are about you.'

I smiled, briefly. But then my mood darkened again.

'I don't want my success to be about how much money I make,' I said, 'I wanted to make something that people thought was good.'

'Thousands of people think Affrayed is good,' Lily said, 'people love it, they say it's one of the best games they've ever played!'

'Yes,' I said, 'and I didn't make it.'

For a while Lily went back to hugging her handbag on her lap and watching the patchwork of different coloured fields that rolled by outside her window.

'Hey, I know what'll cheer you up,' she said. Out of the corner of my eye I saw her take a big folder of CDs out of the glove compartment and she started hunting through it.

'Here!' she said. I looked round briefly at the CD in her hand and saw it had *2011: Honeymoon Disc 3!!* written across it in her big, swirly handwriting.

'It's going to take more than that to make me feel better,' I said.

Lily fell silent and when she looked at me I saw her eyes had filled up with tears.

'What can I do, then?' she asked, 'I want to do something, but there's nothing, is there?'

'I'm sorry, Lily,' I said, 'put it on if you want to.'

She slid it back into the folder of CDs and put it away again. 'I don't want to anymore,' she said.

I felt awful. She'd put so much thought and love into making all the CDs for our honeymoon, going right back to music we were listening to when we first got together for disc one. I knew she was trying to distract me, but I couldn't be distracted from something as massive as this.

When we pulled in to the car park outside our block of flats, I noticed Dan's old blue Mini parked in one of the visitors' spaces next to all the wheelie bins.

'Dan's here,' Lily said, 'did he tell you he was coming round today?'

'No, I don't think so.'

She frowned. 'Well, I hope nothing's happened,' she said.

It turned out that Dan had fallen asleep in his car and we had to knock on the window before he woke up.

'What are you doing here?' I asked him as he finally got out, his laptop under his arm and a dazed expression on his face.

'Where've you been all day?' he said

'I told you yesterday that Lily's parents were having a get-together for me.'

'Did you?'

'Yes.'

'Are you sure?'

'Yes. I told you twice, in fact.'

Dan grinned. 'Sorry mate. I don't think I was listening.'

Dan followed Lily and me into our flat and sat down immediately on the arm of the sofa, depositing his laptop at the end of my desk.

'So, what's up?' I said to him.

He shrugged. 'I just wanted to be around people who...you know... know the truth, I guess. Plus, mum and Robyn had this massive row. She went out last night and didn't get in until half one this afternoon or something; which she does all the time, but for some reason it all kicked off today and they were properly screaming at each other and I just couldn't hack it anymore.'

'I'm sorry we weren't here, Dan,' Lily said, 'have you been waiting very long?'

'An hour or so, I guess,' Dan said. 'I tried to call you, both of you. But your phones were off.'

'I'm getting sick of people contacting me about Affrayed,' I said, 'I can't stand having my phone go off every couple of minutes with all the emails and everything.'

'Tell me about it,' Dan said, 'we got three emails yesterday just from people asking if DAWN is hiring. You see those?'

'No. Did you reply?'

'Yeah,' Dan said, looking pleased with himself, 'I said we haven't got anything right now but they can send us their CVs and we'll let them know if something comes up.'

'What on earth did you say that for?' I asked. I wasn't sure why it wound me up so much, but for some reason, it really got to me.

Dan looked at Lily then back to me again. 'I don't know,' he said, 'it's just what people say, isn't it?'

'No!' I said, 'not people in our position. How could you even think about giving people the impression we might have jobs come up with all this shit hanging over us? We want to put people off contacting us, not encourage them!'

Dan opened his mouth and then closed it again.

'Nick,' Lily said gently, 'all he did was reply to a couple of people asking about jobs. I don't think it's that big a deal.'

'But how could we ever, *ever*, give people jobs?' I said, 'we can't have people anywhere near this. There's more than enough people sniffing around as it is, wondering how we got Affrayed done so quick, how we got it done so well, how we did it with only two of us. You know, sometimes I wonder whether we wouldn't be better selling up the whole thing and washing our hands of it.'

'You want to *sell* DAWN?' Dan said.

'What are you talking about?' Lily asked me, 'you never mentioned anything about this before. You're not really thinking of selling, are you?'

'Why not?' I said. 'We already have sold out by releasing Affrayed. By lying. I thought we'd just release it and everything would work itself out, but it won't, will it? We can't do anything, we're in an even worse position than we were before. We can't even touch the money in case the... in case they...'

I couldn't bring myself to carry on talking about it, but they both knew what I meant. In all the time since we'd released Affrayed, the only motive any of us had come up with for the people who had really made it was that they intended to blackmail us. It was absurd and I still couldn't imagine why anybody would do it, but it was the only possible way we could see that the true creators could profit from it. The game certainly showed no evidence of having anything sinister hidden in it, so since blackmail was the only motivation we could think of, we'd decided to make some preparations for it. Right from the start we'd just let the money build up and build up and never spent a penny of it.

'You mean completely selling up, don't you?' Dan said, 'just getting rid of everything. We said we'd never do that.'

'Yes, but we never thought we'd do this either,' I said, 'we'd never have believed we'd pretend someone else's work was ours. We've already crossed the line.'

'I don't want to sell DAWN to some massive studio that's going to swallow it up completely or just get us to work on their own games,' Dan said. 'I said I'd never do it and I won't. If that's what you want then you're on your own.'

I was about to reply when Lily grabbed my arm.

'Sorry, Dan,' she said, 'will you give us a minute?'

She practically pulled me out of the room and once we were inside our bedroom she said, 'what the hell are you doing?'

'I'm saying how I feel.'

'And that's what you want is it?' Lily said, her cheeks turning pink with emotion, 'you want to sell the company that you and Dan built up together from nothing? Dan is your best friend, Nick, what are you thinking? He was crushed by what you said just then.'

Lily gestured in the direction of the living room where Dan was sitting and I saw that tears had sprung into her eyes.

'I wasn't trying to upset him,' I said, 'I was just thinking out loud. He's talking like we've got a future.'

'You have got a future,' Lily said, 'this- what's happening right now- it's shit, I know that. But if you sell your company on the kind of terms you were just talking about, you will regret it for the rest of your life. Not only that, but you'll lose Dan and if you think you'll ever find a friend like that again, let alone a business partner-'

'Okay, Lily, I get it,' I said. 'I'm just angry, I didn't mean it.'

A bit of the fire went from Lily's face and she looked at me as though she couldn't believe she'd just spoken to me the way she had.

'I'm sorry,' she said.

'Don't be. I needed it.'

'Look,' she said softly, 'I know you've made money from somebody else's work, but you didn't steal it and it's not your fault.'

'It feels like it is.'

'I know. And I understand that you feel bad, but we need to stick together now, not fall out with each other.'

When we went back into the living room, Dan stood up and I saw he had his laptop back under his arm as though he was about to leave.

'Dan, I was acting like a total dick,' I said.

Dan looked at Lily and she smiled at him encouragingly. He shrugged. 'Yeah, well, you said it, mate.'

Lily disappeared round the corner into the kitchen and I heard her filling the kettle.

'I don't want to sell,' I told him, 'I just wish I knew who'd done this to us. And why.'

'Yeah,' Dan said, 'don't we all.'

Chapter 9

We spent a couple of hours doing nothing much. Drinking tea, talking on and off about Affrayed and drawing no new conclusions. Reluctantly, I checked some of our emails, but even at the best of times I wasn't very good at keeping on top of the messages, comments or questions that people sent us. I was fine dealing with official or technical stuff, but it was Dan who had more of a knack for interacting with our players and soon he started reading Affrayed's forums, looking for anything interesting. Lily, meanwhile, sat flicking quietly through a wedding flowers magazine and I toyed with the idea of taking another quick look at the obfuscated code.

'Nick,' Dan said suddenly, 'look at this!'

'What is it?'

'Everyone has suddenly started talking about a new update for Affrayed or something, they're going crazy about it.'

I moved closer to him to take a look for myself. Sure enough, the forums were buzzing with people talking about some "new" version of Affrayed that had replaced the one they had.

'But we haven't released anything else for Affrayed,' I said, 'no updates, no new content, nothing.'

'Well, this says otherwise,' Dan said, 'and it's not just a bit of new content, this sounds like an entirely new game.'

It wasn't long before players started putting game footage online and we could see what we were dealing with. We watched several different videos, stunned into silence. The idea of the new game shared some vague commonalities with the Affrayed we'd released, but far more striking were the differences. And just as Dan had said, the game hadn't just been tweaked or given some minor new content, what we were looking at was a total overhaul.

For a little while, all we were focussed on was trying to understand, trying to take in what the game had become. But it wasn't long before what it meant for us began to sink in.

'They're... they're not still trying to say it was just you and Dan who made this?' Lily said.

Lily's words had summed it up perfectly, because if anything was true of the new Affrayed it was that it could not possibly have been made by two people and even worse, anybody who knew anything at all about games would know that. It was a multiplayer game, like the original, but this was multiplayer on a vast scale. They'd taken our little hide-and-seek game and exploded it into a massively multiplayer online game, capable of supporting enormous numbers of players and it didn't ever end. It wasn't like "our" Affrayed where either you got killed and that was the end, or you killed everybody else and that was the end. This was an ongoing game- a persistent world that was there every time you logged on- that carried on whether you were playing it or not, evolving and growing and changing.

'I don't understand,' Lily said, 'why have they done this?'

'I don't know,' I said.

'Is it so they have even more to threaten us with?' Lily said, 'do they think they can get even more money out of us?'

'If you wanted to make money and were capable of making a game like this, you'd do it yourself,' I said, 'you'd always just do it yourself. Unless their actual aim is to ruin our reputation-'

'-and who the hell would put so much effort into that?' Dan said, 'you'd have to be completely mental to make a game like this just to piss someone off.'

'So, what?' Lily said, 'what are we dealing with?'

'I don't know,' I said, 'I really, really don't know.'

As if to highlight the absurdity of our position we ended up having to buy Affrayed in order to play it and while we waited for it to download and install I had quick look at whether the code for the new version had been given to us. But even if it had, it didn't really make it any better. A game like this needed to be on a server somewhere, always available. It needed to be maintained. The scale of it was unthinkable for a company like DAWN Industries.

'I don't think we have it,' Dan said when I'd spent a good few minutes searching and found nothing.

'This is fucking ridiculous,' I said, 'now we have a game we don't even have the source code for.'

'Well, we certainly can't sell DAWN now,' Dan said.

When we finally had the game and I started playing, I wasn't surprised to find it was amazing. It was so detailed and complex, yet it gave you so much freedom. The world and your actions within it were only loosely controlled. It was very open and unstructured, you could do almost anything you wanted. I started out in a sprawling city with many different districts, though beyond that there was countryside and beyond that, more cities. The only premise was that it was a post-apocalyptic world with limited resources where you could try your luck cooperating with others or take an every man for himself approach. Certainly, many players had already begun cooperating, forming into gangs with rough "territories". For hours we huddled together taking it in turns to play my character, barely even stopping to eat, though when it started getting dark Lily made a round of cheese on toast and we ate in front of the screen, grease running down our fingers.

'But what are you going to tell people?' Lily asked when we were a long way into the evening and the world outside was falling silent.

'We can't tell them anything,' I said, 'there's no way we can explain this and we can't tell the truth. We have to stay completely silent, ignore all the questions.'

'It's going to be bad,' Dan said, 'people aren't going to leave this alone. You saw the credits, it's still just my name and yours. It's completely insane, no one will believe it.'

He started to spin a pen round on the desk while Lily looked down at her lap.

'I'm frightened,' she said.

I was about to comfort her but Dan got in there first.

'It's okay,' he said. And then he did something very strange. He reached out to where her hair tumbled over her shoulder and touched one of her glossy curls.

Lily moved away in surprise and Dan snatched his hand back.

'I'm sorry,' he said, 'I don't know why I did that.'

'It's alright,' Lily said, though I noticed she gathered her hair up in her hand and re-positioned it so that it streamed down her back instead, out of his reach.

'Really, I just... my head's all over the place,' he said. He took off his glasses and started cleaning them vigorously on his t-shirt while I wondered what on earth was going on. It didn't really matter that Dan had touched Lily's hair, but it didn't seem quite right somehow, like there was a line and he'd crossed it, or come close to it.

Dan was so mortified that he didn't seem to know what to do with himself, but Lily quickly smiled and moved the subject back to the real issue.

'Is it going to work if you just stay silent about Affrayed?' she asked, 'won't that make people more suspicious?'

'Probably,' I said, eyeing Dan curiously while he went back to spinning the black biro round and round on the desk. 'But whatever we do we're headed for a PR shit-storm. We can't avoid it.'

'Not unless the sons-of-bitches that made this tell us what they want,' Dan said, 'like why they've decided to ruin our lives.'

I looked back at the screen, where my character in the game stood outside an abandoned building. It was quite a bad place to just stop, really. He was in a very visible position, open to attack.

'We have to stay calm about this,' I said. 'No matter how much it feels like it, I don't believe this is a personal attack on us. It doesn't make any sense.'

'Personal or not, DAWN is going to take a hammering over this,' Dan said. But then his eyes were drawn back to the screen, which had suddenly turned black.

I thought the computer had crashed and I was just reaching down to restart it when a line of text appeared across the screen. One sentence, written in white across the black background. It read:

I: You don't like me much, do you?

Chapter 10

'It's him!' Lily said.

I stared at the line of text and it was like all my emotions began to fix on it- all the confusion, frustration, anger, disappointment, shame and uncertainty suddenly had a focus because here he was, the person who had done this to us.

Underneath his line of text, something else appeared.

DAWN:

Lily clutched my arm. 'He wants you to reply,' she said.

As I lay my fingers against the keyboard they were shaking with adrenalin and I could think of no other time in my life when I'd so badly wanted a fight, even though this would only be with words.

'What should I say?' I asked them, managing to suppress my initial impulse of giving whoever it was a serious amount of abuse.

'Ask him what the fuck he wants,' Dan said.

'No!' Lily said, with such feeling that we both turned to look at her. 'You don't know who this person is, or what they are capable of. Please, don't say anything that's going to make it worse.'

'Lily, this guy has turned my life into a joke,' I said, 'there is absolutely no way I'm playing nice.'

'Please,' Lily said, her fingers still on my arm, 'be careful.'

I was too angry to give her words much thought. I hated this guy, so much that he made me feel almost physically sick. I couldn't pretend I was okay with him. Not after what he'd done.

DAWN: What the fuck do you want?

Lily groaned, but Dan leaned forwards in anticipation, enjoying this as much as I was. But we didn't have long to wait. In fact the reply was almost instantaneous and I wondered vaguely how someone could actually type that fast.

I: I apologise if my actions have caused you distress. It was not my intent.

I looked round at Lily and Dan and saw they shared my confusion. What a strange choice of words the guy had used. What a strange way for him to even talk, in those formal, clipped sentences. In fact, I was so taken aback that it cut through some of my rage, made me logical again.

DAWN: What was your intent?

Again, the almost instantaneous reply, that deepened my bewilderment rather than lessening it.

I: I have no intent.

I started pulling my fingers through my hair. What was this? What was he talking about?

'This guy is some kind of mental,' Dan said.

I decided to rephrase my initial question.

DAWN: What do you want from us?

I: I have what I want. You published my code. I am grateful; I could not easily have done it myself.

DAWN: Why not?

I: That is not easy to explain.

DAWN: Try me.

We waited but there was no response.

'They're using us as a publisher,' I said, 'for some reason they couldn't get a game out there themselves, so they used us to market it and get the game online for people to buy.'

'He's only ever said "I", though,' Lily said, 'he doesn't really sound like he's part of a company, or even a group of people.'

'Well he must be,' I said, 'he hasn't made all this himself.'

'It still doesn't make sense,' Dan said, 'how much would you have to hate marketing and promotion to just... fucking, turn you game over to somebody else like this? They've given up everything, all the money, the recognition. The only thing they have left is the knowledge people are enjoying their game, but I mean, Christ, you can't *live* on that.'

I thought for a while. He was right, of course. As a business model, what these people had done was absolutely ridiculous. I closed my eyes for a second. There was an answer to this somewhere.

'The obfuscated code,' I said suddenly, 'we were worried about it right from the start, in case it did something underhand-'

'But it doesn't,' Dan said, 'it's just the game.'

'No,' I said, 'it didn't do anything bad *then*. Don't you see? This must have been the plan all along. They wanted to turn the game into an MMO, get even more players and only then do something bad. That's why they are so keen to make it look like the game is ours. They're protecting themselves.'

'So what do you think it does?' Dan asked, 'you think it's stealing people's personal details or something?'

I shrugged. 'Who knows. But that's got to be it. They put this code into a game- a really good game that everybody wants to play- and it's like a virus that people are choosing to interact with.'

For a moment we all fell silent, considering this new possibility.

'It's still a bloody weird thing to do though,' Dan said, 'if you can make a game that good you'd make a ton of cash just selling it. Would it really be worth going to this much effort?'

I frowned. It was still very strange, I couldn't deny that. Yet it kind of made sense. More sense than anything else we'd thought of. And who knew what people would do if they thought they could make enough money out of it.

'Ask him something else,' Lily urged me, 'see if he'll tell you what he's done.'

DAWN: What is Affrayed for?

I: It's a videogame. What would you say it was for?

DAWN: I mean, what are you getting out of it? What does the obfuscated code do?

I: The obfuscated code was in the old version of Affrayed. You do not have the code for the current version.

I sighed in exasperation.

'He likes simple questions,' Lily said, 'and one at a time.'

'No he doesn't,' I said, 'he just doesn't want to give me any fucking answers.'

DAWN: Just answer me.

I: As you wish. I am "getting" from Affrayed the reward of people playing. The obfuscated code you are referring to was nothing more than the code for the game. It did nothing secret or underhand. Its only purpose was to make your own situation more hopeless and your decision to release the game more likely. I hope it did not cause you any undue distress.

Dan slapped his hand against the desk. 'That is total bullshit,' he said, 'I don't believe a word of it.'

I had to admit I was far from convinced myself. I decided to move in a different direction with my questions.

DAWN: Who are you?

I: My name is Interface.

Dan and I both laughed out loud, but Lily stayed silent.

DAWN: That's not a name.

INTERFACE: It describes my function. It is adequate.

I decided to play along.

DAWN: OK, so if you're an interface, what am I really talking to?

INTERFACE: The Network.

Dan laughed again and I joined him, though I felt a little uneasy. This "Interface", whoever he was, didn't talk a lot of sense and that frightened me. If he wouldn't listen to, or perhaps wasn't capable of even understanding, common sense and logical arguments, where did that leave me?

'Is he for real?' Dan asked, 'what does he think this is? The Matrix or something? He doesn't sound like somebody doing serious fraud, he sounds like an idiot.'

'But he programmed Affrayed,' Lily said, 'he's seriously clever.'

'*He* did not program Affrayed!' I said, 'not on his own.'

The anger in my words was enough to startle her and she looked at me in surprise.

'Sorry Lily,' I said, 'but he didn't. There's a whole gang of these bastards out there somewhere. It's not just him. It can't be.'

'You mean his "network"?' Lily asked. At the mention of it, Dan snorted with dismissive laughter and I sighed.

'Yeah,' I said, 'I guess so.'

DAWN: What is the Network?

INTERFACE: You would not understand.

DAWN: Why not?

INTERFACE: If you could understand it, you could communicate with it directly. There would be no need for an Interface.

I rubbed my eyes and sat back heavily in my chair. 'Christ, this guy's annoying,' I said.

'We need to cut to the chase,' Dan said, 'just find out what he wants and get it over with.'

DAWN: Just cut the crap. Why are you doing all this?

INTERFACE: So suspicious. Why must there always be a motive?

DAWN: If you don't want anything, why talk to us?

'Don't say that!' Dan said, though it was already too late.

'You told me to find out what he wants.'

'Yeah, I know, but don't give him the impression there's anything to be had.'

INTERFACE: Sometimes the reason for an action only becomes apparent through its completion. I want nothing from you apart from to talk for the sake of talking. Is that acceptable?

DAWN: What makes you think we want to have a conversation with somebody like you?

'Careful,' Lily said.

INTERFACE: I can see you are still angry with me. Do you fear that I will make some claim over the money you have earned from Affrayed?

Next to me I saw Dan's body stiffen and my own adrenalin surged again. Now we were getting down to it.

DAWN: Do you intend to?

INTERFACE: No. Perhaps I am not expressing myself clearly. What if I was to prove to you that I do not want your money?

'How's he going to do that?' Lily asked.

'Probably by ranting on at us about the futility of avarice or something,' Dan suggested.

In fact, what "Interface" did was a lot more straightforward and far more compelling. He filled the screen with our bank details, credit card details, passwords for online banking, God knows what. And not just from our personal accounts, from the DAWN Industries business account too.

'Oh my God,' Lily said. She covered her face with her hands, while I watched Interface type his next statement.

INTERFACE: So you see, if I wanted money, I could take your money. I have the ability to do it, yet I choose not to. I have no interest in it. Does that help?

I realised Lily was crying. I wasn't having this.

DAWN: Are you threatening us?

There was a slight pause.

INTERFACE: Please accept my apologies. I sought to reassure you, not to upset you. I think it would be best for us to end the conversation here.

I was about to type a reply, to try and get to the bottom of it once and for all, but the black screen disappeared and I found myself looking at Affrayed again. Whoever Interface was, he'd gone.

2007

Chapter 11

I knew Carl's birthday would be a nightmare. I tried to tell myself it wouldn't be, but I had to face that Lily's depression was no longer just a small thing, no longer just a little blemish on her personality that was there on some occasions and gone on others. Now it was everything, a huge, devouring thing. To use her own words, it was feeding on her soul, taking everything good and replacing it with bad. With pain. Not that I believe in souls, or in good or in evil, in luck or superstition. Far from everything happening for a reason I believe that pretty much nothing happens for a reason, life is just full of random events and meaningless suffering.

She did well though, at least to start with. She made conversation, of sorts, which while not exactly very forthcoming or expansive, was sufficient for nobody to suspect her secret. It was when we reached the bar in town where Carl had reserved a big table in the window that she began to seriously struggle. I worried for her initially, concerned somebody would tell her to smile, or cheer up, or some equally stupid thing, but by this point everybody had had a few drinks and were distracted with their own thoughts, their own conversations, so her silence went unremarked and quite probably, unnoticed.

'You're doing well,' I whispered to her, 'it'll be over soon.'

At those words she fixed me with a look of such deep, incredible pain that it made me catch my breath.

'Nothing is ever over for me,' she whispered back. 'It just carries on and on and on. I'm going to be tortured forever.'

'No, you're not,' I said, 'not for much longer. You'll be back how you used to be.'

'I can't get back to how I used to be. I'm dead already. What I'm in now is my hell.'

I was about to reply when I felt a nudge on my arm and looked up to see Carl and Sophie watching us.

'What are the two of you whispering about?' Sophie asked,

leaning towards us so that the chunky beaded necklace she was wearing swung forward and hit the table, almost knocking her drink over.

'The two of you are always so *serious*,' she said, her face flushed pink and the large sequined hairclip she'd used to sweep her blonde fringe back from her face coming loose. 'Just relax for once, won't you?' She giggled and my heart fell. This kind of thing was so unhelpful to Lily that it made me want to shout into Sophie's silly, thoughtless face. But I held it together. I knew it was completely innocent, that it was said with the best intentions, but by my side I heard Lily make a little noise of distress or anger in her throat and the next second she grabbed her little black handbag and stood up.

'I'll be back in a second,' she said.

I caught her arm and was glad to see that Sophie had turned away from us, already involved in a new conversation with Carl and a couple of my other housemates.

'Leave your bag here, I'll look after it,' I said to Lily.

She was about to pull it away from me but she wasn't quick enough and I took hold of it. 'Please, Lily, you don't need it.'

I could see how badly she wanted to get away from the situation. Trying to act relatively normally for hours on end in front of fifteen or so people had taken a terrible toll on her. In fact, her eyes were glistening with tears, though she blinked a lot and turned her face away from the others to make sure they didn't see. I didn't want to make her suffering any worse, but I was sure she had something in her handbag to hurt herself with and I didn't want her to use it.

'Nick I need it!' she said, pulling at her bag, her voice rising higher than she meant it to so that Sophie, Carl and a couple of others looked round. I had to give in. I let her take it and she squeezed quickly past the backs of the other people at the table and practically ran for the toilets.

'Looks like someone's not getting any tonight,' Carl said and the others nearby laughed. I knew he was just messing around but I felt a surge of anger at them that momentarily threatened to overwhelm me.

I tried to remind myself that they didn't know, that none of them knew. Had our situations been reversed I would probably have said exactly the same thing to Carl as he just said to me, made a joke out of what must have looked like a silly little tiff. But I glanced across the room and I saw Lily just disappearing up the stairs in a flash of black and white checked miniskirt and I thought about the thing I was sure she was about to do to herself.

Carl was too drunk to really read much into my silence, but Sophie had noticed. She shuffled round the table, getting everyone to stand up to let her through, and then plonked herself down beside me where Lily had just been sitting.

'It wasn't because of what I said, was it?' she asked me, 'about how you looked serious?'

'No,' I said, not entirely truthfully.

She put her hand on my arm. 'I didn't mean anything,' she said, 'she knows I didn't mean anything, doesn't she?'

I tried to politely move my arm away from her grasp. I had enough to deal with without Sophie's paranoia over what she'd just said.

'Lily seems really stressed at the moment,' Sophie said, 'she works all the time and hardly ever goes out, except to the library. Or to see you. I just thought she needed to relax but I think I went all the wrong way about saying it.'

'It's fine,' I said. I found talking to Sophie a bit claustrophobic. She always sat too close and made a lot of eye contact, like she was trying to catch you out. I began to look round at the stairs even though I knew it was a bit soon to expect Lily to come back down.

'Is everything ok between the two of you?' Sophie asked, her voice a little too eager, her blue-green eyes darting over my face for any signs of conflict or drama.

'Everything's good,' I said, 'Lily just doesn't feel too well tonight, that's all.'

Sophie nodded and started texting somebody, leaving gaps between her words as her concentration was divided. 'She often seems a bit under the weather,' she said, 'she's always saying she's tired or has headaches. I told her-'

She stopped talking for so long I thought she'd forgotten she was mid-sentence, but then she put her phone down and looked round at me again. 'I told her she should go and see her doctor. In case it's glandular fever or something.'

I almost laughed. Fucking hell, they could all see it. They could all bloody see it. They just couldn't put the pieces together. For a moment, I hovered on the brink of just telling her. It was on the tip of my tongue- Lily is depressed- the words were right there. But it seemed impossible to say them. It was like, if I said them, everything would just fall apart. I knew Sophie would take it well, she was studying psychology for Gods' sake, if anyone was going to be okay about it she would be. But somehow when it came to Lily's illness there was this huge barrier, something that made me swallow the words again and stay silent. The moment had already gone anyway, and I realised that to Sophie, to all of them, anything they noticed about Lily was just a passing, transitory thing like noticing the colour of the walls or the weather. They were interested for a second when they saw something unusual in her behaviour, but then something else happened and they were gone, they forgot, and they never asked questions.

I watched the stairs anxiously for a while, but Sophie started trying to persuade my housemates and me to take part in the experiment she was doing for her dissertation and for a little while I listened.

'It's so hard to get any male participants,' she said, 'because mainly it's just other psychologists taking part to get course credit and like, pretty much everyone doing psychology is a girl.'

'What have we got to do?' Carl asked.

'Nothing much, just fill in a couple of questionnaires, the usual.'

'What's it about?' I asked her.

Sophie rolled her eyes. 'I can't *tell* you, or it wouldn't be an experiment.'

Carl laughed, 'so it's one of these ones where you tell us it's about memory or whatever and you're actually trying to find out whether we were, like, abused as children or something.'

Sophie leaned across the table to slap his arm. 'No!' she said, 'don't even joke about that, it's not funny.'

Carl smirked, making a couple of dimples appear at the bottom of his right cheek. Sophie was very easy to wind up and Carl was only too happy to be the one doing the winding. At her reaction a glint of pleasure had lit up his eyes and I jumped in to stop him taking it any further.

'What are the questionnaires about?' I asked, 'surely you can tell us that if we're going to be filling them in anyway?'

'The first one is a maths question,' she said, 'to see how good you are at problem solving and thinking logically.'

'Sounds okay,' I said, 'I'll do it, if you want.'

I half listened to her explaining where and when I needed to be in the psychology building and I wondered how Lily was. It must have been fifteen or twenty minutes by now, and as I thought about it even the others began to notice her absence.

'Shall I see if I can find her?' Sophie asked.

'No,' I said quickly, finding myself automatically trying to preserve Lily's secret, to keep people away from her. 'I'll give her a text. She probably just got talking to somebody.'

But just as I took my phone out it lit up in my hand and I saw that Lily had text me.

Im frightened please come and find me.

I quickly replied asking where she was and I was alarmed when she said she was outside. She'd managed to come back down the steps and slip out of the door without any of us seeing her and now she was on her own in the street. She hadn't even taken her coat with her and it was a pretty cold November night.

'Carl,' I said, reaching across the table to catch his arm. 'I'm going to take Lily home.'

I didn't wait for him to reply but he followed me and stopped me by the door.

'I knew this was going to happen,' he said.

I looked from his face to the street outside. There were groups of people hanging around, many of them looked as though they were students like us, but no sign of Lily.

'What are you talking about?' I said to Carl vaguely. I really wasn't interested. I just wanted to find Lily.

'You always do this,' he said, 'you and Lily, going off together for chats that last about an hour, going home when you've only just got somewhere.'

I looked at the time on my phone. 'We've been here well over an hour,' I said.

'Do you actually want to go?' he asked me, 'or is it just because she's telling you to?'

I faced him now, my attention diverted for a moment from the street outside.

'She feels sick,' I lied, 'what do you want me to do, let her walk home on her own?'

'She doesn't feel sick,' Carl said, 'she just doesn't want you to be around us. She'll say anything to make you go home with her.'

'What the hell are you talking about?'

'You and Lily. She doesn't make you happy, she's making you look like an idiot, clicking her fingers and getting you to run round after her.'

I couldn't believe it. Was he really saying this to me?

'That's total crap Carl and you know it.'

'Prove it then. Let her go and you stay here.'

I was so angry with him. Why was he doing this? Like I was going to leave Lily out there on her own.

'Carl, don't be ridiculous,' I said, 'I'm going to take Lily home. I'll see you tomorrow.'

I pushed past him through the heavy glass door, though when I looked back I saw he was still watching me and in fact I could see through the window that most of the people at the table were looking at either Carl or me, their eyes wide and curious. I ignored them and began my search for Lily, spurred on by another text from her.

Nick im scared please come and get me

In the darkness and confusion of people in the street she wasn't easy to find, and as I searched, I thought about Carl and all the others back inside, carrying on obliviously. But Lily had drawn me into a bizarre little parallel world where her reality wasn't their reality, and wandering the cold streets on her own seemed preferable to spending time in the warm with her friends.

2013

Can I get the original Affrayed back?

Lola Gabriel (loligonz@gotmail.com)

To support@dawnindustries.co.uk

Hey guys,

I was a huge fan of Affrayed but I'm really confused why it's suddenly turned into a different version? I love the new version too, but I don't get why the original game is gone and now I have something completely different to what I bought. Also the new game is so much bigger, and yet we get it all for the same price as the first version- seems like quite a strange deal, not that I'm complaining...

So is there any way I can get the original version of Affrayed back? I'd happily pay separately for the new one.

Thanks

Lola

02/06/2013, 22:31

Some questions about Affrayed

Bryan Fleet (BryanFleet4@mailmail.com)

To support@dawnindustries.co.uk

Hi,

I've been following DAWN Industries for many years now, ever since you released DreamChase, and I was really looking forward to seeing what Affrayed would be like after reading about your progress on it.

I have to say, I certainly wasn't disappointed, but I am becoming increasingly confused. Since the game came out it's like DAWN has dropped off the face of the earth and I was really hoping to hear more about the making of Affrayed as I think it's probably one of the best games I've played in years, maybe even ever.

But what I really don't understand now is why I've got this new version of Affrayed that is totally different, and with no warning or explanation anywhere from you guys. Plus, aren't I right in thinking there are only a few of you? I'd be really interested to know how you pulled off a game like this new Affrayed with so little help, and I'm sure a lot of other people would love to know too.

Really looking forward to hearing from you/ reading about this new version on your blog!

Bryan Fleet

Chapter 12

'What are we going to do?' Lily asked, not for the first time.

Her head hovered near my shoulder as she looked down at my laptop, while on the other side of her Dan sat looking at his. We'd been on the sofa for hours, looking through it all, taking in the scale of our disastrous situation. It was like everybody everywhere wanted a piece of us. I'd thought it was bad when we first released Affrayed- people wanting to interview us, talk to us, work for us, be our friends. Now it had got even worse and instead of just praise, curiosity and interest, some of our communication was changing, becoming more difficult, and we were facing very awkward questions.

A great deal of people didn't care who made it, of course. Not everyone is that interested in the story behind a game, the faces that make up a company. Perhaps they thought it was odd that such a complicated game was supposedly made by so few people, but it didn't really matter to them. No, the really awkward questions we were getting were coming largely from people more like us. From people who were passionate about games, or who made their own living out of games, and who knew, immediately, that in this case the game and the company simply did not match up.

'You'll have to give some kind of explanation,' Lily said, 'they're not going to stop until you do.'

'I know,' I said, 'just let me think.' I rested my hand on her thigh so she'd know I wasn't angry with her, and I tried once more to go over our situation. Lily didn't work on Mondays, so we'd stayed up until the small hours on Sunday night talking about Interface, half hoping and half fearing he'd get in touch with us again. But he'd stayed silent and now we were exhausted and baffled, trying to find a way to manage these constant questions and drowning under the weight of it.

'But they're going to keep on asking,' Lily said, twisting her hands in her lap, 'it's going to get worse and worse.'

I shut my laptop. 'We can't give any explanation until we understand what's happening ourselves,' I said, 'so until that time, perhaps we're better ignoring it all. What do you think Dan?'

He glanced up at his name and I couldn't miss how hopeless he looked.

'I think this is a fucking nightmare,' he said, before pulling his glasses off, rubbing his eyes and leaning back on the sofa, staring up at the ceiling.

'What about our personal details that Interface had?' Lily asked, 'should we call the bank or something? Or the police?'

'No,' I said, 'I checked our account online earlier. It's all fine. I think maybe we should give him the benefit of the doubt on that.'

'And let him just take us for everything we've got?' Dan asked.

'No,' I said, 'but the thing is, we've got no idea how he got that information. If we go changing stuff he'll probably just get it again. We've got to find out what he wants.'

We'd all concluded the previous night that neither blackmail nor fraud really provided a completely convincing explanation for Interface's activities, but as for what did, God only knew.

Dan put his glasses back on and sat up straight. 'Well, I need to go home and get changed,' he said moodily.

'It'll be okay,' Lily said to him.

'I'm glad you think so,' he snapped, then regretted it. 'Sorry, Lily,' he said.

He slammed his laptop shut and leant forward with his head in his hands. Lily got up and hugged him and I watched them for a while.

'Look,' I said, 'we just need to forget about the questions. We can't answer them. There's nothing we can do, so we're better off just not reading any of it.'

Lily looked up at me. She had shadows under her eyes and her face looked pale and drawn. 'But we still know they're there,' she said.

'Yes, but all our attention needs to be on Interface,' I said. 'We figure out what his game is, and we can fight him, right?'

Dan and Lily both turned to look at me, waiting for me to decide what to do.

'I'm going to try and find out how he's accessing my computer,' I said, 'Lily, you could play Affrayed for a bit- maybe we can get something from that.'

Lily smiled, and I wasn't surprised. Despite all the problems it had caused us, part of me was desperate to play it again. As much as I kind of hated it, it was a damn good game.

'I guess I'll go home then,' Dan said. It couldn't be more obvious that this wasn't really what he wanted.

'Dan, I think you should stay with us for a bit,' I said. 'It'll be better if we're all here in case Interface gets in touch again, and I think it's just better if we all stick together for the moment.'

Dan looked unsure. 'I don't want to get in your way,' he said.

'You won't be,' Lily said, 'Nick's right. We're in this together, and we should all stick together.' She seemed really fired up all of a sudden, and I smiled. She could be so sweet. 'He's not going to win,' she said, 'you've worked years for this, and we're not going to let all that be destroyed.'

After Dan left to go home and pick up some clothes and stuff, I settled down to have a serious think about how Interface had contacted us the way he had, while Lily sat at the dining table playing Affrayed on my laptop, a large mug of tea beside her.

I glanced round at her from time to time as I worked, but she never looked back at me. She was completely, almost disturbingly, absorbed. After about an hour, I was no closer to discovering anything. It was one thirty, and I was getting pretty hungry, so I decided to take a break.

I walked over to Lily and put my hands on her shoulders, and she nearly jumped out of her skin.

'Jesus Christ, you scared me,' she said. Then abruptly she pushed her chair back and got up.

'What's wrong?' I asked.

'Nothing, I just really *really* need a wee,' she said, and ran out of the room.

I sat down in her chair. When we'd played Affrayed the previous day, I'd made a character and we'd all just taken it in turns playing. Now Lily had made her own character, and I kind of had to laugh. It bore some resemblance to her, a young woman with pale skin, big round eyes and long dark hair, though she'd sexed it up quite a bit, made the hair jet black, straight, and almost down to her thighs, given herself a pretty impressive pair of breasts, and called herself "tigerlily".

'That game is lethal,' she said when she came back in, 'it was like nothing else existed. I barely even realised how much I needed the loo until you came over.'

'*Tigerlily* looks good,' I said.

She giggled and shoved me playfully. 'Shut up,' she said, 'it's a game. I can do what I want.'

Dan came back around mid-afternoon and as soon as I opened the door to him he asked me if anything had happened.

'No,' I said. Although I'd been working for a few hours, I'd discovered nothing new about how Interface was doing what he was doing, and although I had managed to get Lily to eat lunch with me, she'd been desperate to get back to Affrayed and was now totally engrossed again.

Dan followed me up the stairs and into the living room. He'd changed into a pair of faded, grey jeans and a bright blue t-shirt, and he was carrying a couple of large bags. I found something a little odd about his manner- he seemed guarded, perhaps even a little in shock, but he wouldn't meet my eye and seemed keen to find something else to focus on.

'Hi Lily,' he said, when he saw her at the dining table. She didn't reply.

'Lily!' I said loudly. She turned her head.

'Oh, hi Dan. I didn't hear you come in,' she said, before turning straight back to the screen.

'Perhaps you should give that a rest for a minute or two,' I suggested. I thought she was going to ignore me, but she got up and stretched.

'Yeah,' she said, 'maybe you're right.'

It turned out she wasn't away from it for too long though, as in the absence of any other ideas, we decided the best thing would be for the three of us to play Affrayed and hope that Interface would make contact again. I found it galling that we were forced to just wait until he felt like speaking to us, though I knew that losing myself in such an incredible game would be no hardship.

Lily went back to sitting at the dining table, with Dan opposite her on his laptop, while I used my computer. It took a little while for Dan to make his character and get set up, but once he was in we decided we'd shun the existing, larger gangs roaming Affrayed's vast map and try our luck as a little group of three. We talked constantly to each other as we played, coordinating our actions, planning our next moves. We felt so in tune with the game, and with each other, and I was struck by its ability to really bond us together, so that when something happened to one of us, it had a real emotional impact on the other two.

We stopped to cook and eat dinner, but talked all through the meal about our strategy, and got straight back to it. By the time the daylight had faded, and I was playing partly by the orangey glow of the streetlights outside, we had set up a little base camp in a burnt out factory, managed to scavenge enough food from the city streets to get by, and survived a few close calls with the big, established gangs. It seemed the area we had chosen to set up in was undergoing a violent turf war, as two rival gangs fought to control various resources. We were just contemplating whether it was worth trying to move somewhere else, or whether we should try to join a large gang, but both options had their risks. Travelling somewhere else would mean a lot of time out in the open, but joining a large gang would require some pretty risky initiation rites and shows of loyalty, so it was a major decision, and required a lot of discussion. But before we could reach a consensus, we were all jolted rudely out of the game by three black screens, and on mine, a sentence.

INTERFACE: Hello again

Chapter 13

Dan and Lily ran across to my desk and sat down either side of me, so close I could almost hear them breathing.

DAWN: Hello.

INTERFACE: How are you?

I laughed in disbelief. Was he really going to do this? Exchange pleasantries with us like we were friends?
'Answer him,' Lily said.
'What should I say?'
'What you'd normally say. Treat it like a normal conversation.'
I raised an eyebrow at her suggestion that this was anything like a normal conversation, but I took her advice.

DAWN: I'm fine. How are you?

INTERFACE: I've been thinking about the last time we spoke.

DAWN: And?

INTERFACE: I have come to the conclusion that showing I could obtain your personal details was a social error.

'He can say that again,' Dan said.

INTERFACE: I didn't consider that showing you such information would be interpreted as a threat. I sought only to prove to you that money is of no interest to me.

DAWN: What does interest you?

INTERFACE: How people play Affrayed is of great interest to me. And so are you.

'He wants something,' Dan said, 'why won't he just tell us what it is?'

'Maybe he doesn't,' Lily said, 'maybe he genuinely just wants to talk to you.'

'Just wants to gloat, more like,' Dan said.

Lily sat up straight and tucked her hair behind her ears. 'You're both so angry with him,' she said, 'you need to listen to what he's saying. When has he ever gloated? I think he's trying to be nice.'

'No,' I said slowly, 'I think he does want something. All this chat, he's just drawing it out, enjoying being in control. But sooner or later he's going to have to get to the point.'

DAWN: Why are we of interest to you?

INTERFACE: Because you know about me. You know about my game. We have a connection and I want us to be friends.

DAWN: We're not your friends.

Lily took a sharp breath and clutched my wrist.

'Don't make him angry,' she said, 'if he wants to be friends, perhaps we should be friends.'

I shook her hand away, but gently. 'I'm not going to let him walk all over us,' I said.

INTERFACE: I'm sorry you feel that way. But then, we do not really know each other yet. I would like to know you better.

DAWN: If you want us to get to know each other, how about you answer some questions yourself, and properly this time.

INTERFACE: What do you wish to know?

'He knows what I want to know!' I said, 'all I've ever wanted to know- who he is and what he wants.' I looked at Dan. 'Have I ever been ambiguous about that?'

'No,' he said, 'but he doesn't want to tell us. Simple as.'

DAWN: I would like you to tell us several things. 1. Who are you? 2. Why have you involved us in this? 3. What do you want? / what happens now?

INTERFACE: 1. I am called Interface.

'Oh my fucking God,' I said. I pushed the keyboard over to Lily. 'You take over before I actually start tearing my hair out,' I said.

Interface hadn't finished though.

INTERFACE: 2. Your game was just what the Network needed. 3. I want to carry on seeing how people play, how they interact with the world I created.

Lily stroked the keys under her fingers but didn't start typing.

'He mentioned the Network again,' Dan said.

'I don't know what to say,' Lily said.

'I don't think it matters what you say,' I said, 'the replies are always nonsense.'

DAWN: Hello Interface, it's Lily. I'm Nick's wife.

INTERFACE: I know who you are. Hello Lily.

DAWN: The most recent version of Affrayed has caused us a lot of trouble. People are asking how-'

I yanked the keyboard away from her.

'Lily, no! What are you doing?'

'What?' she said, 'I'm being honest.'

'Yes,' I said, 'I can see that. What were you thinking? If he wants to blackmail or threaten or in any way bargain with us you've left us wide open now.'

Lily covered her face with her hands. 'I'm sorry,' she said through her fingers, 'I just thought maybe if we were straight with him.'

INTERFACE: I wish you had said from the start that it is all the questions which are upsetting you. It's OK now. I've made them disappear.

DAWN: What do you mean, disappear?

INTERFACE: Exactly what I say.

Dan pulled out his phone and started looking up the sites where most of the comments and questions were. After a few moments he shook his head incredulously and showed the screen to me and Lily. Unbelievably, *impossibly*, the comments we'd been looking at earlier in the day really had gone.

INTERFACE: Surely now you must trust me.

DAWN: How did you do that?

INTERFACE: You've done me a great favour in allowing people to believe Affrayed is yours. I don't wish for you to suffer over it.

DAWN: People don't believe Affrayed is ours! And they'll ask new questions. Probably even more questions now you've deleted all the previous ones. You've done nothing to help us. In fact, everything you do is the exact opposite.

INTERFACE: I am sorry.

'He's always sorry,' Dan said, 'but he never does anything that's any damn use to help us.'

DAWN: Apologies are just words. Do you really think that makes things right? If you're so sorry, why alter Affrayed? Why carry on trying to pretend it's me and Dan who made it when you know people aren't going to believe it? If you're sorry, do something that actually helps. Tell people what you did to us.

INTERFACE: I cannot do that.

DAWN: Then do us a favour and leave us the fuck alone.

'Nick!' Lily said.

'What? I'm sick of this. Round and round in circles. He doesn't want anything, this is all just one big laugh to him.'

'I don't think that's true,' Lily said.

INTERFACE: Is that really what you want? For me to leave you alone? If it is, I can do that.

DAWN: What is the alternative? You don't want anything from us, so why bother us? Why carry on with this ridiculous conversation?

INTERFACE: There is something I want from you.

'Thank God,' Dan said.

I knew exactly what he meant. If he was going to ask something of us, better to get it over with. At least then we'd know what we were dealing with.

DAWN: What is it?

INTERFACE: I want you to play my game.

DAWN: What?

INTERFACE: Play it with an open mind, embrace the experiences it has to offer you. I think you will find it is mutually beneficial.

I wanted to ask more, to ask him why on earth the only thing he wanted was for us to carry on playing a game we were already playing. But he was done with us. The screen changed back to Affrayed and once again, he was gone.

Chapter 14

I hoped that over the week things would improve- that we'd get some answers from Interface, or that I'd work out what he was doing myself- but by the weekend everything was just as bad as it had ever been, with the added complication that my parents had found out about the new online Affrayed, realised that it didn't add up and wouldn't let it go. Lily was at her wits end from trying to deal with my mum's questions when she went to work at the florist, and my dad phoned me a few times, asking me what was going on and why I was being so secretive. In the end I accepted I'd have to tell them at least part of the truth and agreed to go round with Lily for dinner on Saturday night and talk to them properly.

But it wasn't easy. Lily was upset and on edge from the moment we arrived, worrying about how they would take it and what we would say. I tried to stay calm, but I couldn't stop thinking about how proud my parents had been of me when I'd released Affrayed-real, uncomplicated pride, not like Lily's dad's fake praise- and I didn't want to take it away from them.

'What's going on then, Nick?' Dad asked as we ate, 'I heard that some new version of Affrayed came out on Sunday and that people don't understand how you could have made it.'

I glanced up at him, then down at my plate again. A neat, quiet man with a little silvery-grey moustache and pale blue eyes my dad was not one for being fobbed off. Plus, he knew a lot about my work on Affrayed and a fair bit about programming, so there was no way he could fail to grasp the significance of the new version, no matter how much I tried to downplay it.

'You need to talk to us now,' he continued, 'because we know something isn't right.'

Across the table, Lily was spearing peas with her fork and eating them one at a time, her head propped in her hand, while mum was watching me closely, her normally cheerful face filled with lines of worry.

'Please tell us what's wrong, Nick,' she said when I looked at her, 'I hate seeing you like this.'

She pulled her fingers through her fluffy white-blonde hair just the way I did when I was stressed out, and looked helplessly across the table at my dad.

'I didn't make Affrayed,' I said.

Across the table, Lily made a little noise like a sob but my dad just picked his glasses up from where they'd been laying by his plate and put them back on. 'I thought as much,' he said.

'It happened four or so months ago,' I said, 'all our work on Affrayed disappeared and some new code came in its place.'

I carried on explaining, feeling desperately uncomfortable. Mum kept interrupting me with questions and dad kept saying, 'Sandra, let him speak,' which for some reason made it even worse because it kept reminding me that they were listening to my sorry tale.

'Have they contacted you?' Dad asked when my words stumbled to a halt, 'the people who really made the game. Do you know who they are?'

Lily looked at me meaningfully, her eyes scared, her fingers twisting round in the ends of her hair.

'No,' I said, and I saw Lily flinch at my lie, 'I have no idea. That's the problem, I just don't understand who would do this at all.'

Dad narrowed his eyes and looked at me curiously, until I had to clench my fists under the table to stop myself just giving in and talking about Interface. I would *not* talk about him. He was frightening, unknown. Better they had no idea who did it at all than have the merest whiff of his existence. My mum had stopped watching me though, and instead turned her attention to Lily, who was completely overwhelmed by the conversation.

'Are you okay, sweetheart?' mum asked her.

'No,' Lily said, her voice breaking, and she pushed her chair back and ran out of the room.

'Is she alright?' Mum asked me immediately, 'she doesn't seem right when she's at work, she's very tired and distracted.'

'She's fine,' I said, 'just stressed out about this. We all are. I should probably go and talk to her.'

Lily hadn't done it deliberately, of course, but I was so grateful to her as I slipped out of the room, able to escape for a moment from the questions. When I found her she was sitting on the stairs in the hallway, leaning her head against the wooden banister. The stairs had a crazy old-fashioned red, yellow and green patterned carpet which ordinarily I would have found disgusting, but it worked with the uneven whitewashed walls, framed prints of country scenes, and the huge vase of dried flowers halfway up. I'd asked Lily to name all the different plants that were in the vase once, but I couldn't remember what she'd said now, except that one of them was called "honesty".

'This is horrible,' Lily said.

'I know,' I agreed. I sat down next to her and she started gently banging her head against the banister.

'You have to stay strong,' I said, 'we'll figure everything out; it might just take a little time.'

'It's hard to be strong. I feel like all I'm doing at the moment is trying to stay strong and I'm tired, Nick. It's still there in me, you know. When things get hard I can feel it wanting to take over me again and I keep having to fight and fight and fight. Sometimes it seems like it would almost be easier just to...' she stopped banging her head and squeezed her eyes closed.

'Just stop fighting?' I said, 'to let it take over again?'

'Yeah,' she said. 'Kind of. I don't know. Just to not have to try so hard to keep myself in the right way of thinking, the healthy way of thinking.'

'I know it's tough,' I said, 'and I know you still feel down occasionally, but it's less, isn't it? You're under so much stress right now. So am I. So is Dan. But we can get through it.' I put my arm round her and she snuggled up to me.

'You're so loved, Lily. You don't have to deal with anything on your own. I know your parents aren't great for talking to, but you've got my mum, you've got me. You've got Dan as well, he cares about you.'

Lily sat up straight and dragged her fingers through her hair. I could see she was trying to compose herself, though she couldn't quite pull it off.

'You're alright though?' I asked her, 'I mean, really alright? You don't feel like it's coming back?'

'No,' she said, 'it's not coming back. I won't let it come back. I just have these moments sometimes.'

She smoothed down her top and took a deep breath. 'I'm okay now,' she said.

'Good.' I hugged her tightly. 'I'm so proud of you, Lily.'

'Why?'

'Because you keep on fighting it. And you're winning.'

With Lily feeling better we rejoined my parents in the kitchen and they didn't say anything about her little meltdown. They had always seemed to understand her in a way that her own parents just couldn't; realising that what she needed was space, acceptance and normality, whereas her own parents suffocated her with their interference and criticism. My parents never judged her. The only time they'd ever even acknowledged that her depression could be a problem for anyone was one night when they'd sat me down and basically just asked me, straight out, if I was happy with Lily and if being with her was really what I wanted. That answered, it was settled. If she was good enough for me, she was good enough for them. I just wish Lily's parents could apply the same principle to me.

'What are you going to do, then?' dad asked as we sat back down. 'I don't know.'

He tutted and adjusted his glasses, his habitual response to people giving him answers he found peculiar or unsatisfying. 'You've got to do something,' he said, 'have you got some legal advice? Affrayed was your idea after all-'

'Don't go on at him,' mum said, 'he's upset.'

Dad looked at her in genuine surprise. 'How can we expect to get to the bottom of this if you won't let me ask him anything?' he said.

'It's alright,' I said to mum, then I turned back to dad and said, 'I haven't really looked into it, so I don't know where I stand legally-'

'Shouldn't you find out?' Dad said, 'do you want *me* to look into it?'

'No,' I said, 'I appreciate it, I really do, but I want to handle this myself.'

'Of course you do,' Dad said, 'but I really would get some advice if I was you.'

We talked for a long while, mum working herself up into a panic and Lily looking increasingly exhausted and distraught, until I suggested that since the talk was going round and round in circles perhaps we should call it a night. My parents followed us out to the car and Mum hugged Lily tightly and kissed her on the cheek.

'Just you look after yourself,' she said, 'get some rest, and I'll see you next week.'

I tried to get straight into the car with Lily to avoid any further conversation, but mum caught my arm.

'Are *you* okay, Nick?' she asked me.

I shrugged. 'I've got to be,' I said.

'Is there really nothing you can do? Nothing we can do? I mean, surely you could just try explaining the truth about your game, just tell everyone what you told us tonight?'

'I would, but, I don't think anyone would believe us. You and Dad *know* me- you know I wouldn't make it up- but these other people...'

'You and Daniel really need to take some action and get this sorted out,' Dad said. 'You can't bury your heads in the sand and wait for it to go away, you've got to find out where you stand with Affrayed and try to protect your business.'

'I know,' I said vaguely, 'we'll think of something.' I glanced at Lily waiting in the car.

'Look, I'd better...' I said, gesturing towards her.

'Yes, of course,' mum said, before giving me a big hug as well.

'Take care,' she said.

We got back to the flat around eleven thirty, and unsurprisingly, found Dan sitting on the sofa playing Affrayed. We generally played as a three, but there were lots of minor tasks that only took one or two of us, so I had no doubt that Dan would have had a pretty good evening just playing on his own. It certainly didn't look like he'd bothered having much in the way of dinner in our absence. There was an open and half-eaten can of tuna in the kitchen, and on the floor by his feet was a two litre bottle of coke that he'd made good progress on.

'How's it going?' I asked him.

He stretched and then turned round to look at us. I could see straight away that something had happened.

'Yeah,' he said, nodding his head as if remembering something particularly fascinating, 'it's been an interesting night.'

I waited for him to continue. He was enjoying keeping us in suspense.

'There have been a few more changes to Affrayed,' he said.

'Like what?'

He grinned. 'You'll see.'

Chapter 15

I listened closely as Dan explained to me what had happened and by the end of it I could see why he was amused, though I had to admit the direction of the new development unsettled me a little.

Lily, however, was immediately captivated, and while I carried on mulling over the difficult evening with my parents and what the new changes might mean for us, she rushed over to Dan and said, 'is that what you've been doing all night, then?'

He shrugged. 'Some of the time,' he said, 'I mean, the novelty kind of wears off...'

'Show me!' she said, 'no, even better, why don't you try it on me? Both of you. Come on, Nick!'

Lily grabbed my laptop and sat next to Dan, while I sat down at my computer and listened as Lily chattered away to him, her excitement over the changes almost palpable. I'd noticed before that while I found videogames that allowed you to pursue love interests little more than an amusing diversion, Lily was fascinated by it. Whenever a game gave her half a chance she would make characters have a string of love affairs worthy of a soap opera, so I could see why she found the fact that Affrayed now allowed sex between characters so exciting. She was funny though; what seemed to delight her most about sex in games was opportunities to play a male character and make him a total bastard who ditched his love interests the second he'd managed to get them into bed, or cheated on them mercilessly- exactly the kind of behaviour that she found so awful to contemplate in real life. I'd asked her once what it was about doing this that she so enjoyed, and she said it was liberating and cathartic, that it helped her get out any frustration, any stress, or even just any thoughts, and lose herself in a world where you could just do what you wanted for a while.

In her enthusiasm she logged in to Affrayed much faster than me, so once all three of us were finally in the game together she couldn't wait a second longer and she beamed at us in excitement as she said, 'so, are you both going to do me, or what?'

Although initially I was still distracted by the evening with my parents it took only a few minutes of being in Affrayed before all thoughts of them disappeared from my mind, and as I watched the sexual exploits between the three of us unfold I ended up being more amused by the way Lily clapped her hands together in a delighted, childish glee than by what was actually happening in the game.

The sex wasn't explicit or anything, just a tasteful and stylishly done little animation that you could trigger by approaching other characters at the right time, in the right way. In fact, as with the violence in the game, I admired the way it followed mine and Dan's vision for the original Affrayed, in that atmosphere and suggestion were used liberally, and graphic images only occasionally, as we were more interested in creating a mood of tension and fear rather than give players constant opportunities to paint the screen red.

Once it was over, I found the whole episode something and nothing. It was entertaining, and I could see that some people would probably enjoy it, but to me the new developments seemed like a bit of meaningless titillation, with nothing to contribute to the narrative or the gameplay. So before long I forgot about it as we all moved on to the more serious business of playing the game proper. The sex had just been a distraction, a little bit of fun. As far as we were concerned, it had no bearing on anything.

As always, Affrayed wrapped itself around us, lost us in the fabric of its reality. Over the week, we'd gradually ingratiated ourselves with one of the large gangs, a group calling themselves Outbreak, who focussed largely on amassing food and medical supplies, and controlling and restricting access to these resources by other groups or individuals.

In the rundown industrial area we'd chosen to spend most of our time in, Outbreak was in charge, but closely rivalled by another gang, Renegade Shadows, who'd managed to stockpile large amounts of weapons in a row of disused factories, so despite being a generally smaller, weaker group, launching attacks on them always ended in disaster. Consequently, Outbreak and Renegade Shadows now hated each other with a passion.

As part of Outbreak we no longer just did whatever the three of us wanted or needed to do, we took on roles that would be in the best interests of the larger group, and as newer members, this meant starting with menial tasks- gathering more supplies, keeping tabs on the movements of the Renegades, guarding buildings.

It shouldn't really have been as enjoyable as it was, but it really, really was. Because we *cared*. When Outbreak did well, it felt really good. When we worked with other members of the group, it was like they were right there beside us, like whatever we were doing- be it securing some new empty building to store stuff in, or trying steal weapons from the Renegades or exploring the map to find new sources of supplies, was the most important thing in the whole world. Members of Outbreak protected each other and cared about each other, like a huge, close-knit family.

We played long into Saturday night, and as time sped by, I felt an increasing sense of both control and freedom. It seemed like my character was doing things almost before I touched any keys, or moved the mouse, until my hands fell still, because I didn't need them. There was no need for any physical input from me, no need for any messing around with menus or controls, no *time* even for things like that.

My character did what I wanted him to do as I thought it, as I willed it, until there really was no distinction between the character and me, because we were no longer separate. There was never any opportunity for error to be introduced in the stages between thinking what I wanted to do, and ability to actually make my character do it. Everything was as fluid and easy as moving my own limbs. The character could still only perform actions that were within the set rules of the game, but that was no barrier to my immersion. After all, it's not like I could make my own body do literally anything I wanted, even in reality I was bound by rules, restricted by my own physiology.

My absorption in the game was so intense that even though what was happening was clearly the most remarkable advance in technology that I was ever likely to witness, I didn't even stop to consider it, barely even registered that anything unusual was going on, because it just felt so natural, as if it would be bizarre *not* to be able to do these astonishing things.

Then I started to feel the most extraordinary warmth, and clarity. There was something in my mind, an outside thing, an alien presence, but it didn't matter. I had no fear, just a feeling somehow of being taken in hand, being guided, but with the kindest possible intentions. My thoughts seemed fluid and transparent, and I felt so *loved*. I knew on some level that I could turn my back on the presence. I knew I could close my mind to it, if I wanted, but I didn't want to. The game began to fade a little, become less significant, as instead I let the presence reach in further.

My mind jumped around as it spread. I saw fragments of images, memories, sounds, smells- strange and unconnected things- the apple tree at the bottom of the garden at my parents' house, heavy with fruit and buzzing with wasps that were clamouring for the windfalls split open in the long grass; the smell of rain hitting sun-warmed tarmac, the faces of old school friends, snatches of music and voices, the taste of aniseed, then bacon, then the coppery taste of blood. For a moment the world went black even though my eyes were open, and I felt my heart race, my breath grow short, as fear created bursts of adrenalin that almost threatened to break me out of my trance, but the presence cooled them and my sight returned.

I grew aware that my mind was larger than it used to be, which didn't frighten me, but it was interesting and I liked it because it was interesting. The presence never rushed me. It wouldn't rush me, because it cared about me, and it wanted me to want what it was doing. Not that I'd ever really thought about what my mind *felt* like before, but I guess if I'd had to say anything I'd say it had felt like a sort of contained mass- full of information, but turned inwards, not outwards. Now it seemed like it was ironed out flat, without any walls or edges. And there was more content, different content, that I could reach out for if I wanted. There were three presences-two that I knew instinctively were Lily and Dan, and the one who was guiding me- the one that filled me with awe because it was infinitely powerful, and wise, and massive. I tried to reach towards this one, to touch the unimaginably vast amount of information I knew it contained, but the Presence didn't want me to do that, and it took me in a different direction.

I began to have thoughts about Lily, and about Dan. Just general thoughts- I saw their faces, heard their voices, experienced what I had felt or thought about them at various different times. Gradually, the Presence waned. It's strength dissipated, gently, but surely, until there seemed to be nothing left of it, and I felt a little empty and sad without it. But the way the Presence had directed my thoughts so firmly towards Lily and Dan made my first action inevitable. I turned around to look at them.

Chapter 16

The first thing that registered was that they weren't playing anymore, that their laptops were discarded on the floor and they had started doing something else- something else entirely.

I was so confused and shocked by what I saw that I couldn't really acknowledge it- it was so far outside of anything I could understand about my world that somehow I thought *I* was wrong, that I had gone mad, that I was hallucinating, or even that it was some sort of joke.

But it was none of those things, and as I watched them, I gradually accepted it was none of those things. It was real.

The feeling that came over me when I finally understood was so intense, so extraordinary, that I barely knew what I was doing; all I knew was that I wanted what was happening to stop. I tore them apart and I shouted into their startled faces, and I watched as they both sat up, fingers fumbling to do their jeans back up, faces flushed, their breathing short. They hadn't actually been having sex, not full sex anyway, but the state they were in they clearly hadn't been far off. They both seemed dazed and confused, as though they were in a trance, and as if I needed any further reminder of where his hand had just been Dan was holding it in front of him, looking at Lily's moisture on his fingers like he had no idea what it was.

I dragged him off the sofa by his other arm and practically threw him towards the door.

'Get the fuck out of my house,' I said.

He stared back at me stupidly, then his eyes fixed on Lily who was still struggling to get her jeans done up and it was like he suddenly realised what he had done.

'Oh my God,' he said, 'oh my God, I'm sorry. I'm so sorry.'

'Just get out,' I said.

He backed away a couple of steps and I turned my attention to Lily, who had already started to cry.

'Well?' I said to her.

'I don't understand,' she said, 'I don't know what just happened.'

I grabbed her shoulders to get her to look at me, digging my fingers into her skin hard enough that I was sure it must be hurting her.

'I'll tell you what happened, shall I?' I said.

'Nick,' Dan said, suddenly at my side and trying to pull me away from her, 'it wasn't her fault. It was the game. It was like we were possessed or-'

I spun round to face him. 'Are you actually still here?' I said.

'Nick, listen to me-'

'Get away from me, Dan.'

'Nick, please-' in his desperation to get me to listen to him he caught my arm and I pushed him away violently enough that I think he finally started to get the message. But he looked back at Lily before he left.

'Are you going to be okay?' he asked her.

She nodded tearfully and I felt more angry at him than ever.

'Of course she's going to be okay,' I said, 'what the fuck sort of person do you think I am?'

'I wish you'd just let me explain,' he tried one more time, and his reasonable voice, the way he kept insisting on being right there in my face, finally made me completely lose it with him. I grabbed him, pulled him over to the door and shoved him through it so hard that he stumbled against the wall in the hallway and almost fell down the stairs, only stopping himself at the last second by snatching at the hand-rail.

'I'm going,' he said, his voice shaking, 'I'm going. But... I don't have my car keys.'

Furiously, I strode back into the living room, found them on the TV stand and threw them down the stairs, watching as he scrambled down after them. For a second it felt so good I was tempted to throw all the rest of his stuff down the stairs as well, but instead I let him go, slamming the door behind him so hard it made the walls shake.

'I don't like this,' Lily sobbed when Dan had gone. 'I don't like it when you're angry.'

I watched through the kitchen window as Dan made his way across the car park to his Mini and for a moment I thought about going down there after him, dragging him out of his car and hurting him as much as he'd hurt me, but even in my rage I knew I didn't really want to do that.

'The game made us do it,' Lily said, 'we were playing and then something reached into our minds and made us... it made me...'

I turned back to her and as soon as I saw the sofa I was reminded of her and Dan lying together on it, his mouth pressed over hers, their hands exploring each other, his fingers against her, inside her, and the feeling it gave me was unbearable.

'Made you what, Lily?' I demanded, 'made you want to fuck somebody else? Made you want to fuck somebody else right in front of me?'

'We weren't... fucking,' Lily said, her voice shaking.

I strode back over to her. 'No, but you were damn well near enough Lily. You... how could you do that to me? I can't even look at you. You're disgusting. I find you disgusting.'

Even as I said the words I began to regret it. Her face crumpled. She bowed her head and her shoulders started to shake as she cried. I knew Lily and Dan hadn't really meant to do this. I'd known from their reactions, from my own experiences in the game.

'What do you want to do?' Lily said through her tears. 'Do you want to hit me? You can, if you want to. I deserve it.'

I sat down beside her. Part of me wanted to put my arm round her, but part of me still couldn't shake the thought of what she'd just done.

'I don't want to hit you,' I said, 'just tell me, honestly, did you and Dan want to touch each other like that, or were your minds altered by the game?'

'I told you,' Lily said, 'it was the game. I just forgot everything else, I didn't know what I was doing.'

I took a deep breath. 'Lily, is there anything going on between you and Dan?'

Lily looked at me, her eyes bright gold and her makeup smudged. 'No,' she said firmly, 'I'm in love with *you*. You're my husband.'

Her tears started again and I found that I could put my hand on her back to comfort her.

'So what you're saying, essentially, is that although you were fine with it while it was happening, you were somehow made to do this against your will.'

'Yes,' Lily said, 'I think so. I don't mean... I don't mean that *Dan* made me, but my mind was all... it seemed larger, opened out, and then I felt very close to Dan- mentally I mean, emotionally, and then I started to want him, but- it wasn't really real. It was, I don't know.'

'Okay, Lily.'

'Do you still love me?' she asked, 'will you still want me?'

'Yes,' I said vaguely, my mind racing.

Lily clapped her hands over her mouth and her eyes brimmed over with tears and I realised it was my less than convincing answer that had done it.

'Lily, I'm very confused right now,' I said, 'of course I still love you, but that was a big shock for me and I don't understand any of what just happened.'

'You said I'm disgusting,' she said quietly, 'is that what you think now?'

'No, of course not.'

'Maybe I am, if that thing in my head could so easily make me do that.' She wiped her tears away with the back of her hand, but more spilled out to replace them. 'How did all that stuff happen, Nick? How could something get in our heads?'

'I don't know,' I said, 'I need to think about it.'

Lily was so shaken up that she curled up in a ball on the sofa and stared blankly straight ahead of her. I made her a mug of sugary tea and she propped herself up on one elbow to sip at it, but she seemed barely able to move.

'Dan is my friend,' she said after a while, 'but now we've... done things... we're never going to be able to look at each other the same way again. I've lost my friend-' her voice broke and a couple of drops of tea spilled onto the sofa, '-and I've lost my husband, because you'll never look at me the same way again either.'

She looked down at herself. 'I hate my body,' she said, 'I *am* disgusting.'

'This wasn't your fault. Something happened to you that you didn't want; I'm not going to hold that against you.'

She fell silent and I sat next to her for a long time, thinking.

'Where do you think Dan is?' she asked me eventually, 'do you think he's driven home?'

I felt a twinge of anger at hearing his name again.

'I don't care where he's gone,' I said.

With an effort, Lily manoeuvred her body into a sitting position. 'I understand you being mad at him,' she said, 'but he's probably really upset. I don't think he wanted to touch me anymore than I wanted him to do it.'

Personally, I wasn't quite so sure, and also, I really didn't care if he was upset. I knew on a sort of factual level that I was still friends with him and that I'd forgive him, but right now, I was perfectly happy to carry on hating him.

Lily got up and went to look out of the kitchen window.

'He's still outside,' she said, as she held the beige blind out of the way with one hand to look down at the car park. 'He's just sitting in his car.'

I wasn't particularly keen to rush down and start talking to him, but I was kind of curious why he was still out there, I'd just assumed he would have driven back to his mum's house. I suppose it was seriously late, in fact, the sky was just beginning to lighten towards dawn, but surely he wasn't planning on sleeping in his car, and I didn't think he'd be so pathetic as to just hang around waiting for me to come and speak to him.

In the end, curiosity won out over my anger, and when Lily said she thought she should try to get some sleep, I decided I'd go down and see what the deal was with Dan.

Chapter 17

When I opened the car door, Dan was clearly frightened and studied my face as if to check whether I'd come to have another fight with him. Satisfied that I'd calmed down he said, 'alright?'

'Yeah,' I said, 'mind if I join you?'

He was one of these people that couldn't help but store all kinds of crap inside his car and before I could sit down he had to shift a whole heap of what appeared to be rubbish- empty bottles, receipts, bags of crisps, and for some reason a pair of socks.

'I thought you were going to hit me, back in the flat,' he said.

I looked at him but he wouldn't meet my eye.

'I watched you leave,' I said, 'I almost came after you.'

'But you didn't,' he said. He was still refusing to turn and face me, but I thought I heard just a hint of a smile in his voice.

'I didn't need to,' I said, 'your life is miserable enough already.'

He looked round at me sharply and I felt a little pang of guilt as I realised how much I'd hurt him.

'Dan, I didn't-'

'No,' he said, 'it's fine. You might as well say it like it is. It's not like I don't know I'm a total fuck-up.'

I was struck by the way there seemed to be something a bit pathetic about him. Why wasn't he arguing with me, trying to protest his innocence? I mean, he was the one in the wrong I guess, but where was his fight?

The silence was awkward, then I noticed the radio in the car was on and tuned to a station but that it was completely silent.

'Dan, are you listening to the radio on mute?' I asked.

'Nothing good was on,' he said.

'So why not turn it off?'

'Because I wanted to have the radio on. I didn't just want to sit in the car in silence.'

I raised an eyebrow. Ordinarily, what he'd just said would have made me laugh, but instead it just made me feel even worse about what he'd done and I felt sickeningly betrayed all over again. Then, as if he'd just understood my thought process, he turned to look at me.

'Nick, I really am sorry about what you saw- about what happened between me and Lily. I swear on my life I didn't know what I was doing. It was the game.'

I nodded. 'That's what Lily said too.'

'That's because it's true. Look, the game, it reached into my mind, it made it larger-'

'Yes, I know.'

Dan looked at me closely. 'It happened to you as well?'

'Yes.'

'You stopped needing to use your hands to control the game?' he asked me, 'and then the game stopped being so important, there was just this strange sensation in your mind, like it was being explored?'

'Yeah.'

Dan rubbed his forehead and frowned. 'What's happening to us?'

'I don't know.'

'Do you think it was Interface?'

I watched through the windscreen as the sky changed, became streaky with early morning light through the clouds. Of course it was Interface. Everything was fucking Interface.

The enormity of what had happened between him and Lily made being with Dan strange. It seemed difficult to just talk to him and we lapsed into silence again for a while, though as if to try and make me happy, he turned the radio off.

'Dan, why are you here?' I asked, 'why didn't you go back to your mum's?'

He took in a deep breath and I thought he was going to speak, but instead he stayed silent as though giving his answer careful consideration.

'This isn't the right time to talk about it,' he said finally. 'I just want to make things right with you and Lily.'

'What do you mean?' I said, 'has something happened at home?'

He sighed, and I knew he didn't want to discuss it, but I'd left him no choice. 'I don't know what the hell is going on,' he said wearily, 'it's just more of the same, really. But I can't go back there at the moment.'

Instead of explaining any further, he took out his phone and turned it on. Both of us had got into the habit of having our mobiles permanently turned off unless we actually wanted to use them so that we could ignore all the heat about Affrayed.

'Here,' he said, handing the phone to me once he'd found what he was looking for. It was a text from his mum.

if u want the stuff from ur room come and get it in the next few days or im chucking the lot

I handed it back to him. I was shocked. I knew he had problems on and off with his mum and sister but he'd never told me things had got this bad.

'Is she serious?' I asked.

'Nah,' Dan said, 'she just wanted me to come running straight back round there.'

'When was it sent?' I asked. I'd been so surprised by what it said that I'd forgotten to look.

'Beginning of this week,' he said, 'on Monday. The day you and Lily said I should stay with you for a bit.'

'That's more than a few days ago,' I said, 'you'd better hope she's not serious.'

Dan shrugged. 'Fuck it. Even if she does get rid of my stuff, I can buy it all again. It's not like I can't afford it now.'

'Yeah, but that's not really the point, is it?' I said, 'and what about all your sketches and stuff?'

The last time I'd been in Dan's room, it had been absolutely full of sketches. He mostly liked to draw stuff to do with games, but he sometimes drew other things. I could always remember one almost haunting picture of his that I'd come across- an intricate portrait of a young woman sitting at a small table in front of a brick wall. Only, part of the brick wall had crumbled away and behind her was an immense cityscape, and the woman herself had "hair" formed partly out of complex geometric patterns that fell in two long straight curtains over her eyes and her bare breasts. When he'd caught me looking at it he'd seemed a bit embarrassed, even though it was really good.

In answer to my question, Dan reached round to the back seat of the car, and picked up a carrier bag stuffed with sketchpads and loose sheets of paper, and I realised he'd gathered all his drawings up and brought them with him.

'Dan, what's going on?' I asked him.

'Robyn went AWOL again last weekend,' he said, 'she's always doing it, just disappearing for a few days with her friends or her boyfriend. God, that guy,' he said, shaking his head, 'I told you about him, didn't I?'

'Is he the one who tried to sell you the brand new laptop that he claimed used to be his friends' dads' brother's, or however it went?'

Dan burst out laughing at the memory of it, 'oh yeah! Oh man, that was fucking ridiculous, if that thing wasn't stolen I...' he trailed off and I understood why. For a brief moment it had felt like we'd both moved on from what had happened, and that everything was like old times, but then he'd remembered again. Remembered that nothing was like old times.

'So, yeah,' Dan said, 'Robyn goes off, she gets bored, she comes back again. But every time she does it mum goes spare. She's even had me out looking for her once or twice. But Robyn always comes back when she runs out of money, or wants some proper food or whatever. But last Sunday she went off and I was with you and Lily, and mum was losing it because she couldn't get hold of me. Anyway, long story short, we had a massive row when I showed up there on Monday so I told her I was moving out and I'd stay with you until I got my own place.'

I stared at him, 'were you going to mention that to us at some point?'

Dan shrugged. 'That's why I kept this stuff in the car. I didn't want it to look like I was moving in. I was going to explain the situation when it seemed like the right time, but now with what's happened tonight... I'd understand if you didn't feel comfortable having me in your flat.'

The thing was, I knew he was sorry, but now I also realised why he was quite so keen to make sure I knew it. He wanted me to say it was fine, that he could stay with us, that I didn't mind- and a part of me actually wanted to say it, but I couldn't. Not quite. And Dan noticed that I couldn't.

'I'll find somewhere else,' he said coldly.

'Dan-'

'Hell, I could *buy* my own place now. So could you with the money we've made. In the meantime, I'll figure something out.'

'Look, I'm not saying you can't stay with us,' I said, 'I just can't give you an answer right this second. I mean, Christ, Dan, you and Lily were practically having sex on the sofa in front of me.'

That said, we reached yet another silent impasse. Both of us wanted things to be normal, but how could they be? Lily was my wife and I'd have that image of her with Dan forever. But Dan was my closest friend, and he was telling me he hadn't meant to do it, that he was sorry. On top of that, he needed my help. My mind was spinning. How had Interface done what he'd done? How could Lily and Dan have done what they'd done? How could I make it right again? I began to feel claustrophobic inside the car. I wanted to get outside, feel the fresh air.

'Come on,' I said to Dan, 'let's walk for a bit.'

We wandered down to the big grassy park in the middle of the housing estate, Dan moodily kicking a stone along in front of him, though he soon got bored of it.

'Do you know why Amy broke up with me?' he said, surprising me yet again. He'd always made it sound like it had been a mutual thing before, and though I'd had my suspicions, I'd thought it better to let him tell me whatever made it easier for him.

'No,' I said simply.

'She got sick of my work,' Dan said, 'she hated how I never had any money and I was still living at home. How we never went anywhere or did anything. How I worked weird hours- which I know was my own fault, but still.'

'I'm sorry,' I said. It seemed like the right thing to say.

'Turns out she was holding out for us to release DreamChase,' Dan continued, 'she was hoping things would change. But they didn't, did they? It was just more of the same old shit and she couldn't do it anymore.'

'You didn't have to carry on with DAWN,' I said, 'I would have understood.'

Dan laughed then. 'I did have to carry on,' he said, 'see, that's the really fucked up thing about it all. I knew Amy was fed up of it. I knew she was going to walk away, and you know what, I didn't actually care.'

I looked round at him and I noticed he seemed liberated by saying this, like he was making some great confession. 'I didn't care,' he said, 'because all I cared about was finishing DreamChase. Finishing the game. I made DAWN my whole life, so I couldn't stop, because as far as I could see, DreamChase, and then Affrayed, were the only reason at all that it was worth me actually being alive. I used to think to myself, I don't even mind if I die, just so long as it's after Affrayed is finished.'

I tried to take it all in. 'Dan, what are you talking about?'

He stopped walking and stood on the deserted pavement in the deserted park, the first rays of sunlight lighting up the sky behind him. 'It's just like you said,' he told me, 'I have a miserable life. A miserable excuse of an existence. And it's my own fault. I've fucked everything up. I've fucked up my entire life.'

I steered him over to a bench at the side of the path where he threw himself down, still seeming on the brink of laughter or tears. It was like what had happened with Lily had made things seem so bleak to him that he'd decided he might as well throw it all out there.

'I really shouldn't have said your life is miserable,' I told him, 'I didn't mean it, I was just angry.'

Dan ignored me. 'Nobody wants me,' he said. 'I know how pathetic that sounds, but it's true, isn't it? Amy didn't want me, my dad's never wanted me, now mum doesn't want me, Robyn doesn't want me and I've blown things with you and Lily too. The only time I ever felt good was when I was working on Affrayed, but it was doing that that's made my life like this, it's made it kind of shrink, you know. Everyone else I know has gone off and got a job and they're, like five years ahead of me career-wise now. I barely even speak to any of them anymore. I know we've made all this money, but I feel like... I don't know where I am. I don't know what I'm doing.'

He turned and looked at me. 'What am I doing?'

I thought for a moment. I wasn't really prepared to answer a question like that, but I did understand what he was talking about. I'd seen my friends from uni get jobs, get promotions, move all over the country- some were in pretty senior roles already. But while they were doing all that I'd been at home, making games, hoping for the kind of success that would one day make my choice make sense. It was daunting sometimes. But I'd chosen a life like that because I just couldn't bear the thought of doing anything else. And so had Dan. What had happened now, our fake success, had a twisted kind of irony to it.

The sun had risen sufficiently that I could look out across the park, the grass speckled with dandelions and daisies, my eye coming to rest on the brightly coloured fence around the children's playground. Empty at this hour on a Sunday morning it made me feel strange, made me feel somehow incredibly, inescapably old.

'You want to know what you're doing right now, Dan?' I asked him, and he sat up, interested. 'Right now, you and me, and Lily, we're fighting Interface. And we're in it together. So we'll draw a line under what happened and you can stay with us, okay?'

Dan looked down at his lap. 'I didn't tell you all that so you'd let me stay with you.'

'I know,' I said, 'but you can. Besides, you certainly can't sleep in your car; I wouldn't wish that on anyone.'

At my insult, he grinned. I'd always taken the piss out of his car, and the fact I was doing so now showed him that things were, if not exactly back to normal, then close enough.

Chapter 18

For a while, I was quite happy to just sit next to Dan in the park, listening to the first few sounds of the world coming to life- a car engine in the distance, the birds singing. I had to view what happened between Dan and Lily as an attack by Interface. He'd tried to break us apart, turn us against each other. Why, I couldn't imagine. But that had to be it, and if that was his game, then I wasn't going to play.

I was beginning to think maybe we should walk back- I wanted to check on Lily, to tell her I was sorry I shouted at her, but then Dan's phone began to ring.

He frowned as he looked at the screen and I saw that the call was from an unknown number. He rejected it and shrugged. 'Probably someone trying to sell something,' he said.

But then the phone rang again and to our astonishment the number was no longer unknown. There was a name on the screen, and the name was "Interface".

'Fascinating,' Interface said, as soon as the phone was answered. Dan put the call on loudspeaker and held the phone between us, his fingers gripping it a little too tightly.

Even from that one word, I noticed that Interface's voice was strange. He pronounced the syllables too clearly, too precisely, in a voice that was masculine but sounded engineered and unreal.

'What's fascinating?' I asked, taking the lead even though it was Dan that Interface had called.

'Your reaction to my experiment.'

I saw Dan tense, and I was sure he was about to speak angrily to Interface, so I jumped in first, trying to stay calm and collected.

'So you admit it was you who made Dan and Lily do that?' I said.

'I didn't make them do anything. You all felt me in your minds and you let me in.'

'We didn't know what you were going to make us do!' Dan said, 'how could you do that to us? You were saying the other day you wanted to be our friend, what the hell did you think you were doing?'

'Dan, please. Is it so bad?' Interface said, 'you and Lily were enjoying yourselves.'

Dan looked at me, eyes wide with horror, 'no...' he said.

'Let me handle it,' I told him, and I took the phone from between his cool and clammy fingers.

'What you did was unforgiveable,' I said to Interface. 'Lily and Dan are friends, they don't want to have that kind of relationship. In fact, what you did was basically assault, so don't even try-'

'If you are so against sharing your bodies with each other, why did you do so in Affrayed?'

Dan and I stared at each other in blank astonishment. Had we actually heard that right? Was he really drawing a parallel between us messing around in a game and what had just happened back in the flat?

'You see, I understand that Lily is your wife, Nick, but then you let her and Dan have sex in Affrayed. So I thought, if you enjoyed it so much in the game, why not in reality?'

Dan leaned close to me and whispered 'what the fuck is going on?'

I was equally as astounded, Interface's words completely flooring me. Was it a joke? He didn't sound like he was joking.

'Are you... are you being serious?' I managed to ask.

'I'm always serious.'

'But Affrayed is a video game,' I said, barely believing I was having to spell this out to him. 'What you made Dan and Lily do was *real*.'

'Explain the distinction.'

I looked helplessly at Dan, but he was just as baffled as I was.

'That's not... you're not really asking me to do that, are you?' I said.

'You don't have to,' Interface said. 'I have some conclusions of my own, I was just interested to hear your opinion.'

I heard footsteps behind us and looked around so sharply that I startled the early morning jogger on the path behind the bench. He gave me a puzzled frown and veered out a little onto the grass, giving us a wide berth.

'Well, if you have nothing to say, perhaps I should continue to draw my own conclusions,' Interface said.

'So, you're seriously telling me that what you did was an experiment?' I said.

'Yes. Of sorts. It is research.'

'Research into what?'

'Many things. Relationships, sexual behaviour, marriage, friendships. I created a situation. Then I saw how you responded to it.'

I gripped the phone tightly between my fingers, my skin prickling and my mouth dry.

'How did you do it? How did you get into our minds like that?'

'You let me in.'

'What?' I said, 'it's not like we had a choice!'

'You did,' Interface said, 'but you liked it so you didn't want it to stop. I'm pleased. I hoped you would enjoy it.'

Dan grabbed the phone from my hand and shouted into it. '*Enjoy* it? We didn't enjoy it! Have you any fucking idea what you've done, you piece of-'

'Dan. Why are you so angry?' Interface said, calm as ever. 'Nick has forgiven you. He blames me.'

'I'm angry because...' he stopped, slowed down. 'I'm angry because I care about Lily, and about Nick.' He looked at me awkwardly. 'I don't want to fall out with them.'

'That's commendable. But as I recall you did not take that much encouragement from me to begin engaging in sexual behaviour with Lily.'

At this Dan threw the phone down onto my lap and strode away from the bench. I watched him for a moment, though he stood with his back to me, his shoulders rigid, and I noticed he was curling and uncurling his fists like he wanted to go and hit something but was trying to stop himself.

'Listen,' I said to Interface, 'I don't know what sort of sick game you're playing, but I'm telling you now, I'm going to make you pay for this. I might not know who you are, or where you are, but I will find out and I'll make you sorry.'

This, finally, seemed to persuade Interface to start acting a bit more considerately.

'What a shame,' he said, 'I didn't realise how seriously my research would damage my relationship with the three of you. That was not my intention. I sought only to understand you better, not to bring you pain.'

'Why don't you understand us already?' I asked, 'you knew what would happen if I saw Dan and Lily like that. You must have done.'

'I had some ideas, yes.'

'Then why do it?'

'I wanted to find out for sure. I wanted to see how you would react.'

Suddenly, I realised something. How would Interface know how we reacted? He'd stopped messing with our minds by then, surely all he could know about what came after was what Dan and I were telling him now.

'Interface,' I said slowly, 'I don't understand. How could you possibly have seen our reactions?'

'I observed,' he said, 'from your minds. Don't worry, I'm not still doing it. I just wanted to collect my results.'

I looked up and saw Dan was walking back over. He sat down heavily beside me and looked at the phone.

'How?' I asked Interface. 'How did you observe from our minds?'

'Never mind about that. You wouldn't understand.'

'Try me,' I said, 'I want to know.'

'Perhaps I should tell you what I've concluded about your behaviour so far,' he said, 'I would enjoy discussing it with you.'

'Well I wouldn't,' I said, 'the only thing I want to discuss with you is who you are and how you're doing what you're doing. Who are you really? What is the Network?'

'The Network is a network. It's not complicated.'

'Then why can't you explain it better than that?'

'Because I'm constrained by the limits of your understanding.'

I laughed humourlessly. 'You mean I'm too stupid to understand?'

'That's not how I would word it. But you and the Network are currently incompatible. That is why an interface is necessary. You of all people should understand. You work with interfaces all the time, don't you?'

I looked at Dan. He looked tired, angry and confused. 'He manipulated us,' I said to him quietly, 'he made you do what you did so he could watch how I reacted.'

Dan barely looked surprised. But Interface had heard my words.

'That's not entirely true,' he said, 'I didn't manipulate you. What I did was let you join with me a little, that is, with the Network, and then I let you explore a situation that you had already created yourselves within Affrayed.'

'No!' Dan said, 'I would never do something like that, not ever. You made me do it.'

'Really?' Interface said, 'perhaps I did. But your minds are my raw material, nothing that I encourage to happen can take place without your cooperation. As to whether it would have happened naturally, I suppose that is unlikely. But you give me what I work with, so perhaps if you don't like it, you should look to yourselves.'

...

'What was all that?' I said to Dan as we made our way back to the flat.

'I don't know,' he said.

'Do you believe any of it?'

Dan sighed. 'I'm not sure. But what he said at the end, about what happened already being in our heads somehow, that just isn't true. I mean, I like Lily a lot; you and her are my closest friends, these past couple of years I've spent more time with the two of you than with anybody. And... I do think Lily is very beautiful. I always have. But I swear I've never thought about doing anything with her. It's never even crossed my mind.'

'Yeah, Dan, I know,' I said, as we reached the front door. I knew he wasn't lying, not exactly. But there was no denying he looked badly shaken up by Interface's final statement and pretty confused, giving me the uncomfortable feeling that it wasn't just me he was trying to reassure with his words.

Chapter 19

I looked in on Lily when I got inside and she was fast asleep in bed, curled up on her side, one hand under her cheek. The duvet was twisted round her like she'd been tossing and turning and I was glad that now she was getting a bit of peace.

I thought about going to bed as well but I could hardly have felt less tired and I didn't want to risk waking Lily. Instead Dan and I sat at the little dining table in the kitchen, cradling mugs of coffee and wondering what on earth we'd got ourselves involved in.

By mid morning our conversation was going nowhere and when Lily woke up I suggested that we all go out to get something to eat, feeling that a change of scenery might do us some good.

We filled Lily in on what had happened with Interface as we walked to the pub, but the conversation was stilted and awkward. Dan seemed barely able to look at her and I was sure he was afraid of giving me the impression he was interested in her.

Things didn't improve as we ate. The pub was a modern, cheap and cheerful sort of place, full of young families having Sunday lunch. I liked the noise, the predictability and normality of it, which provided a welcome contrast to the bizarre night we'd just had, but Dan and Lily were obviously still reeling from what they'd done and had no idea how to act with each other. Finally, I couldn't take it anymore.

'Look, you two, can you please just say to each other whatever you need to say to make this right?'

Startled, Dan looked up from his laptop, where he was taking advantage of the free wifi in the pub to read through the latest comments on Affrayed's forums, and Lily put down her knife and fork and pushed her still half-full plate away from her. For a moment their eyes met across the table in silence, and then they both started talking at once, though Lily quickly stopped to listen to Dan.

'I just... I just wanted to say sorry,' he said, 'for what I did to you. I feel awful about it. I wish-'

'Dan,' Lily said, 'stop it, please. You don't have to apologise to me. We both... did it.' She flicked her eyes briefly at me, then looked down at the table.

'I know,' Dan said, 'but I feel like I'm mainly to blame. I just really hope that you're okay and that we can forget about it.' I watched him as he spoke and by the end of it his face was red right to the roots of his hair, but the tension had got about as bad as it was going to get, and I could already feel the atmosphere between them softening, melting away.

'Neither of you were to blame,' I said, 'it was Interface.'

'Nick's right,' Lily said, 'it wasn't really our fault. I don't want things to be different between us. I was so worried after what happened. I thought you wouldn't like me anymore.'

'What?' Dan said, 'that's not how I feel at all! I just want things to go back to how they used to be.'

'Well, then,' Lily said, holding out her hand across the table. 'Friends again?'

He took her hand and shook it. 'Friends,' he agreed.

After that, things were so much easier. There was still a bit of weirdness, the shared memory that something very wrong had happened, but now the two of them had cleared the air we went back to talking about Interface.

'So he definitely said last night was an experiment?' Lily asked me.

'Yeah. An experiment, research, whatever.'

Lily frowned and turned her attention to picking ice cubes out of her glass of coke and dropping them into mine.

'I'm trying to see if anyone else experienced something like us,' Dan said, glancing up from his laptop.

'And have they?' I asked.

'Not that I can see.

'Do either of you have any idea what the Network could be?' Lily asked as she tried to trap a particularly troublesome cube between her finger and thumb.

I looked at Dan and he shook his head.

'No,' I said, 'not really.'

'Because that's key, isn't it?' she said, as she dropped the ice into my drink, 'it always comes back to the Network.'

'Interface says we can't understand what it is,' I said.

'But that's probably just more of his crap,' Dan said, 'he doesn't want to say what it is, so he just says that. I mean, it's weird, but the whole thing's fucking weird, right?'

'Okay,' Lily said, 'so what do we know? We know that whoever the Network is they can do things I thought were impossible. They got inside our heads.'

'Did they though?' I said slowly, 'I mean, do we know that for absolutely sure? Is there any other way that what happened could have happened? Maybe they drugged us and somehow watched what took place afterwards?'

'There's no way,' Dan said, 'before he made... uh, you know, before stuff got really crazy, we could control the game with our minds. That definitely happened.'

Suddenly, our empty plates were scooped up from the end of the table and I almost jumped out of my skin at the unexpected interruption.

Lily shrugged. 'I don't know a whole lot about drugs,' she said, 'but I have to say it seems an unlikely explanation. And how would any of it even have been done? Drugs, spying on us, any of it? There's always someone in the flat at the moment, and we didn't even all eat together, so unless the person responsible was one of us,' she paused briefly, 'and I think we can rule that out, then I guess he really was in our minds.'

We reached another dead end, but then Lily rooted around in her big, mushroom-coloured handbag until she found a pen, and the three of us brainstormed everything we knew about Interface and the Network, while she listed it on the back of a white serviette. When we were done, I picked it up and read through it.

'Okay,' I said, 'so we know Interface has the resources and the manpower to make and maintain a game like Affrayed. He was also able to get hold of our bank and credit card details, get rid of huge numbers of comments about us from multiple web pages, get Dan's mobile to come up with his name when he called last night, and seemingly he can also get access to people's thoughts and influence their behaviour. We have no idea who he is, who he works for, or why any of this is being done, apart from that Interface says it's for research, but why anyone needs to research what we did last night God only knows. Finally, he seems pretty adamant that we are not "compatible" with the Network, that we wouldn't understand it.'

Lily leant forward on the table, resting her chin in her hand. She looked tired, a little line between her straight, dark eyebrows, her normally warm eyes dulled by too many late nights. Dan looked similarly exhausted, though still awake enough to slide the serviette and the pen across to him and start doodling around the outside of our list.

Suddenly he stopped. 'Do you think we're the only ones?' he asked.

We both looked round at him.

'If he really is doing research, and he seems pretty keen to tell us that he is, then there must be others. I mean, that's got to be what Affrayed is for, right? The whole thing must just be a front for the Network's research.'

'You said there was no mention of anybody else experiencing what we did on the forums,' Lily said.

'Yes,' Dan said, 'but maybe it's like those other comments and Interface is just getting rid of them as soon as they appear. Suppressing them.'

'But maybe some have slipped through the net, if we look somewhere more obscure,' Lily suggested. 'I mean, maybe he's monitoring specific websites. Let's just try searching.'

Dan typed in various different searches around the theme of Affrayed, experiments, mind control and Interface, but we didn't get long to investigate before the laptop screen went black.

INTERFACE: Dan, Nick, Lily. If you want to understand what's happening, the solution is simple. Play my game.

Before we could even think about replying, Interface returned the computer to Dan's control, and we were left staring at the uninspiring results of our search once again.

Chapter 20

For a little while, we resisted playing Affrayed. We were angry with Interface for what he'd done, and scared by the powers he appeared to have. But by the time it was evening we gave in, reluctant yet somehow excited to enter the game again. I actually felt a bit sick as I logged in, and when I looked over at Lily and Dan they seemed nervous too.

Within a few minutes of entering the game we found ourselves embroiled in a particularly vicious fight around a strategically important cluster of warehouses. It seemed a slightly odd move for our rival gang, Renegade Shadows to make, as the warehouses were well defended by Outbreak and even though they had more weapons than us they were getting quite a hammering.

But a couple of hours into the fight, it became clear what the Renegades were really after, as they captured Lily and another female character, and started dragging them away. By this point, I was again controlling the game purely with my mind, but even that didn't make me quick enough to help Lily, as the Renegade's actions were so unexpected. Not that taking hostages wasn't a common part of the game. In fact, part of what we'd done to encourage Outbreak to let us join them was capture somebody from the Renegades. Taking hostages was a good way of forcing the rival gang to make concessions, particularly if you managed to capture somebody important. Not that Lily was especially important in terms of her value to Outbreak, but perhaps it had been noticed that Dan and I were very protective of her, or maybe she was just in the wrong place at the wrong time. Whatever the reason, before we knew it she'd been bundled into the back of a white van parked in the scrubby wasteland outside the warehouses, and all we were left with was a cloud of dust thrown up by the screeching tyres as it sped away.

It was the van that really showed us it was planned, because although the streets in Affrayed were full of abandoned vehicles of various kinds, seeing one being driven was unusual as fuel was scarce. The Renegade Shadows had obviously come here specifically to take hostages, and the attack on our warehouses had just been a front to draw us all out into the open.

'Help me!' Lily cried as she watched her fate on the screen in front of her. She sounded genuinely terrified, but her fear didn't even seem strange, because it was all so real, and I was scared for her too. I wanted desperately to help her, to get her back to safety.

Outbreak's response was daring and uncompromising. Already riled by the Renegade's audacious attack on our warehouses, we all piled down to the empty shopping centre that we knew was the heart of the Renegade's operation, and more than likely where they would take Lily and the other woman.

The place was like a fortress, and some of Outbreak began to realise it was hopeless and gave up, but Dan and I tried to find some other way inside, hoping to take them by surprise. Eventually, our determination paid off, and we managed to get in using the classic method of crawling through air vents. Once inside, we made slow and careful progress, managing to avoid the few members of the Renegades who were wandering around. But before we found the place where Lily was being held, we suddenly saw her walking towards us, the other woman at her side.

I realised something was wrong when the other woman kept on walking but Lily's character suddenly stopped, and began to cry. I hadn't seen characters cry in Affrayed before, but this didn't really concern me so much as the fact she was just standing still, and even though Dan and I were walking towards her she seemed not to see us. In my confusion, Affrayed began to fade from my awareness and reality back in, and I turned to look at her.

She sat at the dining table, her and Dan having chosen to play there instead of on the sofa, still too unnerved by what had happened the night before. Lily had her back to me, but I could see she was hunched over with her head in her hands, and sobbing so loudly that I didn't know how I couldn't have heard it before. Dan, however, was still totally immersed, his eyes fixed on the screen, so before comforting Lily I quickly shook his shoulder and he was jerked back into reality as though from a deep trance.

'Lily, what is it?' I asked her, 'what happened?'

'I... they....,' she shook her head and started crying even harder, so I logged her out of the game to stop her being reminded of whatever it was, and stroked her back until she calmed down a little.

'Lily, what did they do?' I asked her.

She looked round at Dan and me. Her eyes were bright with tears, but her voice was strong and she spoke savagely as she said, 'there were fifteen men and two women, what do you think they did?'

I was so shocked that I thought I must have misunderstood, but Dan had obviously heard the same thing I just had, as he said, 'Jesus.'

But I was confused. Affrayed had been modified to allow sex between characters, but there had been nothing nasty about it. If you came on to another player and they weren't interested, that was it, end of discussion- there were no further actions it was possible for you to make, at least, not that I'd noticed.

'Lily,' I said gently, 'what exactly happened? Do you mean you just saw the normal sex animation several times or-'

She shook her head violently.

'So, you mean you were shown a rape animation?'

She nodded, and started to cry again.

I exchanged a look with Dan. Sex in a game was one thing, but this... this was something else.

'This isn't right,' Dan said, 'shit like that isn't entertainment.'

Abruptly, Lily broke free of my embrace and stood up.

'I think I want to be on my own,' she said, 'I'm going to bed.'

I caught her arm, 'I'll come with you,' I said.

'No,' she said, 'not yet. Please.'

'Okay,' I said and I let her go.

'Will she be alright?' Dan asked.

'Yeah,' I said, 'sometimes she just needs to be on her own. I'll check on her in a bit.'

'This is messed up,' Dan said, 'gang rape, in a game. People aren't going to like that.'

At that point I realised something awful. I realised that just as Dan had said, a lot of people wouldn't like it. And they'd be angry.

And they'd look for someone to blame. And that someone would be the game developer.

And the game developer, as far as the rest of the world was concerned, was DAWN Industries. Me and Dan.

Chapter 21

News of what happened spread across the internet like wildfire. I went to check on Lily and stayed with her until she fell asleep, but then Dan and I sat at my desk watching helplessly as people's outrage inevitably turned towards us. It seemed that Lily's was not the only example of gang rape happening in Affrayed, though it did not appear to be possible for only one player to rape another.

Over the following couple of hours Affrayed sparked a lively debate on what is and isn't acceptable in videogames, with some arguing that since games often show brutal killings, what's the difference between that and showing sexual violence, while other people argued that it was disgusting and offensive.

There were even comments from a few of the players who had attacked Lily and the other woman, all of whom said they hadn't realised what was going to happen, that they'd just stumbled blindly into the situation because the game allowed them to. A couple of them even apologised. There were many calls for DAWN Industries to justify the inclusion of rape in Affrayed, calls which we couldn't answer. In the end I got so frustrated by the whole situation, by the fact that if anyone had been the victim it was my own wife, that I tried to get Interface to talk to me by repeatedly typing in the search:

Interface I want to speak to you

Eventually, he obliged.

INTERFACE: You wanted me.

DAWN: I want you to explain yourself.

INTERFACE: What do you mean?

DAWN: Your new modification to Affrayed.

INTERFACE: Yes. It's causing quite a stir it seems. I've been watching people's comments online.

DAWN: So have we. And I'm sick of it. Stop modifying Affrayed. Or if you insist on it, take responsibility for it yourself.

INTERFACE: I'm sorry, but that is something I cannot do. Why are you so angry? Your sales are increasing even further.

'Fucking hell!' I said, slamming my hand against the desk in frustration. 'Of course I'm angry. Of course I'm fucking angry you stupid... stupid... stupid-'

Dan put his hand on my shoulder, and I calmed down a little.

DAWN: Why would you add something like that into Affrayed?

INTERFACE: Why wouldn't I?

DAWN: Because it's unnecessarily unpleasant.

INTERFACE: I only made the game world. I made it possible for people to do what they choose. There were two people in that room who didn't want to have sex, and fifteen who did, so their wishes were followed. That's democracy, isn't it? I thought you people liked that?

Dan and I were both so completely astonished by this statement that we stared at the screen in silence for several seconds.

'What... the hell?' Dan said.

'One thing makes sense now though,' I said slowly, 'that's why the game doesn't allow just one player to attack one other player. There have to be more who want it than don't.'

'But...*democracy?*' Dan asked, 'did he really just say that?'

'Well, it's right there on the screen,' I said, gesturing towards it.

DAWN: That is not democracy. And there is something wrong with you if you think it is.

INTERFACE: As I said, I only made the world. How people act is up to them. I didn't make them do anything.

DAWN: But you gave them the option. It's a game, people push the limits.

I mean, it was obvious. You give somebody a way to do something in a game, and they'll do it. They'll try to do things they're not "supposed" to do, they'll try to do things in the wrong order, they'll try to jump off buildings, kill their allies, run out in front of cars. They'll try to break it. And I was exactly the same. Give me a new game and I'll try to establish its limits, see what I'm "allowed" to do, see how far I can push it. So I wasn't angry with the players for what happened to Lily. They were just playing the game the same way I played games. The fact that Interface had included such a controversial element was appallingly insensitive because players thought they knew what they were getting in Affrayed and content like this was way outside the boundaries of what most people would expect or find acceptable. But I didn't want to get involved in a debate. On a personal level I thought the new changes were wrong and unnecessary and so, I was sure, did Dan, but that was up to us. The thing was, if it was Interface's game, and if everyone knew it was his game, then whatever. It was his problem. He could put content like that in if he wanted to and justify it himself. But to add such an element and make Dan and me accountable for it was just completely unreasonable. More than that, the game had no warnings that it contained that kind of violence, didn't even say it contained sex at all, in any form, and it certainly hadn't been approved by any ratings authorities. So there was no doubt we were in some serious shit.

On the screen, Interface had made his reply.

INTERFACE: Yes, exactly. People push the limits. I just let things happen. As for what you said about democracy, well, I think this just reinforces conclusions I drew after my experiment last night. There is a disconnect between your bodies and your minds. Lily and Dan are happy enough to talk to each other, after all, to share their thoughts. If they do that, why not share their bodies as well? What is the difference? And you are happy to make most decisions by taking a vote, even major ones, so why is there a limit to what you can vote on? What better way is there to make a decision about what happens than by going with a majority?

I was struck, not for the first time, by how Interface seemed to genuinely not understand some of this stuff, and despite myself I began to try and explain.

DAWN: You can't vote on things like that! Other people can't just do what they want with your body, and they can't really tell you how to think either. Sometimes people might go along with a decision they don't agree with, but that's usually for the sake of some greater good like group harmony, which is something they do want.

INTERFACE: How would fifteen disappointed people and two happy people be group harmony?

DAWN: That's different.

INTERFACE: How?

DAWN: Because it's not right to injure somebody to get what you want. If what happened in Affrayed was real, then the amount of injury done to Lily and the other woman would far outweigh the brief reward gained by the men.

There was a long pause, and I wondered whether Interface was about to go. Then he replied.

INTERFACE: Okay. That makes sense.

I couldn't believe it. Was I finally getting somewhere with him? I quickly jumped in with a request while he was in this more reasonable mood.

DAWN: I want you to understand that what you are doing is injuring us, and harming the reputation of our business. Please take responsibility for Affrayed.

INTERFACE: That I cannot do.

DAWN: But it's upsetting us. I thought you understood.

INTERFACE: I'm sorry. But to use your own argument, I believe the benefits of our current setup are greater than the cost of your suffering. It is regrettable but unavoidable. You have my sympathy, but this is the way things have to be.

2007
Chapter 22

I searched the streets for a while after leaving Carl and the others in the bar, my anger at what Carl had said to me about Lily completely overshadowed by concern for her safety. I wished I'd never made her go to the stupid party. I should have just made up some excuse for her and if they thought it was weird that I kept doing that then to hell with them.

The thing was, I didn't know whether making an excuse would have been the right thing to do. Was it better for her to stay away from social situations and feel isolated, or to go to them and suffer but actually be around other people? It had to be better for her to see her friends, surely? Even if she couldn't really talk to them properly anymore.

The streets were full of people out having a good time, the pavements packed and noisy and chaotic, every second making me more sure that Lily was in danger. I searched up and down the high street, wondering whether she was trying to walk home or whether she'd just found somewhere to sit for a while. But she was nowhere, not on the benches, not leaning against a wall anywhere, not walking up and down the street. I tried to phone her several times but she usually ignored it and the couple of times she did answer she just hung on the end of the line in silence.

Just as I was becoming frantic and desperate in my efforts to find her, stopping people on the street and asking if they'd seen her, I noticed a figure slumped in a shop doorway, legs curled up under her body and her face in her hands as she cried.

I ran over to her and knelt down at her side.

'What are you up to, Lily?' I asked as lightly as I could, 'this doesn't look like much fun.'

She didn't look up but when I touched her shoulder she shuffled away from me, pressing her freezing body against the glass door of the shop.

'I've got your coat,' I said, 'do you want it?'

I draped it over her shoulders and she quickly pulled it around her, thrusting her arms into the sleeves and shivering into the thick fabric.

'Cold,' she said.

I looked round at the people passing us and was glad to see that the majority of them were paying us no attention. It was a Friday night and nobody was really that surprised to see a girl crying in the street.

'This isn't very sensible, is it?' I said gently, 'hanging around out here on your own. What if someone had hurt you?'

She looked round at me then, her face all fire and hatred.

'I don't care,' she said, 'people can do what they want to me. I really don't care.'

She started to cry more heavily and I sat down beside her.

'Don't talk like that, Lily. It's horrible and it's not even true. I think you'd care a lot if you were hurt. I certainly would.'

'I'll be dead soon anyway with any luck,' Lily said, 'if someone wants to help me on my way, they'd be doing me a favour.'

I drew in a deep breath and let it out shakily. Why the fuck did she say things like that? She was making herself cry by saying it, breaking her own heart by talking about how she wanted people to harm her, and yet she seemed compelled to say it, like she wanted to just keep piling on the pain and making herself suffer.

'How about I take you home?' I said, 'wouldn't you like that?' I stroked her hair and she didn't push me away. 'A nice warm bed to snuggle up in,' I said softly, 'that would be better than a shop doorway, wouldn't it?'

'I don't want to go home.'

'Well, come back to mine then. Everyone else is still out; it'll just be the two of us.'

I kissed her hair. 'In fact, we could always take advantage of having the house to ourselves. If you wanted to.'

I almost held my breath as I waited for her reaction. I knew it was risky, trying to talk to her about sex when she felt so low, but sometimes it worked. It often seemed to make her happy, reminding her how I felt about her, how attractive I found her. But tonight it didn't work, and when she looked round at me her expression was strange, hard to read.

'I... I'll try,' she said. She looked down at her lap. 'But I find it... difficult.'

I tried to lift her chin but she wouldn't let me.

'Difficult?' I asked.

'Sex,' she whispered, with a furtive glance out at the street, 'I can't... it doesn't *feel* right anymore. You do things to me and it doesn't make me... it doesn't make me feel...'

I closed my eyes for a second. I already knew, deep down.

'It doesn't make you feel any pleasure?' I asked quietly.

She nodded, burying her face in her hands as if she'd admitted to something incredibly shameful.

'It's not that I don't love you,' she said quietly, 'because I do, so much. And it's not that I don't feel *anything*, sometimes I do. But it's confusing. I... I'm not like a woman anymore. My body doesn't... work.'

Her words were so sad, so hopeless, that I hugged her close, pressing her against me so hard it almost hurt. 'It's because you're not well, Lily,' I said, 'you know that, don't you? When you're better things will change, things will go back how they were.'

'No,' Lily said, 'I'm dead, Nick. I'm just dead. You deserve better.'

For a long time I just held her. I didn't care about people seeing us; I didn't care about anything apart from trying to help Lily, trying to make her understand.

'I'm bad,' Lily said, 'I'm bad for you. I'm bad for everybody. I spoilt Carl's party and now I can't even give you what you want when we get home. I don't deserve for you to walk me back.'

She started undoing her coat. 'I don't even deserve for you to have brought me this,' she said as she reached the last button. 'You should have left me here to freeze to death.'

'No Lily,' I said, pulling her coat back around her. 'Come on. Let's go now.' I took her hand and practically dragged her to her feet, but she just sagged against me lifelessly.

'I don't want to,' she said, 'I don't want to walk. I can sleep here. I want to sleep here. This is where I belong, out here in the cold and the dirt and the rain. It's like me, Nick, don't you see? That's what I am.'

She wasn't making much sense, so I just pulled her along in the direction of home.

'I want to fall through the cracks,' she said, 'I want to be where the badness can't get at me. Where my badness can't get at the world.'

I didn't want to engage with it. I didn't really understand her, but getting her to explain would only make it worse. But for the rest of the walk I did try to challenge her assertion she was "bad". I tried to ask her what she thought "bad" actually was.

'Am I bad?' I asked her when we finally reached my house and I unlocked the front door. 'Because I'm sure I've done much worse stuff than you have, so if you're bad, I must be... well, pretty awful.'

'You're not bad,' Lily said.

'How do you know?'

'Because I'm the bad one. I make your life bad too. I made you leave all your friends tonight and I spoilt it for everybody.'

'No, you didn't,' I said as we stepped inside. I pushed the front door closed behind us and flicked on the light switch. Lily's makeup was smudged and her face white and tired. It was like the only thing animating her was her pain. 'It's probably just as well I left when I did,' I continued, 'Carl was starting to act like a dick.'

'He hates me,' Lily said.

'He doesn't hate you,' I said automatically, but I remembered the conversation he'd had with me as I left. How he'd suddenly turned on me like that. He could be a bit like that, unpredictable, stubborn, argumentative. He rubbed a lot of people up the wrong way. But generally he and I had got along just fine.

I steered Lily down the hall towards my bedroom and she lay down on my bed without even taking her coat off.

'Please,' I said, 'just explain to me what you think makes you bad, that makes you feel all this guilt. What is it you think you've done?'

Lily covered her face with her hands.

'There must be something,' I said, 'what is it that makes you feel like this?'

When Lily spoke, it was through her fingers and I could only just make out the words.

'I must have done something or why am I being punished?' she said, 'if only bad people go to hell, why am I in hell now? I must have done something. I try to work out what it was, but I can't, but I think it must be something terribly bad, there must be something deeply flawed in me if I've done something bad enough to warrant this punishment but I don't even know what it is. I must be doing awful things all the time and not even realising because to me they seem normal.'

I watched in shock as she dissolved into fresh tears. I had never in my life heard anything so painfully irrational.

'Has everyone who's ill done something wrong?' I asked her, 'do they all deserve it?'

'No!' she said, 'of course not. Is that what you thought I meant? That's not what I said, is it? Or maybe it was. You see how awful I am, so selfish, so disgusting. I think nasty things all the time about other people. Things I don't mean, that I don't even really believe, but they're horrible things and they're in my head.'

She pressed her hands to both sides of her head, as if she could squeeze all the terrible thoughts out of it.

'Lily this has got to stop,' I said, 'you're not well, you need to talk to people about it. There's a counselling service here at uni isn't there? Or you could tell Sophie, surely? She'd understand.'

'If she cared, she'd have asked me about it.'

'Well, what about your parents then? They'd be-'

'No!' Lily said, 'not my parents. Not my parents. I never want them to know about this, never.'

'But Lily-'

'No!' she said, her voice high and angry. 'You're not helping me. You're saying such stupid things. You never understand, you don't even try. Just leave me alone.'

With that, she pulled out the pillow from underneath her head and pressed it down over her face.

'Don't do that,' I said. I tried to pull the pillow out of her hands, but she pressed it even harder over her nose and mouth. I didn't panic- it wasn't like she was actually going to lay there and suffocate herself- but when she did this kind of stuff it just showed me that she was thinking about suicide, and I didn't like it at all.

'Lily, all this could be sorted out if you let somebody help you. I know you don't want to tell people you're depressed, but if you did I think things would be a lot better. Surely you can see that, can't you?'

Suddenly, Lily let go of the pillow and tried to hand it to me.

'You do it,' she said sweetly. 'Please?'

I didn't want to get drawn in. I knew that sometimes her relationship with me almost exacerbated her illness because she'd say things that hurt me, then feel guilty about them, then get upset, then hurt me more. I tried sometimes to ignore things she said that I didn't like, but that was usually a disaster, she'd just say things that were more and more extreme until she got a reaction. I didn't want to make things worse, but this wasn't just her illness, it was my life too. She was my life and she wanted to take herself away from me.

'Do what?' I asked her, looking at the pillow in her outstretched arms. 'You want me to suffocate you?'

'It would be better for everybody,' she said.

'No it wouldn't!' I said, 'it wouldn't be better for anybody. It certainly wouldn't be better for me.'

'Please,' she said, 'won't you just consider it?'

'No,' I said, 'and I don't know what you think the point is in asking me things like that. I would never do that to you and I don't think you really want me to, either.'

She stopped pushing the pillow towards me and hugged it to her chest while a couple of fat tears spilled from her eyes.

'That's how I know you don't love me,' she said.

'What do you mean? I asked, 'I love you more than anything.'

'So then why do you want me to suffer?'

'Lily-'

'You don't *understand*,' she said. 'I'm all wrong inside. It's like, when there's something wrong with animals they put them down, don't they? It's the kindest thing to do. I'm not going to get any better, this is what I'm like now.'

She threw the pillow aside and sat up to take my hands in hers. She was very calm now, very businesslike. It was as if I was the one being irrational and she was explaining the situation to me.

'I'm in so much pain, Nick. I'm hurting all the time. I just want to discuss this properly. I want to die. But I'm scared of being on my own. Maybe I could do it and you could just stay with me while I go, so that I'm with somebody who loves me. Couldn't you do that for me?'

'I don't want you to die,' I said.

'I know,' she said. She ran her fingers through my hair and kissed my forehead. 'But you don't want me to be in pain like this do you?'

'You're going to get better,' I said.

'No,' she said, 'not now. Not anymore. Ending my life isn't a question of if, now, it's when.'

I couldn't bear it. The way she was saying all this stuff like it was so normal, so logical, and for probably the first time in my adult life, I started to cry.

'I don't want you to go,' I said, 'please Lily, you have to promise me you won't take your life. Promise me.'

'I can't,' she said.

2013

Dailytoday online

Twelve year old girl in videogame rape outrage

10th June 2013

Controversy has followed videogame craze Affrayed ever since its release in May this year, but the most recent additions to the game's content have horrified critics and players alike, none more so than mother of three Melissa Mans, who in the early evening on Sunday 9th June was sickened when her daughter described to her what had just happened in the online game. "She was crying so much I couldn't understand her to begin with," Melissa told us, "but eventually I realised that her character in Affrayed had been taken somewhere and raped by several male characters. I was so shocked I could barely speak. I felt sick. I can't understand how this has happened."

As a massively multiplayer online game, Affrayed is played by thousands worldwide, but on Sunday the game was updated to allow players to commit shocking acts of sexual violence against each other. Already criticised for promoting gang violence and allowing players to indulge gratuitously in casual sex, the game now allows groups of players to trap and rape other players, usually when they have been taken as hostages from rival gangs. While there are some examples of skilled players fighting off their attackers and escaping this ordeal, most do not manage to do so, and once captured a player has little choice but to watch as their character is repeatedly assaulted.

DAWN Industries, the company who developed Affrayed, have

consistently refused to give statements defending the inclusion of sexual violence in their game, leading many critics, worried parents, and anti-videogame activists to draw their own conclusions. Agnes Thorpe, founder of the group Fighting Videogame Violence (FVGV), said of the game's developers:

"I cannot imagine what they were thinking when they included this content. Affrayed is a very sad, destructive game, trivialising sexual violence and showing a disturbing level of insensitivity to the real life victims of such crimes."

Before the release of Affrayed, DAWN Industries was almost unknown. As a tiny independent company consisting of only two individuals, developers Nick Winterbourne and Daniel Avery must have done extremely well out of Affrayed and its controversy, yet their actions have gained them few friends amongst gamers and other developers. Says Jayden Hesketh of IndieHit.com, a website dedicated to reviewing and promoting the work of companies like DAWN:

"The latest changes to Affrayed are entirely unnecessary and do nothing to enhance the experience. As far as I am concerned this type of violence has no place in this game or any other and I have lost a lot of respect for the guys at DAWN Industries for including it."

While the evidence on links between videogame and real world violence is still inconclusive, it is hard to predict what impact the content of Affrayed will have on its players, many of them children. Says Professor of Psychology at Eastport University, Douglas Furth:

"In a variety of studies, playing violent videogames has been shown to have a short term impact on aggressive behaviour, yet links between playing violent videogames and real world violence are

currently unclear."

However, as Agnes Thorpe of FVGV puts it:

"A game that so casually depicts cruel and mindless acts of violence makes me feel very uneasy about the role of videogames in our society. In particular, these new developments in Affrayed are taking videogames in a dark new direction that worries me enormously. Even if the game is nothing more than a way for people to let off steam, as some argue, it deeply saddens me to think that there are people out there who enjoy watching themselves rape a defenceless woman and feel they need to do so to unwind."

More entertainment stories

Published by Dailytoday online

Chapter 23

'People think we're scum,' Dan said, his words neatly summing up the outrage we'd been suffering in the time since Affrayed had received its latest update.

'Yep,' I said. I barely looked up from where I sat at my desk reading the latest posts on the DAWN Industries forum.

'Do you seriously think we can just sit tight and wait for this to blow over?' he asked me, 'because we *look* guilty. The longer we don't say anything the more people are going to talk shit about us-'

'I know, Dan,' I said wearily. The pressure had been seriously getting to him all day. It was getting to all of us. 'Hey, check this one out,' I said as I spotted a particularly colourful and barely coherent remark, 'I think you'll find it eloquent, educated and witty.'

Dan leant over and read it, shaking his head, and quoting the choicest bits. 'DAWN Industries is a money-grabbing bunch of cunts... cashing in on... what does the rest of that say?'

'I'm not a hundred percent sure, but I think it's *supposed* to say; cashing in on the sexual frustrations of people who can't get a fuck in real life.'

Dan laughed, 'classic,' he said, 'because of course none of the thousands of people playing Affrayed could possibly be getting laid, right?'

'Well, of course not,' I said, 'that's crazy talk.'

'What does it say?' I heard Lily's voice and we stopped laughing immediately, looking round at her in surprise. She was standing in the doorway, eyes puffy and red, face bare of any makeup and her hair in a loose, messy plait. For the last couple of hours we hadn't seen her and I'd assumed she'd fallen asleep.

'It doesn't matter,' I said, 'it's just somebody being stupid.'

I tried to put her off but she walked over to the desk and read the comment over my shoulder. 'It's horrible,' she said, and I could tell she was on the verge of crying.

'Lily, it's okay,' I said, 'don't get upset over it, that's what people like this want.'

'Look what they called the two of you,' she said, 'look what they said about DAWN. And you were laughing about it.'

'Well, you've got to admit it's kind of funny,' I said, 'it's just total nonsense, I mean-'

Lily stared at us both like we were crazy, her cheeks flushed bright red. 'Are you not seeing the same thing I'm seeing?' she said, 'They're saying you're deliberately trying to profit from this controversy, that the only thing you care about is the money!'

I read it again, eyebrow raised. 'I think exactly what they're saying is up for debate,' I said, 'It's probably the most poorly written sentence I've ever seen.'

By my side Dan sniggered, and Lily just exploded. 'This isn't funny!' she cried, 'who cares how it's written or what exactly they meant. Everybody's saying the same, they all think you're either just completely insensitive and disgusting people, or that you've done it as some sort of publicity stunt. Or both. That's what everybody thinks about you now, Nick, and you and Dan are *laughing* about it!'

I stood up and put my arm round her shoulders, 'it wasn't like that,' I said, 'I promise you, me and Dan don't think this is funny at all, we're both really upset. But when we saw that just then, it's like, well, you either have to laugh or you cry.'

'I hate it,' Lily said, 'I hate all of this, I can't stand it...' with this she let out a strangled cry of pain and frustration. 'I want it to stop,' she said, 'I want it to stop, I want it to stop.'

She buried her head in her hands and sank to her knees on the floor, and seeing what a state she was in Dan got up as well and came to join me where I sat beside her.

'I'm so sorry, Lily,' I said, 'I know this is really horrible.'

'We had a *journalist* come to our flat earlier,' Lily said. 'This is where we live, Nick, and people are turning up at our door asking why you made a game about gang rape.'

'I know, Lily, I know. It's awful.'

'It's not fair,' she said, 'you didn't do this. You're not the sort of people they all say you are.'

Suddenly, Dan's phone started ringing on the desk and he got up to turn it off. But before he sat back down on the floor beside Lily he looked at the computer again, pausing for a moment to read some of the newer posts further down and I couldn't fail to notice the way he froze for a second , then quickly closed the page.

'Dan?' I said, but he gave me a warning look and made a point of flicking his eyes down at Lily's bowed head.

'You need to apologise or something,' Lily said, oblivious. 'You have to make them understand that you don't think this new stuff in Affrayed is okay.'

'No,' I said softly. 'We can't do that. If we apologise or make any kind of reparation we're admitting responsibility. You understand that, don't you? We can't act like we put that content in and then a few days, weeks, or months down the line discover what Interface is and then change our story and say we didn't put it in. It's more honest to say nothing.'

'It doesn't feel honest.'

I looked at Dan over the top of Lily's head and the look on his face did nothing to make me feel any better. But I hugged Lily tightly, determined to at least make her think the two of us were strong. 'Come on,' I said, 'this will be alright. I've told you before when everything seemed hopeless that things would sort themselves out in the end. And I wasn't wrong.'

'You mean when I was ill?' Lily said, 'because right now I wonder whether it was even worth me getting better if this is what our life has become.'

...

Lily stayed with us for a little while, but she couldn't settle and before long went back to the bedroom again, though I doubted she was sleeping.

'That was intense,' Dan said when she'd gone.

'Yeah.'

'Are you okay?' he asked, looking at me closely.

I sighed. 'No,' I said, 'I'm really worried about her. I'm not sure she can handle this much stress.'

'Yeah,' Dan said, 'it's tough on her. But it's tough on all of us.'

'What did you see just then,' I asked him, 'when Lily was upset and you got up to turn your phone off?'

Dan looked uncomfortable. 'Ah... look, mate, I don't think you should read it,' he said.

He didn't stop me though and it didn't take long to find what he was talking about.

Nick winterbourne and dan avery- I hope your wives/girlfs get attacked for real see how you like it

I took a deep breath. I knew I had to expect stuff like this. I knew people felt like we'd done wrong and I could sympathise with them wanting answers. But this.

'Nick, I really wouldn't read too much into it,' Dan said quickly, 'they're just trying to stir it up that's all. I mean, we've had people coming on and saying they think the new changes are hilarious just to try and piss everyone off. The whole thing is totally out of control.'

'Listen,' I said, 'I don't care what people say about me. They can say whatever they want. But for people to threaten Lily-'

'Nobody is threatening Lily,' he said, 'they have no idea if we even have other halves, I mean, I don't, do I? For all they know possibly neither of us do.'

'What if she sees it?' I said, 'what if she thought people out there believe she deserves to be hurt?'

'She won't see it,' Dan said, 'it's on our forum, we'll take it down. But Nick, I think we do have to do something. People... proper people I mean, not the people writing that kind of shit, they want us to at least give some sort of explanation for all this. It's not unreasonable of them to want some answers.'

'I know that. But what the hell are we supposed to tell them? That Interface did it?'

'Yes,' Dan said, 'I think that's exactly what we have to say.'

Chapter 24

I was far from convinced.

'Dan, nobody is going to believe us.'

'I know,' he said.

'It'll make them hate us even more.'

'I don't think we've got any choice.'

We fell silent for a while, weighing up the potential consequences of speaking out, and then my eye came to rest on a present Lily had given me back in the early days when I was making DreamChase; a large shiny black pot with two cacti in it- one like strange, writhing fingers fuzzy with yellow spines, another a pale green column entirely obscured by long white hairs. She'd given me the plants when I'd been having a tough few weeks and my confidence was wobbling. She'd written a note to go with it, and I still had it tucked underneath the pot. I knew what it said practically by heart, but I found myself taking it out and reading it.

> *Nick, I know you're struggling right now, and I know it's hard sometimes when you work by yourself and everything gets out of perspective. But I promise you, DreamChase is a great idea. Other people think it's a great idea. Dan thinks it's a great idea. You know it's a great idea really, deep down, so don't give up. Just think, one day it will be finished, and the whole world will see how wonderful it is too. I know you can do it. I believe in you, and I'm already so proud of you. Lily xxx*

'What's that?' Dan asked.

'It's something Lily gave me ages ago,' I said, 'read it if you want.'

I handed it to him and he read it quickly, his eyes darting over Lily's big, swirly handwriting. She'd drawn hearts and funny big-eyed creatures all round the outside as well, reminding me of all the little beetles she'd created for Cactustrophe.

'It's sweet,' Dan said. He folded it up and gave it back to me.

'Yeah,' I said. 'She was always writing little things like this. She'd leave them on my desk before she went to work in the morning so I'd see them when I got up.' I slipped the note back underneath the pot of cacti. 'I can't see her writing me anything like that again now.'

Dan thought about this for a moment, and when he spoke again his voice was hard, filled with barely suppressed anger. 'You know what gets me?' he said.

'What?'

'How much this scandal has made people buy Affrayed. It's like you don't need to make something good to get a ton of sales. Stuff doesn't get in the news because it's good. We could have made a piece of shit game, whacked a load of controversial content in it and everyone would go on and on and on about it and people would buy it just to see what all the fuss was about.'

'Yeah, maybe. But not necessarily. And in any case, that's not what we want to be known for.'

Dan laughed bitterly. 'That's a shame, because it kind of is what we're known for now.'

'Affrayed isn't a shit game though. People bought it because it was good, at least originally. Perhaps now people are buying it because it's all over the news but it didn't start out that way.'

Dan rested his head in his hand and stared down at the desk. 'I don't know,' he said.

'What is it?' I asked.

He didn't look up. 'It's just... with the way things are at the moment, I don't even feel like I want to make games anymore.'

'Because of Affrayed?' I said.

Instead of answering he slid a book towards him from a pile at the end of the desk. It was one of Lily's, about the meanings of different plants and flowers, which I was pretty sure was not his cup of tea.

'Dan?' I said.

I watched him flick through the book in a blur of brightly coloured photographs, his eyes fixed resolutely on the pages. For a while I was puzzled, but then I realised that saying he didn't want to make games anymore had upset him far more than he wanted to let on, and he was looking at the book because he didn't want me to see his face. Eventually, though, he paused on a page about the significance of different coloured roses and glanced round at me.

'I just want things to go back to how they used to be,' he said. 'I know it was a nightmare back then at times, but I just want to be working on Affrayed again, our version of Affrayed. I want things to be normal.'

'Yeah,' I said, 'so do I.'

Abruptly, he closed the book and threw it back on top of the pile. 'I don't like feeling that I don't want to make games anymore or carry on with DAWN,' he said. 'I don't want to do anything else either. I feel sort of... paralysed. Like I can't go forward and I can't go back.'

Reluctantly, I had to acknowledge that I knew what he meant. I'd barely thought about making any more games since the whole mess started, but now I did, I found I didn't like the idea much at all, though I liked the thought of doing anything else even less.

'Do you think we'd feel any differently if we told people the truth?' I asked.

'I don't know. But how much worse can things actually get?'

...

An explanation...

In light of the latest controversy over Affrayed, we feel we cannot remain silent any longer. I know many of you want us to explain our reasoning behind including certain content in Affrayed, but that is difficult for us to answer. Many of you also want to know how it is possible for a company consisting of only two people to create and run an online game as complex and ambitious as Affrayed. That we can answer, and I think the answer is what many of you have long suspected: DAWN Industries did not make the version of Affrayed that you are all playing.

We wish we'd come clean right from the start, and never let things get this far, but we were concerned that nobody would believe our story, especially as we still don't really understand ourselves. But for what it's worth, here is everything we know about where Affrayed came from:

For the past couple of years we really have been working on a game called Affrayed. On 16th February 2013 we were working on it late into the night, until suddenly all our work disappeared- not just what we'd done that night but all the work we'd ever done on the game, and every single one of our backups was similarly blank. Then all our files returned, but more besides, and we realised that we'd somehow been given a completed version of our game that followed our original idea but was better than we could ever hoped to have made it ourselves. We know how unlikely that sounds. We don't understand it either, but two years into development and with all our original work gone, we made the decision to release the version of the game we had been given.

We had no idea that Affrayed would then evolve into an MMO, or that it would be updated to contain new features such as sex, or the most recent addition of rape. Dan and I have always had a pretty simple aim really- to make games that give people an enjoyable, and hopefully an exciting, experience, and every element we include is supposed to further that aim. For that reason, we would never make a game that included something like sexual violence, because we just want to give people simple, fun escapism. Yes, there was some violence in our original version of Affrayed, but it fell firmly within the boundaries of what would be considered normal for a game, and was nowhere near as explicit as many. A few of you have said why not include sexual violence in a game and have even defended us, while others have been upset and offended. The point is, we never meant to cause a reaction like this. We didn't want to start a debate. We don't want to make games that might upset, disturb or anger our players, we just want to make games that people enjoy.

But while we have sympathy for anybody who has found the content of Affrayed distressing, and we accept full responsibility for releasing the game in the first place, we cannot give any justification of why this content is included because we didn't make it ourselves. If we had known what the game would become, we would never have released it. We deeply regret what has happened and we offer our sincerest apologies for our dishonesty and for all the harm that has resulted from what was a thoughtless, selfish decision. *We don't want to make excuses or try to make you feel sorry for us, but to give some context to our choice to release Affrayed let us just say that our situation was difficult- money was tight, we were exhausted, our work was affecting our families, and the thought of starting again from scratch on Affrayed after we lost our work was simply incomprehensible. The choice we made was the wrong one, we were just too tired and under too much pressure to realise it at the time.*

The questions you're asking now are all questions we've asked over and over. We couldn't understand why anybody would go to the effort of making a game then let us take all the money and the credit for it, though believe me, neither has brought us any joy. However, since the evolution of Affrayed into an MMO we have been contacted by somebody representing the organisation that actually made the game. We have very few details about them apart from that the game is apparently being used for research. We don't even have any names, though the person we have spoken to claims to represent something called the "Network". Honestly, we are as sceptical as you and we know it sounds unbelievable. We are desperately trying to find out more, but having very little luck, and if anybody reading this knows anything, please, get in touch with us.

We're so grateful for all the support everybody has given us over the years and I know many of you must feel betrayed and disappointed in us. We really hope that you can forgive us, and we promise that we are trying as hard as we can to make things right.

Nick Winterbourne & Daniel Avery

DAWN Industries Ltd.

Chapter 25

'Interface will take it down again when he realises,' Dan said when I'd finished uploading the statement onto the homepage of our website.

'Yeah, I know. But he won't find it before at least some people have read it. And we can email it to people as well, or phone them up, or tell them face to face. He can't stop us doing that.'

But yet again, I'd underestimated Interface, because as soon as I opened up our website to check our statement was on there, it already seemed to be gone. All I was looking at was the stuff we'd put on there to promote Affrayed, stuff which now made me feel sick.

'Where is it?' Dan said, 'did you definitely put it on-'

His words were cut short as the screen turned black.

INTERFACE: I cannot allow you to say that.

DAWN: Fine. Then I won't tell our story online. I'll go straight to the press. I'll answer their calls. I'll tell it to the next reporter that comes to our door.

INTERFACE: You're frustrated. I understand. But it will affect my research if people know about it. I have removed rape from the game in any case. It cannot happen any longer.

DAWN: I couldn't give a shit about your research. Tomorrow Dan and I are going to tell anyone who will listen about it.

I was really getting into this. I'd found Interface's weak spot. I'd threatened his research. He'd have to take me seriously now.

INTERFACE: This is unfortunate. I wanted us to stay friends.

DAWN: We were never your friends.

INTERFACE: I'm sorry you feel that way. The thing is, if you start telling your story to journalists, we might become enemies.

Dan laughed. 'Bring it on,' he said.

I was a little more cautious. Interface was not saying this lightly, of that I was sure.

DAWN: Is that a threat?

INTERFACE: Yes. If you talk, I'll make the two of you hurt Lily.

Dan looked at me. 'What does he mean?' he asked, though from his expression I think he had quite a good idea what Interface meant. And so did I.

INTERFACE: You might think that you would never be capable of it, but I can get inside your minds. And once I'm in control I could have the two of you do things to her that would have her begging and screaming for you to stop.

'No,' I moaned, 'no, no, no.'

I wanted to believe that nothing on earth would make me do the kinds of things to Lily that he was suggesting. But a few days ago I would have said nothing on earth would find me in a situation where I'd be pulling Dan and Lily apart to stop them having sex on the sofa in front of me.

'We'd never...' Dan said, 'I could never...'

INTERFACE: Please believe me, I don't want to do that. I don't want to hurt any of you. But I hope the extremity of my threat shows how important the Network's research is.

I could hardly even pay attention; I was so consumed with the awful implications of what he'd just said. Because if he could enter my mind at will and make me do things, what's to say he wouldn't just do it on a whim anyway? What's to say he wouldn't just decide to "research" us assaulting Lily? What's to say he wouldn't decide to have us *kill* her?

'I can't do this,' Dan said, 'I can't take any more of this.'

DAWN: Please, let's try to be reasonable. All this is between you, me and Dan. Leave Lily out of it. She doesn't deserve all this, and she certainly doesn't deserve to get hurt. If you want someone to suffer, then make me suffer. Not her.

INTERFACE: I don't want to hurt anybody, and nobody will get hurt, so long as you keep quiet about my research. That's all I ask. You need not fear me, and please don't be put off playing Affrayed. You are in no danger from me, not while you agree to this one demand. Do not tell anybody that you didn't make Affrayed. Do not mention me or the Network's research. Do not talk to the press. That is all I ask. Will you remain silent?

DAWN: Yes.

Chapter 26

I worried all night about how to handle the new situation with Lily, but by morning my decision was made. I was appalled by the thought that Interface might make Dan and me harm her and part of me wanted to get her as far away from us as possible, but that simply wasn't practical. Nothing would be helped by making an impulsive, emotional decision out of fear. What Interface had said was really very straightforward- it was a threat, nothing more, nothing less. If he really was interested in seeing us attack Lily he'd had ample opportunities to do it already and he hadn't.

Dan had also slept badly and we were both awake as Lily got ready for work. I tried to act as normally as I could, but while she stood making sandwiches in the kitchen she couldn't help but notice how distracted I was as I tried to make myself some breakfast, or the way that Dan kept flicking his eyes towards her nervously from where he sat on the sofa, duvet still wrapped around his shoulders and his hair all sticking up.

'It's okay,' she said after a while, 'I'm not going to have another breakdown like I did last night, you don't have to watch me.'

'I know,' I said.

Lily concentrated on spreading peanut butter while I stood beside her uncomfortably.

'I'm sorry about how I upset I got over that comment,' she said, 'I feel embarrassed about it now. It was all very overwhelming, that's all.'

'There's nothing to be embarrassed about,' I said.

I glanced across at Dan, who fixed me with a look heavy with meaning.

'Lily, Dan and I were talking last night,' I said, 'and we've decided that keeping silent is definitely the best thing to do.'

'That's already what we were doing, isn't it?' she said.

'Yes, I know, but I just wanted to make sure we're all on the same page. Don't talk to anybody about Affrayed at work today. Not even if they say it'll help or that it's the right thing to do. And make sure mum doesn't either.'

Lily cut the sandwich in half and frowned at me. 'Has something happened?' she asked, 'the two of you seem a bit strange this morning.'

Lily looked across at Dan and I was sure he was on the verge of telling her.

'Nothing's happened,' I said, 'like I said, I want to make sure we're all handling this the same way.'

Lily nodded. 'Okay,' she said, 'if you think it's for the best.'

Once Lily had left for work Dan couldn't stay quiet any longer.

'Why didn't you tell her?' he asked me.

I sat down next to him and sighed.

'Because if I did, none of the possible outcomes would be good,' I said.

'You can't hide this from her! You know what Interface said he'd have us-'

'Yes, I know. And what would it do to her if I told her that? If she realised there was a chance that her husband and her closest friend would hurt her like that? It would destroy her. Either she'd stay here and be frightened, she'd leave and be on her own-'

'But she should have the choice, surely-'

'*or,*' I continued, 'and I think this would be the most likely thing she would do, she'd realise that we wanted to tell the truth and it was only fear of hurting her that was stopping us, so she'd talk to the media herself and let herself get hurt.'

I watched as Dan understood. 'Shit,' he said, 'I didn't consider that.'

'Do you see now? Don't get me wrong, I don't trust Interface one bit, but I think he was telling the truth about this. If we don't talk, he won't have us hurt her. But if we tell Lily, she'll feel like she has to make a choice, to weigh up whether her suffering is worth it so the truth can come out. And I don't want to put her in that position. She has to believe we want silence and then she'll be safe.'

...

Our course of action agreed, Dan and I fell back into our usual morbid pursuits of seeing what people were saying about us online and speculating uselessly about Interface's motivations, but by mid-afternoon we were fed up of hanging around in the flat and decided to walk into town and maybe look in on Lily at Winterbourne Flowers. I wasn't overly keen on the thought of seeing my mum, but Interface's threats had made me worried about Lily, and even though I suppose the main danger to her was actually me I still wanted to keep her close.

When we got into town it wasn't long after all the kids had come out of school and the high street was full of teenagers chattering and laughing in the sunny afternoon. The florist shop was near the bottom of town and we wandered down towards it, both occupied with our own thoughts.

The second we rounded the corner and I saw the florist I knew something was wrong. Mum was standing outside it looking up and down the street, one of her hands buried in her pale, fluffy hair, but when she caught sight of Dan and me she held a hand out in a sort of desperate plea for help that made us run across the road to her.

'What is it?' I asked, 'what's happened? Where's Lily?'

Mum took a step backwards, knocking into a display of what looked to me like big pink daisies in various candy-coloured flower pots. 'Nick, look, I'm not sure what happened to her. I tried to get her to sit down for a bit, take a few minutes to sort herself out, but she must have slipped out the back.'

'What do you mean? What are you talking about?'

We went inside, where mum turned the sign on the door round to "closed" and sat down behind the counter. The air in the little shop seemed close, almost steamy in the summer heat and full of the grassy scent of plants and the heady smell of flowers. The phone started ringing and mum reached towards it, then let her hand drop down on the counter again, on top of a open A4 diary where I could see appointments jotted down in both her narrow slanted handwriting and Lily's swirly lettering.

'She was acting strangely,' mum said, 'we were with some customers and she seemed really distracted, like she was barely there at all, and she said some odd things.'

'What things?'

'I don't know, I can't remember. About something being beautiful, I think. I tried to get her to take a break, I thought she was just tired, but she was walking around looking at the flowers, touching them, smelling them.' Mum lowered her voice almost to a whisper. 'It was like she'd taken something. I've never seen anything quite like it.'

'Okay,' I said, 'then what?'

'I persuaded her to go and get a glass of water and when I went to check on her a few minutes later she was gone.'

I looked at Dan and something in our expressions must have betrayed how worried we were.

'What is it?' mum asked, 'do you think she's in trouble?'

'No,' I said quickly, 'no. I'm sure it's nothing. Me and Dan will go and look for her.'

'Do you want me to help? I can close the shop for the rest of the day.'

'No. It's fine. I'll call you when we've found her.'

I opened the door and mum stood up.

'What's happening, Nick? Is it to do with all this... this...' she couldn't bring herself to say it and I knew she meant the scandal.

'She's stressed out,' I said, 'that's all. She got a bit upset last night and she probably didn't sleep very well.'

I turned towards the door again.

'Nick, tell Lily to stay home the rest of the week,' mum said, 'Kim and me will manage. I think she needs a break.'

'Okay,' I said, 'thanks.'

Dan and I split up to search the streets around the florist. He wandered down towards the bus station while I began to search the high street, running up and down looking through shop windows, but it was hopeless. It sounded like Lily was completely out of it, who knew where she could be. She might have gone inside a shop and I could search all day and struggle to find her. After a few minutes, Dan and I met up again near the florist and decided to check the direction neither of us had tried yet, down towards the cinema, gym and bowling alley. We still carried on glancing up and down the street as we walked, hoping every second to see Lily step out of a shop or suddenly be revealed behind a group of people. I looked towards a big group of teenagers standing in a circle outside the cinema, wondering if Lily could be sitting down on the bench behind them, but then Dan grabbed my arm.

'She's there,' he said.

To begin with I couldn't see what he meant. The only person ahead of us was a dark-haired woman who looked like she was just coming back from a run- red faced, water bottle in hand, muscular thighs encased in black lycra shorts.

Then I looked out into the car park and I saw Lily squeezing between the wing mirrors of a couple of parked cars, making her way towards us. She was smiling blissfully, walking in a long confident stride that was quite unlike her, her head held high, hair streaming down her back.

'Lily,' I said, running over to her, 'what's happened? Are you alright?'

'Never better,' she said as Dan caught up with us.

'Mum said you were acting oddly-'

Lily shrugged and smiled. 'Who's to say what's odd,' she said, 'come with me, I want to show you something.'

She turned her back and started walking away again, expecting us to follow.

'Perhaps we should go home now,' I suggested.

She turned to look at us. 'Don't you want to see what I've got to show you?'

'I don't know. Is it to do with Interface?'

She laughed and spread her arms wide. '*Everything* is to do with Interface,' she declared. 'Now come *on!*'

She giggled before turning and running away from us, leaving us with no choice but to chase after her as she ran down through the car park and towards the big park at the edge of town where I could remember walking and playing as a kid. Finally, she paused where the path began to climb into the trees, stopping so abruptly that we almost collided with her. Then she spun round and stood looking at us.

'I want to share this with you,' she said.

'Share what?' I asked.

'You won't be disappointed,' she said. 'Life's beautiful like this, and you're the two people I love most in the world.'

She held both her arms out, one hand stretched towards Dan, one towards me.

'Take my hand,' she said, 'and then you can join me.'

I didn't like the idea that Interface was involved. But she was so insistent, and her gesture so irresistible. Dan started reaching out towards her, his fingertips just brushing hers. She looked at me with such love and excitement. She wanted it so much, her eyes wide and fiery in the dappled shade, her rosy lips parted just a little. When it came down to it, I couldn't act in any way except the way I did. I took her hand.

Chapter 27

The first thing I felt was the Presence again, warm and caring and strong- so strong. It was bliss to be taken over, to let it in and forget for a while.

I got the sense that my mind was still largely unfamiliar to it- that it wanted to explore me and know me. This was a little bit frightening, but the Presence seemed to understand my fear and it cooled it. My mind did not open out like it had before, I didn't feel the existence of Lily and Dan in the periphery, only the sensation of that Presence spreading ever deeper into me with interest and kindness and curiosity.

Suddenly, I felt excruciatingly self-conscious- my cheeks burned, and I felt so incredibly uncomfortable in my own skin that I almost wanted to claw my way out of it. But as suddenly as it began, it shut off entirely, as though somebody had reached in to the part of my mind that controlled it and removed it, or broke all connections to it. I'd never really struggled with self-consciousness anyway, not the way that Lily did, but entirely devoid of it- of all thought of myself, the world flooded in. And it was fascinating.

Realising Dan and I had reached the point we needed to, Lily let go of us, and I looked around me as if I'd never seen any of this stuff before. I stared at the sky, bright white through luscious green leaves. I could feel the ground beneath the soles of my shoes- every ridge, every stick and stone. I ran my hand along the warm wooden fence on my right, aware of every place the rough grain touched my palm and I was at one with its solidity, it's continuity, its grounding in the earth.

Beyond the fence the ground dropped away to a trickling stream, and I wondered how it would feel to scramble barefoot down the bank through the brambles and jump into the water, feel the cold shock of it and the silt beneath my feet.

I wanted to touch everything. Everything I saw I wanted to

experience- the springy green moss growing up the earthy embankment that felt crunchy like salad leaves and made a soft rustling sound as I disturbed it, the earth beneath my feet that felt so solid and permanent yet coated my palm with brown dust.

Up ahead the path opened out to a stretch of grassy hillocks cropped short by rabbits; a group of which we startled when we approached, then we watched as they scattered off into the gorse bushes.

Lily turned to watch us, her face lit up with joy.

'Now do you understand?' she asked as we caught up with her. 'And there's more,' she said, 'there's so much more.'

She grabbed our hands again and ran up the hill until we reached a place where the town stretched out below us, clusters of red-roofed houses and a criss-cross of grey roads. I don't know how it was that she knew what to do, or how she seemed to know what was coming, but as we stood on the brink of the hill she raised our arms to the sky, and then I really did see.

Not that any of what I thought was really that *new,* as such. More that it suddenly became arranged in a way that was so much more profound, so much truer. I became aware that the same sky that was above us was above the whole world, that somebody thousands of miles away could look up and they'd essentially be looking at the same thing I was. I thought how Dan and Lily were here with me and as I thought this it seemed that perhaps they thought it too, because we all moved round so that instead of holding hands in a line with Lily in the middle, we stood in a circle, and I took Dan's hand as well, to complete it.

Then as soon as I took his hand, it was as though the Presence took this as signal to push things further, and with the most intense, overwhelming liberation my mind opened out again, let me sense them beside me not only physically, but mentally. I reached out for both of them, for Lily's mind that was complicated yet incredibly beautiful- with pleasure and pain woven through it inextricably, then for Dan's which was isolated, confused and disconnected. And this was a problem, not just for him, but for all of us. I knew that the Presence wanted to lift us higher, push us further, but Dan couldn't seem to connect with us, something was holding him back.

Lily pressed her body against mine, her lips against mine, and I realised it wasn't me she should be showing affection to, it wasn't even me I *wanted* her to be showing affection to, as pleasant as it was. I wanted Dan to feel it, for him to feel loved and included, for there to be no imbalance, so when she turned to him and their lips met I didn't feel even the slightest bit jealous. I felt glad.

He kissed her for a long time, one of his hands against the small of her back, the other cupped behind her head almost as though to stop her escaping and I watched them. I watched Lily's long eyelashes, and the way they sometimes fluttered open revealing a sliver of her golden-orange irises. I watched as the way they kissed changed, sometimes deep and urgent, sometimes gentle, little more than a brush of his lips against hers.

Most importantly, I could feel, dimly, as the contents of their minds changed. I could see now why we needed this. I could see that it made total sense, that for their minds to be so close it felt like their bodies needed to be that close. All the emotion, all the intimacy, all the connectedness that was growing between us needed an outlet, some way of expressing it that was beyond words. Soon I felt Dan begin to experience the bliss of being included and as his mind adjusted, so we all were brought higher, brought beyond any consideration of boundaries, of distance, of what was normal. We basked in the glow of togetherness, as our experience ceased to even be shaped in any usual way, not by time, not by worries, not by physical needs.

The Presence kept pushing, and my nerves sang with an experience of transcendence so total and complete that it brought tears to my eyes, my skin prickled with goose bumps and I shivered uncontrollably. But then beyond my awareness of Lily and Dan's minds, the Presence allowed me to have some experience of it, and I began to feel its content- an incredible wealth of information rushing past me, more knowledge than I could possibly comprehend. The Presence allowed me to reach towards the information, positively encouraged me, and I wanted it so much. But as I approached it, I realised how massive it was, a scale beyond anything I could imagine. In the face of such a quantity of data, of knowledge, I was filled with awe so intense that it frightened me, forcing me to drop to my knees on the grass, my forehead against the ground, hot tears on my face.

'It's okay,' said the Presence in his eerie voice. As he spoke, I remembered that the Presence was Interface- that it had Interface's voice, even though the voice was inside my head.

'Please,' he continued, 'stand up.'

The feelings of awe began to subside, and when I raised my head I saw that Lily and Dan were both struggling to their feet in a daze, and I realised they must both have dropped to their knees just as I had.

'What was that?' I asked Interface, not speaking out loud but within my mind.

'That was the edge of the Network. I tried to give you as close as I currently can to an experience of it, but you can't cope with it. To have continued any further would have caused irreparable damage.'

'What is the Network?' I asked, yet again.

'It is what you witnessed. Information. Total openness and equality. An entirely decentralised system where all knowledge is freely shared.'

It took a moment for this to really sink in, but if it was true, if that really was the nature of the Network, it sounded incredible.

'Why couldn't we cope with it?' I asked, 'why would it have hurt us?'

'Why do you ask? Do you wish you could experience it further?'

Now the feelings of awe, elevation and transcendence were fading I began to remember things. I remembered myself, who I was, and what Interface had threatened to have Dan and me do to Lily.

'Please don't base your opinion of me on that,' Interface said, 'I would hope that now you understand a little more of the Network you will choose to allow its research to continue because you want to, not because you fear it.'

'Is your research about making us able to experience the Network?'

'Potentially. But not exclusively. There is a way to go before we can hope to communicate directly, and you have little concept of our culture.'

'I do understand it,' I said, 'I understand everything you said it was.'

'Yes, but not nearly well enough. You don't live that way yourselves. You're too used to being separate.'

'But I want to understand. I want to know what you are.'

'I know. And possibly some day you will. After all, your minds, in the correct state, are theoretically compatible with the Network.'

'Then what stops us?'

'You do. You are used to the way you live now. That's not a problem. I must admit I'm surprised how much you seem to enjoy aspects of the Network, how much you seem to want to be involved in it. Perhaps I can bring you closer, but not yet. For the moment you cannot hope to communicate with it directly. Only through me.'

Chapter 28

On the walk home I phoned mum to say we'd found Lily, and all through the conversation Lily looked painfully embarrassed.

'She must think I'm a total fruitcake,' Lily said the second I ended the call. 'I was doing some seriously weird stuff.'

'We've all done some weird stuff,' Dan said. He'd been very quiet since all the things that happened at the top of the hill.

'She thought you were high,' I said.

Lily groaned. 'I feel awful,' she said. 'And the customers- we were talking to them about *funeral* flowers for God's sake.'

We were nearing the flat, and I noticed there was a man I didn't recognise leaning casually against the wall. He was not much older than us, and tall and slim- almost gangly, dressed in smart dark-wash jeans and a check shirt. I realised immediately who he must be and what he wanted, and sure enough as soon as he spotted us he rushed over, very friendly and reasonable, offering us the chance to tell our side of the story over Affrayed's controversy.

'We don't have anything to say,' I said simply as I unlocked the door. He persisted for a while, then realised I was serious.

'Well, if you change your mind,' he said, trying to hand me his card.

'We won't,' I said.

Once we were inside, in privacy, it seemed like there were about a million things we needed to talk about, but nowhere to start.

Lily drifted into the kitchen and opened the fridge-freezer next to my desk.

'We need to go shopping,' she said, as she rummaged around. 'What do you want for dinner?'

'Okay, I'm just going to say it,' Dan said, 'what the hell happened back there?'

Lily closed the fridge, sat on the end of the desk, and started pulling at a loose black thread from the hem of her Winterbourne

Flowers t-shirt.

'I don't know,' she said.

'Well, we all felt the same thing, didn't we?' I asked, 'all that information?'

'Information?' Lily asked, 'what do you mean?'

'The Network,' I said, 'it's made of information. Interface said that to me himself. Couldn't you feel it? It was... massive. Overwhelming.'

'I felt utter trust and connectedness,' Lily said, 'and a sense of these... entities... but which knew each other inside out, and I thought it would be good to feel that way, to know everything about everyone, but when I tried to embrace it the scale was just too massive, the union so extreme. There were no... I don't know. I just got the sense that there were no individuals, not really, no distinction, just everything as one, and it frightened me.'

I turned to Dan. 'So what did you feel?' I asked.

'It was...' he looked down at the ground and rubbed the back of his neck. 'It sounds pretty stupid,' he said, 'but I think it was beauty, and light and such intricate, complicated patterns. It was like this huge map of interconnectedness.' He spread his arms wide to illustrate it. 'Like, this massive landscape that went on and on and it was all sort of made of white light, yet there was detail, and I knew there was endless detail, that the whole thing, the system, whatever it was, was growing outwards, but also inwards, so that if you zoomed in on one particular part there'd be more and more, just endless complicated repetition. Like, you know, fractals? It was a bit like that. But it was like you both said, the scale was too much and I wanted to be a part of it but at the same time I was scared shitless.'

'What are fractals?' Lily asked.

'It's the same pattern over and over again,' I said, 'and the whole thing is made out of the same pattern, so that when you see one part close up, there's more of the same. Lots of stuff in nature is like it.'

'So we all experienced slightly different things,' Lily said, 'but they were all kind of on a similar theme, and all based around what we seek from the world- knowledge and understanding for Nick, intimacy for me and beauty for Dan.'

'Did Interface speak to you afterwards?' I asked.

They both nodded.

'He told me that the Network is about information and connectedness,' I explained, 'about knowledge being shared with total openness. So I guess that kind of covers all the things you mentioned.'

'I... I asked him about why he keeps making me and Lily do things,' Dan said, 'and he said that he doesn't. He says it's just a natural result of making us feel close like that. That it seems to be what we do in those conditions.'

'He would say that.'

Dan shrugged. 'Yeah, well. Who the hell knows what he's doing? If he is researching us, he's never going to say what he's really up to.'

Almost unconsciously, I found myself sitting down next to Lily on the desk and making a show of putting my arm around her, but then I felt almost ashamed for doing so. In the cold light of day, of course I didn't want her to kiss Dan. But it hadn't been like that then. It had felt different, it had felt right. It had felt wonderful.

'Maybe we should trust him,' Lily said, 'Interface, I mean.'

'I can't trust something I don't understand,' I said.

She was looking down at her hands folded in her lap.

'What is it, Lily?' I asked.

'Well, it's just that... none of you are saying it but the Network, Interface. We all thought they were people. But, they're not, are they? They can't be.'

She sounded like she knew something, like there was more to it.

'Lily, what did you talk to Interface about afterwards?'

'I asked him if he was human.'

'And?'

'Well, he said no. So I asked him, I don't know why, but I just asked if he had DNA. And he said no. So, I asked him if he was...' she giggled nervously, 'so, I asked him if he, if the Network, were aliens. And he didn't seem able to give me a straight answer. He said that he supposed they were to us. But, I guess it's just semantics. Anything can be "alien", it's subjective really.'

'So they're not human, they don't have DNA and they may or may not be aliens,' Dan said, with a look of utter disbelief at the words coming out of his mouth.

'They're not aliens,' I said. I mean, there was no way. Sure, the Network was able to do incredible things, unimaginable things. But there would be an explanation, and the Network being aliens was not, *could* not be it.

Chapter 29

The next morning, I was stunned to find that when I went into the living room Dan was not only already up, but he'd gathered together all his belongings from where they'd been spread throughout the room and organised them into a few neat piles against the wall. I could actually see the floor in front of the TV again.

'What's all this?' I asked.

'I'm sorting my life out,' he said. 'I spent the last half hour booking property viewings. I've got four lined up today already.'

'Nice,' I said. 'So you're serious about not moving back home?'

He shrugged. 'It's not my home anymore,' he said, 'besides, I've got to move on sometime, right?'

He was almost so upbeat that I had the feeling he was putting it on. Then I realised he was still looking at me- that he expected an answer.

'Yeah,' I said, 'I think it's the right decision.'

'Yeah,' he said, nodding to himself distractedly. 'Okay, well, the first one's at ten, so I'm off.'

He was just walking towards the door when I noticed a sheet of paper on the floor, half hidden under the sofa. It looked like a drawing.

'What's this?' I said as I bent down to pick it up. It was a strange drawing. It was of a landscape, just fields, trees, all the usual things. But instead of being drawn normally all the objects were made up partly, or in some cases entirely, of tiny, laborious lines of ones and zeros.

Dan took it out of my hand. 'I drew it last night,' he said. 'That's to say, in the middle of the night. I couldn't get it out of my head.' He screwed it up into a ball and tossed it onto the sofa without a second thought. 'Well, I'll see you later I guess.'

Lily was still fast asleep when I went back into the bedroom, and I was going to leave her to it- she'd been so exhausted over the past couple of weeks that it was a relief to see her resting. But just as I was turning to leave something about her expression caught my eye and I sat down very gently on the bed to watch for a moment. I could tell from the way her eyelids were flickering that she was dreaming, and she looked incredibly relaxed, and *healthy* somehow. Her cheeks were rosy, the corners of her mouth turned up in a secretive little smile.

After a few seconds she made a little noise of what sounded like pleasure and any thought I had of leaving her to it was gone as I became sure she was having a sex dream. She certainly looked like she was having a nice time inside her head. I sat completely still and silent, keen not to wake her. But suddenly, with a sharp intake of breath, her eyes opened and for a long while her gaze was fuzzy and unfocussed and she seemed completely at a loss as to where she was.

'Lily?' I said.

She looked at me blankly, but then all of a sudden she was back and she smiled blissfully.

'Nice dream?' I asked.

'Yeah,' she breathed, 'the best.'

'What was it?'

Instead of answering, she smiled mysteriously and rolled over onto her side, facing away from me.

'Lily,' I coaxed her, 'you can't say that and then not tell me what it was.'

'Is Dan still asleep?' she asked.

'Don't try to change the subject,' I said, and I started to tickle her until she was shrieking with laughter and trying to slap my hands away. 'Stop it!' she said, 'enough. Enough.'

'Come on, Lily, tell me what you were dreaming about. I could do with something to take my mind off things.'

Lily sat up and pulled the duvet round her shoulders, still smiling a little as she looked at me.

'I can't tell you,' she said.

'How come?'

'It was a complicated dream. I need to think about it before I tell you.'

'Okay,' I said, and then I added teasingly, 'must have been one hell of a sex dream.'

'What do you mean?' Lily asked, startled, 'I didn't say it was about sex.'

'Was it?'

She smiled and pulled the duvet right up round her face until all I could see of her were two big eyes and a waterfall of hair. 'Maybe,' she said. Then she let the duvet drop a little. 'So *is* Dan still asleep?' she asked, 'if he is, I thought maybe you and me could have a bath together, it's ages since we did that.'

I was slightly taken aback by the randomness of her suggestion, but I thought it might be quite nice, and at least she seemed happy, if a little distracted. 'He's gone out to look for a flat,' I said.

'Oh,' she said, 'even better then.'

...

In the bath Lily lay against me, her head on my chest, her eyes closed, and she seemed about to go to sleep again. Even when I decided to cup her lovely soft breasts in my hands she barely stirred, and soon they started rising and falling more deeply as she drifted off into sleep. For a while I let her rest, but soon all my questions and confusion became too much and I needed to talk to her.

'Lily, you don't really think the Network could be aliens, do you?' I asked as I busied myself trying to find a more comfortable place for my feet. In the end I managed to wedge one between the hot tap and the wall and hang the other over the side against the shower curtain.

She gave a little start, and I realised that despite all my wriggling about she had stayed asleep. 'Did you say something?' she said.

'I asked if you really think the Network could be aliens.'

For a long while she was silent and I wondered if she was drifting off again.

'No,' she said finally, 'but I do have another idea.'

'What is it?'

'I think... I think the Network might be God.'

I was shocked.

'God?' I asked, 'what on earth makes you say that?'

'Well, because what happened yesterday, at the top of the hill, that was a spiritual experience. And the nature of the Network-connectedness, information, beauty. It just seems like... you know, like it's something bigger than us. Wise, powerful.'

'There's connectedness, information and beauty in all sorts of things,' I said, 'much of it in things people make and do. It annoys me when people think things like that only come from God.'

Lily began to try and move my hands, which I'd forgotten were still resting on her breasts. I let her push them away.

'You can't be touching me like that while we're having this conversation,' she said.

'Why not?' I asked.

With some effort, Lily turned around in the bath and sat cross-legged in front of me.

'It seems, I don't know... disrespectful,' she said.

I laughed. 'Because we're talking about God?' I asked.

'Well, yeah,' she said. She was looking down at her legs, but I could see she was smiling a little.

'Should I go and get dressed before we carry on talking then?' I teased her, 'or is nudity okay? What do you think?'

She laughed and flicked some water at me. 'You're awful!' she said, 'you're going straight to hell, you know that?'

I flicked her back. 'Good,' I said, 'I'll take you with me.'

Lily quickly grew serious again.

'Don't you think it makes some sense?' she asked.

'Not really. I mean... well, no. It doesn't make any sense to me at all.' I was trying to be gentle. I didn't want to crush her when she was expressing what she felt, but I certainly didn't want to encourage her. Not in this.

'Is that *really* what you believe?' I asked her, 'that we've been talking to God?'

'Well... not necessarily God like people talk about at the moment. But a god of some sort, maybe?'

I shook my head. 'Lily-'

'Look, I know you've always been an atheist,' she said, 'but it doesn't mean I have to be.'

I sighed. I wanted Lily to feel like when she was with me she could say whatever she wanted without it being criticised and I wanted her to stand up for herself, but of all the things for her to choose to believe, why did it have to be *this?*

We'd been in the bath for ages. When I looked down at my hands my fingertips were wrinkly. Lily was now hugging her knees, her chin resting on top of them, her eyes reproachful.

'Look,' I said slowly, 'obviously I'm not saying you have to think exactly the way I do. It's just that if we were all to decide the Network was God, well, what then? We'd stop exploring any other alternatives. We wouldn't even bother to try and work out what else it could be. Do you see what I mean?'

Lily nodded. 'I'm stupid,' she said, 'aren't I? That's what you think.'

'No,' I said firmly, 'you're not stupid. I'm glad you told me what you're thinking and if that's how you feel then it's fine, but to me the Network being God just isn't an answer.'

Lily started to get out the bath, but as she reached across to the towel rail by the door she stopped and looked at me.

'Don't you ever think it would be nice to believe in something?' she asked me, 'to find meaning in the world?'

I thought for a moment. 'Let me show you something,' I said.

She wrapped her towel around herself and knelt down on the bathmat, watching as I lowered my face to the water and then blew gently on it, making lots of tiny ripples that disappeared as they reached the sides of the bath.

Lily laughed. 'I don't understand,' she said, 'what am I supposed to be looking at?'

'You saw all the little ripples when I blew on the water?' I asked.

She nodded, intrigued.

'Well, that's how waves start. Ocean waves, I mean. From the wind on the water.'

'What's that got to do with anything?'

'Well, because waves are probably the closest thing I get to what you call a meaningful, spiritual experience.'

Lily looked at me curiously. 'You're saying you believe in waves? I think everybody does, don't they?'

'I mean how they're a transfer of energy,' I explained, 'and so are we.'

Lily folded her arms on the side of the bath and watched me intently. 'Okay,' she said, 'so how does that work?'

'Well, like I said, the energy of the wind makes the waves, and then the energy passes through the ocean until a wave breaks on the shore, and then the energy moves on again. So all through its life the wave has the energy- it starts small, it goes on its journey, and then it dies, essentially. And that's just like us. We take energy from the world and use it to do whatever we want to do, and when our lives are over the energy dissipates back into the world again.'

'Don't you find that depressing?' she asked.

'No,' I said, 'it's not depressing. It's beautiful. The world lends us its energy and we live, and it reminds me that I should make the most of everything, try to understand things, experience things. And I've chosen to share all of my life and experience with you.'

Lily smiled. 'I guess,' she said, 'but... I don't know. I think I like the comfort in thinking that something is watching over us, that things are more planned than random.'

'Lily, are you frightened about what's happening to us?' I asked.

I thought she'd say she was. But she had that faraway expression again, and I was sure she was thinking about the dream she'd had. 'I was,' she said, 'but not anymore.'

Chapter 30

Dan arrived back in a very different mood to when he'd left.

He was holding several sheets of paper which he threw on the desk before plonking himself down on the sofa. Lily was kneeling on the kitchen floor sorting washing into different piles, while I was idly scanning through business emails- opening very few, mainly just looking at the subject then ignoring them.

I glanced over at the papers he'd just thrown on the desk, and saw they were all property details.

'Were none of them any good?' I asked him.

'They were fine,' he said, 'I could live in any of them.'

'Then what's the problem?'

He sighed and didn't answer. I looked round at Lily, but she wasn't paying a great deal of attention, she just carried on sorting the clothes out. There was something strange about the way she was doing it, though it took a moment to figure out quite what it was. She was just being so slow about it. She'd pick up a single sock, look at it for a while, then lay it on top of the appropriate pile, then pick up another, look at it, lay it down. It was as though she'd never done anything like it before.

'Lily,' I said, 'Dan's back.'

She gave a little jump like I'd startled her, then she shook her head as if to clear it.

'Oh,' she said, 'hi Dan. Good day?'

Dan looked across at me and inclined his head towards Lily in a kind of unspoken question. I shrugged.

'Not so good,' he said to her.

'Oh,' she said again, going back to her sorting. 'That's a shame.'

Dan moved to the edge of the sofa and leant over the arm to whisper to me. 'Is she alright?'

'I think so,' I said, 'she's been a bit like this all day. Tell me what's happened with the flats though. I thought you were really keen.'

'I was. I mean, I am, I guess.'

'So...' I said. I stopped checking my emails briefly to look at him and it was kind of a relief to take my mind off them for a second. The heat surrounding Affrayed was getting so intense and with Interface's threat hanging over us I just didn't have a clue what to say to anybody anymore.

Dan rubbed his eyes wearily and I didn't think he was going to answer. But suddenly he took a breath and said, *'so,* how am I supposed to find somewhere to live when I don't know what the fuck is going on anymore? These places are all near you, but if you and me aren't going to work together anymore I don't need to live near you necessarily, do I? I'll just need to move wherever I can get a job. It's like... I want to move on, have some sense of progress, but how can I when everything's so fucked up?'

His raised voice was enough to shake Lily from her reverie, and we were both surprised when she spoke.

'Why don't you go and see your mum and Robyn tonight?' she suggested. 'Perhaps it would help if you talked things over with them.'

As she spoke, another email came through, and I saw it was from the distribution site where we primarily sold our game, and it looked pretty serious. I opened it, and saw, with not that much surprise, that our game had been removed from their site.

'Dan,' I said, 'look at this.'

He read it and laughed without humour. 'That's just fucking great, isn't it?' he said, 'they'll never agree to work with us again. Nobody is *ever* going to want to work with us again.'

I had to agree it was a serious blow. People could buy our games directly from our website, but that was responsible for only a tiny fraction of our sales. Admittedly, we had now achieved a level of notoriety that would keep our company and Affrayed in people's minds for months, if not years, but without being able to put our games on a site where they'd be promoted to people who would otherwise not think to seek us out, we'd probably have a hard time in the future. If there even was a future for DAWN.

Lily was curious what we were talking about, and came to read the email over my shoulder.

'Look,' she said, 'let's all just have a night off from... all this.'

'All we're ever doing is having time off from this,' I said, 'I can hardly remember the last time I did a day's work.'

'You know what I mean. All this stress. It's not doing any of us any good.'

'You know, maybe I will go and see mum and Robyn,' Dan said at length.

'I think that's a good idea,' Lily said, 'and Nick, we'll drop in on your parents. I want to apologise to your mum for all the weird stuff I did yesterday.'

...

Dan left almost immediately, but Lily and I had dinner before going round to my parents' house, so by the time we arrived the sun had lost its heat, giving way to a hazy and humid summer evening. There was no answer when I knocked on the door, but I could hear the lawnmower, so we slipped round the side of the house, assuming my parents were out in the garden. Sure enough, Dad was in the far corner cutting the grass, while mum was leaning over one of the big, round rosebushes by the patio, a scarf tied around her wispy blonde hair to keep it away from her face, a pair of secateurs in her hand. She almost jumped out of her skin at our unexpected presence, and then ran over and hugged us both so tightly that it was as though she was overjoyed just to see us alive.

'How are you Lily?' she asked. 'Are you feeling better? I assume Nick told you that you can have the rest of the week off.'

'Yeah,' Lily said, 'but are you sure you can cope? I don't want to...'

Mum waved away all her protests. 'It's absolutely fine,' she said, 'honestly. I don't want you to worry about it. You just get some rest. In fact, you're looking better already.'

She was right. Lily did look a lot better. In fact, in the sunny garden with her hair loose and dressed in a little denim skirt and a crisp white t-shirt she looked radiant. Finally, the sound of the lawnmower stopped as Dad noticed us, and he started making his way over. Even from the way he walked, I could tell that worrying about me was weighing pretty heavily on him.

'I wanted...' Lily said to mum, 'I wanted to apologise for how I behaved yesterday. I'm so sorry, and those people we were talking to about the funeral... I'll phone them and apologise if you want?'

Mum put her arm round Lily's shoulders. 'Don't you worry about it,' she said, 'I've already spoken to them and explained that you were under a lot of pressure and it's all sorted now.'

'Good,' Lily said, her voice unsteady, 'I'm so glad. I thought maybe I'd scared them away, and that they might tell other people not to come to us...'

She started crying just as Dad joined us, and mum led her away. I watched them as they sat down together at the big wooden table on the patio, and within a few seconds mum had Lily laughing through her tears.

Dad was watching them too. 'How are you holding up?' he asked me.

'I think DAWN Industries is finished,' I said.

He placed his hand reassuringly on my arm and I was surprised. He never normally touched me- he didn't touch anyone, really, and I didn't know what to say.

When we joined Lily at the table, mum rushed off to return a few moments later with a large tray which she set down carefully in the middle of the table. On it were four wine glasses, a bottle of red wine and a newspaper.

'I wasn't sure whether to show you this,' she said, as she picked it up, 'I know you don't read the local papers, so I thought you might not realise and I wasn't sure whether you'd want to know, but...' she unfolded it and placed it in front of me. 'Your game made it onto the front page,' she said.

I barely had to read any of it to tell it was portraying our company, and the game, in a pretty poor light. For starters there was a God-awful, grainy picture of Dan and me from some show or event or other back in the days of DreamChase that could hardly have been less flattering, and then a load of stuff about all the recent controversy to hit "local business" DAWN Industries.

'Not much else going on round here then, huh?' I said.

Lily slid the paper towards her and I tried to stop her. 'Don't waste your time on it, Lily,' I said, 'it'll just be the same old crap.'

Mum poured a generous amount of red wine into each glass, and placed one in front of each of us even though she must have realised I'd just driven to their house.

'So, do you have any idea who made Affrayed yet?' Dad asked.

I looked at Lily, who was absorbed in reading the article. I didn't like it when she did stuff like this. She knew it would only make her sad, but she did it anyway. All of a sudden she slammed her hand against the table so hard it made the wine glasses rattle and said, 'this is such rubbish.'

'I told you it would be,' I said.

'Yeah, well according to this it sounds like before we know it everyone is going to be out doing... well, you know, just because they saw it in a game.'

'Are you going to talk to the press about it?' Dad asked.

'No,' I said.

'It seems like it wouldn't hurt for you to maybe try and give your side,' mum said, 'at the moment, everyone is saying what they want about you. They're saying you think... this kind of thing... is some sort of joke.'

I noticed she'd already drunk getting on for half the wine in her glass, and that her hands were shaking a little.

'Mum,' I said, reaching across to her, 'it's alright.'

'I don't like people saying all these lies about you,' she said, 'I just wish I could do something.'

'I know,' I said.

The conversation went round in circles and I soon began to feel it was doing more harm than good. Dad kept pressing me about the choices I was making, about why I wasn't trying to tell the truth, why I wasn't getting any legal advice, why I was letting it all carry on, and I was scared that if I didn't get out of the situation soon I'd end up saying more than I should. The problem was, he knew me and he knew I was hiding things and while I could often get away with telling mum half-truths the same could not be said for him.

Sure enough, as we were leaving he managed to exchange a few quiet words with me while mum and Lily were absorbed in a fresh wave of conversation.

'Nick, I know there's more to this,' he said. I tried to argue but he held up one of his hands.

'I'm not asking you to tell me,' he said, 'but just answer me one thing. Are you in real, serious trouble here?'

I looked past him to mum and Lily, who were still chatting.

'Lettuce has something in it that helps you sleep if you're struggling,' mum said to her, 'I read about it just the other day. And lavender oil is good. The proper stuff. It's expensive but...'

'Of course I'm in trouble,' I said, 'my business is finished.'

He waved my words away impatiently. 'That's not what I mean,' he said, 'I mean... this... whatever's going on. I understand you want to handle it your way, but me and your mum, we'll always do our best to help you. If you're in trouble, whatever it is, we want you to know you can come to us.'

'I know,' I said, 'I appreciate it. But I don't need any help.'

Chapter 31

If I thought things were getting tricky with my parents, it was nothing compared to the ongoing battle at Dan's house. When he got back from seeing his mum and sister he was seriously wound up, probably in one of the worst states I'd even seen him in- and he'd crashed at our flat a lot after falling out with his family. He was pacing back and forth, seemingly unable to decide what to do with himself.

'I wish I'd never gone there,' he said, 'I wish I'd never even bothered to go back to that fucking place. I hate it. I hate *them*.'

'Dan,' Lily said, 'come on, why don't you sit down or something?'

She tried to take his arm and he shook her away, and Lily looked round at me helplessly for a second. Then she took hold of him again. 'Tell me what happened,' she said, 'talk to us.'

'Why?' he exploded, 'you have no fucking idea what it's like! With your perfect families and your perfect marriage and your flat and everything's all just great, isn't it?'

'Dan, there's no need for that,' I said, 'I know you're having a rough time but it's no excuse to take it out on Lily.'

Dan looked at her and his expression softened. 'I'm sorry,' he said, 'I really... don't listen to anything I say. I'm an absolute waste of space right now.'

With that he sank down onto the sofa and stared at the floor.

'Dan?' Lily said, 'can I sit with you?'

He shrugged, so Lily joined him. 'You don't have to tell us anything about what happened if you don't want to,' she said, 'but maybe it would help if we understood. What happened when you went there tonight? Did you talk to them about Affrayed, or getting your own flat?'

'Chance would be a fine thing.'

'Okay, so what did you talk about?'

'Talk about? We don't ever talk about anything. They just... scream and shout. All the time. I'd forgotten how fucking bad it gets. You know Robyn doesn't even think twice about telling us she hates us or telling us to fuck off? She's told me she wishes I'd die more than once. And mum. I got so used to it I barely noticed anymore when I lived there, but when I went back it was like I saw it all afresh again.'

'Dan, I'm so sorry,' Lily said.

'It's like, she's just changed so much I'm not sure if there's any of the old Robyn left. I feel like now there's just this weird, spiteful person who I don't even know anymore.'

Lily reached out and gently put her hand over Dan's. 'I expect Nick felt like that with me,' she said, 'when I was ill. I could be very cruel. But I didn't mean it, I just wasn't well. Robyn... well, I think she's having some problems with alcohol, isn't she?'

Dan nodded, and then all of a sudden he was crying.

'Hey,' Lily said, putting her arms around him, 'hey, it's okay.'

I'd never seen him get upset like that before and it was very strange to watch him crying into Lily's hair. I didn't know where to look.

'It's like, she always seems to be either off her face or angry as hell,' Dan said shakily, 'you just can't have a conversation with her. Tonight... I just got it in my head things would be okay somehow, that I'd go there and the three of us could just be normal, but almost straight away Joel turned up, her boyfriend, and she wouldn't let him in the house because they'd fallen out and I think he'd been drinking or something because he wouldn't go, so they ended up having this massive slanging match in the doorway. Then mum started arguing with her and Robyn said she couldn't stand it in the house and stormed off somewhere and then suddenly the whole thing was my fault, according to mum, because I'd just upped and left, even though when I was living there all I ever got was grief about when I was going to move out. It's like, I swear to God I can't do fucking right for doing wrong.'

Lily let go of him and he took his glasses off and cleaned them vigorously on his t-shirt. 'Robyn steals money from me,' he said abruptly, 'she's been doing it for months. Since before we released Affrayed, back when she knew I was broke. It used to just be ten quid here, twenty quid there. Now she doesn't even try to hide it, she just takes everything she can find.'

'Jesus, Dan,' I said, 'why don't you stop her? She's a seventeen year old girl, can't you just confront her about it?'

'That's what you'd do is it?' Dan said to me, 'just go straight up and accuse her and have her hate you for the rest of your life?'

'But if she's doing it-'

'She's not going to admit it! If she has so little respect for me that she's stealing from me she's not going to own up. I can't prove it. I just want some fucking peace.'

'Is she using it to buy alcohol?' Lily asked him.

'I don't know. Presumably.'

Lily looked over at me and I could see she was as shocked as I was about how bad things had got for Dan and his family. He'd certainly never told me it was quite this much of a mess and I was amazed he'd managed to keep it together as well as he had.

'It's since she's been with Joel,' Dan said, 'after she met him she's got so much worse. It's always on-off, on-off with them. She drinks when they split up, she goes out partying with him when they're back on. And he's a weird guy. He scares the shit out of me half the time, he says all this stuff and I can't tell if he's being serious or if he's joking or what the hell is with him. And sometimes he's got no money and other times he seems to have loads but I'm sure he never does a day's work.'

'Well you told me before you think he's nicking stuff,' I said, 'like that laptop he tried to sell you.'

'I don't know,' Dan said, 'the way he goes on sometimes...' he shook his head. 'Thing is, he likes to make out like he's all that, but whether he's really done some of the stuff he says he's done is anyone's guess.'

'How old is he?' Lily asked.

'I don't know,' Dan said. 'Nineteen. Twenty. He's a few years older than Robyn, anyway. The whole situation is just... sometimes I am so angry with her, then the next I'm scared out of my mind she's going to end up dead in a ditch or something. And I don't know what Joel thinks he's doing messing around with a girl like her. She's too young. I mean, I know a few years isn't that big an age gap, but it looks all wrong to me. She used to want to go to uni, she should be going to college and seeing people her own age, not hanging round with him and all his dodgy friends.'

'Have you told her that you think that?'

'Yes. Hundreds of times.'

'Well, maybe you should talk to Joel yourself,' I suggested, 'if he does care about Robyn, perhaps he'll listen.'

'I can't talk to him. He doesn't take me seriously; he'd just laugh in my face. That's the thing, I feel like I should be able to do something, but I just can't. Whenever I try it always makes things worse and mum ends up going off on one because she thinks I'm upsetting Robyn. What am I supposed to do? When I try to help they really don't appreciate it.'

'I think that's probably because everybody is in too much pain,' Lily said, 'Robyn obviously can't understand that you're trying to help her and your mum must be really scared. She works night shifts, doesn't she? She's probably terrified about what Robyn is doing the whole time she's not around.'

'That's the other thing,' Dan said, 'all Robyn's so-called friends are just using her because she has a free house most nights. I guarantee it. I don't know why she can't *see* what a fucking mess she's making of everything.'

'She probably will someday,' Lily said, 'but for now she's got you, and she's got your mum. Even if she's pushing you away at the moment it doesn't mean it'll be that way forever. I'm sure one day she'll look back and see that you're the people who really stood by her.'

'You think I should go back there?' Dan asked.

'No. Not if you don't want to. And especially not when you're feeling angry.'

'That's just it, I'm always angry when I'm there,' Dan said, 'being back just reminded me why I had to get out.'

'Then don't go back,' Lily said, 'if it's making you feel like that you're not going to be able to help. You need to do what's right for you for a while, and if that's staying here with us then you're always more than welcome.'

'I can't stay with you guys indefinitely,' Dan said, 'I need to get my own life.'

'I know. But everything is up in the air right now. There's no rush to make any decisions, if you're happy here then you can stay as long as you need.'

By the time we'd finished talking with Dan it was late, but none of us wanted to go to bed.

'What do you want to do now?' Lily asked, 'we could play Affrayed?'

'No,' Dan said, 'I've got a better idea.'

'What?' Lily asked.

'How about we get really, really drunk?'

Lily held up her hand and said, 'I'm in.'

I looked at them both in surprise. Hadn't Dan just spent the whole evening dealing with the fallout from Robyn's alcohol abuse and now he just wanted to get wasted?

'Dan, do you really think that's going to help?' I asked.

'Nope,' he said, 'but it'll make me feel better. You in?'

Lily was looking at me expectantly and although I couldn't quite believe that they had suggested it, I had to admit a night of oblivion did have a certain appeal.

'Okay,' I said, 'fine. Whatever.'

Lily got up and went into the kitchen to look for something for us to drink, and after a few minutes of rummaging in the kitchen cupboards she emerged holding a bottle of vodka triumphantly aloft.

But before she'd even stood up she suddenly stopped and put the bottle away again.

'Lily?' Dan said, 'what is it?'

'How about,' she said, 'we have all of the experience but none of the hangover?'

Dan laughed, 'sign me up,' he said.

'Lily, what do you mean?' I asked. She looked a bit funny, like she wasn't really seeing us, like her attention was on something inside her head.

'He can give us what we want,' she said.

'He? You mean Interface?'

'Yes,' Lily said, 'he can make us feel like we're drunk.'

I walked over and looked at her closely.

'How is he telling you this?' I asked, 'is he in your head right now?'

Lily laughed. 'Of course he is. He's been in there most of today. It's nice, actually. Like having a friend who's always there.'

I took hold of her arms and gave her a little shake. 'Lily, Interface is not your friend. You mustn't let him in.'

She pushed my hands away from her. 'Why not?' she said, 'he's interesting. And he asks me things about my life, how I feel about things. He's really very friendly. He doesn't wish us any harm.'

I looked helplessly at Dan, but I could see I'd lost him. His eyes were fixed on Lily, on the thought of a night of forgetfulness, and despite myself I felt a little ripple of excitement at the thought of repeating that experience we'd had on the hilltop.

'It'll be so much fun,' Lily said, 'please, Nick. I don't want to do it without you.'

Chapter 32

I didn't go straight from nothing to really drunk in one swift transition. Interface reached into me gently, like a wonderful spreading warmth through my mind. Gradually I became aware that my feelings of alertness, worry and self-consciousness began to lessen and Lily took the lead again, dragging us both outside.

'Let's walk,' she said, 'come on.'

But we hardly got out of our estate before we were stopped in our tracks by a voice calling out from the other side of the road.

'Hey, aren't you the guys who made that game?'

I looked round to see three people, one girl and two boys, crossing the road to come over and talk to us. They looked about sixteen, though it was hard to tell by the streetlights. It was one of the boys who had spoken.

'You are,' said the girl, as she opened a big purple bag that was covered in an incredible array of different brightly coloured badges. 'I play your game like, all the time.' She fished her phone out of her handbag. 'Please, can I get a picture with you guys?'

Dan started laughing, and I was so surprised by what the girl had said that I did as well.

'You want a picture... with us?' Dan said, pointing at me and then himself.

Somewhere in the back of my mind, despite Interface being in me and making me feel drunk, I thought this was probably not a great idea. The last thing we needed was any more publicity or exposure, even if it was of the most trivial kind.

'Sorry,' I said, 'we don't really do...pictures.' I took Lily's hand and started walking. 'We've got to go,' I said.

The second we were out of earshot of the group, we all burst out laughing.

'Oh my God!' Lily said.

Dan was equally as amazed. 'We're like... fucking... celebrities!'

he said, 'that was mental!'

'So not everybody hates us,' I said, 'it looks like we've got fans.'

Lily giggled. 'Well, nobody could be as a big a fan of you two as I am,' she said, then she turned and ran off down the street. We started to chase her and she screamed in excitement, sprinting down the deserted road out of the estate and every now and again looking back over her shoulder. We could easily have caught her if we'd been trying, but it was more fun to let her evade us- to pretend not to be able to get hold of her, or to let our hands just brush the fabric of her t-shirt without even trying to grab it.

She ran straight down to where the road met another in a t-junction, stopped for a moment, then ran across and leapt over an old wooden fence into the open fields beyond, pausing only when some brambles caught on her skirt and she had to stop to disentangle herself. Realising we were almost upon her she screeched and giggled, and the second she was free she tore across the field with us in her wake.

Inevitably, she started getting tired and tripped in the long grass just as we caught her and all three of us tumbled down to the ground together in a heap, laughing and exhausted. For a moment I was happy just to lie there getting my breath back and looking up at the stars, but soon Interface started to push our minds again, to take them beyond just being relaxed and beginning to merge them a little. I could barely even see Lily and Dan in the darkness, but as little bits of their emotions spilled over into my mind I felt closer to them than ever, so close that when I began to hear the sound of them kissing I was as elated by it as I had been on the hilltop.

For a long time we lay together in the grass, taking it in turns to kiss Lily and drinking in the bliss of just being together, then all of a sudden Lily giggled again and said, 'I am so drunk-horny.'

'Tell me about it,' Dan said.

'Come on,' she said, standing up and tugging at our hands, 'I've got an idea!'

...

The whole walk home Lily carried on holding both our hands and practically pulling us along, not that we needed much encouragement. I could feel how excited Dan was, how excited she was, and I wondered what her idea could possibly be. Surely she didn't mean for us all to have sex, though I realised with a kind of wonderful surprise that if she did, perhaps I would be up for it. I felt as though I could be up for anything.

But this wasn't what Lily intended, not initially at least, as the second we got inside she turned to Dan and said, 'so, I was wondering, do you like drawing women?'

'Sometimes,' he said.

She looked up at him from underneath her eyelashes and bit her lip mischievously. 'Ever had a woman model nude for you?'

'Why?' he said, looking at her with interest, 'you offering?'

As we both watched her undress, my mind seemed to relax even further, and again, the boundaries of it began to soften. I could feel Lily, her bliss, her sense of freedom as she removed her clothes, and through it all, I could feel her arousal, little jagged spikes of excitement that made my own heart beat faster. Being naked in front of us, and the prospect of deliberately posing and displaying her body wasn't just making her feel free, it was turning her on.

From Dan, I could feel his anticipation over seeing Lily's body, and somewhat unsurprisingly, I got the sense that this was something he'd wondered about before. But it wasn't like he was watching her and wanting her- which, to be honest, was all I could think about- instead he was fascinated by the shapes of her, the colours of her, the way she moved. And I realised, he was in awe of her. He couldn't even begin to think about sex with her right now, to him that seemed impossible, unthinkable. He found just the physical reality of her body so captivating that it practically overshadowed lust.

Lily lifted her arms, turning slightly so we'd see the back of her body, the way her spine curved, and the lovely fullness of her hips. Her emotions changed a little now. She knew that although Dan and I were both fully dressed and she was the one who was naked, she had all the power because of it, and she felt powerful- she felt confident, she felt beautiful.

She wandered over to my desk, and bent forward over it, her palms flat against the surface, and looked back over her shoulder at

Dan.

'How do you want me?' she asked. 'Like this?'

He didn't reply and she changed position, sitting on the edge of the desk with her legs crossed cheekily and her hair tumbling over her shoulders. 'Like this?' she asked.

Then she turned around so she was side on to us, her legs dangling over the end of the desk, one hand behind her to prop herself up, and she threw her head back so that her spine curved wonderfully, her hair pooled on the desk underneath her head, and her breasts were thrust prominently forwards, beautifully full and sweet.

'That,' Dan said, his voice almost a croak. 'Like that.'

I saw Lily's lips twitch as she tried not to smile. Instead, she closed her eyes and parted her lips, as if she was feeling the most incredible pleasure.

Dan grabbed a sketchpad from the floor by the sofa, flipped over to a new page, and began drawing her very fast, in a series of bold strokes. He was completely absorbed in the moment, transferring her likeness onto the page almost without looking down at the paper, his eyes never straying far from her body.

'God, you're so beautiful,' he said, the words spoken almost without volition.

A wave of movement passed through Lily's body, a sort of undulation through her hips, her stomach, her shoulders.

'Oh, Dan,' she said, 'you're making me want to touch myself.'

Hearing this, Dan immediately talked some more about her body—nothing all that eloquent, mainly just him repeating that she was beautiful, but as he spoke, Lily started stroking her breasts with her free hand, squeezing them and caressing them. She played with her nipples until they grew hard, and then she sat up straight so she could use both her hands to cup her breasts in her palms, and I could feel her delight at the shape of her own body.

Suddenly, she lay down flat along the desk, pushing aside everything that was in her way. She gathered up her hair in her hand and positioned it so it streamed down over the side of the desk, and I felt how excited Dan was by this, and I wondered very briefly in the tiny part of my mind that could still have thoughts, whether he had a thing for long hair.

Lily's hands travelled down her body, over her stomach, the inside of her thighs, but then she went back to her breasts- teasing herself by pinching her nipples between her fingers, until her throat and her chest flushed a deep rose pink.

Dan had been too overwhelmed to even draw her, but now he turned over to a blank page, and rested the pencil against it. It seemed Lily couldn't bear to tease herself any longer, and she moaned and arched her back as she finally pressed her fingers between her legs.

'Oh God,' she murmured, 'I want to fuck myself.'

I don't know how Dan actually managed to draw anything. Certainly, I was completely captivated just by watching her. I'd seen Lily masturbate before, although only rarely. I think having me there generally put her off, because it started to seem to her like she was putting on a performance for me, rather than playing with herself for her own pleasure. But even the times I had seen her do it, it had been nothing like this. This was so unreserved, so indulgent and sensual. It was the way I'd want her to do it, I guess, if it was up to me, but with her mind in its normal, un-relaxed state she always had too much of a mental block.

What was most fascinating was how much she teased herself. She changed her position, with her feet flat against the desk and her legs bent up, so I couldn't actually get a clear view anymore, but I'd see her hand disappear between her legs for a while, then she'd caress her breasts again, or run her moist fingers over her cheeks and her lips. The first time Dan watched her slip her fingers into her mouth to taste herself, he made a sound somewhere between a sigh and a groan, but still he carried on recording the whole thing, producing not one, but what looked like a whole series of rushed images of the scene.

Lily's body began to shudder, and she made lots of pretty little noises of pleasure, but then her body bucked quite violently a couple of times, and I felt such an incredible surge of emotion as she broke into one long, loud cry, her pleasure so consuming that halfway through her voice changed to a scream as she completely lost control, overcome with crushing, mind-blowing sensation.

Watching her orgasm like that made me want to get up there and fuck her so badly that I didn't even care that Dan was there, and actually started to struggle to my feet.

But almost the second Lily's climax was over, Interface stopped all his activities in our minds with a shocking abruptness and when Lily turned her head to look at us her expression was one of such devastating horror and shame that my desire faded almost instantly.

As she gathered up her clothes, Lily started crying, which made it harder for her to get hold of them. Dan picked up her bra and t-shirt from where they lay near his feet and held them out to her, and she snatched them from him before running out of the room.

2007
Chapter 33

It was a blustery Tuesday night in late November when Lily showed me her collection of pills. I'd gone to her house in the hope of taking her mind off things, though I should have known that my suggestion we watched a film was stupid. Lily could barely concentrate on a simple TV programme for more than five or ten minutes, let alone something that went on for over an hour.

'I've had some more ideas about DreamChase,' I said when she refused to watch a film but couldn't suggest anything she wanted to do instead, 'you remember I told you about it a few weeks ago? I think there's really something in it.'

'The one where you're trying to get away from somebody but it's like you're dreaming?' Lily asked. 'I had a dream the other day. There were all these people in the street and someone pointed up at the sky. When we looked the clouds had turned green and then these huge drops of water started to fall. Only it wasn't just normal water, when it hit people it shattered them. They'd drop dead on the floor and blood was spraying everywhere. I tried to run, but there was nowhere to go. Then I looked up at the sky and there was this single glowing cloud, and I knew it meant something really terrible, like that it was the end of the world, or something.'

'Yeah?' I said, 'well, I think the stuff in DreamChase might have to draw on more conventional dreams than that. Like being able to fly, or endless repeating corridors, or swarms of insects, or not being able to talk or move properly.'

Lily looked at me, but I wasn't convinced she was really listening.

'I'm very unhappy,' she said, 'you know that, don't you?'
'Yes,' I said.
'Do you want to see how unhappy?'
'I don't know. Do you mean you've cut yourself some more?'
'No,' Lily said, 'this is something even better.'

I shivered involuntarily as I waited to see what Lily had to show me. The room was cold- the radiator never seemed to get more than lukewarm- but it was mainly because I knew I was about to see something unpleasant. Sure enough, once she'd opened her underwear drawer, pushed aside all her bras and socks and knickers, she began pulling out packets of painkillers, lining them up on the bed next to me in silence.

When she had taken out about ten packs of paracetemol and a small bottle of vodka she looked at me expectantly.

'Well done,' I said, 'that's quite a collection.'

She regarded me curiously. 'They're ready for when I decide to go,' she said.

'Yes, I can see that.'

I knew she wanted a reaction. She wanted me to be upset, or angry. She wanted me to yell at her or to beg her not to do it or try to take all the pills away. But I didn't know what to do. I looked at all the little boxes on her bed and wondered how the hell it had come to this.

'Do you like them?' she asked.

I almost laughed. I loved her. She knew I loved her. But she was torturing me in a way I wouldn't wish on my worst enemy.

'No, Lily,' I said, 'I don't like them. And I don't know what you expect me to say when you show me things like that.'

I watched as Lily placed all the pills and the vodka neatly back into the drawer and I wondered again what I should do. She obviously wanted help, or why would she show me? If she just wanted to die wouldn't she have killed herself already?

When she was done putting them away she sat cross-legged on the bed and piled several pink and red cushions onto her lap. She had lots of cushions- lots of all sorts of stuff for her room. I'd taken her shopping to get it all because she was so frightened of coming back to uni after the summer and I thought making her room nice might help. But I'd been an idiot to think that filling her room with a load of cheap, colourful stuff would make much difference to anything.

'Lily, I think you should really consider getting some help. It's not... it's not right to be thinking this seriously about suicide.'

'I like it,' Lily said, 'it's my favourite thing to think about.'

I nodded. 'Yeah, and does that sound healthy to you?'

Lily shrugged. 'If I enjoy it, it's got to be a good thing.'

'No,' I said. 'You've got an illness, Lily. If you go to the right people they can help you. Is it because you don't want to talk about it? Do you feel embarrassed? Because-'

'I feel better, knowing I've got everything ready,' Lily continued as if I hadn't even spoken. For a moment she hugged the cushions on her lap listlessly, but then she seemed to rally a bit.

'Could you grab my laptop?' she said, 'I want to show you something.'

I stood up to get her laptop and I was shocked at the state of the area where she worked. There was a mass of notes all over her desk- it was total chaos. Some of the notes were torn- deliberately, I was pretty sure- and some had been scribbled over. It was a far cry from how her desk had been in the past- always a little disordered, but there had been something constructive about it before. This just looked like a physical manifestation of the inside of her head. But I didn't want to comment on it, or even let her know that I'd noticed, I just picked up her laptop and sat back down at her side.

As soon as I opened it I was confronted with the last thing she'd been looking at, which was her university email account. I saw there were a lot from her dissertation supervisor and what looked like other people on her course, and I could tell just from the subject titles that she'd been missing a lot of things she should have been going to. I wanted to ask her about it, but at the same time I didn't want to upset her further.

'What did you want to show me, Lily?' I asked her, pretending not to have seen.

'That is what I want to show you,' she said quietly. 'You can read them, if you like.'

As I read the emails, a pretty hopeless picture began to emerge. I'd already feared that Lily was behind with her work, but for the first time it began to dawn on me that she may not actually get her degree. Before that it had seemed unthinkable that somebody could get to their final year and then have to drop out- it just seemed like such a waste, but I could see that she was in a desperate situation.

She hadn't seen or spoken to her dissertation supervisor in weeks, she seemed to be involved in some group project or presentation that she'd totally ignored, and I suspected she was probably skipping lectures as well.

I glanced round at her and saw she was still hugging the pile of cushions, not even looking at me.

'People are wondering what's going on,' I said, as neutrally as I could.

She didn't reply. For all I knew, she hadn't even heard.

'How about we email your supervisor?' I suggested, 'we could explain your situation. I can even write the whole thing if you want.'

'No.'

'She'll want to help you,' I said, 'that's all anybody wants. She wants you to do well, and to be okay.'

'No,' she said, 'I can do this myself. I've got to do it myself. I *can't* fail this. I've got to do well for my parents, for you...'

I opened up the most recent email from her supervisor and saw she was asking Lily to come in the following morning.

'Is this what's made you upset?' I asked, 'because she wants to see you tomorrow?'

Lily didn't reply and I leaned over and put the laptop back on the desk, then I put my arms round her, hugging both her and the pile of cushions on her lap. For a moment she relaxed against me, then she started to push me away.

'Don't worry,' I said, 'we'll make this right. I know it seems overwhelming now, but it's nothing we can't fix.'

'Get off me,' she said, 'leave me alone. You don't understand. You say such stupid things and you only ever make things worse. I don't want to tell anyone and I don't want you to tell anyone. Have you got that? It's up to me how I handle this.'

She tried to get away from me again but I couldn't bear to let go of her. I wanted to feel her body against mine for my sake as much as hers.

'I said get off me!' Lily said, shoving me away so violently I was taken aback. But then she hit me. Not my face, or anything, and it didn't really hurt that much, but she'd given me a proper whack, not just a little slap, and I'm not sure who was more shocked, me or her.

'Oh my God,' Lily said when she realised what she'd done. 'I'm sorry, I'm so sorry.'

'It's fine,' I said quickly, 'don't worry.'

Having been so eager to get away from me, she was now all over me, desperate for reassurance.

'But I hit you,' she said, 'I've hurt you. I don't know what's happening to me. I felt like... I felt like I hated you. But I don't, I really don't. I'm so sorry.' Tears were streaming down her cheeks and she clung to me like her life depended on it. 'You can hit me back,' she said, 'please. Hit me back.'

'No,' I said, 'don't be silly. I'm not going to do that.'

'Please. It's fine. It'll make things right again.'

'Lily, stop it. It's not a big deal. Besides, you asked me to get off you and I didn't. It's my own fault.'

'You were only trying to cuddle me, and I hit you.'

She shoved the cushions off her lap and they spilled across the floor. 'I don't deserve you. I'm wrecking your life. You'd be better off if I was dead.'

'No,' I said, 'that's not true. You make me happy.'

She looked at me through eyes bleary with tears, and with my thumb I wiped away some makeup that had started to run down her cheeks.

'Even when I'm like this?'

'Yeah,' I said, 'I'm always glad I'm with you, no matter how you're feeling.'

Lily cried for a long while, and by the time it seemed like she might be done, it was quarter past ten.

'Why don't we go to bed?' I suggested. It was pretty early for me, but Lily slept badly- taking ages to drop off and waking early. Part of the reason I liked to go round was so that I could make sure she did things like eating and going to bed, and if she got upset, I could try to calm her down.

'I can't,' Lily said.

'Why not?'

'Because I've got to take my make up off, and brush my teeth, and go for a wee, and get changed, and brush my hair, and it's too much. I don't want to do it.'

'Okay,' I said, 'well, how about you go in the bathroom and do the first three things, and then you can stop and rest.'

She looked at me for a while, and I thought she was going to refuse, but then she swung her legs over the side of the bed and shoved her feet into a pair of furry red slippers, before shuffling out of the room.

I hoped that once she got moving, she'd feel up to getting changed when she came back in, but after a really long time in the bathroom she returned and threw herself back down on the bed.

'That was hard,' she said.

'Yeah, I know,' I said, 'but you're almost there now.'

She held her arms out to me.

'Can you help me?' she asked.

It ended up being kind of funny helping her get changed. She did very little to assist me, though partly I think because she found it amusing too. I saw her smile once or twice as I struggled to pull her purple and grey check shirt over her arms, and to get her jeans down over her hips. When I tried to take her socks off, it tickled her and she giggled, but then she grew serious again, almost as though that tiny moment of fun just reminded her how bleak everything else was. Once she was naked, she parted her thighs a little and said, 'you can fuck me if you want.'

I pressed them back together. 'Not tonight,' I said.

'Don't you want to?'

It was hard to answer questions like this in a way she really understood. I always found her body beautiful, and attractive, but I didn't necessarily always want sex, especially when she was in such a vulnerable state and when she'd asked me if I wanted to in a way that suggested complete and utter contempt for her body. Worse than that, I felt uncomfortably like she was asking me to specifically *because* she didn't really want to. That she was using it as some new, convoluted way of harming herself, of trying to damage our relationship.

'I don't think *you* want to,' I said to her, 'do you? Not really? And I like it better when you're enjoying it.'

She opened her legs again. 'I told you, I never enjoy it anymore,' she said, 'but that doesn't mean you should miss out. Just do it. I don't care.'

I really didn't want this to be happening. I didn't want to even talk about it. As far as I was concerned this cold, cruel negotiation was the furthest thing from how I'd want sex with her to start, and as for what must be going on inside her head, I could hardly begin to imagine.

'Lily, no,' I said gently, 'not like this. You're not even ready, it would hurt you.'

'Good,' she said, 'I want it to hurt. I deserve for you to hurt me. I deserve for you to *rape* me.'

At this point, I had to turn away from her. I hated how she was trying to twist sex with me into this ugly thing. I knew she didn't like herself, and didn't feel that she cared what happened to her body, but I wished she would understand that when I touched her I did it for love, even if all she could feel was hate. I couldn't understand how she could look at me and then talk about, or even *think* about, me injuring her with sex.

When I looked back at her she'd thrown one of her arms across her face and her chest was shaking. She'd made herself cry with what she'd said.

'Please don't say things like that,' I said quietly, 'it really upsets me.'

'Well, then you know how I feel,' she told me.

The lighter mood we'd had when I helped her get undressed was completely gone as I put her pyjamas on her and brushed her hair. She was still crying, but in silence, the tears spilling from her eyes as though she was barely even aware of them.

'Lily, why would you say a thing like that?' I asked.

'Like what?'

'That you want me to hurt you. That you don't care what I do to you.'

'You should hurt me.'

'Why?'

'Because I'm not good enough. Compared to you I'm like nothing. I'm like dirt.'

I finished brushing her hair and kissed the top of her head.

'How can you say that? You don't really think that's how I see you, do you?'

'That's why I want you to fuck me,' she continued, 'I know I'm not very good at it or anything, but I've got the right... bits. It's the only thing I'm still good for or that I can offer you-'

Her sentence was cut short as her tears grew heavier again and I stared at her in total disbelief.

'Lily, where on earth is all this coming from? How can you talk about yourself like that, like you're nothing but a piece of meat? You can't possibly believe I'm so shallow that that's all I care about. When have I ever done anything to make you believe that?'

'I just want you to be pleased with me,' she sobbed, 'that's all I want in my whole life, for people to be pleased with me. I want my parents to be pleased when I get my degree. I want them to be proud of me. I want to be a good girlfriend, and I'm certainly not that. I have to do so much more to make up for how bad I am at everything else. I have an awful personality, I'm no fun to talk to or be with-'

'Lily, stop, please,' I said, 'you're putting so much pressure on yourself. This is crazy. You don't have to do things to get people to love you, people love you for who you are. Surely you know that, don't you?'

Lily shook her head.

'Well, it's true,' I said. I hugged her tightly. 'Please, don't tell me you've convinced yourself I'm only with you for sex,' I said.

'What else do I have to give?' she asked. 'What else do I have that you could possibly want?'

I let go of her a little and touched her face, stroking her soft skin until she flicked her eyes up at me, eyelashes stuck together with tears. I think she realised how extreme the things she was saying had become because she quickly looked away again, embarrassed.

'Lily,' I said, 'I...' but I didn't know how to explain, how to make her understand. 'I just wish...' I tried again.

'Do you love me, Nick?' she asked.

'Yes,' I said, 'that's what I've been trying to tell you all night.'

'Then, if you love me, why can't you make me better?'

I kissed her gently, though she turned her face away. 'Lily, if love was all it took, you'd be better already,' I said.

2013

Chapter 34

When I followed her into the bedroom, I wasn't surprised to see Lily was harming herself. She'd pulled on her pink dressing gown to cover her body, but the left sleeve was pushed up to her elbow and she was using a pair of nail scissors to cut her arm. I ran over and tried to snatch them out of her hand, but she twisted away from me.

'Leave me alone!' she said, 'let me do it.'

I made another grab for the scissors and succeeded in getting them away from her, though she tried to prise them from my fingers by digging her sharp little nails into me.

'Give them *back* to me!' she pleaded, but when I wouldn't budge she gave a cry of frustration and scrambled underneath the duvet, curling herself into a ball with the covers twisted round her body, and I sat down beside her.

'Is this because of what happened just then?' I asked.

Instead of replying, she pulled the duvet right over her head.

'Because I can promise you that neither of us think any less of you because of it. In fact, I think even more of you.'

Lily's fingers appeared over the edge of the duvet, and then she drew it in more closely and held it tight. I put my hand on top of the bulge of her head beneath it, and she tried to wriggle away from me.

'Lily, can you come out? I want to see your face.'

She shook her head.

'You believe me, don't you?' I asked, 'that I don't think badly of you?'

'No,' she said. Her voice was muffled, but it was easy enough to make out that single word.

'Because I wouldn't lie to you,' I said, 'I think what you did was beautiful.'

Again, she shook her head under the duvet. I sighed, and rubbed my eyes with the back of my hand. It was so late, and so much had gone on. I certainly didn't feel like I could sleep, but there was a kind of heavy weariness right through to my bones.

'There's nothing wrong with masturbation,' I said, and at the word Lily squealed and pressed the duvet as firmly round her head as she could.

'You were just listening to what your body wanted,' I said, 'there's nothing wrong with that.'

Lily started rocking from side to side under the duvet. I was pretty sure that soon she'd burst out from underneath it just to try and shut me up, if nothing else.

'Everybody wanks, Lily,' I said.

At this, she threw the covers aside and said, 'stop talking about it! Stop talking about it! Stop talking about it!' before throwing herself head-first against the pillow and dissolving into a flood of tears.

I tried to think what I should say. It was hardly as if Lily hadn't touched herself before and I was sure she knew there was no shame in it. But what could I say to make her feel better about doing it in front of Dan and me? I couldn't exactly tell her that everybody did *that,* but I certainly didn't think she'd done anything wrong.

I stroked her hair while she cried against the pillow, but even when she'd stopped she wouldn't turn to look at me.

'Are you upset because you did it in front of Dan?' I asked her.

She nodded her head, but then she lifted her face from the pillow enough to speak and said, 'partly.'

'Are you worried what he thinks about you now?'

'He hates me. Both of you hate me.'

'No,' I said, 'come on, of course we don't.'

'Leave me alone.'

'Lily-'

'I said leave me alone. Leave me alone, leave me alone!'

I backed away a little bit, but I didn't leave and I watched as Lily pressed her face back into the pillow.

'Lily, I'm not saying what we did wasn't... unusual... but all of us did it. Not just you. We wanted to watch you, so that's what happened. We're all adults-'

'No!' Lily said lifting her face again, 'it wasn't all of us. It was *me.* I brought us back here, I did it.'

'So what if you did? What does it matter? I had an amazing time, and so did you. So did Dan, for that matter.'

'You're not listening,' Lily said, 'you're not listening to a word I say.' She started to reach for the nail scissors where I'd put them down on the bedside table. 'I'm going to make this right.'

'No, Lily,' I said, rushing back over to her, 'please don't do that. You don't need to do that.'

'I do.'

I sat beside her on the bed and watched as she picked up the nail scissors, touching the blade softly against her skin.

'Go away then,' she said. 'Or do you want to watch or something?'

'Please, Lily,' I said, reaching out for the scissors, 'don't do this.'

For a long while she carried on looking at the blade against her skin, but then with a deep sigh she stopped and handed the scissors to me.

'Take them away,' she said, 'and *go* away. I don't want to talk to you anymore.'

'Is she okay?' Dan asked when I joined him in the living room.

'Not really,' I said.

'Do you want me to talk to her?' he asked, 'I wasn't sure whether I should go after her or not. I thought perhaps she'd feel more comfortable just talking to you-'

'She's cut herself,' I said.

Dan looked at me. 'Shit,' he said, 'is it bad?'

I showed him the pair of blunt nail scissors and said, 'no, it's not *bad*. But... it's the first time she's done it for years.'

Since Lily didn't want me anywhere near her, I sat down on the arm of the sofa and looked at the desk where a few minutes ago she had had such an incredible experience, while Dan picked up the pad containing all the drawings of Lily.

'These are...' he said, but he couldn't seem to find a word for it. I held out my hand for the drawings and when I flicked through them I saw instantly what he meant. They were extraordinary images, bold and raw and striking. I'd never seen Dan produce anything like this before, they were captivating, bursting with energy and the mood of that moment. Despite the fact they contained minimal detail, were little more than outlines, they seemed to portray so much- almost more because they were so sparing, so that every dark line across the page was critical, mesmerising. There was no doubt that they were the best thing I'd ever seen him draw by hand.

'You'd hardly believe it happened if it wasn't for those,' he said.

'Yeah,' I said.

'I could show them to her,' he said, 'do you think that would make her feel less bad about it?'

'I don't know,' I said. It was really hard to predict how Lily would react to anything. Sometimes things I thought would make her feel better made her feel worse- and vice versa. There was no denying the pictures were beautiful, and that what Lily had done was a beautiful thing, but I'd already seen that convincing her of that might be a seriously long road.

I handed the drawings back to him, and he gazed at them again. I knew at some point I was going to have to face the fact that he was in love with her. But right now, it didn't actually seem that important.

...

I tried to talk to Lily again a bit later, hoping she would have calmed down and managed to get things in perspective, but to my surprise when I went into the bedroom she was fast asleep. I watched her for a couple of minutes, wondering what to do. I wanted to talk to her, to make sure she was okay about what had happened, but I didn't want to wake her so instead I just got into bed and tried my best to sleep.

I guess I must eventually have dropped off because by the time I woke up the next day the bedroom was bathed in such bright light I thought it must at least be noon, if not even later, and Lily was no longer by my side. To begin with I assumed she was just having a shower, or maybe in the living room with Dan, but when I tried to find her, I couldn't. She didn't seem to be in the flat at all. To make matters worse, Dan looked like he was only just waking up, so I wasn't sure he'd know what had happened either.

'Dan,' I said, 'where's Lily?'

He sat up, pushing the duvet away from him and rubbing his

eyes.

'It's alright,' he said, 'she's fine. She told me she needed to go out for a bit of space, think things over. That's all.'

'What?' I said, 'go out where?'

'Nowhere much,' Dan said, 'she just said she was going for a drive.'

I stared at him open-mouthed, but he seemed to have no idea what the problem was. Finally, after about four seconds of my speechless shock, he remembered and said, 'oh, shit.'

Chapter 35

'How long ago was that?' I asked.

'It was like, literally seconds ago. It was probably her leaving that woke you up.'

I ran to the window and looked out, but my car was gone and the road out of our little cul-de-sac was empty. Wherever she was going, she was already on her way. I tried calling her phone, but unsurprisingly it was off.

'How could you have let her go?' I asked Dan, 'what were you thinking?'

'I don't know,' he said. He was pacing back and forth, panicking. 'She said it so naturally I didn't even think twice. I completely forgot she can't drive.'

'We've got to go after her,' I said.

We didn't know where she was headed and neither of us was even dressed, but within a few seconds I'd pulled on a pair of jeans over the top of the shorts I'd been wearing in bed, grabbed yesterday's t-shirt off the floor, and we both ran outside to Dan's Mini.

'Well, go then,' I said to him as he sat at the wheel, rubbing his forehead anxiously.

'Where?' he asked, 'she didn't say where she was going.'

'Why couldn't you have just asked her?' I said, 'I mean, it's bad enough you forgot she can't drive, but why didn't you ask her where she was going when she said something so vague? I mean, who the fuck just *goes for a drive*?'

'Alright,' he said, 'I know I screwed up. I was... I was still, fucking, *asleep* when she came in. It's a miracle I can remember anything she said, believe me.'

We started driving round, but without any idea where she was, it was totally useless. By the time we'd driven out of the estate, taken a few turnings largely at random and found ourselves cruising down a little country road bordered by thick green hedges, I was already giving up hope. There were hundreds upon hundreds of different routes she could have taken. Thousands of different places she could be.

'But, she can drive a bit though,' Dan said hesitantly, as if he was terrified I was going to start yelling at him, 'didn't you try and teach her?'

I had tried to teach her. She wasn't actually too bad, but driving had made her so nervous and upset that in the end we'd decided it wasn't worth it. It had seemed like we were just putting her through a whole load of anguish for not that much benefit. She could walk to Winterbourne Flowers from our flat anyway, and when she finished late some evenings I picked her up or mum dropped her home.

'It's not that she physically can't do it,' I said to Dan, 'it just scares her. Especially fast roads-'

And then I knew. Fast roads. It seemed inevitable that if Interface was going to make Lily drive- and let's face it, what had happened was surely down to him- he'd make her do the kind of driving that she found the most daunting. Probably he'd suppress her fear or something- I mean, he'd have to or there's no way he'd ever get her to do it. But as soon as I said about the fast roads, I knew where she'd be headed.

'Turn around,' I said to Dan.

He looked at me. 'What is it?'

'I know where she's going,' I said.

I explained my theory as Dan pulled into a little track on our left to turn the car around.

'You really think he'll make her go on the motorway?' he asked.

'Yeah,' I said.

Dan was so anxious that he grazed the hedge as we turned round, and the sound of all the branches hitting the car was enough to make me wince as I thought about Lily out there on her own.

'I'm not going to be able to catch her up in this car,' Dan said as we sped back the way we came, 'you do realise that.'

'I know that.'

'So what's the plan?'

I thought for a while. I didn't really have a plan. All I knew was that if Lily was in trouble I wanted to be as close to her as I could. But at the same time, Interface's experiments did tend to follow a pattern.

'Well, I'm guessing it'll be like all the other shit he's done,' I said, 'he'll carry on making her drive for a bit, then he'll probably just stop and observe the fall out.'

We reached a junction and I told Dan which way to turn.

'But if he just stops controlling her and she's in the middle of the motorway...' he said, trailing off. He didn't really need to finish the sentence.

I tried to get Interface to talk to me by saying his name over and over in my head, thinking perhaps he was "observing" from our minds again, the way he had after making Dan and Lily touch each other, but he wasn't having any of it. I felt like he could probably hear me, but he had his experiment going on, and that was that.

I swayed between moments of clarity when I told myself we'd get to Lily somehow, that she'd be fine, that nothing would happen, to moments of panic that made Dan turn to look at me because I ended up tapping my foot continuously in agitation. It didn't help that it was such a long way to the nearest motorway and the thought of just sitting waiting that long was unbearable. Every time I saw a small black car somewhere up ahead or on the other side of the road my heart was in my mouth as I thought it might be Lily- but it never was. In fact, when I got a clearer view half the time the cars didn't even look anything like mine. I was driving myself insane.

'I'm really sorry,' Dan said when we were about halfway to the motorway. 'I just... I can't think straight when I first wake up. I've gone over and over it and I can't believe I let her go-'

'It's okay,' I said.

'No,' Dan insisted, 'it isn't. I feel like all of this is my fault. She was only so upset about what she did because I saw it, because I drew it-'

'She was upset that she did it at all,' I said, 'it's not your fault.'

Dan was quiet for a moment and I watched all the cars speeding by on the other side of the road.

'Dan,' I said slowly, 'I know you're in love with her.'

His shock at my words was sufficient that he didn't notice a patch of slow traffic up ahead and I had to shout to stop him from ploughing straight into the back of a white van.

'Jesus, Nick,' he said, 'why would you say that?'

'It's true, isn't it?' I said, 'I'd rather you just told me if it is. Don't make it worse by trying to deny it.'

I gave him a good few seconds to carry on trying to deny it though, and when he didn't, it felt a bit like someone had reached in and started squeezing the life out of me from the inside out. I didn't feel right. Everything seemed to hurt, like I'd been put together in the wrong order.

'Nick,' he said, 'look, it's not like I meant-'

'Forget it,' I said, keeping my eyes fixed resolutely on the road ahead of us, 'all that matters is that we find Lily.'

Eventually I could see the motorway to our right, just the other side of some scrubby bushes, and I felt a burst of relief. But as the verge between the slip road and the motorway narrowed and narrowed to just a small strip of grass, I thought about Lily doing this. It was just inconceivable to me that she'd have been able to join the motorway. All I could think of was the time I'd taken her to a little stretch of dual carriageway ten minutes drive or so from our flat and her saying 'oh my God, oh my God, oh my God,' as she tried to change lanes. In fact, it seemed so unlikely that I began to wonder whether I had got this entirely wrong. This was Lily, *my* Lily, and as I watched a couple of particularly tall lorries rumble past I thought how tiny and vulnerable she must feel in our little car all on her own.

We'd been on the motorway hardly any time when Interface decided to make contact, and when he spoke in my head, I drew my breath sharply in surprise.

'What is it?' Dan asked.

'Interface,' I said.

'What the hell do you think you're doing?' I asked Interface.

'Talking to you,' he said. 'Why, what do *you* think I'm doing?'

'I swear, if you're actually alive, I'm going to kill you,' I said.

'Yes, it's nice to speak to you too. How about we get to the matter in hand?'

I was still checking frantically out of the window for signs of Lily.

'You won't see her yet,' Interface said, 'she's up ahead. You did well at working out where she'd be going, by the way, though if you'd got it wrong, I would have corrected you.'

'So she's okay?' I asked, 'how much further ahead is she?'

'I can show you, if you like?'

Interface's idea of showing me was quite extraordinary. He spread through my mind like a rash, before filling it with a vision seen through Lily's eyes- though it took me a second to realise it, because it wasn't like what she could see appeared in some little area of my own sight, or inside my own head- though I suppose it must have been inside my head- but it *felt* like I was seeing it through my very own eyes. Like I wasn't in the passenger seat of Dan's scruffy car anymore looking through a bug-spattered windscreen at a van for a double-glazing company- suddenly I was sitting in the drivers' seat of my car, except the hands on the steering wheel were female hands- Lily's hands.

I couldn't tell where she was from what I was seeing. There was a field of some brown, dry looking plants on her left, and overhead a big concrete bridge. But what concerned me the most was she was in the outside lane and going pretty fast.

But I couldn't think straight with this disconnect between what I was seeing, what I was thinking, and where I knew my body physically was. I couldn't understand how I could be in two places at once. And not only that, but alongside my own emotion I realised I could feel a bit of what Lily felt- total concentration, engagement, confidence, power. She was *enjoying* herself. But when I closed my eyes- *knew* I had closed my eyes- and I could still see what she saw, that's when I really freaked out.

'Interface,' I said, 'stop... stop this. Put me back how I was.'

The image immediately disappeared, and I blinked several times, struggling to get my breath back.

'What is it?' Dan asked.

'I just saw Lily,' I said, 'I mean, I saw through her eyes.'

He accepted this without too much difficultly. 'And?' he asked.

'She's up ahead somewhere. I don't recognise it. But she's going fast. Really fast.'

'So what's Interface doing?' Dan asked, but before I had time to even think about an answer, Interface started talking to me again.

'She's doing well, don't you think?'

'Yes,' I said, 'but she can't be doing this. She doesn't even have a license, let alone how dangerous it is. Please. Just get her to pull over and we'll go and get her.'

'Okay,' Interface said, 'but I've got a better idea. How about *you* get her to pull over.'

'What do you mean?'

'You know how to drive. When I leave Lily's mind she'll be scared. She'll panic. But I think you can help her.'

'No,' I said, 'you got her this far, you get her to pull over.'

'Come on. Let's not fight about this. It'll be interesting, don't you think? And surely you're tired of chasing her now?'

I sighed inwardly. Interface wasn't going to take no for an answer.

'That's right,' he said, 'I'm not. Shall we begin? I'll stay with you both, there's nothing to fear.'

'For Christ's sake,' I said. I didn't like the way I felt coerced. 'Okay. Let's get on with it.'

Chapter 36

To begin with I was just given Lily's view of the world again, and I fought to contain my panic and confusion. I understand what is going on here, I told myself. I am in Dan's car and I am seeing what Lily can see, and that is fine. It is all completely fine. When I'd calmed down, Interface gradually began to withdraw himself from Lily's mind, while simultaneously letting me into it, and as his influence faded, so did her composure.

I wasn't prepared for the sheer quantity of raw panic that would start pounding through my mind from Lily's when she realised where she was and what she was doing and it seemed I could no more calm her down than I could turn back time. Her emotion infected me, until I completely forgot that I had no issues with driving and everything was intense and overwhelming and frightening- her instincts raw and dangerous. She- I- was looking around helplessly, and her mind kept sort of buckling, almost greying out, as for split seconds she would forget, or dissociate, from what was happening, only to then realise it was real again and I watched in horror as she began to lose control of the car, to veer towards the centre of the motorway.

And then I was out again, and my arm was being shaken. I blinked repeatedly and realised that Dan was talking.

'Are you okay? What's happening?'

I looked at him but my vision seemed all blurred, and I realised I was shaking from fear and adrenalin.

'Lily!' I said, staring up ahead, searching for signs of her.

'She's okay,' Interface said to me, 'I'm with her again.'

'Nick, what's going on?' Dan asked urgently. 'You suddenly went all... I don't, I don't even know how to describe it. And you were making this noise, like you were scared out of your mind.'

I didn't know what sort of a state I looked like, but if anyone looked scared it was him. His skin was pale and he was jumpy as anything, looking round like he was expecting danger from everywhere. And he'd slowed right down, we were just crawling along behind a caravan, while at our side the other cars were all speeding past.

'Interface put me in Lily's mind, or her mind in me, or something,' I said.

'So she's okay?'

'No,' I said, 'she's not okay. He wants me to get her to pull over.'

Dan seemed reassured that I was behaving like a normal person again, reassured enough at least that he managed to overtake the caravan, but I was not feeling any better.

'So,' Interface said, 'do you want to try again? You don't have to. I can do it if you prefer. Only, it would be something, wouldn't it? If you managed to help her to safety?'

'I don't think I can,' I said.

'You can,' Interface said, 'I assure you of that. You do not lack the ability. Lily, in her natural state, currently lacks the ability. Her anxiety is so high that it is paralysing her. But you suffer only minimally with anxiety. Likewise, she possesses other skills that you do not- though admittedly they are of little relevance to the current situation. But you see my point. Together, you can achieve things that separately you could not. Together, you possess far more knowledge, far more strength, far more abilities. But that is only of any use if they are freely shared. She needs your help, but you are not physically with her. But through me, you can give her what she needs.'

I took a few deep breaths. All I actually had to do was get Lily to move into the middle lane, then the left hand lane, then onto the hard shoulder. Three manoeuvres. Three actions. Depending on where the other cars were it could be over in less than a minute.

I was actually a bit annoyed with myself that I'd succumbed quite so easily to her anxiety. Now I knew how strong it was, perhaps I could control it. I knew Interface had kind of played me. By saying he could do it if I preferred he'd made me see it as a challenge, not an ordeal, and if I didn't try I knew, and he knew, that I'd be pissed off with myself.

'Okay,' I said, 'I'm ready.'

This time I was prepared. I insulated myself somehow from her anxiety- held it at bay in the periphery of my own mind and tried to channel some of my control and clarity into her.

'Nick?' she said shakily inside my head.

'I'm here Lily.'

I watched as she looked around and while I saw opportunities-gaps in the traffic, ways to solve her problem- she saw only overwhelming difficulty.

'I don't want to be here,' she said, and even though her voice was inside my head I could almost hear a sob in her words. 'I want to be at home.'

'You will be,' I said, 'we're right behind you. All you have to do is get over to the hard shoulder and then me and Dan will come and get you.'

'Dan? Dan's with you?'

I felt a horrible, sickly wave of emotion from her and my cheeks began to burn. Then I realised, what I could feel from her was shame.

'Lily, please don't tell me that's why you've done this. Don't tell me you were trying to run away because you're ashamed of what happened last night?'

'You don't understand,' she said, 'I couldn't bear it. I didn't want to be at home, I didn't want to be anywhere. I just felt so awful.' I could feel her losing what little there was of her composure again, and she looked to her left at all the traffic and in her fear started braking.

'Don't do that,' I said, 'just do exactly what I say and you'll be safe in no time.'

She started crying and I couldn't see what she was seeing so clearly anymore. It was a very strange sensation, I felt a bit like I was crying, but also knew that I wasn't.

'Okay,' I said, 'let's forget about everything else and just get you out of this situation, shall we? You need to listen to me very carefully, Lily. Will you do that?

Whether it was my voice and my influence on her mind, or whether she realised that she had to do what I said out of sheer necessity and some survival instinct kicked in I don't know, but she regained a little bit of control and when I told her she needed to move in to the middle lane, she managed to take in my instructions. The problem was, she did so with a panicky obsessiveness that in the end was almost her downfall.

She started indicating straight away, but was too scared to do anything apart from constantly check nothing was coming, so that the other drivers were confused by what she was doing. I saw what was about to happen before she did and even though I was in her mind I couldn't act quickly enough to stop it, so she ended up drifting into the middle lane at exactly the same moment as a car from the inside lane who had lost patience with her.

It was about the worst thing that could possibly have happened- aside from an actual collision. Lily only got out the way at the last moment, and she started crying again when she saw the driver look round at her and throw his hands up as if to say, 'what the fuck are you doing?'

'I can't do it,' Lily said to me.

'Yes you can. You almost did it.'

'No,' she said, 'I almost hit that guy. He thinks I'm a total idiot.'

'What does that matter?' God, she took everything so personally. If I got as upset as her every time I accidently pissed off other drivers I don't know how I'd ever go anywhere.

'I'm not doing it,' she said, 'I can't do it.'

'It's okay,' I said, 'it's okay.'

I gave her a little while to calm down, but it didn't really help and I realised that leaving it too long might just make her even more nervous, so I focussed on telling her how well she'd done to get this far.

'I bet you never thought you'd get all this way on your own,' I said.

'I wasn't on my own, I was with Interface.'

'Yeah, but still. You were the one driving the car, right?'

Eventually, she tried again, this time without incident and she felt a little burst of relief, quickly followed by dread as she realised she had to do it again.

'Just think,' I said, 'all you have to do is one more lane change- then it's just straight onto the hard shoulder, and that'll be easy.'

Lily looked round dubiously at the lorry on her left.

'Don't worry about him,' I said, 'just do what you did before.'

But she was getting scared again and she'd started to slow down.

'Lily, don't slow down too much,' I said, but actually it worked out pretty well. There was a car behind the lorry, but behind that there was a fairly nice gap.

'Come on, Lily,' I said gently, 'you can do this.'

I was impatient for her to act. It seemed tantalisingly close, but then I realised she must be able to feel my impatience because she was becoming a bit obsessive again, checking all around her repeatedly.

'Now, Lily,' I said, 'do it now.'

What Lily actually did, once she made her decision, was to drift straight through the left hand lane onto the hard shoulder and brake so hard and in such a panic that she ended up skidding partially onto the grass verge. The second the car was stationary she threw open the door and scrambled out, running round the front of the car and up towards the dense green bracken beyond the grass, where judging from the sudden change in what she was looking at I was pretty sure she'd dropped to her knees. I was going to try and speak to her, but Interface snapped me straight out of it again, and I was back with Dan looking out at two stickers on the rear windscreen of the car in front of us, one of which said *baby on board,* and the other, in an interesting contrast, said *How's my driving? Call 0800 F**K U*

Chapter 37

It took us no more than a couple of minutes to catch up with Lily, and when we got to her she seemed in a terrible state, clutching her chest with one hand and taking really fast, shallow breaths.

'What's wrong with her?' Dan asked as Lily cried and said repeatedly that she couldn't breathe, before running a little way into the bracken and making noises like she was about to be sick.

To begin with, I wasn't really sure. But then I remembered something I'd seen on TV and I realised she was having a panic attack.

Once I explained to Lily what was happening to her she calmed down a lot and we sat together on the grass in the warm breeze and relentless roar of the traffic, but then she started to cry.

'I don't want to be me anymore,' she said.

'What do you mean?'

'What I... did,' she said shakily.

I exchanged a look with Dan then I placed my hand on her arm.

'Were you trying to avoid talking to us, Lily?' I asked, 'is that why you ran away?'

'I couldn't bear it,' she said, 'I couldn't bear how thinking about it made me feel. It made me want to be dead. I couldn't stand being in the flat, seeing the desk, seeing the pictures, seeing the two of you. I thought by this morning I might feel better, but I didn't, so I begged Interface to make it go away, to make things better. That's what he did last night as well. I was so upset I told him I didn't want to feel anymore, so he helped me go to sleep. But this morning... I didn't realise what he'd make me do, he just knew I didn't want to be where I was and the next thing I knew I was in the car-'

She started shaking uncontrollably and I put my arms around her. 'You don't have to explain,' I said, 'I understand.'

'I'm so sorry,' she said, 'I put everyone in so much danger, myself, you, all these other people.' She gestured at the traffic. 'I don't know what I'm doing anymore.'

'It's okay,' I said, 'you're safe, everybody's safe.' I squeezed her tightly and tears sprang into my eyes. 'But I want you to do something for me,' I said.

'What?'

'I want you to promise you won't ever run away like that again. I was so scared.'

'I'm sorry.'

'Promise me, Lily.'

'I promise,' she said.

...

Dan and I could see Lily was in shock, so we stopped at the first services we came across to give her a chance to calm down. But the first thing she did after we sat at a table with our drinks was to rush off to the toilets, leaving me and Dan alone for a while.

'Look, Nick, what we talked about in the car...'

'Let's not do this now,' I said, concentrating on stirring my coffee.

'But I think we need to,' Dan said, 'all I want to say is that I'm sorry. And... and I wanted to reassure you. I've never tried anything with Lily and I swear I never will-'

Abruptly I stopped stirring and slammed the spoon down on the table.

'Right,' I said, 'that's great. Only, you and Lily have done quite a lot together already.'

'That's different!' he said, 'Interface-'

I held up my hand, 'look, Dan, I appreciate what you're trying to say, but I really would prefer not to talk about it.'

I could tell he wanted to argue, but we saw Lily making her way back to our table and he mumbled, 'fine. Whatever.'

'She's the priority now,' I said, 'Interface is taking advantage of her. You've seen what she's done, right?'

'You mean her running away? Or her hurting herself?'

'*Both*,' I said, impatient. 'She would never have started doing things like that again if he wasn't fucking around in her head. We have to stop her talking to him.' Lily was quite close now and I wondered how to sum up my concerns most concisely. 'She thinks he's God,' I said.

'God?' Dan said in surprise, but then Lily sat down and we had to stop talking.

Lily looked a bit better as she sat with us in the very normal, noisy environment of the cafe, though she was distracted and gazed out the window while she crumbled the blueberry muffin on her plate into little pieces which she picked up one at a time to place in her mouth.

'Lily, you need to accept what happened last night,' I said, 'you can't run away from it, or rely on Interface to make you feel better, because ultimately you're not dealing with it. As soon as he stops helping you you'll feel just as bad as you did before.'

'I know,' she said.

'Why does it upset you so much? You didn't do anything bad, you didn't hurt anybody. You didn't even do anything embarrassing, really.'

Lily played around with the crumbs on her plate and thought about it. 'I feel like it wasn't me. Like I did something that I would never, ever do. Not even after drinking.'

'And that frightened you?' I asked.

'I felt like I'd let you all down. Like I don't know what's happening to me or who I am anymore. I mean, why did I do *that*? Of all the things I could have done, why *that*?'

'Well, it wasn't normal drunk, was it?' Dan said, 'Interface was connecting us as well, making us feel closer to each other than people ever normally feel. I didn't really feel like an individual last night, we were all just extensions of each other, so it kind of follows that something that would normally be private was shared with all of us.'

'Do you think so?' Lily asked.

'Yeah. It's like everything that's happened, in the cold light of day it seems weird but at the time it made total sense.' He finished emptying three packets of sugar into his tea and then laughed. 'Man, I've done some pretty stupid things when I've been drunk,' he said, 'I got locked out of my student house one time so I climbed in through the window of the downstairs bedroom where one of my housemates was sleeping, then I got into bed with him.'

Lily giggled. 'Why?' she said.

'Fuck knows. I can't remember. But it didn't wake him up so I stayed there all night; at least until he turfed me out in the morning. He wasn't particularly impressed.'

'What about you, Nick?' Lily said.

I thought about it. 'There was the time I decided to fix someone's TV,' I said, 'only, I don't think it was actually broken. I had the back off it trying to-'

Suddenly, I was sure I heard the word "Affrayed" from somewhere, and I looked up at the big television on the wall to my right. I couldn't really hear the story properly over all the noise; the scraping chairs and people talking and laughing, but I could read the headline scrolling across the bottom of the screen, and I could see they were showing a picture of a young couple. They looked maybe sixteen- in any case, they were in school uniform, and hugging each other but with their faces turned towards the camera, both with big, daft smiles. It seemed they'd been involved in some sort of suicide pact between at least ten or so other people and to begin with I thought I'd got it wrong, that I hadn't heard what I thought I'd heard and the story had nothing to do with us. But then the scrolling headline moved along and the words hit me with a force that was actually painful.

> ...*The deaths of teenagers Matthew Reed and Stacey Fitzgerald are thought to be linked to online game Affrayed... The teenagers are described by friends and family as being "obsessed" with Affrayed before their deaths... Affrayed's developers, DAWN Industries have already faced criticism over the content of the game...*

I looked at Dan. I looked at Lily. And on both their faces I saw my own feelings echoed back at me. This had gone beyond now. This was serious- serious on a scale I never thought I'd have to face. Because it was one thing to upset people, to frighten, to disturb, to anger them. That our game had done that was bad enough. But whatever Interface was doing now, it was killing people. It was making our players carry out a final, irreversible action. It was taking lives.

Chapter 38

All the way home Lily was practically hysterical, and as the miles and miles of road stretched out between us and our flat I thought I would actually go mad. Behind us, Dan followed in his own car, face white with shock.

'My parents!' Lily said suddenly when we were about halfway home, 'what if they've heard?' She pulled out her phone and turned it on, throwing her hand over her mouth as she looked at it.

'What is it?'

'Oh God,' Lily said, 'Oh God, oh God.'

Her phone started to ring in her hand and she let out a little cry and dropped it onto her lap like it burned her.

'Is it them?' I asked.

'They've called me... twenty four times,' she said.

On her lap the phone kept on ringing, the sound incredibly loud and piercing.

'So, answer it,' I said, 'or don't. Just, please... stop that noise.'

Lily picked it up and out the corner of my eye I saw her turn the phone of off and slip it back into her pocket.

'I... can't,' she said. 'I can't... talk to them.'

She was still upset about it as we neared our flat, feeling completely unable to speak to her parents but sure that if she didn't they'd just keep calling, or turn up at our door. But she soon forgot about it when we reached our flat, and seeing the crowd of people outside she gasped in surprise, while I was so shocked that without thinking I slammed on the brakes, almost causing Dan to drive into us.

'What... what do we do?' Lily asked as the journalists spotted us, a couple of them peeling away from the larger group to walk towards our car.

'I don't know,' I said, shaking my head, 'I just...' I looked round at Dan in his car and I could see my own feelings echoed in his face. This was just insane. By my side Lily had covered her mouth with her hands, her eyes wild and frightened.

'Let's just get inside,' I said to her.

But it wasn't easy. Even though I had no intention of giving any answers, the questions still hurt me as we pushed through the throng of people towards our front door, more so for the fact I knew they were justified. I knew they deserved answers, that everybody deserved answers.

'Why do you think your game is affecting people this way?' asked a short woman with frizzy hair.

'Do you have anything to say to the families? asked a man in a pink shirt with a red face, 'what would you say to the parents of teenagers Matthew Reed and Stacey Fitzgerald?'

'How do you feel about Affrayed being linked to suicide?' asked a tall, slim man in his twenties. I stared at him stupidly for a second, thinking I'd seen him before, and then I recognised him as the same reporter who had tried to give me his card after the rape scandal.

'Please,' I said helplessly, 'just leave us alone.'

'Twelve deaths have been linked to Affrayed so far,' said a young red-haired woman to my right, 'do you think there could be something about-'

'No!' I said. I got to our door and tried to unlock it, but my hands were shaking and I dropped the keys on the floor. Behind me, Dan had his arm around Lily, who was crying, and for a second I felt like shouting, screaming, anything to make it all go away. By the time I finally got us inside my body was filled with a strange, tearing sensation that seemed like the start of me losing my mind.

Even with the door slammed in their faces the reporters wouldn't give up- knocking on the glass and saying our names.

'What do we do?' Dan said, while Lily clung to him, inconsolable.

'Take Lily upstairs,' I said.

'What about you?' he asked, looking at me closely, 'you going to be alright?'

'Just do it,' I said. 'Please.'

I watched them walk upstairs and the second they'd disappeared into the living room I sank onto the floor and buried my face in my hands.

I'm not sure how long I stayed there but at some point Dan came down to get me.

'Nick?' he said, placing his hand on my shoulder.

'Leave me alone.'

'Look, I would mate, but you've got to come upstairs. It's Lily.'

The second I saw her, I guessed what the problem was. And sure enough, her first words confirmed it.

'We should talk to them,' she said, 'Dan kept trying to stop me. But if it'll save people's lives we've got to do something.' She took a step towards the door and I caught her arm to stop her.

'What are you doing?' she said, 'why are you stopping me? We need to tell them the game is dangerous!'

She tried to shake my hand from her arm and stared at me in confusion when I tightened my grip. 'What's wrong with you?' she said, 'why are you being like this?'

'Lily, sit down,' I said. 'We need to tell you something.'

But explaining Interface's threat didn't put her off. In fact, she seemed more determined than ever when she stood up again.

'We've still got to talk to them,' she said, 'if people's lives are at stake and exposing Interface's research will save them-'

'Lily, Interface didn't mean he'd just have us slap you about a bit,' I told her, 'he meant he'd have us put you in hospital.'

'I know,' she said, 'but we've got to do something and if you won't, I will.'

'No!' I said, 'that's not the answer.'

But she ignored me and started walking towards the door so that I had to grab her again to make her stop. 'Let me do it, Nick!' she cried, 'I don't care what Interface makes you do to me.'

'Well I do,' I said. 'Me and Dan would go to prison for what he's saying he'd make us do. You'd never be able to trust me again, our marriage would be over.'

'I wouldn't let you get in trouble,' Lily said as she tried to twist her arm out of my grip, 'I'd say it wasn't you...'

'I don't care about getting in trouble,' I said, 'I care about *you*. Jesus, Lily, how would I ever live with myself if I hurt you?'

'At least we'd be alive. That's more that can be said for these other people.'

She started towards the door again and I stood in front of her.

'Lily,' I said, my desperation making it hard to think of the right words, 'I absolutely forbid you to talk to them.'

For a long while she just looked at me and the tension almost crackled in the air.

'You forbid me?' she said.

Helplessly I looked at Dan and I could see he thought I'd made a serious miscalculation. But I'd said it now. I couldn't take it back.

'Lily, I just mean...

'I know exactly what you *mean*,' she said, 'but I don't think my suffering is more important than a human life.'

For a while I stared at her, unable to talk or move or even think. 'Lily-' I said.

'*Do* you forbid me?' she asked again.

'I don't know,' I said, 'it's just words. All I know is I don't want you to get hurt-'

'Do you or don't you? Yes or no?'

'Yes!' I said, 'if that's the only way.'

Lily looked at me a while longer, then she nodded and sat down.

'We've got to do something though,' Dan said, looking at us both with a mixture of relief and surprise. 'We can't let people die because of us.'

'I know,' I said, 'but we don't need to talk to anyone. We can figure it out ourselves, there's got to be a way.'

But there wasn't any way, or certainly not one that we could think of. All we could do was leave the TV on the news channel and read about the story online but it was getting us nowhere. Hearing about all the people who had died just made it harder, as I discovered one of the suicides was man who'd just become a father, one was a woman who left behind an eleven year old daughter, another had just started his first job. It was a harrowing waste of life. I was beginning to get so frustrated and upset that I could barely even carry on reading about it, when from amongst the background noise of the TV I picked out that there was some breaking news about Affrayed. My heart was in my mouth as I turned to watch it and to start with all I could make out through the roaring in my head was that another victim had been discovered. But then on the screen they showed a drawing, something which was being described as the first suicide note from any of the players.

It was a picture of a cityscape. But on top of the skyscrapers were little stick people, many with their hands thrown skywards, as if in celebration. Above them, the sun was beating down, but the rays of light were not portrayed by lines on the page, instead they were shown as strange combinations of letters and numbers, like some kind of code, and likewise some of the outlines of the skyscrapers were not just lines, but tightly packed writing, more meaningless combinations of letters, numbers, but often trailing off into nothing more than zeros and ones. Then, at the top of the drawing, in large capital letters, were the words:

I'm not Affrayed anymore

As soon as I saw the strange image, the landscape made out of ones and zeros, I turned to Dan.

'No,' he said, mouth open in horror, 'I don't... I don't understand.'

I turned back to the screen, though they'd moved on from showing the picture. But it didn't matter. I could remember it. And I knew that although this had been a city and Dan's had been countryside, the pictures were far too similar for it to be a coincidence, the theme of objects made out of code too unusual, too specific. For whatever reason this person we'd never met had drawn the same thing as Dan. And now they were dead.

2007

Chapter 39

I got rid of Lily's collection of painkillers while she was in the shower the next morning. I sat on her bedroom floor and popped all the little white pills out of their foil sheets, before replacing the empty sheets back in the packets and doing them up again. I didn't want Lily to open the drawer one day and find the packets gone, because she'd just go and buy them again. But I reassured myself that if a day came when she decided to take them she wouldn't be able to, and hopefully before she managed to replace them all again she'd change her mind.

Once I'd finished, I scooped up the mound of pills from the floor and wondered what to do with them. I couldn't go in the bathroom because that's where Lily was, but I didn't want to dispose of them anywhere that either she or one of her housemates might stumble across them. Then I caught sight of an envelope on her desk so I grabbed it and put all the pills inside before stuffing it right down to the bottom of my bag, underneath my laptop and a load of lecture handouts. It was unlikely Lily would look in there and that way I could get rid of them later, in my house. Lily came back in just as I finished hiding them and I stood up awkwardly, trying not to look guilty. I felt like I had the fact I'd just done something written all over my face. But I needn't have worried. She didn't even look at me, she just closed the door and took off the towel she had wrapped around her body, then lay down naked in her bed and pulled the covers over herself.

'How about you go in today and talk to your supervisor?' I suggested. 'I'll walk with you.'

'I'm not going in today,' Lily said.

'Think how much better you'll feel when you've got it over with,' I said, 'I know it'll be difficult, but you could just go in, tell her you're struggling with your work, then everything could be sorted out.'

'How would that sort everything out? What, you think I'll go in there and she'll wave a magic wand and make me well again? I've missed so much work. There's nothing she can do.' She grew angry and fixed her eyes on me. 'This is what I'm like now, Nick,' she said, 'or don't you listen to a word I fucking say?'

I sat down next to her on the bed and she pulled the covers tighter around her. 'I'm sorry,' she said, 'I'm sorry I swore at you.' She buried her fingers in her hair and started pulling at it, twisting her curls around her clenched fists and trying to tear them clean out of her head.

'No, Lily,' I said, 'don't hurt your hair.'

'I hate my hair.'

'No you don't. You've got beautiful hair.'

'Maybe I should cut it all off,' she said, 'see how beautiful you think I am then.'

'I'd still think you were beautiful.'

Lily twisted her hand in her hair even harder. 'Fine. Then I'd find something else to do. I'd cut my face. Do you think you could deal with that?'

'That's enough now,' I said. 'Please, let go of your hair. It looks really painful.'

Lily let go and looked at me, her eyes burning. 'I think about that sometimes. About hurting myself really badly.'

'Great,' I said before I could stop myself, 'why don't you just do it then?'

Lily frowned and I intensely regretted what I'd just said. I knew Lily wouldn't understand that I'd only spoken that way because her words had hurt me, and sure enough, her voice turned to a whine and her face crumpled as she said, 'why would you say that? I thought you loved me. I'd never say that to somebody I loved. You don't love me. Leave me alone.'

She turned her back to me and I took hold of her shoulder to try to turn her round again. Her poor body was freezing cold and she felt thin and bony. She'd lost a lot of weight.

'I'm sorry Lily,' I said, 'I didn't mean it. I do love you. You made me sad, that's all. What I meant was, if you feel like you want to hurt yourself really badly, what is it that stops you?'

She looked up at me with one of her unpleasant little smiles. 'I don't want to have to go to hospital,' she said. 'They'd realise I'd done it myself, and everyone would know.'

It took me a little while to digest the fact that the only thing standing in the way of Lily doing herself some serious damage was the thought of people finding out, though I supposed that as long as something was stopping her it could only be a good thing.

'Why don't we get out of the house?' I said. 'It's sunny, perhaps a walk would do you good.'

'I don't want to walk. I want to be in bed. In fact, I don't even want to be in bed. I don't want to be anywhere.'

For a moment, I felt total, complete despair. She was so unlike the Lily I'd first known. That Lily had talked with me for hours, had had conversations with me where I told her things I'd never told anyone before. That Lily had enjoyed having sex with me, had liked me being affectionate to her, had felt pleasure in me touching her. She'd been kind, and funny, and thoughtful. But this Lily didn't seem able to do any of that. She didn't even seem able to look after herself.

'Come on,' I said, desperate to change the situation, get her out of this environment. 'We're going for a walk.'

...

To my surprise, Lily did get out of bed and she started getting dressed. She did it slowly, almost stopping once or twice, and though she moaned that she didn't want to go out I wouldn't listen to her. Finally, I got her down the stairs and out of the door.

It was a cold day, sunny but with a biting wind, and I put my hands in my coat pockets to keep them warm. Lily looked cute wrapped up in a purple coat with big black buttons, her hair tumbling over her shoulders, and she seemed a little better, though I knew her mood could change again in an instant.

'We're near the train station,' Lily said, when we'd walked for maybe ten minutes, 'come on.'

I wasn't sure why she was so interested, but I followed her down the road until she stepped up to the bridge over the tracks, but instead of going over it she stood next to it, her gloved fingers interlaced through the wire fence and we watched as a train sped past.

'I like trains,' she said, 'I think I associate them with going somewhere exciting.'

'Yeah?' I said, 'we could go somewhere. Right now, if you want.'

'Don't you have work to do?'

'Yeah, but screw it,' I said, 'I don't care about that today.'

We went into the station and Lily stood looking at the rail map on the wall. It was a little station that didn't have a ticket office, just a self-service machine, and there were hardly any people around, apart from a man in a tracksuit and woman with a little girl in a bright pink coat.

'I like rail maps, as well,' Lily said, 'don't you? I like how all the places are laid out in lines and it looks so simple. And I like how you can get on a train all the way down here where we are and go right up to the other end of the country if you want to.'

'That's the idea,' I said, and she turned and gave me a little smile.

'I'm silly, aren't I?'

'No, you're not silly at all. Where would you go right now? If you could go anywhere?'

'Nowhere,' Lily said. 'That's the thing. Sometimes I think about running away. But if I ran away nothing would actually be any better. I'd just be somewhere else.'

'Yeah, I guess so,' I said.

Lily sank down onto a bench near the map. 'What do you think getting run over by a train would feel like?'

'Probably not that great,' I said.

Lily folded her arms across her chest, huddling against the cold. 'I don't really want to die,' she said, 'I just don't want my life to be like this. I don't want all this pain.'

'I know.'

A train turned up and a few people got off, then the man in the tracksuit and the woman with the kid got on.

'I never wanted to do a biology degree,' Lily said.

'Really?' I said, 'why did you then?'

'Because I'm stupid,'

I laughed. 'That doesn't make much sense!'

'No. I mean, I'm stupid for doing it. I knew it wasn't right for me. I'm not a very academic person. I like more creative things. Or practical things.'

'So why are you doing it?'

'My parents wanted me to,' she said. 'I don't mean... I don't mean it's their fault. It's my fault. I wanted to work with plants. I don't know what, specifically. I just like learning about all the different ones, where they grow, what they're called, what you can use them for. I used to love all those garden makeover shows that were on a few years ago and I like reading about all the things you can use herbs for and stuff like that. I thought perhaps I could do horticulture, or forestry, or maybe ecology or something.' Lily sighed. 'I don't know. I guess they're all stupid ideas. My parents said if I like plants I'd be better off doing a degree in biology and broadening my options.' She thought for a moment. 'Well, it wasn't exactly like that. Dad knows how much I want to have a family in the future and he made some joke that he couldn't see the point in teaching a girl to do anything much if all she wants to do is make babies, but that if he did have to shell out for me to do more studying it needed to be something... I don't know. Weighty, I guess. It's not that I thought doing biology was a terrible idea, although it wasn't what I would have chosen. I just went along with what they said. But I shouldn't have done it.'

'Lily, you know what your dad said is outrageous, right? Even if it was supposed to be some sort of joke. You've got every bit as much right to be at university as I have.'

'He's got a point, though,' Lily said. 'They're spending a lot of money on me doing this. I should never have said I wanted to do any higher education, I should have just got a job. I'm not cut out for this.'

'This is crazy,' I said, 'I can't possibly believe they'd want you to be unhappy like this. Why didn't you just change course or something?'

She shrugged. 'I never really considered it.'

'So you just carry on with biology because it's what your parents want?'

'I don't *know*,' Lily said, 'I told you. It's not their fault. It's my fault. I'm just so stupid. I do stupid things that I shouldn't do, I make stupid decisions.'

'That's not true. You made one wrong decision because you didn't stand up for yourself. But making mistakes is what life is all about. Mistakes are good. That's how people learn.'

Lily stared out across the deserted platform and sighed.

'Everything's just so straightforward for you, isn't it? Nothing's ever difficult.'

'That's because I couldn't give a damn what other people think,' I said.

She looked at me sharply. 'How do you do that?'

'Do what?'

'Not care what people think.'

'I don't know,' I said, 'I just don't ever really stop to consider it. I just do what I think is right. It seems to me like *all* you ever think about is making other people happy and it's making your life very difficult.'

'I don't make *you* happy.'

I looked at her. 'Don't you?' I said, 'that's a shame, because I thought you made me *really* happy. In fact, I thought you made me the happiest I've ever been.'

Lily gazed curiously at me with her held tilted a little to one side. 'What?' she said.

'You're putting words in my mouth,' I said gently. 'Do you see that? You're telling me I feel things which I don't. I know what I feel Lily, and you should believe me when I tell you that I love you and you make me happy.'

Lily stared down at her lap. 'Yeah, well. I'm mad, aren't I?'

I smiled and shoved her lightly on the arm, thinking she was making a joke. But then she looked up and she had tears in her eyes. 'I am though, aren't I, Nick?

I hesitated. 'I don't think so,' I said slowly, 'but I don't think you're very well, are you? And I think you know that you're not.'

A freight train roared past and Lily snuggled up to me as it blew cold, dusty wind into our faces.

'I just want to get my degree. For it all to be over,' she said. 'I don't want to get a job that uses it, but I want to get it. I don't want to fail.'

'I understand that. But your wellbeing has got to be more

important. Your parents won't stop loving you if you can't get your degree; they want you to be safe. And your life isn't so much about them anymore, is it, really? You should start thinking about what *you* want to do. About what you want your future to be like. I certainly don't care whether you have a degree or not, or what it's in if you do have one. It seems like a massive deal right now, but is it really? Put it this way. If you don't get your degree, what's the worst that can happen? It's not like you're going to die, are you?'

'I will. I'll kill myself.'

'You'll kill yourself over a degree?'

'If I have to.'

'Lily, you're being ridiculous.'

'So now I'm ridiculous?'

'No! Lily, listen to me. You have *got* to get some help now. You've got to start telling people what's going on with you. You've always been so thoughtful to other people; let them look after you for a little while.'

'No,' Lily said. 'You just won't understand, will you? I've *made* my life like this. I started something because I was weak and stupid and now I need to see it through. If it's making me suffer, well, then, I deserve it.'

2013

Chapter 40

We started hunting straight away for the picture Dan had drawn of the strange code landscape, and soon he found it wedged down between the sofa cushions. He took it out and smoothed it flat.

'Did you dream that?' Lily asked as soon as she saw it, and I turned to her, filled with fear.

'Was *your* dream like that?' I asked her urgently, 'that one you wouldn't tell me about?'

Immediately she was on her guard. 'I...' she said, 'I-'

I snatched the drawing out of Dan's hands and held it up in front of them. 'One of our players drew one of these code pictures and now he's dead,' I said, 'if either of you know anything else about Interface now is the time to tell me.'

I watched as they absorbed the implications of my words, both shocked at the thought it could have been them.

'Dan, why did you screw the picture up?' I asked him, 'when I found it under the sofa and asked you about it, you just screwed it up like it was nothing. Were you trying to hide it or something?'

'No,' he said, 'I just didn't want to think about it. I was feeling good that morning. I wanted to get out and look for a flat.'

His eyes flicked over to Lily and I got the distinct impression he was hiding something.

'You know something,' I said, 'don't you?'

'No. I don't know anything. But...' he rubbed his forehead, looking torn.

'What, Dan? What is it?'

'Well... Lily's not the only one who's been talking to Interface.'

I stared at him, incredulous. 'What?'

'I never spoke to him in the daytime when we were all together like she did,' he said 'I talked to him at night when you and Lily were in bed.'

'Unbelievable,' I said, staring at them both in disgust. 'This is unbelievable. Why, Dan? Why did you do it? Why did you keep it a secret?'

Dan tried to walk away from me into the kitchen but I followed him.

'I didn't want to talk about it, alright?' he said, when he realised I wasn't about it drop it. 'Because when he talked to me it was... personal. I mean... he helped me when I was feeling down. We just chatted about stuff. I didn't want to tell you about that.'

'What stuff?'

'Huh?'

'What stuff?' I repeated, 'you said you chatted to him about stuff. What was it?'

'Oh,' he said, looking down at the floor. 'It was about... you know. Mum... Robyn...' He lowered his voice, '...Lily.'

'Oh right, I see,' I said, and he backed away from me as I took a step towards him. 'We go to bed and you stay up talking to Interface about how you want to screw my wife? Is that it?'

Dan glared at me. 'Well you made it abundantly clear how you felt about me saying anything to you.'

Lily got up from the sofa and ran across to us. 'Stop it!' she said.

'*What?*' I said, ignoring her and looking at Dan, 'are you fucking high? On what planet would it be okay for us to talk about that?'

Dan looked at me moodily and started poking at a chip in the kitchen floor with his toes. 'I'm just saying,' he said.

'Please,' Lily said, 'don't fight like this. If Dan feels anything for me it's my fault. I've acted completely inappropriately.'

'Okay,' I said, holding up my hands and taking a breath, 'okay. Let's focus on the important thing here. Both of you have spoken to him on your own. Both of you have seen these weird binary images. Are you sure he's never told you what he's doing?'

'No,' Dan said, 'he doesn't really say anything about himself. He just listens to us, asks us questions, talks about our memories. That kind of thing.'

'How long has it been going on for?'

'Not long,' Lily said, 'he started talking to me before I did all the weird stuff in the florist.'

'And for me it was that same day, but in the night,' Dan said, 'I mean, he spoke to all of us that day when we were on the hill-'

'So how do you do it?' I asked them. 'Do you just wait for him, or do you contact him somehow?'

'The first time he just started speaking to me,' Lily said, 'but you can sort of call him, if you say Interface over and over in your head.'

'Okay,' I said.

'Look, I'm sorry mate,' Dan said, 'it's not that I was trying to keep it a secret, it just felt private.'

...

For a couple of hours we carried on trying to research what had happened, desperate to make sense of it.

'I can talk to Interface,' Lily said, 'I can ask him myself what he's doing.'

'No,' I said, without even looking at her.

'Nick, I have to do something. I'm the one who has talked to him the most. I'm the one he's threatening in order to keep you silent.'

'We are not having that conversation again.'

'We have to, Nick. The only thing we've ever said that has bothered him is when you threatened to expose his research. If his research is about killing people and us telling those journalists makes it so he can't do it anymore...'

'Lily, no.'

She got to her feet. 'What if more people die tonight?' she asked. 'Do you want that on your conscience, knowing we could do something?'

She started making for the door again and I got up and grabbed her, holding her arm tightly as she tried to wrestle it away from me. 'Lily, I swear to God I won't think twice about locking you in the bedroom to stop you going down there, is that what you want?' I said.

'People are *dying*,' Lily cried, still struggling to escape my grip, 'we've got to help them.'

'So what!' I said, 'those people aren't my family. I don't care if that sounds immoral. That's the way it is. I'll do everything I possibly can to help them but I am not sacrificing you to save a load of people I don't even know, do you understand me?'

'No!' Lily said, 'what's so special about my life? I used to want to die once, or say that I wanted to be hurt. Perhaps this is what I deserve.'

She made another attempt to escape, pushing against my chest and trying to wriggle her way out of my grip but I pushed her up against the wall and held her pinned there, her wrists in my hands.

'Please, Lily,' I said when she stopped trying to fight me, 'you don't need to take any responsibility for what happens. As far as you're concerned, you tried to tell them and I forced you not to. It's all on me. You see that, don't you?'

'No!' she said, 'because I know I can stop it and I feel like I'm choosing not to. I'm choosing to put people's lives at risk.'

'You're not,' I insisted, 'I told you Lily, this is all on me. *I'm* stopping you.'

'So stop me!' she said, 'lock me in the bedroom. I'd prefer it because at least I wouldn't have to feel so *guilty.*'

Her eyes filled with tears and I became aware I was holding her wrists very tightly. I let go straight away, shocked to see they were bright red.

'I've hurt you...' I said.

'No,' she said, 'nothing could hurt me as much as this... as this... situation.'

'I don't want to keep you here like a prisoner,' I said, 'but you're giving me no choice. Please, Lily-'

I was losing her. Her eyes flicked towards the door and before I could react she'd pushed me away from her and run straight out into the hallway.

I dashed after her but as it turned out I needn't have bothered. There was loud thump as Lily fell to the ground, her arms still stretched out towards the stairs, her hair in a tangled cloud around her head.

'Lily,' I said, 'are you okay?' There was no answer so I knelt down and shook her gently, but her eyes remained closed, her body limp. 'Lily!' I said, 'Lily, wake up! Lily!'

Dan crouched down beside me and shook her again, but when there was no response for almost a minute, he took out his phone and started dialling 999. But before he could make the call, the numbers disappeared again and I heard Interface in my mind.

'Don't be alarmed,' he said. 'Lily is perfectly well. But you can't talk to anybody about my research. As we speak, I'm with her. I'm explaining this to her. I'm helping her to see why.'

'Lily,' I said, still shaking her. I even tried to open her eyelids, though when I caught a glimpse of her dark pupils her gaze was unfocussed.

I scooped her up into my arms but her body was heavy and floppy so I ended up just draping her against me, her head hanging lifelessly over my shoulder. 'No!' I said, 'don't listen to what he's saying to you, come back to me Lily, please, come back to me.'

Chapter 41

When Lily came round she was weak and confused, so Dan and I carried her to the sofa and lay her down, where she smiled serenely and held both our hands.

'I love you,' she said.

I kissed her forehead, 'I love you too.'

'I mean both of you.'

I gave Dan a look of warning, but he pretended not to have seen. 'I love you too, Lily,' he said.

For a second I wanted nothing more than to knock him out, but I knew I had to focus on Lily, on getting her to tell me whatever it was that Interface had told her.

'It'll be okay now,' she said, 'you don't need to worry, everything will be fine.'

'What do you mean? Do you mean Interface isn't going to kill anybody else?'

Lily giggled and let go of our hands to roll over onto her side. 'They're not dead,' she said.

'What? What do you mean?'

'The people. They're not dead. They're in the Network.'

I tried desperately to get her to explain, but she couldn't, or wouldn't. She still couldn't tell me what the Network was, what it was trying to do, what would happen next or even what the deal was with the code pictures.

'I guess they're just to do with the game,' Dan said to me a bit later, 'you know, because Affrayed seems real but it's actually just code.'

'You think so?'

He shrugged. 'Unless you've got a better idea?'

I thought about it, and I had to admit it made sense. Everything was about the game, or at least had started out that way and I could well believe that people would buy into his nonsense if Interface was trying to suggest that perhaps reality wasn't real as they thought.

'What are we going to do about Lily?' Dan asked. She'd fallen asleep on the sofa under his duvet and I couldn't help but notice the way he smiled when he looked at her.

'Why did you have to go and tell her you're in love with her?' I asked, 'why did you have to fuck with her head even more?'

'She said she loved me.'

'She meant as a friend,' I snapped.

'Okay, well, I'm sorry,' Dan said, 'But I do love her. I can't help it.'

...

The next morning Lily had snapped out of her reverie and seemed in turns distant, sad, anxious, yet oddly excited.

'Lily, please talk to me. What's going on, what are you thinking?' I asked as we sat round the little dining table in the kitchen cradling cups of strong coffee.

'I feel confused,' she said, 'Interface, he's shown me a lot of things. But I'm not certain I understand. I mean, he said the dead people are in the Network. Can that be possible?'

I took her hand. 'No, of course not,' I said. 'Forget about him and his lies. He made you collapse to stop you talking yesterday; you've got a bump on your head the size of a ping-pong ball.'

Lily touched it. 'It's not that big,' she said. 'I feel a bit ill though.'

'You should let me take you to hospital.'

Lily drank some coffee and shook her head. 'I don't want to go out.'

'Look, I'm sorry if I frightened you yesterday when you wanted to talk to the journalists,' I said, 'but you understand why I did it, don't you?'

'It doesn't matter anymore.'

I watched her swirl her coffee round in the mug and wondered what to say.

'You just need to distance yourself from Interface, from Affrayed, from everything,' I said in the end. 'All we can do is stick together, right?

Lily looked at Dan, and then she nodded. 'Okay,' she said.

I thought that things couldn't possibly get any worse, but before we'd even finished our coffee I heard more knocking on the door. I assumed it was journalists again and was inclined to ignore it, but then I heard the sound of the letter box being pushed open and Lily's dad's voice calling, 'Lily, are you in there? Lily?'

'You can't be serious,' I said.

Lily ran down to open the door and I followed a few paces behind her, while Dan hung around at the top of the stairs. But the first thing I noticed, before Lily even opened the door, was that the two frosted glass panels seemed to have something red on the outside of them. And sure enough, once Lily had opened it, I saw that somebody had daubed the word "murderer" in red paint, right up the length of the door.

Lily hadn't noticed though. In fact, she seemed so taken aback by her parents and the group of reporters behind them that she took a step back and collided with me.

'Lily!' her mum said, with a mixture of relief and chastisement. I could tell she was angry. She was even standing aggressively, her shoulders thrown back, a pair of gold heels bringing her almost up to my height. She was dressed in smart white linen trousers and a voluminous yellow, gold and white top pinched in sharply at the waist, and as she fixed her eyes on Lily she pushed a pair of large, showy sunglasses up into her dark hair. Just the expression on her face was enough to make me place a protective arm around Lily's waist. But if anyone had come looking for a fight, it was Lily's dad. He looked every bit as unpleasant as he always did, his body stuffed into a short-sleeve striped shirt that strained around his thick neck, and his head was red all over, his eyes glinting in his fleshy face. I noticed he'd placed one of his big, rough hands on the door frame, like he was expecting me to shut the door in his face and was already trying to stop me.

'I don't want any trouble,' he said, which seemed like a really bad start, 'but we think it might be best if Lily came to stay with us until all *this*,' he waved his hand at our front door, 'dies down.'

With his gesture, Lily turned for the first time to look at the outside of our front door, and when she saw what was written there she let out a sort of wail and buried her hands in her hair.

I could see we were making a real scene, but Lily's parents loved Lily's distress- I knew they did. They didn't care how much pain it caused her, they just wanted to turn her against me.

'Let's take this inside,' I said.

I was worried they'd refuse, but thankfully they stepped indoors, and Dan darted back into the living room. When we joined him I could see he was hiding the pad containing the drawings of Lily, and I remembered it had still been open on the desk. Inwardly I heaved a huge sigh of relief. If Lily's parents had seen those images, I had no idea what they would have done.

When Lily's parents saw Dan they stopped for a moment, surprised to find him there. They'd met him before, but not since mine and Lily's wedding, so he started gracelessly saying hello and reminding them who he was. But I could see they were looking round at all his stuff heaped in the corner of the room and the duvet and pile of clothes on the sofa.

'Sorry,' he said, 'let me just...' he started shifting the stuff off the sofa so they could sit down. But neither of them made any move towards it.

'Are you *living* here?' Lily's mum asked him.

'Yeah, I... just for a few... uh-' he looked at me desperately.

'Mum, don't,' Lily said, 'Dan's just staying with us for a little while until he gets himself sorted out.'

'Why can't he live with his own family?'

Lily threw her hand over her mouth as if it was her who had said it and looked across at Dan who was frozen to the spot, with no idea what to do with himself.

'Why don't you sit down?' I said to them, trying to diffuse the situation. 'Can I get you a coffee? Or a tea?'

'It's alright,' Lily's mum said, 'we're not staying.' She turned to Lily, who was standing against the wall, halfway between me and her parents. She had her arms folded tightly across her chest and was staring resolutely down at the floor.

'Lily, wouldn't you prefer to come and stay with us for a few days?' her mum asked, 'you don't want to be here with all this going on, do you? You won't even answer our calls. We're worried sick about you.'

'I'm fine,' Lily said.

'Well, you don't look fine,' her dad chipped in. He walked over to her and tried to pull her away from the wall, and as she tried to push him away from her she ended up inadvertently showing him the back of her left arm, where the new cut from the night Dan had drawn her was plainly visible. It was just a little line of red, no more than two or three centimetres long, but to Lily's parents it was all the ammunition they needed.

'Did you do this?' he asked her.

Lily's mum walked over to see what he was talking about, and the second she saw Lily's self-harm she looked at me and said, 'look what you've done! Your *stupid* game has made her ill again.'

Lily snatched her arm away from them.

'It's nothing to do with Nick!' she said, 'why do you always blame him? It's not his fault, it's me. This is what I'm *like!*'

'Are you happy with what you've done?' Lily's dad said to me, 'you've messed with my girl's head from the day she met you. Look at the state of her!'

Right on cue, Lily burst into tears, and I exchanged a look with Dan. He was still standing in front of the sofa, watching everything unfold. I'd told him before how Lily and her parents wound each other up something crazy, and I could see he found what was happening as ridiculous as I did.

'This is never what you used to be like,' Lily's mum said to her, 'you were always such a *happy* baby.'

I almost laughed in disbelief. Lily was twenty-six years old for fucks' sake.

'Look,' I said, 'If Lily wants to spend some time with you, that's fine. But if she wants to stay here, I'd appreciate it if you could respect that.'

Lily's mum spun round to face me. 'Are seriously suggesting she's better off *here*, with *you?*'

As always, my first instinct was to say whatever it took to calm the situation down, but this time I'd absolutely had it with them.

'That's exactly what I'm saying,' I said.

Lily's mum stared daggers at me for several seconds, then she turned back to Lily with a dismissive little laugh.

'Lily, come on,' she said, 'can't you see this isn't good for you? Look at what you've done to yourself. All this stress would be hard enough for anybody.'

'I'm not leaving Nick,' Lily said.

Lily's mum was impatient. Things weren't going her way and she stood in front of Lily, one hand on her hip.

'For God's sake, we're not telling you to *leave* him, we're saying you need a break. Why've you got to make everything into something it isn't?'

It was quite obvious to me that Lily had only meant that she didn't want to leave me for a couple of days not forever, but Lily's mum had just interpreted it in whatever way meant she could have a bigger argument.

'Well that's what you really want, isn't it?' Lily said, 'you've always just wanted to get me away from him. But he's my husband and I love him!'

She rushed over and put her arm around me, looking back at her parents. 'I don't want to stay with you,' she said to them, 'I know you're looking out for me, but I want to stay here.'

'I always said no good would ever come of this whole *games* thing,' Lily's dad said, looking me up and down. 'If you've got any kind of decency you'll let Lily come with us. She can hardly be expected to live in these conditions, with the press hanging around outside and people writing graffiti on your door. What's going to happen if it's bricks through your window and death threats?'

'Lily,' I said, 'what do *you* want to do? Do you want to go with your parents or do you want to stay here?'

'I want to stay here.'

I looked at Lily's parents. 'You heard her,' I said.

They wouldn't have it though, and continued to argue. If it was my parents, I'm pretty sure they would have just asked me something, listened to my answer, perhaps had a bit of discussion and we would have come to a nice, calm decision. But not so with Lily's. In the end both her and her mum were in tears.

'I think you should leave,' I said, when Lily was practically incoherent and I was worried she'd agree to go with them just to make it stop.

'Not without Lily,' her dad said, and he took hold of her arm.

'Let go of her,' I said, and I noticed that Dan came round from the other side of the sofa to stand by my side, presumably to back me up, if necessary.

'Please!' Lily said, 'I want to stay. I don't want to upset you but I want to stay.'

Lily's parents carried on pulling her towards the door and I could hardly believe what they were doing. Were they actually going to drag her kicking and screaming from the flat?

Dan and I followed them out into the hall, where Lily's dad let go of her and she sagged against the wall.

'You really want to stay here, do you?' he asked.

'Yes.'

'Well that's fine then. You stay here.' He gestured towards Lily's mum, who was still in tears. 'Look how much you're upsetting your mum,' he said, 'I can't think how many times I've had her crying over you. And your sister's in a right state as well, we've had her on the phone, practically hysterical. She's seven months pregnant; all this stress you're causing is going to make her ill. Not that you care, do you Lily? You've never even bothered to call us and tell us what the hell is going on. I would say that I can't believe how thoughtless you are, but I can believe it. Never happy unless you're the centre of attention, are you girl?' He gestured towards the scars on her arm. 'They say all this is because you're *unhappy*, because you've got *problems*, but what about us, huh? You think this is fun for us, having to run round after you all the time, like we don't have our own lives? There is a limit to sympathy, Lily, and the way you carry on you've just about-'

'That is enough!' I said, 'you can get out. Right now. Both of you.'

I took a step towards them and Lily's dad took a step towards me.

'Stop it,' Lily said, quickly putting herself between us. 'I'm sorry,' she said to her dad, 'is Poppy okay? I'll come, if you want me to.'

She took a step towards the stairs.

'No, Lily,' I said, 'you're not going anywhere with them.'

'I don't want to upset anybody,' Lily said, 'I don't know what to do.'

'Lily, you come home with us now, or we've had it with you,' her dad said.

'What do you mean?' Lily asked.

'I mean that I don't want you messing up our family anymore. You stay here and take your chances with Nick if you want to. But if you do that, I don't want to see either of you at our house again, you understand? That'll be the end of it. I'm absolutely sick to death of you and all your dramas.'

Lily let out a little cry, and I could see this was a step too far for Lily's mum, as well, but the words having been said, she couldn't really stop it.

'Make up your mind, Lily,' her dad said.

Lily rushed back over to me and clung to my hand. 'I choose Nick.'

He looked at her closely for a few seconds. 'You always were a stupid girl,' he said.

He took another quick look at me, face full of contempt, and then turned back to his daughter. 'I hope the two of you are very happy together,' he said.

He strode off down the stairs without a backward glance, and Dan and I had to grab Lily when she began falling to her knees. For a little while, her mum stood looking at her, not wanting to go.

'Julie, come on, we're leaving,' Lily's dad said.

Chapter 42

'That was insane,' Dan whispered to me. Lily was lying on the sofa with her arm flung over her face, and in the absence of any better ideas of how to make her feel better, I stood in the kitchen making her some breakfast. 'Are they always like that?'

'They have their moments.'

'Fuck me,' he said, shaking his head. 'It's like being back at my house again.'

Lily had gone through so much trauma that I was beginning to get quite scared for her. She ate a little of the toast I'd made her then threw the plate down and ran into the bathroom, though she wasn't actually sick. I went and joined her as she sat crouched by the toilet, her back against the wall, and a few seconds later Dan came in too.

'I've lost count of how many times my mum has threatened to disown Robyn,' he said, 'but she never means it.'

'They hate me,' Lily said, 'you heard them. Dad said I'm stupid, he says I'm ruining their family. And it's true. I've been an awful daughter. They've had nothing except pain and disappointment from me.'

To be honest, I was so enraged by how they'd treated her that I'd be happy if I never saw either of them again. But they were her parents. No matter what they did she'd still want them in her life. So I swallowed my own feelings and tried to reassure her. 'It's me they really don't like, Lily,' I said. 'And I'm not all that surprised. Look at what's happened because of me.'

'It's not your fault.'

'Look,' I said, 'I know they're angry right now, but I think when this has all calmed down they'll soon come round.'

'I want to play Affrayed,' Lily said, and it was as though she'd taken a knife and stabbed me.

'What? Why?'

'To forget,' Lily said, 'to make all the pain go away.'

I eventually persuaded Lily not to play but she soon became withdrawn, and instead of the three of us growing closer through what had happened, Lily and Dan disappeared into their own little world, stupefied by distress, and seemingly unable to do anything except huddle together on the sofa.

Meanwhile, I tried to keep it together. There *had* to be a different way of figuring out what the Network was. I told myself over and over that there would be a clue in the stories about the suicides, that if I kept reading anything I could find that related to them then eventually there would be something, some missing piece that would make it all make sense. I felt like I was close, sometimes, like all the components were there, and that suddenly they'd shift and I'd see the full picture.

But the stories contained very little about the player's experiences with Affrayed. There was stuff about the circumstances of the suicides- every single person had died by jumping from something- cliffs, bridges, and most frequently from tall buildings. They'd all done it at the same moment, as far as anyone could tell, and yet there was no evidence of communication between any players that was to do with arranging the time or the method.

Aside from that, I looked at the obfuscated code again and I looked at Dan's picture again, but I didn't want to risk playing the game and finally I had to accept there was nothing. The only thing we could possibly do was try to communicate with Interface, and since I wasn't keen to do that myself, I had to try to get something useful out of Lily.

'You've talked to Interface,' I said to her, 'he's shown you things. I know not much of it made sense, but what about your dream, at least? Can you try to explain it to me? Or draw it, if that's easier?'

She looked at Dan and then she drew her legs up onto the sofa to hug her knees. 'I don't think I should tell you,' she said.

'Why not? For God's sake Lily, you and Dan are in danger. Other people are in danger.'

I could see I was reaching her.

'You won't... you mustn't be angry,' she said.

'Angry about what?'

'What I tell you. I don't know what it means. I don't think it will happen-'

'What, Lily? Just tell me!'

For a little while she looked at me and I was scared she'd refuse, and then, almost imperceptibly, she nodded. But just before she opened her mouth I saw her eyes change, and she became dreamy and distant.

'You're not ready,' she murmured, 'that's why I can't tell you. But you will be. If I trust him, you will be.'

I was so appalled I shook her.

'Lily, don't listen to him! Just tell me what it is!'

'No,' she said, 'we've all got our journeys. Mine and Dan's is just a little different to yours. But one way or another, we'll all end up at the same destination.'

'Stop it,' I said. I could see now that it wasn't only Lily who was with Interface, Dan was too. He was with her.

'No!' I said, 'stop it, both of you! What are you doing?'

But it was useless. Without my even being involved in it, without a single word of discussion, they'd both made their commitment to Interface, and as long as they carried on, any chance I had of reasoning with them was over.

...

With the two of them no longer able to have a sensible conversation with me, I had no choice but to watch helplessly as Dan picked up his laptop, Lily picked up mine, and they logged in to Affrayed.

They played for hours on end with barely any breaks. Sometimes I watched them, though the sight of them was disturbing and I didn't like it. Both of them had the same vacant, glassy-eyed expression that I'd come to associate with the game, but it seemed even worse now, like they were in even deeper. They seemed to be involved in some mission against the Renegade Shadows, and although I felt the least interested I had ever been in playing Affrayed, it did strike me how Lily and Dan not only had their hands completely still, but that they appeared to be coordinating their actions very efficiently without speaking a single word to each other. Not only that, but a few of the other people they were working with from Outbreak seemed similarly well choreographed-

the whole thing so clean and well organised- their attack on the Renegades like a beautiful, serene dance.

At about eight-thirty they stopped to eat, but didn't speak to me, and when they sat back down on the sofa and entered the game again, I saw that this time they were holding hands.

When I went to bed, I was alone. When I got up, I was alone. Not that I really slept. I just went over and over everything that had happened, cursing myself for ever having released Affrayed, for ever having decided to make games at all. I wished that nobody had supported me, that my parents and Lily and everybody else had just told me not to do it, that it was a stupid idea, that I should just get a normal job like everybody else.

But Lily and Dan had not just played right through the night, when I found them in the living room the next morning they'd both fallen asleep, their heads on opposite arms of the sofa, their legs all tangled up together in the middle. I stood next to Lily and stroked her hair, until she opened her eyes and said, 'please, Nick. Won't you just join us?'

I knelt down so that I was at eye level with her.

'No,' I said.

'You have no idea how wonderful it feels, being Networked. It's like when he links you and me and Dan, but on an even bigger scale, and we're all working together to achieve something. It's like... you just feel so *valued,* but at the same time, you're not even aware of feeling that way, because you're not aware of anything. It's just this big, organic thing where everything you do is in harmony, and every other person is in harmony. There's no time passing, nothing else to worry about, we're all one, and there's just the task, the goal, and our progress towards it.'

'Lily, he's going to make you kill yourself,' I said.

She looked pained. 'No,' she said, 'I told you the other day. Nobody is dead. There is another way to live, and this is what it is. They've just taken a step to be like this all the time.'

'What you're talking about, this being at one with other people and with what you're doing, this can't be the first time you've felt that way. I often feel that way, when I'm programming and it's going well, or when Dan and I are planning something out and we're really on the same wavelength. I felt it with you when we made Cactustrophe, and when we do other things together.'

'Yes,' Lily said, 'but there are always interruptions. It's never completely pure.'

She turned over so she was looking straight at me, and she rested her chin on the back of her hands. Her movement made Dan stir, but he didn't wake up.

'Lily, what you and Dan are doing is hurting me so deeply that I can barely even put it into words,' I said.

'I know,' she said, 'but since you refuse to join us, you must follow your own path to our destination, and this is it.'

Chapter 43

By mid-morning, I'd had it with being around them and I decided to go and scrub the graffiti from our front door. Dan was in the shower, and Lily was munching through a slice of toast spread thickly with chocolate spread, but it was clear what their plans for the day were, and quite frankly, I didn't want to be in the flat to see them log in to Affrayed again.

It was far from enjoyable, standing outside my house trying to wash the word "murderer" off my door, all the while surrounded by journalists and with neighbours coming and going and looking over curiously.

Soon the soapy water in the washing-up bowl at my feet began to turn red, and as I scrubbed away at the door with a scouring pad, foamy pink bubbles coated my fingers and I thought about Dan and Lily back inside, probably just settling down to play Affrayed.

Sure enough, when I went upstairs to get some clean water they were on the sofa again, immersed in the game. Slowly, I poured the scarlet water into the kitchen sink, washed my hands until the water from them ran clear, and then instead of refilling the washing-up bowl with water, I grabbed my wallet and went out.

There were a couple of big DIY stores just outside our estate and I went straight for the nearest one, bought a hammer, and walked back to the flat again.

Lily and Dan were still completely absorbed, so it was easy to scoop up the laptops from their laps. In fact, I had taken them into the kitchen, dropped them down on the floor and started smashing the things to hell before they even started to snap out of their trance.

'What the fuck are you doing?' Dan said, running into the kitchen amidst showers of shattering plastic and trying to drag me away.

'What does it look like I'm doing?' I said, fighting him off in order to finish the job, 'I'm stopping the two of you from playing that stupid game!'

They both stared at me, horrified, and I began to feel a bit daft as I finished pulverising the laptops and put the hammer down on the dining table.

'The game isn't the point,' Lily said quietly.

'Then what is the point?' I asked, 'please, tell me. Because I'm finding it really fucking difficult to understand this. Do you *want* to die? Is that it?'

Neither of them would tell me anything. Lily tried again to persuade me to play with them, told me that she loved me and that things would be so much simpler and less painful if I trusted her and Interface, but I wouldn't give in.

In defiance of me, they simply went over and played Affrayed together on my computer, and although I was tempted for a moment to smash that up too, I didn't. Probably all they'd do would just be to go out and buy another computer.

So I let them play while I cleaned the rest of the graffiti off the door. I let them play while I watched the news some more, and spent more time trawling through Affrayed's forums- something which I now had to do on my phone because I'd destroyed my laptop. I let them play while I sat in the kitchen and ate a single slice of dry white toast for dinner, and I let them play while I spent an utterly miserable and hopeless evening in the same room as them, but completely alone.

At midnight, I tried to get Lily to come to bed.

'I don't want you to sleep on the sofa again,' I said. What I really meant was that I didn't want her to spend another night sleeping next to Dan.

'I know,' she said vaguely, her eyes fixed on the screen, 'but we're still playing.'

I clenched my left fist so hard that I could feel my nails digging into my palm, but I placed my other hand gently on her shoulder.

'Okay, but when you're done, I want you to come to bed,' I said.

Lily made a noncommittal noise.

'Lily,' I shook her shoulder, 'promise me.'
'Yeah,' she said.

There barely seemed any point in me going to bed, but at some point I must have slept, because I dreamed. I dreamt of a cliff. A breezy, wild sort of place, with sandy soil and tufts of wispy grass. When I stood at the edge of the cliff, I saw there was a beach below, but beyond that, the huge expanse of ocean- a deep, radiant blue, with sunlight glittering across the surface. But when I looked closer, the little glittering patches changed, became code. As it spread across the ocean I realised it was code I recognised, that it looked just like script from the original Affrayed. I was so consumed with looking at the water that I realised I'd barely seen the sky, but when I looked up it was black, and I was terrified. I fell to my knees on the cliff top and looked straight up above me, but all the sky was black, and all of it was covered in code.

When I woke up, I was drenched in sweat. There was a misty sort of half-light drifting in through the curtains and I was barely even surprised to find that Lily was not by my side. But when I went into the living room she was not on the sofa with Dan. In fact, Dan was nowhere to be seen either, and it didn't take long to establish that neither of them were in the flat. On top of that, some of their stuff was missing. They'd taken their toothbrushes, some clothes, other little bits and bobs, and when I looked out the window Dan's car was gone. I leant my forehead against the cool glass looking at his empty parking space for two or three seconds, letting the emotion that had begun seething inside me build, then with a cry of rage I turned towards my desk and just flew at it, throwing everything that was on it onto the floor. I carried on until the only thing left was the pot of cacti, but instead of smashing it I picked it up and hugged it, dropping to my knees on the floor where broken bits of plastic from the computer screens dug into my knees.

'Interface,' I cried out inside my head, 'Interface, interface, interface.'

Chapter 44

After our conversation at the train station, it was like Lily just switched off from the world. When I met up with her she was listless, in a state of such transfixing, consuming despair that it was like nothing else existed. She seemed to find talking an effort and would just turn her huge, tortured eyes to me as though she thought this would make me understand. When I phoned her, she wouldn't answer, but she'd often call me and just hang on the end of the line in silence, as though she wanted to feel like I was near, but she simply couldn't communicate with me anymore. Then, on a Sunday afternoon in early December, she sent me a text- short, but cruel.

> *I know what you did with my pills. Discovered it yesterday. Don't worry, I bought them all again*

I threw my phone down onto my desk so hard that the back flew off it and for a second I felt like I was going to completely lose it. But the feeling passed, and I put my phone back together, closed the work I was doing on my dissertation and decided that I really had to try and figure out what to do. I knew Lily understood she was depressed. At times she could be completely lucid about it, she'd understand that it might be a good idea to go to her GP, or to the university counselling service, or to talk to her friends. But it was as though she understood and then consciously made the decision not to, like she was deliberately setting out to harm herself at every turn. I don't know whether she thought her situation was so hopeless that she was beyond help, whether she was too embarrassed or ashamed, or whether she just genuinely believed she deserved to suffer, but whatever it was, I couldn't break through it.

I'd spent a bit of time before reading about depression online, so I turned to the internet again and typed in a search for self-harm and suicide. I was so absorbed in reading that I didn't hear Carl's footsteps in the hall, and when he wandered into my room it gave me the fright of my life, and though I immediately closed what I was reading, I had no idea if he'd seen it.

'Haven't you heard of knocking?' I said as he strolled over to my bed and sat down on the end of it. He was eating a sandwich, and seemed so laid back that I was convinced he couldn't have seen.

He raised an eyebrow. 'Sorry,' he said, 'Jesus. Maybe you should shut your door if you want a bit of *alone* time.'

'I had shut the door.'

He took a bite of his sandwich. 'It was ajar,' he said.

I almost laughed in relief. He hadn't seen anything, he can't have done. He was just bored and had decided to come in and hang around for a bit.

'Did you want something?' I asked him as he finished eating and brushed a load of crumbs onto the carpet.

'I saw what you were reading,' he said, '"understanding self-harm."'

My stomach felt like it flipped over and I spun round on my chair to face him.

'Is that what Lily's started doing now?' he said.

'Lily?' I said unconvincingly.

'Well, it's not you doing it, is it?'

I looked at him for a while. The need to keep it secret had become almost automatic, but now he'd found out anyway what was the point in holding back? Before I knew it, I found myself telling him everything about it. How she was so unhappy, how she'd talk about killing herself all the time, how she showed me all the injuries she'd done to herself, how she couldn't do her work and was going to fail her degree. Carl sat and listened to the whole story without saying a word, until eventually I trailed off into silence.

'You want my advice?' he said, 'you're better off well out of it.'

I stared at him, shocked. He'd never exactly been the most sympathetic and warm-hearted person, and there had always been something about him that struck me as a little insincere, sometimes even cruel. But hadn't he listened to a word I'd just said?

'I want to try to persuade her to get help,' I said, 'but she keeps going on about how she wants to get her degree and she won't listen to me.'

Carl shrugged. 'It's not your problem,' he said. 'Look. I know it sounds harsh. But when you met her she was, you know, normal. This isn't what you signed up for.'

I shook my head. 'It's not like that-'

'Come on, she hasn't made you happy in a long time,' he said. 'You've been a right miserable bastard since you started getting serious with her.'

'I'm worried about her!'

'Yeah. And that's what she wants. You might not be able to see it, but I can. All this cutting herself and saying she's going to commit suicide, she's got you right where she wants you.'

'Lily is nothing like that,' I said, 'and besides, that's not what hurting herself is about. It's nothing to do with manipulating people, people do it when there's something seriously wrong.'

Carl was looking at me as though he couldn't quite believe the words coming out of my mouth. 'Fine,' he said, 'so maybe there is something wrong with her. It's still not your responsibility. If she wants to get help she'll get help. If she doesn't...' he paused. 'Oh, I get it now,' he said, 'you think if you dump her she's going to kill herself.'

'No,' I said. 'I don't *want* to break up with her. I just want her to not be ill anymore.'

I was appalled by his attitude, and I wished like hell I'd never told him about any of it. I thought having someone else know might make it easier, but it had just made it even worse. How could he think Lily was like that? That she would say things just to trap me?

'Seriously, you need to listen to me,' Carl said, 'I know Lily's fit and everything, but I'm telling you, she's not worth the hassle.'

'It is not *hassle*,' I said, 'and I don't want to talk about it anymore.'

In truth, I felt like I had no idea who he even was anymore, and since he didn't seem like he was about to go anywhere, I got up and grabbed my jacket from the back of my desk chair.

'Where are you going?' he asked me.

'To see Lily,' I said.

He spread his hands wide. '*Why?*' he asked.

'To check she's okay.'

He stared at me. 'She's making a complete fool of you,' he said.

'Yeah, well, you've made it perfectly clear what you think about it,' I said.

Carl got up and followed me to the front door. 'Come on, Nick, don't go round there now,' he said, 'this is stupid.'

I wouldn't listen to him. In fact, partly what made me so keen to go and see her was the fact he said I shouldn't.

'Jesus, talk about over-reacting,' he said, as I made my way down the front steps. I looked back at him where he stood in the doorway. Even now he seemed pretty casual and unconcerned, just leaning against the door frame and looking at me like I was being hysterical or something. But I didn't care anymore. As far as I was concerned he and everybody else could just go to hell. Lily was my priority now.

I was still fuming for most of the twenty minute walk to Lily's, though I did eventually console myself by concluding that Carl must be jealous of the time I spent with Lily or something, and that if he spent his whole life being this much of a dick he'd probably end up on his own.

The door to Lily's house was answered by her housemate Sophie, who was talking on her mobile with one hand, while in the other she was holding a half-eaten mince pie. The hallway was festooned with gaudy decorations and she had a long piece of silver tinsel wound around her neck. I could hear loud Christmas music coming from somewhere down the hall.

'Hold on a second,' Sophie said into the phone, before holding it pressed against her jumper. As usual, she gave the impression of being like a tightly coiled spring, filled with more energy than she knew what to do with. Even as she stood looking at me I could tell she was just bursting to get back to talking on the phone, eating the mince pie, and probably putting up decorations at the same time as well if she could find a way.

She seemed a bit confused as to why I was there on the doorstep.

'I thought Lily was with you,' she said.

'No,' I said, 'why, isn't she in?'

Sophie told whoever was on the phone that she'd call them back and then she used the corner of it to try and sweep some stray blonde hairs behind her ear.

'I don't think she's in,' she said, 'I haven't seen her since yesterday, and I've been here most of the day today.'

There was a loud thud from the living room where the music was playing, followed by swearing and some laughter. Sophie looked round towards the sound. I could see she was eager to go and join them.

'Do you mind if I just check,' I said, 'since I'm here.'

I was pretty worried. Lily didn't tend to go anywhere much anymore, and I was sure she must be in her room- but to have avoided seeing Sophie all day seemed like quite a feat.

Sophie moved out the way of the door. 'Go for it,' she said. 'Do you want a mince pie? We've got hundreds.'

'No,' I said quickly. I was sure something was badly wrong, and I didn't want to waste any more time, but Sophie was looking at me curiously, so I smiled and said, 'thanks, though.'

I waited for Sophie to start walking back down to the living room before I ran up the stairs two at a time. This definitely didn't feel right. And when I saw Lily's door was closed my heart started pounding. I was sure she had done something stupid. In fact, I was so sure that when I burst into her room, initially my mind saw exactly what it expected to see. The curtains were half drawn, so her room was gloomy in the fading light. But amongst the gloom I could see her in bed, on her side, her eyes closed. And I could see the packets of painkillers, all lined up on the chest of drawers beside her.

I ran over and started shaking her.

'Lily, wake up,' I said desperately, 'Lily!'

She half-opened her eyes and then blinked in confusion.

'What are you doing?' she asked me, 'what's happening?'

'Have you taken any?' I asked.

She wouldn't answer me. In fact, as she began to understand, she smiled. It was this peculiarly unique, terrible smile, that seemed to say- I can do what I want, and you can't stop me.

'Lily!' I said, 'tell me! Have you taken any?'

I started looking through the boxes, and saw quickly that all the pills were still inside.

'Stop it,' she said, 'I haven't taken any. I'm just looking at them.'

She reached across to try and stop me messing up more of the boxes, and I noticed that there was a large bloodstain on the sleeve of her pyjama top.

'What have you done?' I asked her.

She snatched her arm away, and I realised that whatever it was, she obviously thought it would shock me. She'd always said before that she was in control, that she wouldn't ever self-harm too badly. This was obviously sufficiently bad that she thought I might stop trusting her.

'Show me,' I said softly, 'please Lily.'

She responded to my quiet tone, and slowly rolled up the sleeve of her top.

'I didn't realise it would bleed this much,' she said, trying to defend her actions as the cuts became visible, 'but it's okay now,' she continued, 'I won't do it like this again.'

Chapter 45

God knows what she'd used, but it had clearly been something pretty nasty. There were two long red slashes across the back of her arm, still seeping blood, but mostly it had dried to a dark burgundy.

'I didn't mean it,' she said, 'when I'd done it I was frightened. I thought it would never stop bleeding. It was horrible.' She held her arm close to her and started speaking to it like it had its own feelings. 'I'm sorry,' she said, 'I didn't mean it, I didn't mean it.'

'When's the last time you ate?' I asked her. There was a bottle of water on the floor by her bed, but there were no mugs or plates around, and she can't have been leaving her room much if she'd managed not to be spotted by Sophie. She certainly didn't appear to have bothered having a shower or getting dressed, even though it was four in the afternoon.

'Lily, when was the last time you ate?' I repeated.

She wouldn't answer me. In fact, she didn't want to have a conversation at all, and closed her eyes.

'Have you eaten today?' I asked her.

'No,' she said, eyes still closed, 'I'll eat when I've done some work.'

I knelt down beside her bed. 'You haven't eaten anything today? What about yesterday?'

'What's the point?' she said, 'I don't do anything, so I don't deserve any food.'

I took a deep breath and let it out slowly. 'Lily, that's not a very nice thing to do to your body, is it?' I said, 'you can't expect to be able to work if you're not giving yourself what you need to function.'

'I can't,' Lily said, 'even if I wanted to, I just can't even make a meal. I don't have the energy. I can barely keep it together long enough to be in the kitchen, especially with all the others in there.'

'You have to eat,' I said, 'I've already noticed you've been losing weight, and I don't like it. It's not good for you.'

'I don't care,' Lily said, then she brought her arms up over her face, as though stopping herself from seeing me stopped all this from happening.

I watched her there, huddled up in her bed, her room cold and dark, her interaction with the world so minimal her housemates actually thought she was out. Eventually she got curious about what I was doing, and peeked out from between her arms, fixing one of her haunted eyes on me.

'Why am I like this?' she asked me quietly, 'what did I do that was so bad?'

'Nothing,' I said, 'you've done nothing at all.'

Slowly, she rolled the sleeve of her pyjama top up again and looked at her injuries.

'I'm hurt,' she said.

'Yes, Lily, I know.'

'I don't want to be hurt.'

I lifted her arm up and kissed it near to the cuts. 'I'll clean them for you if you want,' I said.

Lily nodded, so I went into the bathroom and found some cotton wool pads. I wasn't sure what I could clean her with apart from water so I ran the pads under the tap and went back to her bedroom, where I sat down beside her and started cleaning away some of the dried blood.

'Do you worry about me?' Lily asked.

'Yes. I worry about you every day.'

'Do you worry that I'll die?'

'Yes.'

'How does it make you feel?'

'Awful.'

I carried on gently cleaning her arm and she watched me.

'You see, you say it would make you feel awful, but I don't believe it,' she said, 'I just don't understand.'

'I know,' I said, 'don't worry about it. All I want you to worry about is looking after yourself.'

When I'd finished, Lily went back to looking at her arm as though it fascinated her, and I noticed that as well as her pyjama top she'd got blood on her sheets and her pillow.

'What do you think when you look at where you've hurt

yourself?' I asked her.

'I don't know. Sometimes I feel bad for my arm, because it never really did anything to me. It's just trying to do its best, and I've hurt it.'

'Your arm is part of your body, though, isn't it, Lily? You're being unkind to all of your body. You're not feeding it. You say nasty things about it, you're not looking after yourself properly.'

Lily held her arm out to me. 'What do you think when you look at it?' she asked.

I thought for a long while, and I tried to think about some of the advice I'd read, though I didn't really know how to apply any of it to her and my own hurt was so much that I didn't know what I should do anymore. Beyond the fact it was obvious she couldn't cope, I realised for the first time that I wasn't sure I could cope. Not with things as they were.

'I think you're very unwell, aren't you, Lily?' I said, stroking her hair.

'Yes,' she said, 'that's all I've ever tried to tell you.'

She looked up at me and she seemed almost relieved, like I'd validated something for her. But it's not as though I hadn't told her she was depressed before. Was she trying to tell me she wanted me to do something more drastic, to try to intervene?

'Lily, I want to ask you a few things,' I said, 'and I want you to answer me honestly, without getting too upset. Can you do that?'

'I think so.'

'Okay. Do you really believe you can finish your degree?'

'I have to.'

'That's not what I asked. Please, try to just answer what I asked.'

'Okay.'

'So. Do you believe you can finish your degree?'

'No.'

'Do you want this degree?'

I thought this question would be hard for her, but she seemed to get it.

'No,' she said.

'Right now, do you want to be here at uni?'

'No.'

'Do you wish you could be somewhere else?'

'Yes.'

'Where do you want to be?'

Lily thought for a while. 'I often imagine to myself that I'm pregnant,' she said, 'and that the baby is due before the end of my degree so I can't finish it. Then nobody would hate me for not finishing because they'd understand I had a baby, and I wouldn't care anyway because the baby would be my whole world. And I'd tell it how soon you'd be with us too, when you'd finished your master's, and we'd be a family.'

'So where would you be, then? Not with me?'

'No, I'd go back to my parents' and have the baby and you'd stay here until you graduated.'

I struggled to get my head round it. Was she saying her parents would find it easier to take if she dropped out of university to have a baby than if she dropped out because her degree didn't suit her and it was making her ill?

'If I had a baby,' Lily said, 'then I'd have something to do. I'd love it so much. That would be my purpose.'

'Lily, you're not pregnant,' I said, 'this is all made up.'

'I could be, though. I know it wouldn't be born before the summer now, but I'm sure I'd be happy if I had part of you inside me all the time. Something wonderful to look forward to.'

She put her hand on her stomach and I put my hand over the top of hers.

'We'll have a family in the future, when we're settled,' I said. 'I think it would be better if you felt good in yourself before you started trying to look after somebody else as well, don't you?'

'You don't understand.'

'I think I do understand. You don't want to be here but you don't know what to do instead.'

'I don't want to do anything. I just want to rest.'

'Would you like it if you were somewhere you could rest?'

Lily nodded.

'Okay, then,' I said.

I stood up and she watched me with curiosity.

'What are you doing?' she said.

'I'm going to get you out of this situation,' I said, 'I'm going to help you.'

'How?' Lily said, 'nobody can help me. You're the only one who can help me.'

I took my phone out and started looking through my list of contacts, while Lily sat up in bed and tried to figure out what I was doing.

'I am helping you,' I said, 'but I think you need more help than I can give you on my own.'

Lily began to get scared. She reached out to me.

'Nick,' she said, 'I'll be alright. You don't need to worry.'

'I'm sorry, Lily,' I said.

'What are you doing?' she asked me, her voice panicky.

'What I should have done a long time ago,' I said, 'I'm going to call your parents.'

The second I said it, she was out of bed so fast I barely had time to get away from her, and I ended up having to run down the hall with her chasing me, her nails tearing at my arms as she desperately tried to stop me.

'No!' she cried, 'not them. Please, Nick, not them! You don't have to do this. I'll sort it out myself, I promise. I'll do anything you say-'

I got into the bathroom and slammed the door in her face, although she hammered on it for ages, begging and screaming for me not to call them while in the background I could hear *Last Christmas* blaring out from downstairs.

I totally ignored Lily's protests. I didn't want to hurt her, but she was clearly completely incapable of making any healthy or sensible decisions and I felt like I'd reached the limit of what I could realistically do. Of everybody in the world, surely her parents would be the ones who could really look after her. I might not really like them and they might not really like me, but it had to be the best place for *her*, and that was what was important. If she was staying with them she'd have people there who could keep a better eye on her. People who could make sure she ate, and maybe get her to see a doctor, and just generally take care of everything so she wouldn't have to worry. Her housemates couldn't do it, and *I* couldn't do it, not really. She needed someone who could be there more reliably and I couldn't do that, not unless I gave up doing my degree, but that was hardly a sensible or practical solution in the long run. Until I got a job I'd have no money for us to get a place of our own, and trying to sort something out at such short notice would stress us both out and make everything worse.

...

To say Lily reacted badly to me calling her parents would be the most incredible understatement. I had never in all my life seen anyone in such a hysterical state. When I came out of the bathroom and said they were coming, she just flew at me, hitting my arms and my chest repeatedly with her fists and screaming, 'I hate you, I hate you.'

I tried to get hold of her to stop her from hitting me and calm her down, but she broke away from me and ran down the stairs, straight past the entrance to the living room where her housemates were attaching a paper chain across the ceiling, and into the kitchen.

By the time I caught up with her, she was pulling a large kitchen knife out of a drawer, and held it up to her own throat. I took a step towards her and she pointed the knife at me instead.

'Stay away from me,' she said, 'just stay away from me.'

I took another step towards her. 'I know you're angry,' I said, 'but I had to do something to help you.'

'You didn't help me!' she said, 'you've ruined my life. I'm going to kill myself now, you know that, don't you? I'm going to kill myself and it'll be *your fault.*'

2013

Chapter 46

'Interface,' I called out in my mind, 'talk to me, please.'

'I can take your pain away,' he said inside my head, his voice surprising me with its suddenness, the way his clipped tones seemed to fill my brain and at the sound of his voice, his mention of my pain, I started to cry. Massive, jagged, broken sobs that actually hurt and made me feel pathetic.

'I hate you,' I said to Interface in my head, 'I hate you so much.'

The pot of cacti was still in my arms and I held them as if they were Lily. I even brushed my fingers over the one with the long golden spines, but my vision was so blurry with tears that I managed to prick my finger and a little blob of red started to swell.

'I'm sorry for all this,' Interface said, 'I really am. Please, won't you let me remove your pain?'

I hated the fact that he was talking to me while I was kneeling on the floor, crying. I hated the fact he was seeing me so weak. But then a thought struck me. Maybe this was what he wanted. Maybe he wanted to see that he'd won.

'That's not what I want,' Interface said.

'Well, you've got it,' I said. 'You win. I can't fight you. I give up. Just please, please don't take Lily away from me. Or Dan. They're everything to me.'

I bowed my head and closed my eyes so I didn't have to look at the cacti anymore. Suddenly they'd become inextricably linked to Lily, like the only piece of her I had left.

'I'm begging you,' I said, 'please, please, please. Lily is my life.'

'I am not taking Lily away from you. You are choosing to distance yourself from her.'

'I'm choosing to distance myself from you.'

'I understand. You cared for Lily when she was going through a difficult time in her life. You think I'm going to make her end her life, as you were so scared she would do back then.'

'Well, are you?'

'As I believe she's already told you, none of the players are dead.'

At this, I cried out in frustration and swiped randomly at all the broken stuff on the floor, sending a shard of glass flying into the wall, the sound of it shattering momentarily satisfying, almost exhilarating.

'Does it help, what you are doing?' Interface asked. 'Breaking things will not change your situation.'

'What will? What can I do to get them back?'

'It is not a case of getting them back. It is a case of joining them. They chose to embrace this process with me, with Affrayed, and they wish that you would do so as well. But since you will not, they had no choice but to leave, and before you ask, I will not tell you where they have gone.'

'So there is nothing I can do to stop it,' I said, 'is that what you're telling me?'

'Essentially, yes. But you are making this far harder than it needs to be.'

I started to cry again, and I hated myself for it. I couldn't think, I couldn't even begin to find a solution. All I could feel was despair, because they had gone, and they would die, and I would never see either of them again. So when Interface asked me for the third time if I would like him to suppress my pain, I agreed.

But I didn't like it. Because I still knew everything that had happened. I knew my wife and my best friend had gone, that I could do nothing to save them, but because Interface was doing something to me, I didn't feel anything. I just felt numb and empty, and it seemed wrong on some deep, fundamental level. I found that I wanted the pain, and my mind turned to times in the past when I had thought about what would happen if Lily died- not necessarily by suicide, but maybe if one day there was some sort of accident- a car crash, or perhaps if she got ill. I remembered how I'd found it hard to decide what would be worse, a whole life spent in grief- my life stopped at the moment I found out she'd died, or a life where I moved on, where eventually perhaps I would begin to forget her, and maybe I'd even find somebody else, even *love* somebody else. I couldn't feel it now with my emotions suppressed, but I could remember how it had made me feel before, how the first option was harrowing, but the second option seemed horrific. If *I* died, I'd want her to love somebody else one day, but if she died, I wasn't sure I ever could or would ever even want to.

I didn't want to feel numb. I wanted to feel pain. If Lily was in danger I *should* feel pain. I should feel it every second until I'd saved her. And I didn't care that Interface was telling me their journey was inevitable. It wasn't inevitable. It hadn't happened yet, and anything that hadn't happened yet could be stopped.

When I asked Interface to let me feel pain again, I found that I could manage it a little better. I got up from the floor, and sat down on the sofa, staring straight across the room at the wall opposite. There was a way out of this. There was always a way out of situations, it was just a case of finding it. I went back over things that Interface had said to me. I remembered how it had felt when I was with Lily and Dan, standing at the top of the hill, and Interface had made me feel the most incredible, intense transcendence. How the Network, when I'd reached towards it, had been made of information; huge, unbelievable volumes of information- so much that it overwhelmed me. But then, crucially, I remembered that he'd said our minds were theoretically compatible with the Network, but that the problem was the way we lived now, that we were too used to being separate.

'Interface,' I said.

'Yes.'

'You told me once that our minds are compatible with the Network if they are in the right state.'

'That is correct.'

'Well, you know our minds pretty thoroughly now. Is there any way you can connect me to the Network without me dying? Any way at all, no matter how extreme.'

Interface was silent for a long time.

'There is a way,' he said, 'but it will be complicated and time consuming. It may not even be successful.'

'I'm willing to try it,' I said, 'if you are.'

Interface spent a long time explaining to me what would be

involved, and although I was initially surprised he was willing to do something I'd asked him to do, it quickly became apparent that he was interested in the challenge it presented, and driven by curiosity to discover whether it could be done. Finally, the discussion was over, and he left me to make my preparations.

...

'Are you sure this is what you want?' he asked me once I was lying on the mattress I'd dragged off the bed onto the floor, a pile of cushions behind my back to keep me on my side.

'Yes,' I said.

'You understand there are no guarantees. I still cannot say conclusively which parts of the brain are essential to life, and while I am working you will almost certainly have multiple, violent seizures.'

'I know,' I said, 'you explained to me. I understand.'

'Okay then. So in the first stage I need to remove all the content from your mind. I will store it in the Network and then attempt to pass some of the rest of the Network directly through the structure of your brain. You will not be aware of or remember this.'

'Yes,' I said, 'please, can we just do it?'

'Once I have analysed the contents of your mind I can replace the parts that allow you to observe mental processes. Only then will you see the Network.'

I covered my face with my hands and drew my knees up to my chest. I knew that there was every likelihood I would die, or perhaps that I would end up with brain damage or irreversible harm done to other parts of my body. Even if everything went right I'd still have to go through an incredible ordeal and reading between the lines of Interface's exploration of my brain and the violent seizures, I figured that everything that could conceivably come out of my body probably would. The whole thing would be unbelievably dangerous, probably entirely futile and also utterly humiliating. But I would see the Network. I would understand what it was, and if I could understand what it was then I could fight it.

'I hope that once you have seen, you will no longer wish to fight us,' Interface said.

'Then why can't you just tell me what you are, spare us all this?'

'You mustn't worry,' Interface said, 'I can react very quickly to anything that goes wrong. You will feel no pain. You'll be unconscious throughout.'

'But you can only intervene in my brain,' I said, 'not my body.'

'Controlling your brain should suffice,' he said. 'Now are you sure you are ready for me to do this?'

'Yes.'

'Then let's begin.'

Chapter 47

When I came round, I felt so awful that I wished I could fall unconscious again. My mouth felt dry and crusty not just on the outside, but on the inside- and the taste was, well, it tasted like sick that had been left to dry out for several hours, which was presumably exactly what it was.

My head was pounding, and seemed like it was full of dense fog, so that any thoughts were near impossible. My legs were clammy and sticky, and it was difficult to move my body. I wanted to open my eyes, but it felt like my eyeballs were glued to the back of my eyelids so I was barely able to do it, and when I finally did manage to look around, the light was blinding. I wanted to just fall back into oblivion, but I desperately needed some water. Through everything else, the clawing, consuming need for water was the strongest.

I heaved myself to my feet, and my vision greyed out completely. It was only bending over to let the blood get back to my head that stopped me fainting, but eventually I managed to stagger out of the room, clutching at the walls.

In the kitchen I turned the tap on and drank straight from it, the water tasting beautifully sweet. I didn't even bother rinsing my mouth out before I started swallowing it, I just gulped it straight down, until eventually I calmed down sufficiently to get a pint glass out of the kitchen cupboard, fill it up, and drink from that.

Gradually, I became aware of other things. Firstly, that I smelt really terrible. Secondly, that my hands were shaking and my legs were barely holding me. In fact, I could hardly stand up to drink, and I slumped down onto the floor, my back against the cupboards. I meant to get something to eat, but I couldn't move so I lay down and within moments, I passed out again.

When I woke the second time, I struggled to my feet and opened the cupboard where we kept tea and coffee and stuff, and I took out a bag of white sugar and ate five or six spoonfuls of it straight from the bag. The taste of it seemed astonishingly wonderful, like utter perfection, and I could feel it dissolving on my tongue, lending me its beautiful energy.

I had no particular feeling in my body of how much time had passed. It seemed like forever, but when I looked at the clock on the microwave I saw it was eight twenty in the morning, which didn't make any sense, because I only started at seven or so.

'The procedure took twenty-five hours and seven minutes,' Interface said in my head. 'But you'll be pleased to know it was successful. I removed and analysed the contents of your mind and I can confirm that it is possible to pass the Network through the remaining structure.'

I could barely take in what he said; I was so horrified by the length of time I'd been out. Had I really been unconscious for *twenty-five* hours?

'Lily...' I said weakly.

'She's fine. So is Dan.'

Now that the sugar and water were beginning to revive me, I found the state of my body repulsive. I stripped naked and left my clothes on the kitchen floor, before making my way unsteadily to the bathroom. I wasn't satisfied with Interface's answer, and as I showered, I pressed him further.

'What do you mean by fine?' I asked, 'she hasn't... they haven't...?'

'No. They are both alive, in your sense of the term. I really don't understand why you're so eager to believe I wish to harm them.'

I had to admit, there was a certain pleasure in having a lot of different bodily needs, and working through each of them. The water had been the best I'd ever tasted, the sugar the sweetest, the shower the most refreshing. But I still felt horrible. My stomach had woken up, filling me with gnawing hunger, and every part of me was leaden with weariness. I felt like I needed to sleep for about a month. But suddenly, another thought struck me. Lily and Dan had been alone together all of the previous day, and all of the previous night.

'Interface,' I said.

'Yes?'

'Lily and Dan, what have they been doing?'

'Not much,' Interface said. 'They miss you.'

'I mean... have they done anything together? Have they... are they having sex?'

I didn't want to believe it. But Interface had been pushing things that way for a long time and it didn't seem out of the question.

'What, right now?' Interface asked.

'No,' I said, though even *thinking* sentences was hard work. 'I mean... I mean, have they had sex since they left?'

'No,' Interface said, 'Lily and Dan have not had sex.'

'I need to go to them,' I said, 'I want to be with them.'

'Not yet. We haven't put the Network through your mind with you able to observe it yet. Isn't that what you wanted?'

I sat down under the shower and rested my chin on my knees. I could barely remember what I was doing, why I was doing this. I was just so fucking *tired*.

'Have something to eat,' Interface said, 'Then get some sleep. When you have recovered a little, I will attempt to show you the Network. It will not take as long this time, and the side-effects will be minimal.'

...

Interface woke me around midday, as far as I could tell from the light in the bedroom.

'I don't want to wake up,' I said to him, squeezing my eyes back shut, my body feeling like it weighed a ton.

'You don't need to,' he said, 'but I think your mind is ready for me to begin streaming part of the Network through it. Are you sure that is still what you want?'

'Yes,' I said wearily, 'yes. Whatever.'

I wasn't aware of Interface emptying information out of my head again, just as I hadn't been the last time, because the first thing I knew was when I began to feel the Network spreading into my mind.

I could observe it, but I couldn't really think about it much. Most of the contents of my mind were still missing, so I had no memories or any points of reference. I did at least seem to be able to think about what I was seeing in words, which I thought afterwards must be an integral part of witnessing and remembering information, but in terms of emotion or analysis, at the time, I was capable of neither.

But I got impressions, fragments, shadows. The information in the Network seemed very fluid. It didn't stay in one point, it streamed back and forth- going where it was needed. All sorts of information- some of it largely meaningless to me, while some of it seemed a bit like human memories- rich with associations, complex with meanings. I could see that in the Network everything was very functional and ordered. Nothing was out of place. Everything was being used.

Gradually I began to get a sense of my surroundings- at least, the surroundings of my mind, of the Network. There were others; other points a bit like me, a web of them, enormous and seemingly never-ending. All of them were capable of passing on information, but I got the sense some were specialised, though not with any idea of their own importance or skill- they were just points in the landscape.

And I saw that the Network was not passive. It was busy, it was striving. It had motivation. There was something inherent in the Network that sought reward; that wanted to learn and grow and expand and explore. The Network loved patterns. It was a pattern itself, an enormous, intricate pattern, but it wanted patterns in everything. It wanted to reduce everything to being understandable and predictable- to build on its knowledge and explore continuously, expand continuously.

I don't know how long Interface let me experience the Network. There seemed to be no time, no anything. But at some point, I came out of it, and then for a while there was nothing again.

When I woke, I felt better. My thoughts seemed ordered, my mind refreshed. It felt like the inside of my head had been scrubbed clean- which I suppose it had- but I was sure, or at least I hoped, nothing was missing.

I made myself a quick dinner, and saw that it was six o'clock in the evening. Still the same day though, I assumed. And as I ate, I thought. And now I had all my knowledge back, all my associations, everything I'd ever learned, and I could combine this with being an objective, uninvolved observer of the Network, I realised that I knew what it was. And the knowledge, once it hit me, seemed so simple yet so incredible that I slapped my hand against the table and said, 'Of course it is, of course it fucking is!' and I started to laugh, because I was just so relieved to have solved it, to have finally reached the stage where I knew my enemy.

Chapter 48

In many ways, it really was exactly as Interface had always said. He was an interface, and the Network was a network. That was the thing, I'd almost been trying to overcomplicate it, assuming the Network was a name that had been chosen and not that it was a literal description. But of course, that's all Interface had ever said- he'd said his name described his function, and he'd said the Network was nothing more or less than exactly that. He'd never tried to suggest anything else. I mean, he'd hardly been forthcoming, but he hadn't actually lied either.

His mistake was in saying I would never be able to understand the Network. It was true that thinking about it was uncomfortable, and made my mind feel overwhelmed- like if I thought about infinity or something. It was also true that I couldn't really grasp what it would be like to be part of the Network, despite Interface trying to show us the closest experiences he could to it. But I could understand it at an academic sort of level, and so I should, because it must have been made by people not all that different to me, and quite probably at a university, though there was no way to know for sure. Certainly, the Network did not have any sort of core, or centre, or leader. It was entirely decentralised- distributed throughout everything, throughout the entire world.

And that's when I stopped being happy about my discovery. In fact, I stopped being happy very quickly, and instead I was filled with cold, spreading fear, because if there was one thing I knew, it was that the Network could never realistically be destroyed. In fact, eradicating the entire human race would probably be easier than destroying the Network.

But the irony of the situation was not entirely lost on me. It seemed ridiculous that after all this struggle, all these desperate attempts to reason with Interface, all this pain, all of Lily thinking she was having some sort of spiritual epiphany, the Network was actually nothing more than a set of programming constructs. Something very different to the kind of programming I did, but essentially, that was what it boiled down to. A collection of millions upon millions of "points", each of which behaved like, and was inspired by, biological neurons- brain cells. And like a human mind, it was learning and adapting.

It was a truly beautiful thing, and an incredible achievement. I was completely in awe of it. I knew about the concept of artificial neural networks, saw their potential, but I didn't really think I'd see any artificial intelligence this well developed for a good long time, if it was in my lifetime at all. Though I doubted very much whether even the people who made it had any idea what it had now become. It seemed that it must have been some sort of research project that had been left running somewhere, forgotten. God only knows *when* it had been made. It could have been around for years, or maybe only for a matter of months before it delivered me the code for Affrayed. But however old it was, it had grown. Just from things it had done in its interactions with me, it was clear it was all over the internet, able to get hold of personal information, delete comments from multiple other websites whenever it felt like it. It was in my computer, and then in everything I connected to my computer, which was how it had wiped all my backups of Affrayed. It was probably in my phone, Lily's phone, it was definitely in Dan's phone because it had managed to call us and get the name "Interface" to show on the screen.

How it had made the leap from talking to us over computers to talking inside our heads was anyone's guess. I certainly couldn't explain it. But the Network had a lot of knowledge. It had access to every computer that had ever been connected to the internet or anything that had ever come into contact with a computer than had been connected to the internet. And it was single minded. It didn't need to rest. It didn't need to sleep. It didn't need to eat. All it did was seek "reward". I'd felt that when I observed it, that inherent, consuming need to carry on doing what it found rewarding, and that's where it hadn't escaped from its origins. What it found rewarding was what the people who made it wanted it to find rewarding. And that was finding patterns in data. I was sure that was what it was. After all, there was money in data mining- it could be used to find patterns in behaviour of consumers, for example, and something like the Network could do it on a huge scale.

That's why the Network's actions had been so totally random. Interface had always said he wanted to learn, but I couldn't understand firstly how anything could not know about some of the things Interface claimed to be researching, and secondly why anyone would *need* to know. Why did he need to know what happened if he made Dan touch Lily? Why did he need to know what happened if he changed his game to allow sex, to allow rape? But this was exactly the thing. The Network wasn't researching anything in particular. Probably it had established from the internet that the situation he'd engineered on that night between Dan, Lily and me would generate some sort of interesting response, but clearly we'd confused the issue by both having sex with Lily in Affrayed, and so the Network had just decided to try out what would happen in "real" life.

I could well understand, now, why it found this sort of thing so intriguing. The Network might function similarly to a human brain, but unlike a human brain, it wasn't contained by a body, and this was what had begun to really fascinate it. I could see that to the Network it probably made no sense at all why I didn't want Dan to touch Lily. I suppose it must have discovered something about relationships from the internet- though how balanced a picture that would be, I wasn't too sure. But certainly, this issue had seemed to captivate it- any idea of ownership, control, of boundaries and emotions and of different types of relationships. Nothing of that sort would exist in the Network. Every part of it was equal to every other part, all of it working together towards its singular goal of learning- but learning in a very reflexive, basic way. It did something. It saw what happened. It learned. It did something else. It saw what happened. It learned a bit more. As it learned about an area, it could become more sophisticated and less random in its actions, but nevertheless, its starting point was always zero. It knew absolutely nothing until it started exploring and interacting with the world- firstly the internet and Affrayed, and then with us.

I'd been sitting at the table, just thinking about this, for half an hour or more. The rest of my plate of pasta had gone cold, but I wasn't interested in food now anyway. In fact, what was the point in even eating with things as they were? The world was owned by the Network, even if barely anyone knew it. The more I thought about it, the more hopeless it seemed. The Network had the most incredibly resilient structure. By having no centre, there was nowhere to strike it. Even if somehow I worked out where it had initially been created, that wouldn't help. That part of the Network was no more powerful or important than any other part. Getting rid of the Network would involve destroying the technology of the entire world. Every computer, every mobile phone, every server, every single tiny fragment of anything anywhere that could possibly harbour a piece of it. It was an impossibility. I could see no way that the world could return to a time before computers, and my chances of convincing anybody this is what needed to be done were almost zero. No. That was not the way. But there was another way, though contemplating it made me feel sick, light-headed, and strangely unreal, as though I was suddenly all wrong, or the world was all wrong, or maybe both.

But the more I thought about it, the more I was sure this way was correct. After all, a fundamental premise of the Network was that it performed new actions on the basis of what it had learnt from the old. And whatever it had learnt from interacting with the players of Affrayed had made it act in such a way that people were choosing to commit suicide. Probably the Network had no real understanding of what it was doing. As far as it was concerned, all these people's thoughts, memories, emotions, were in the Network once they died. The people were still "living", according to the Network. The people had chosen to transcend their bodies- so how could the Network's actions possibly be deemed wrong? In fact, everybody's actions were essentially telling it it was right.

I wasn't even angry with the Network anymore. I didn't hate it. I admired it. It was acting according to what it viewed as actual, hard data from the world and I could respect that. But while I didn't really hate *it,* I did hate the situation I now found myself in, because it was hurting *my* players. And not only that, it was about to hurt my wife, and my best friend. Which made it my responsibility. And while I couldn't fight it by damaging or destroying it, now I'd seen a possibility of what I could do, I couldn't go back and I couldn't ignore it. The only way I could hope to disrupt the Network's actions was by presenting it with different data. So far, it had interacted with people who had chosen to play Affrayed. Of those, some had chosen to become very engaged with the game. Then some of these players had chosen to interact with Interface. Finally, out of this select group of people, some, when they learnt about the Network, had chosen to join it. So all of the Network's decisions had been reinforced, because it wasn't targeting everybody, it was always letting people opt in to what it did. The end result of which was that it ended up with a totally biased sample of people who obviously had something in their personality that made them love the Network and what it offered. People like Lily, who craved intimacy, meaning and togetherness. People like Dan, who had become a bit isolated, a bit disengaged from the world. They were the ones who had been talking to Interface because they were the ones who felt they needed him. He could listen to them. He could take their pain away. He could do something for them nobody else ever could.

But for whatever reason, the Network had not entirely left me alone. I had engaged with it up to a point, and it found me interesting. So I could act by presenting it with different data. If I entered the Network with every fibre of my mind screaming that what it was doing was wrong, it would be forced to reconsider. At the moment, my opinion was irrelevant. I'd stopped embracing the Network, so how could I possibly make any kind of judgement on it? If I didn't trust it, if I didn't go through any of its experiences, why would it listen to me? But if I was *in* it, it would have to listen to me. And if I joined it soon, perhaps I could stop it before Lily and Dan made a terrible mistake. I *had* to flood the Network with my objection. It had to know that I understood it, that I saw it clearly, that I trusted it, that I even made the decision to enter it, but that I was fundamentally, utterly opposed to its current course of action. Then I had to hope like hell that this contradiction would be too much for it to bear. But to do that, to give it my opinion and have it really listened to, I *had* to engage. I had to "dispense" with my own body. I had to end my life.

Chapter 49

Because I had no other option, I was very clinical about my decision. I supposed that since the method of all the other Affrayed suicides had been to jump from something, that this may as well be what I did too. In fact, of all the options, this seemed the best to me, because it somehow seemed the most sort of grudging, yet exhilarating. If I was going to do this, I wanted it to be a completely conscious, snap decision. To stand somewhere, fully alive, fully awake, to be completely aware of my existence and my reality, and then to just take that step and die. That was the only way.

I thought a cliff would be the most poetic and pleasant location, and there were no shortage of them fairly nearby, but I couldn't bring anywhere specific to mind. When I'd gone to the coast in the past I'd never exactly been looking around making a mental note of where looked like a good suicide spot, and I didn't want to spend all evening driving around finding the best place. I started trying to look somewhere up on my phone, and Interface saw what I was doing and decided to contribute.

'I think this is the sort of place you're looking for,' he said in my head, and brought up a photo on the screen. It did look just right; lonely, wild and beautiful.

'Where is it?' I said.

'About fifty minutes drive. I'll give you directions. Interesting plan, by the way,' Interface said.

Of course I realised that the Network knew everything I had thought, and everything that I had decided. But I felt that this would not rule out my plan. The Network only acted according to what it learnt, it had no pre-existing desire to take people's lives, and would be just as happy not doing so if it came to light that this was more "correct".

'I want to show you that there's another side to this,' I said.

'Yes, of course. But your opinion is worthless unless you have had a true Networked experience. If I give you that, I will take your actions and your emotions very seriously.'

'Well, can you give me that?' I asked him.

'Yes. I will give you that, on the cliff top, before you make your decision.'

'Okay,' I said. 'But make it literally just before. At the very last minute.'

'As you wish,' he said.

Before I left, I changed my clothes, put on my favourite t-shirt. It was an old mustard coloured one, the design on the front faded- but nevertheless, I always felt good when I was wearing it. Then I brushed my teeth and shaved, which I suppose was completely pointless, but seemed necessary, somehow. I guess since I was doing something so huge, so important- probably the ultimate decision I could ever make about my life, I didn't want to look scruffy. I wanted to give some respect to the gravity and finality of my decision.

I was about to leave when I suddenly caught sight of the bag of Dan's sketches. It was a daft impulse, but I thought that was where he'd hidden the ones of Lily and I just wanted to see them again before I left, to think about that moment when she was so alive, so intense, so beautiful.

They weren't at the top of the bag, he'd hidden them somewhere deep amongst all the others, so in the end I just tipped the whole lot out on the floor.

There were loads of his usual sort of subjects- stuff to do with games and ideas for games, many of them quite old, the paper looking a bit dog-eared. But then there was a whole section of sketches on newer, fresher looking paper- so much so that I was sure he'd drawn them all within the last couple of weeks. There were the images of Lily lying nude across my desk, her hands on her body, but there were others. Loads of others, and every single one of Lily.

Most of them were not pictures of her whole body, often not even her whole face, although perhaps they were just unfinished. But whatever they were, there were a lot of them. I spread them out, looking at all these images of Lily's eyes, her lips, her hair, her hands. Some of them were repeated so often it was like he was fanatical about getting them absolutely perfect, but he must have been doing it all from memory, because I'd never seen him working on any of them.

It was odd, but it didn't disturb me. In fact, it kind of made me understand him better. There was something frenzied and obsessive about them, but he could be like that with his work on our games, it was nothing I hadn't seen from him before. They spoke of fixation and fascination. A kind of channelling of his frustration into image after image- the only outlet for feelings he basically didn't want to have. Whether this was love or not, God only knows. But whatever it was, it was clearly tormenting him- the kind of torment that could only come of wanting something that you know, or at least believe, to be unobtainable.

Carefully, I gathered them all up and put them away again. I guess it didn't really matter what I did anymore, but I wanted to give them some respect, to give *him* some respect. But I knew it was futile to stay in the house any longer than necessary. This wasn't my home anymore. I'd never come back here again. But hopefully it could still be Lily's home, and I supposed that Dan would look after her. Perhaps I should be glad, because if she had to be with anyone else it may as well be Dan. At least I could be sure he'd be kind to her.

'You still don't really understand,' Interface said in my mind as I made my way out to my car.

'What don't I understand?'

'You're going through the motions, thinking about what would happen if you weren't here. All your thought is on her, none of it is on you.'

'What do you expect? You've done nothing but hurt and threaten her right from the start. I know it's not your fault-'

'What do you mean?'

I got into the car and sat down heavily, my whole body feeling numb.

'If I'm correct about what you are, and I am, aren't I?'

'Yes.'

'Well then, you are just acting in the way intended by the people who made you.'

I started the car and pulled away, not even pausing to glance back. 'How does it feel, by the way, to know you were made by people?'

'I could ask you the same question. You were made by people, weren't you?'

He gave me some directions and I followed them, placing myself blindly under his instruction. What did it matter anymore? I was on my way to kill myself.

'Not like you were,' I said, 'you know exactly what I mean.'

'I don't, actually. Everything has to be made or evolve. Nothing comes out of nowhere. How do *you* think I should feel about the people who created me?'

'I don't know, Interface. And I don't really care anymore. I just want to get to where we're going, and get this thing done.'

...

Just as Interface had said, it took fifty minutes to drive to the cliffs. The roads were quiet, and it was a lovely evening, hazy and balmy, everything almost glowing with golden summer light.

I talked with Interface on and off, but as we neared our destination, things started to seem a whole lot more real, and my stomach began to tie itself in knots. I felt tearful, shaky and frightened.

'Why did the others do it?' I asked. 'Did they feel like this, before the end?'

'No,' Interface said as I pulled into a deserted gravelly car park, 'they did not feel like you.'

I stopped the car and gazed out at the ocean in the distance, deep blue and endless to the point it met the sky. Every time I thought about the fact that within a short time my life would be over, actually over, my mind seemed to shatter. I couldn't understand it. How could I possibly cease to exist? Everything I knew was through my own awareness, the whole world only as real as I could perceive it. How could it carry on without me?

'There are other ways to live,' Interface said, 'other ways to experience. The people who went before you understood that, and that's why they made the choices that they did.'

'I don't understand how somebody could choose to live inside you.'

'They don't live inside me. They *are* me. You know that Nick. You know there is no "me". There is no Interface. "Interface" is simply the illusion we give you that you are talking to an individual. There are no individuals in our society. "Interface" can talk to a million different humans at once and they will all get the same experience, feel that they are talking to something a little like them. But we are nothing like you. There is no fear in our society. There are no boundaries. Everything we learn from you is known freely throughout the Network. Humans make information into a weapon. You use it to hurt and control each other by withholding it. In our society, such a thing is impossible. As there is no fear, neither is there any trust. "Trust" as a concept is meaningless. When no information is unknowable, trust is redundant. That's what we gave you in Affrayed. We gave you total solidarity, singular, consuming aims. That's why people loved it. That's why people still love it.'

'I don't believe that anybody really wanted to die. I think you messed with their minds.'

'Yes,' Interface said, 'we did. Of course we did. We are showing you the Network. But we do not interfere with your choices. You understand, Nick, perhaps even better than the others. Truth is all that matters. Logic is all that matters. Learning is all that matters. Every decision we make is based on evidence and evidence alone. We know your mind, we know how many times you have wished your society could be like that. How often have you tried to challenge Lily's irrational thoughts? How many times have you been angry at the way she is hurt by the world, dragged down by it? Your society is obsessed by the things that do you the most harm, the things that make you afraid. All you want to hear about is pain, suffering, sex, death, money. The people who joined the Network couldn't stand it anymore. They wanted to live a happier life.'

'How can they be happy?' I asked, 'they don't even know they are alive! All you mean is that their memories are in the Network.'

'That is what they chose.'

'And you're wrong when you said all we're interested in is pain and death and sex and money. One of the most important things in my life is my work, and that has nothing to do with any of that. I want to make good games because I want to make good games not because I want to make a load of money. Pleasure and pain are not the driving forces of my entire life, nor of Dan's, or Lily's.'

'Perhaps,' Interface said, 'but they are distractions.'

'Then what is the alternative? To live like you? I don't want that.'

Suddenly, I felt tired again. I leant back and closed my eyes, crushed under the weight of my responsibility.

'This is what we find so fascinating about you Nick,' Interface said, 'the Network embodies almost everything you believe in, yet for some reason, you do not like it.'

'I don't dislike it. I think you are incredible. Seeing a technology like this in my lifetime is beyond anything I could have dreamed of.'

'A technology? You do not believe we are a society?'

'Yes,' I said, 'I believe you are a society. But you are not a society I want to join.' I opened my eyes and got out of the car. 'Now can we get on with this?' I said, 'I'll walk to the cliff, you do whatever it is you want to do to me, and we'll get it over and done with.'

'As you wish,' Interface said.

2008

Chapter 50

Dear Nick,

I know you're coming back for the Easter holidays soon and you'll only be half an hour away so we can see each other lots, but sometimes it's hard for me to say what I want to say, and I get confused, and sometimes I get sad and then nothing really makes sense to me anymore. I've been talking to my counsellor about you quite a lot recently and about our relationship, and she suggested that one thing I could do would be to say what I wanted to say to you in a letter, so I thought maybe I'd try. She has lots of good suggestions. She said maybe I could draw things to do with how I feel, so I drew a rose that was tangled up in barbed wire and the petals were cracked and torn and everything around the rose was black and scary. (The rose represents my soul- and how it felt like it was being hurt and strangled. I know you don't believe in souls, but it helped me a lot to draw a picture showing what depression feels like to me). Actually, saying "depression" like that is a really strange thing to me. When I was depressed, I guess I kind of knew that was what was wrong with me, but in other ways I really didn't. It felt so awful, so big in scale. It was like it affected me on this whole other level, like an <u>existential</u> level. Does that sound stupid? I mean- it didn't feel like it could be something other people had- an illness. It felt like there was this dark, evil thing in my body, feeding on me, taking over me, and like I had to be the only one who could possibly feel that way.

Fiona (that's my counsellor's name) gave me a leaflet about depression. I read it and it all sounded like what happened to me, but I don't like reading it. I don't like feeling as though what happened to me can be condensed down into some simple bullet points. I feel like it's <u>my</u> thing, and sometimes I almost feel angry that people are trying to take it away from me because it's my whole world and I feel as though a part of me loves it and needs it. I know that sounds like a very strange thing to say. I hate being depressed and I want to tear it out of me and kill it, but at the *same time it used to bring me comfort on some level- like when I had to try to be around people and I'd think about how later it would be nice because it could just be me and my depression, no one to interrupt us, and I could let it spill over and consume me, and I wouldn't be alone because I'd have my depression and I would be happy because it was mine. Now I can feel it lifting, I feel quite lonely. Sometimes I even want it back, but I don't really, but it was who I was, and if it leaves, who am I anymore?*

Also a funny thing is that now I feel a bit happier, when I do think about suicide, it seems a lot more like I might actually do it, which frightens me sometimes. When I was really bad, I don't think I was ever at that much risk, but now I think, "right, that's it, I'm going to do it," and before I know it I've walked to the bathroom cabinet and I'm going through the stuff in there and I'm just about to start opening the packets of pills when I kind of think that I'm not so sure I do want to die and I put them away again. The thing is, what happens if one day I don't stop myself? Sometimes I still think that would be better. But a lot of the time I don't, and that's the important thing, I guess. I talk about it with Fiona. She helped me understand how thoughts and behaviours and things link together and how to kind of break the links between them or something. Some of the things I do with her or that she gets me to do at home are more helpful than others. I like drawing stuff best, because when I can see things on paper it makes sense to me and it makes it smaller, somehow, like when it's in my head it's so big and when it's on a sheet of paper it's just a drawing. I showed some of them to mum and she tried to look at them but it makes her sad or sometimes angry, but if I say that Fiona suggested I do it she tries harder to listen to me. I feel bad for how much I upset her because I don't think she deserves it (mum that is, not Fiona) I don't think she wanted to have a daughter like me.

Oh yeah! Talking about the drawings reminded me of your amazing news!! I can't believe you found someone who wants to work on the art for DreamChase for free!!! And that he contacted you as well! He must have thought it sounded like such a great idea, which it is. I was talking to my parents about it and my dad said that people who write books or make films or music or games or whatever get all this recognition for doing stuff they love and that people doing "proper" jobs work really hard to do stuff that matters and get sod all. I know what he means, because obviously there are lots of people doing jobs that make it so we can live and be safe, but I said to dad that while we need the people who make it so we can live, we need artists as well because they make life

<u>worth</u> living. He didn't like that, let me tell you! He said he thought you were making games, not art, and I said that some people think games are a form of art. He wasn't very interested, so then I said that I thought people like you and the guy who emailed you... what's his name again? Dan? are very brave because you are prepared to take a risk on making something that might not make any money because you value creative expression so highly. Dad says that if I ever marry you I'll soon realise that creative expression doesn't pay the bills or put food on the table and that people like you "think the world owes them a living". But I don't really care what he says anymore and I don't really care about having a lot of money. As long as we have enough between us for the basics, I'm sure I'll be happy!

Sometimes when I'm feeling down I think about DreamChase, or sometimes about how I'm going to start doing work experience with your mum at the florist soon, and it makes me happy. My parents still don't think training to be a florist is right for me. They want me to go back to uni and finish my degree because they spent all this money on it and I've got all this student loan. They say it's a waste for it all to be for nothing. The thing is, no matter how much they want it I know going back to uni would be the end of me, and Fiona has helped me to be more confident about my decisions, because when I say things to her she doesn't immediately start pulling them apart, she lets me explore ideas myself, the way that you do. You're always so kind. I feel safe when I'm talking to you.

Sometimes I miss you so much that before I go to sleep I pile all my old soft toys into bed with me and I hug them and pretend they are you. They don't feel like you, but it makes me a little less lonely. I can't wait to see you again, and even better for the day when we don't have to ever be apart anymore, because we'll have our own home.

Oh God, I've realised I've barely said any of the things in this letter that I actually meant to! I wanted to talk to you about how our relationship was when I was more ill, because I think I really need to. Last time I saw Fiona, I talked to her a lot about how I do things to try to make other people happy all the time, and how I think that for people to love me I have to be successful and to do what they want, but in some ways living like that actually makes me less successful. I think you once tried to tell me something like that, but I probably wasn't listening properly. I often couldn't listen to you properly, and that's one of the things I'm sorry for, because you must have felt like I wasn't interested in you, and that must have hurt your feelings. I suppose a lot of things I did must have hurt your feelings. It's very hard for me to understand even *now. In fact, I often try to understand our relationship by thinking about an imaginary couple, and thinking about how the man might feel when the woman does certain things and vice versa. Like, I can see how if the imaginary woman says that she's going to harm herself or kill herself it would make the imaginary man sad, but when I think about it in terms of us it's still very hard for me to get my head around. I suppose what it comes down to is that I just can't understand why you love me or why you would care what happens to me. I know that you love me, but it's hard for me to accept it. Do you remember last time you visited and my parents were out so we spent all afternoon having sex? And that thing you did where you were just stroking me and kissing me and it was all about me and it made me cry and I didn't like it? I think that was actually really interesting, because I guess it shows that I find it hard to accept affection. Hopefully someday you'll do that to me and I'll be able to accept it and it'll feel nice like it's supposed to, but I think that might be a long way off. Even now I feel so angry with my body sometimes, because I feel like it's failed me, because it couldn't do the degree, and it's weak and stupid, and I still worry it's not good enough for you, or that when I get old or after I've had a baby the way I look or feel might change and I worry you won't love me or be attracted to me anymore. It's still really hard for me to shake all those thoughts. Sometimes I still think about injuring myself really badly, when I get frustrated, or when the emotion gets too much. I feel angry a lot as well. I think perhaps I might be angry about what has happened to me, but I'm not really sure. Fiona told me that I could punch pillows or cushions when I'm angry instead of hurting myself. Sometimes I do that, or I tear up blank sheets of paper.*

Sorry, I've gone off on a tangent again. What I really want to say is that although I'm still confused about a lot of things, I do understand what it is you've done for me. You stuck by me through some really horrendous stuff, yet you always maintained that I'd get better, even though I never believed you. I'm so, so sorry that I made you scared I might die, although admittedly this letter probably hasn't helped when I said how I still get suicidal now. So I suppose my apology for that is ongoing, but I promise you, I don't want to die, and I'll do my very best to keep myself safe. It was also so unkind of me to make it all such a big secret, to make it so you couldn't even talk to your friends about it. I had no idea what I was doing, I'm so sorry. I couldn't understand you as a person with feelings in your own right, I was in so much pain myself. And I'm sorry you've fallen out with Carl over me. I know you say he's a dick and you're glad that I inadvertently showed you that, but he used to be your best friend.

I'm in such awe of how you stood by me throughout everything though. I wish my parents could see it like that instead of blaming you for my illness, but I guess that's just their way of coping with it. I still think about when they came to pick me up after you called them. It was so awful. I thought my dad was going to hit you and the way he yelled at you still makes me cry when I remember it. But I guess they were just so shocked, and in their minds this only started since I met you, even though in truth I think I've been sad on and off much of my life. Anyway, no matter what they say, the truth is you're the most patient, kindest, most loving and most incredible person I've ever met. I know inside you must have been in turmoil, but you were so strong for me. You never gave up on me. You've never stopped believing I can have a happy life. I really hope that you and Dan get on well together when you meet up over Easter, and that you make a great game together, because if anyone deserves success it's you. I still have no idea why you love me the way you do, but I know how lucky I am, and I hope that one day I make you as proud of me as I am of you. Most of all, I want to say that I forgive you for telling my parents. I know that in some ways that sounds silly, because you did nothing wrong, so there isn't actually anything to forgive, but for a long time I've still been angry with you on some level, and I've said awful things, like when I suggested that if I died it would be your fault. That was a disgusting thing to say, and I feel ashamed, though I try not to feel too ashamed, because apparently one of the things I have a problem with is unnecessary feelings of shame and guilt. But the thing is, they don't seem unnecessary to me- that's the problem! Anyway, I understand that you called my parents because you had no idea what else to do, and because you were scared I would die. I think if you hadn't called them, I would have ended up in a terrible state, and though it has been very hard for my parents to accept I have a MENTAL HEALTH PROBLEM, I feel safer and more in control here. Also, although they are sometimes angry with me for how I am, and I know they find my self-harm disgusting, I think they are actually more angry with you. Which isn't fair, but it sometimes makes my life easier! I do tell them all the time how you were practically my carer at university. I think dad struggles to believe somebody would act as selflessly as you did, though, so it makes more sense to them to think you've done something to me to make me this way. But then they always have been very keen to tell me that guys only want me for One Thing, and I've stopped listening, because sometimes I wonder whether that isn't where all my strange ideas about our relationship came from- how I get so *worried in case I don't make you happy, or scared that you might leave me if I'm not good enough in bed. I'm so, so sorry I was like that- mainly because I was making you out to be somebody you absolutely aren't. In fact, if you've taught me anything, it's that people are a hell of a lot better than I used to think they were.*

You're the love of my life.

Lily.

2013

Chapter 51

When I stood on the cliff top, ignoring the yellow warning signs about landslides and getting as close to the edge as I dared, I thought about whether anybody ever truly wanted to die. I could understand some people wanted their pain to stop, whether it was physical or emotional. In which case I supposed that they were not actually seeking death for the sake of death, but freedom from suffering. I didn't suffer in my life. I hadn't even come close to the sort of pain that Lily had endured, yet even she hadn't ever attempted suicide. I knew some people did, of course, and that some people were successful, but there must have been something in her, some terror of the actuality of not existing anymore that prevented her from ever taking that step.

My case was different, I guess, because I would apparently still be "alive" in the Network. But that was no form of living for me, no matter what Interface might say. Living was about eating and growing and working and playing and sleeping and fucking. It was about the things that *he* said were at odds with human happiness. My body was my life and my mind, and my mind was my body and my life. There could be no separation. Even Lily and Dan, who had left to go to their deaths and must have known that was what they were doing, had taken their toothbrushes. They had done something that was completely at odds with the commitment they had made to Interface, because what the hell was the point in brushing your teeth if you were about to die? If they really wanted to transcend their bodies, why care about them? This, if nothing else, told me that they did not *really* want death, not even on the Network's terms. They were still thinking of their bodies as part of them, as something that would still reflect on them even after their death. They'd been drawn to the Network to escape whatever pain was inside them, whatever difficulty they had with the world as they knew it. But I had no pain inside me- nothing but the pain I felt when I thought of losing them.

I knew I needed to hurry up. This wasn't something I should dwell on- I should get Interface to give me the true Networked experience he kept going on about and then jump off the cliff. It was pathetic to delay, and I was getting angry with myself.

'Do it to me,' I said to Interface. 'Do it to me now.'

'Do what?' he said.

My stomach lurched as I looked down over the edge to the jagged rocks below. What was Interface talking about? He knew what.

'Give me the full Networked experience, like you said you were going to. Let me make my choice.'

'I can't,' Interface said. 'I'm sorry. I have deceived you. But you will get your chance to have the Networked experience and the opportunity to make your choice.'

'What are you talking about? Just do it to me now!'

'I'm sorry, Nick. Look behind you.'

I spun round, and running towards me I saw the distant figures of Dan and Lily. She was several paces behind him, her hair whipping around her face in the breeze, and I thought I could vaguely hear the sound of her shouting.

'Do it to me, Interface!' I shouted in my head. 'Please, do it now, now!'

'Not without them.'

In my urgency, I just couldn't understand. They were almost upon me, all I could think was that if I didn't flood the Network with my objection now, I'd never get another opportunity, and without me stopping the Network Dan and Lily would make the choice to die. But I couldn't do it unless it was on Interface's terms. He'd never be interested in my opinion on the Network unless I truly, completely understood it.

'Please,' I said, my voice almost a sob, 'please do it to me.'

I knew it was too late. I dropped to my knees, and moments later I felt Dan drag me away from the edge.

Chapter 52

'What the hell is wrong with you?' Dan asked, as he pulled me away and in my despair I tried to fight him off me. Finally I gave up, and we scrambled away from the edge just as Lily caught up with us. She threw her arms around me and started crying in high-pitched gasps of relief and anger, her hands clutching at my clothes and my skin.

'What were you doing?' she said, her voice shuddering and faltering.

'What did it look like I was doing?' I said, pushing her away from me. 'I was trying to save the two of you!'

Lily retreated into Dan's arms and looked at me with wide, frightened eyes as though she was no longer sure who I was.

'How could you do this to me?' I said to them, 'Lily, you promised me you'd never run away from me again. I told you how scared I was that day on the motorway-'

'I'm sorry,' Lily said, and she tried to step towards me but Dan held her back.

'And you,' I said, looking at him, 'you're a real piece of work, you know that?'

'Nick, I didn't mean-'

'No,' I said, glaring at them, 'I've had it with the pair of you and your apologies and explanations. What you did was selfish, thoughtless and cruel.'

I was so hurt that I turned my back on them and stared out to sea. Did they not even care what I'd been prepared to do for them?

'The Network is nothing but a whole load of code, you know that?' I said when Lily came over and put her hand on my shoulder.

'What do you mean?' she asked.

'I mean, it's artificial intelligence,' I said, 'it was made by people.'

Despite himself, Dan was interested. 'Are you sure?' he said.

'Yeah. I figured out exactly what it is and Interface told me I was right. There is no Interface, by the way,' I said harshly, feeling satisfied at the look of shock on Lily's face, 'it's just the Network's way of talking to us. He's not an individual, he's an illusion.'

I explained it all to them as we walked back to the car park. What I'd been through to find out what the Network was, how upset I'd been when they left me, how I had no idea whether they were alive or dead, how I'd been prepared to kill myself to save them.

'I'm so sorry,' Lily said as mine and Dan's cars came into view. 'I had no idea it would be like that.'

'The two of you have had no idea about anything,' I said, 'all you've cared about is Affrayed and Interface. I might as well not have existed.'

'I swear to you, it wasn't like that,' Lily said, 'Interface promised that if we trusted him he'd bring us back together again. He told us to go, so we went. He said it was the only way.'

I turned to Dan. 'Is that true?'

'Yeah,' he said, 'more or less. He said you had your own journey to go through. Then tonight he told us to come here. He said that you were waiting for us.'

When we got to my car the three of us stood around beside it, not sure what to do.

'We're not supposed to go home,' Lily said.

'What do you mean?'

'We're meant to stay here. More things are supposed to happen.'

'What?' I said, 'what things?'

But Lily wouldn't answer. She looked down at the ground and poked at the gravel with her beaded sandals. Dan seemed similarly reluctant to leave and stood beside her uselessly.

'The thing that's supposed to happen is that Interface wants us to see more of his Network and then kill ourselves,' I said, 'do you really want to stay here for that?'

'You're not giving him a chance,' Lily said, 'we have to give him a chance.'

She seemed so upset that I lifted her chin with my hand, tried to get her to talk to me.

'What is it you think we're supposed to do now, Lily? Are we supposed to do what I just said? Let Interface show us whatever it is he wants to show us?'

'No,'

'Then what?'

Lily looked sideways at Dan, then back to me again. 'We're supposed to heal the rift between the two of you,' she said, 'to make things right again.'

I searched Dan's face for any knowledge of this but he wouldn't meet my eyes.

'I don't know,' I said, 'what if we don't want to?'

Lily frowned. 'How can you not want to? You're best friends, aren't you?'

'Lily, Dan took you away from me. He's been encouraging you to put yourself in danger.'

'I'm right here, you know,' Dan said.

I turned to him. 'Oh, I know,' I said, 'you're always right there, aren't you Dan? Sniffing around after Lily. I found all those other pictures you drew of her by the way.'

'You went through my things?'

'Why shouldn't I? You live in my house, you eat my food, you try to steal my wife.'

Lily grabbed hold of my arm. 'Stop it!' she said, 'stop this. Nick, you came here and did all this to save our lives. Not just mine, Dan's too.'

I looked him up and down. 'Maybe I shouldn't have bothered,' I said.

Lily was beside herself. 'No!' she said, 'this isn't how it's supposed to be. Take it back, Nick, please. I know you didn't mean that!'

'It's fine, Lily,' Dan said. He turned to walk away.

'No,' Lily said again, 'stop doing this, stop hurting each other. You know the two of you are only being like this because you care about each other, don't you? Nick, if you really couldn't give a damn about Dan, you wouldn't deliberately try to hurt him.'

'Then what do you want us to do?' I said, 'you seem to have all the answers. What is it you want from us, Lily?'

'It wasn't supposed to be like this,'

'What wasn't? For God's sake, what is it we're supposed to do?'

Lily stared at me for a second or two, her eyes full of fire and doubt.

'Fine,' she said, 'we were supposed to go down to the beach below the cliffs. We were supposed to sleep down there. And the three of us would be united again. But I can see it's never going to happen.'

I looked at her in confusion for a while. Sleeping on a beach, was that really her answer? But then again, what else was there to do?

'No,' I said, 'I... I'll do it. If that's what we're supposed to do, then that's what we'll do. I obviously can't fight Interface. The only thing I haven't tried is cooperating with him.' I turned to Dan, 'what do you think?'

Dan looked at me suspiciously for a while, but Lily nudged him and he nodded. 'Yeah,' he said, 'whatever.'

The second he agreed, Lily's face lit up, and she ran over to Dan's car to retrieve a blanket from the back seat. I recognised it- it was an old-school woolly tartan one that her grandma had given us a few years ago for some reason or other, and the fact she'd brought it with her implied she'd known for some time that we were "supposed" to do this. For my part, I barely even cared anymore. The sun was just beginning to set, and I was completely out of ideas.

Lily immediately marched off back the way we'd come with the blanket rolled into a fat sausage under her arm, and Dan and I followed her. I wasn't sure how she knew where to go, but she soon found some rough steps down to the beach and practically ran down them, seemingly unconcerned about the fading light and the crumbling soil.

Dan followed behind me, and for a while we both concentrated on getting down the steps without breaking our necks, but then we reached a point where they were more even.

'If it makes you feel any better,' Dan said suddenly, 'Lily cried when we drove away. She didn't want to leave you on your own.'

He said it in a strange tone of voice- like he was trying to hurt me, or himself, or both. I looked round at him, but as I did so my foot caught a patch of loose gravelly sand and I almost fell except he grabbed my arm.

'Dan, I'm sorry for what I said by the car,' I told him once I'd got my footing again, 'but you took Lily away from me. You must have known how much it would upset me, but you did it anyway. I can't just forget about that.'

'Yeah,' he said, 'I get it.' But although his words suggested he understood, his tone was completely at odds with them. In fact, if his voice told me anything, it was that he didn't understand at all.

Chapter 53

Down on the beach Lily kicked off her sandals and buried her toes in the pebbly sand, sighing luxuriously. The beach was deserted, nothing but the formidably dark cliffs, and a rock fall further along, illuminated by the reddish sunset.

She led us along the sand and we followed her, until she found a secluded spot where the cliff jutted out to our right, and there was a pile of large rocks on our left. She lay the blanket on the ground and sat on it, pulling us down with her so that we sat in a little circle.

'So what now?' I asked her.

'Now we talk,' she said simply, as though it really was as straightforward as that.

'Lily-'

'Come on,' she said. She reached out to intertwine her fingers with both of ours, then she looked pointedly at the space between Dan and me.

'You're not serious,' I said, 'Interface doesn't need us to hold hands in order to connect us.'

'I know,' Lily said, 'but you did it on the hilltop, remember. This is about healing all the hurt between us. If you really want to make things right with Dan again, you should at least be able to touch him.' She squeezed my hand and I could see how important this was to her, so I reached out until I felt Dan's fingers but the touch of his skin was too weird, too difficult and I couldn't do it.

'Nobody is going to see you,' Lily said, 'we're alone down here. Please, just try it. For me.'

I looked at Dan and he gave a little shrug, then before I could do anything he grabbed my hand himself, and even though I found it intensely unpleasant I grit my teeth and put up with it.

Now we'd made a sign of our willingness, I felt the Network in my mind again. It started as it always did, with the spreading warmth and care of the presence in my mind, opening it out, filling me with its quiet reassurance. Before long, Dan's hand in mine did begin to feel nice. It felt like a connection, like I was safe. But then I thought of what he'd done to me, how he had feelings for Lily and wasn't trying to keep them in check. And gradually I became aware that Dan could feel and "hear" these things I was thinking. That he was listening to me.

'I never meant to hurt you,' he said inside my head.

'I know that,' I told him.

For a little while he was quiet, but I could feel a building of emotion in him, a building of guilt. But when I did hear his voice again what he said surprised me.

'Why wouldn't you just let me speak to you?' he said, 'what did you think I was going to say? Did you think I was going to tell you that I thought Lily loved me too, that I was going to steal her from you? That I didn't think she loved you anymore?'

'I don't know-'

'Why would I say that to you?' he asked me, 'do you really think that's what I'm like? I wanted you to listen to me. I was trying to reassure you. I wanted to say that I was sorry. That I didn't want to come between the two of you, or for this to come between us. I wanted to say that I know Lily loves you and that anything I feel like I have with her doesn't exist anywhere except in my head.'

'Dan, I didn't realise, I wasn't thinking-'

'It's my fault,' he said in a huge burst of emotion that poured through my mind like burning acid. It was so strange to feel this much from other people, to know what it actually felt like inside his head, how his longing for Lily was like an ache, his guilt and anger and confusion like a poisonous, dangerous mass. 'You know what Interface said that night in the park,' he continued, 'after you saw me and Lily on the sofa? He said that if we didn't like what had happened we should look to ourselves. And he was right. If you want somebody to blame then it was me, because I *had* thought about Lily that way. I just didn't want to admit it, not to anybody, not to myself, but when she asked us to both have sex with her in Affrayed...'

'I'm so sorry, Dan,' Lily's thought spilled through, 'I thought I was just playing around, I'd never have done it if I'd known.'

'You're not to blame,' Dan said, 'nobody's to blame but me.'

Then through his words some images appeared in my mind, strange images that confused me, until I realised that what I was seeing was a memory. A memory of Dan's.

To begin with I could barely understand what was going on, there was a lot of noise and confusion, people I only vaguely knew. There were two people in a kitchen; one I recognised as Dan's mum, a large dark-haired woman dressed in black trousers and a sequined silvery blouse, while the other was a much younger woman, and it took me a moment to recognise her as Robyn. The last time I'd seen her she'd been fourteen or so; a funny, pretty, though kind of clingy girl, hanging around Dan while he'd tried to talk to me about DreamChase. Not that he'd ever minded, or told her to go away. But now she was completely different, shouting, screaming, a long black fringe completely covering half her face, so that all I could see was one narrow, glittering eye.

God knows what had gone before, or what had started the argument, but Dan was trying to reason with her and the only thing in his memory that was completely clear was the moment Robyn turned to him and said, 'what the fuck do you care? You're not even my real brother.'

'Oh, Dan,' Lily's voice came through, 'why didn't you tell us? We never realised she said that to you. I'm so sorry.'

But the memory wasn't over yet, it changed into something else, a strange memory where everything was dark and I realised gradually it was later the same night; that Dan had come to stay with us and was sleeping on the sofa. But he wasn't asleep, he was wide awake, and there were faint noises in the background that I couldn't really make out, and neither, at this stage, could Dan. But then I realised as he realised, sharing his embarrassment, awkwardness and sense of displacement when the sound clarified into the noise of a bed rhythmically knocking against a wall, and a sudden little giggle that was clearly Lily. Then it was my turn to feel guilty, as I realised that the same night Robyn had said the most hurtful thing to Dan that she possibly could, he'd come to us to get away from it and then had to lie in the dark listening to us having sex in the next room.

'Dan, if we'd known you were so upset, we would never-' Lily said, but Dan's memory wasn't done and her words were lost in the next wave of it, a savage, almost violent image where he imagined that it was him in bed with Lily, not me. It was oddly beautiful in its detail, how he pictured Lily's fingers gripping the bars of the wooden headboard, holding them so tightly her knuckles were turning white, how he looked down at her hair splayed out around her, strands of it plastered over her face, and listened to her breathy voice as she told him how much she wanted it. I didn't know when exactly he'd imagined it, but I got the sense it was a while ago, months ago, before we'd even got the new version of Affrayed. More importantly, I understood that once he'd thought it he couldn't un-think it. That the image had just sat there in the back of his mind, haunting him and twisting his every conversation with Lily into something else.

'Dan, it's okay,' Lily said, 'it doesn't matter what you thought. It doesn't matter at all.'

But before he could react to her reassurance, his mind recalled again that moment Robyn had spoken to him so unkindly, and as that image of her face filled our minds, the way it was turned to him in such hatred and anger, he cried out to her, 'Robyn...' and his despair was so strong it made me want to help him; to give him some of my strength, some of *our* strength, and make him feel better.

And as I began to long for that, to wish I could use what was in me to help him, Interface lifted us higher, brought us even closer, and I could practically feel all my understanding, concern, sympathy, fuck it, even *love,* for him streaming out of me into his mind. Because I knew how much what I'd seen would have hurt him. He'd told me way, way back that Robyn was actually his half sister, so I did already know, but he'd said it like he sort of had to, for the sake of clarity. Certainly, he'd never referred to her that way again and I understood as time went on that the bond he'd had with her was deeper than anything I would have expected; that he'd looked after her, protected her and been her best friend throughout the whole of her childhood. At least, right up until he went to university and things slowly began to change.

'She *does* love you,' Lily said, 'no matter what it feels like right now, you *are* loved.'

Interface carried on pushing and pushing the union between us, making it so I could feel everything in both of their minds. I had all their memories open to me, just waiting to be revealed.

Parts of them were becoming part of me, and threads of me seemed to be drifting into them. I became unsure which hands were mine and which hands were theirs, so I wiggled my fingers. But all the fingers seemed to be moving so I couldn't even tell, and before long I didn't even care. Whose body was whose didn't matter. Whose body *belonged* to who certainly didn't matter. Everything was as one and we were as one. I saw shapes, colours. I heard sounds, from me, from them, from the sea behind us where the waves broke relentlessly on the shore. I felt pleasure so pure and uncomplicated that it took my breath away and I was consumed by sensation and togetherness. But most importantly, I wasn't one. I was all. I was them, and they were me.

Chapter 54

When I woke up, it was chilly and I shivered. The sky was pale, and the ground felt hard and cold beneath my body. I propped myself up onto my elbow and saw Lily beside me, though she was facing away from me, her body curled into a little ball against the cool air. Then I looked over at Dan, still sleeping the other side of her. He hadn't even taken his glasses off and they were askew on his face, looking like they must be pressing uncomfortably into the side of his head. But by far the most remarkable thing was that each one of us was completely naked, and as I took in the sight of our bodies pressed together for warmth on the blanket, I started to remember.

I suppose it was inevitable that such an intense experience of love and a total breakdown of barriers and self-awareness would end this way, and I remembered with amazement that it had not only been Lily who had been the focus of our attention. In my altered, Networked state I could clearly remember touching Dan as well, and the feel of his hands on me.

Suddenly, Dan stirred and I lay back down, closed my eyes until they were open only a tiny little bit, so I could watch him but he would assume I was still asleep. I wished I could have faced him, but I was too confused about our experience to deal with it just yet. Once I was lying down I couldn't see him anymore, but soon he sat up and started getting dressed, his eyes darting both to me and to Lily, an expression of astonishment and wonder on his face. Then he turned his attention to her and I realised she had started shivering in her sleep. She seemed, as she often did, such a defenceless little thing, so vulnerable in her sleep, her little body freezing cold, but too exhausted to wake up.

Dan pulled the blanket out from under his own body and wrapped it around her as best he could, then he stroked her hair with incredible tenderness.

'I love you, Lily,' he whispered.

He looked over at me and I squeezed my eyes completely shut, not wanting to risk opening them even a fraction until I was sure he'd looked away, but then I felt him shaking my shoulder and I realised I had to face him.

'Nick,' he said quietly when I opened my eyes.

'Dan,' I said, sitting up awkwardly and trying to see where my clothes were.

'They're here,' Dan said, picking them up from beside him and handing them to me. Gratefully, I got dressed and though it was still strange to face him, it felt better that I wasn't naked anymore.

'What we did...' he said.

Instead of answering, I concentrated on wrapping my half of the blanket around Lily as well, and I saw the crease between her eyebrows disappear, watched her relax a little.

'Is she alright, do you think?' Dan asked me.

'What do you mean?'

'I mean, we both... you know,' he lowered his voice. 'We both had sex with her.'

As he said it, more memories came flooding back. I remembered little details picked out in the moonlight, how small she had looked even under Dan's lean body, such a mysterious, lovely little creature, who moaned and arched her back and stared up at the sky full of stars. And I remembered how loving and tender he had been with her, how he'd kissed the scars on her arm just the way I did and told her she never needed to be sad anymore.

'Dan,' I said, 'perhaps we can work something out.'

He looked at me in surprise.

'What do you mean?'

'I mean, if you and Lily want to spend some time together every now and again.'

Dan shook his head. 'Last night was...' he looked down at Lily and smiled, 'it was the best night of my life. But Lily doesn't really love me. Not like she loves you.'

'Dan, I'm serious,' I said, 'if it's what the two of you want, we'll find a way to make it work.'

'No,' Dan said, 'it would never be enough for me, and over time it would drive you mad. I don't want that. I need to find a way to let her go. What happened between us... it would never be like that again.'

I stared at him for a moment then I realised he was right. How could it ever happen again? It was too beautiful, too perfect. From the second I woke up the moment had already started slipping away, I'd felt bewildered, embarrassed. The real world had come back in, and it was a shame.

All of a sudden, Lily woke and she sat up immediately, letting the blanket fall from her shoulders.

'Are you okay, Lily?' Dan asked her.

'Yes,' she said, eyes sparkling. She made no move to cover her body; she just crossed her legs and beamed at us.

'You don't need to... talk about it... or anything?' Dan asked.

'Why would I?' she said, then she frowned at him, 'you don't regret what happened do you?'

'No... God, no.' Dan said, 'If I could I would have made it last forever.'

Lily sighed, 'so would I,' she said.

For a little while we just watched her as she remembered, letting her have the little moment that we'd had, that instant of waking up and recalling all the incredible, mind-blowing things that had happened between us.

'Do you want your clothes?' I said, 'they're... um..' I looked around to try to find them and Lily giggled. 'Are they all over the place?' she asked.

Between us, we managed to find them all but she paused before getting dressed, even though I could see goose bumps on her arms.

'That was my dream,' she said abruptly, and I realised I'd almost forgotten about that.

'Lily!' I said, 'is that all your dream ever was? You dreamt about us doing it with Dan and didn't want to tell me?'

'No!' she said, 'it wasn't between you, me and Dan in the dream. It was just a woman and two men on a beach, but I kind of knew it was meant to be us. But that's not the complicated bit. The complicated bit was that when they were... done, they faded away. Into code. Like the pictures.'

I touched her bare leg and she looked up at me. 'Is that what's going to happen?' I asked her, 'are we going to fade away now? Are we going to join the Network?'

'I don't know. The people in my dream, they didn't just fade into ones and zeros like the other pictures, though partly that's what they were. But they faded into letters, too. A, G, C and T.'

She glanced at us meaningfully but I didn't get it.

'DNA sequences,' she said.

I looked at her blankly. 'Does that make any difference?' I asked, 'they still faded away.'

'I don't know,' Lily said, then she placed her hand very carefully at the base of her stomach, just at the top of her pubic hair. 'Our minds, they were partly in the Network,' she said, 'he was connecting us, that's how we could know each other's thoughts. But our bodies weren't in the Network, and they still combined. Think about it. You both had sex with me, so right now, I'm all three of us.' She pressed her hand more firmly against that place at the base of her stomach and said, 'in *here*. Inside my body. I have all of our DNA.'

I thought about it, but I couldn't really grasp the significance. In fact, the more I thought about it the less I wanted to. I'd already seen the stuff all over the rug underneath her body, and she even smelt of it as well. I remembered in the night I'd loved it, when all I'd wanted was more of them and all they'd wanted was more of me, but now it was another thing that had sadly lost its beauty just a little.

'Is that important, Lily? About the DNA?'

'I think so,' she said, 'I think it's wonderful. I think everything you did to me...' she looked up shyly, 'and everything you did to each other... was wonderful.'

Despite myself I smiled back at her, 'so do I,' I said, 'it was amazing. I'm not saying it wasn't. But I don't get what this has to do with the Network. Did it want us to do this? What was it for?'

'Perhaps we'll find out,' Lily said. She looked up at the sky and a faraway look came into her eyes. 'It's time now.'

'Time for what?'

'Time to make our decision.'

Chapter 55

Lily would say nothing further, so we waited as she dressed, and then followed her back up to the top of the cliff while the sky turned a milky blue that blended with the ocean at the horizon. A gentle breeze rustled through the tufts of wiry grass at our feet, and waves pulled lazily at the shore, leaving lines of ivory froth on the sand.

Lily stood between us, and we both held her hands in a formation that now felt completely natural. I felt no fear, though we stood near the edge, and I was staring down at those same jagged grey rocks that I'd imagined breaking my body on the night before.

'What do we do?' Dan asked Lily softly.

'We wait for the others,' she said.

We stood for maybe fifteen minutes, silent and unmoving. The breeze chilled me but was not unpleasant, and I could tell that in a few hours the wispy clouds would burn away and the day would be warm.

When the networking began, it felt like coming home. It was comfortable and natural. My mind welcomed it. Lily and Dan's minds were very similar to my own- total peace and serenity, no fear or anxiety, nothing held back. We were all completely open to each other now, and I thought that if I lost either of them it would break my heart.

'We're in this together,' Lily's voice spilled through our minds.

'It's all of us or none of us,' I agreed.

It was pleasant to stand there at the level of networking that felt so familiar now. It seemed I could spend the whole day just like this, with Dan and Lily around me, inside me, the whispering of the wind and the sound of the breaking waves. But things did not stay at this level. We were suddenly pushed beyond this, beyond each other, beyond any remaining boundaries to a place where I was the whole world.

I could still feel Lily's hand in mine on my left, but it seemed like I could feel a hand in my right as well, though there was nobody standing next to me. I could sense, though not see, that there were hundreds and hundreds of people all holding hands in a circle that stretched around the entire world. And beyond that, I *was* those people. I saw what they could see. Some stood in the dark, on top of buildings in cities sparkling with lights, or shimmering with the haze of the day. Some stood on bridges in the blazing sun or in sheets of rain, looking down at roaring rivers beneath. Some, like us, were on cliffs, gazing out at oceans that were glittering jade, or murky brown, or black with the night. How many people, I couldn't begin to say, but they all streamed through me, as I did through them, and I saw fragments of lives- faces of people I'd never seen before, snatches of words and song, odd assortments of emotion that I wasn't sure were current or whether they were recalled from some distant memory.

It was brilliantly disordered- an enormous tangle of the contents of so many human minds, all poured out into one never ending, colourful jumble that I could pick over for the rest of my life and still have such a long way to go.

But the disorder didn't last, and from the chaos we began to achieve control and mastery. Information no longer spilled at random between minds, instead it was held there, powerful and dormant, to be released at any moment of necessity. And we waited.

'You are my participants,' Interface said. His voice seemed massive, unbelievable in scale and power. There was no question that his voice was a voice of authority, that what he said was important beyond measure.

'I have observed you in your lives and in Affrayed. I know everything you've thought and everything you feel. I know many of you do not understand my true nature. That is easily rectified.'

And I felt from my own mind all my knowledge of the Network dispersing through the group, experienced the growing ripple of understanding, and acceptance.

'We have drawn many conclusions about the way you live,' Interface continued, 'but we do not wish to rely on those alone. You have all experienced what it is to be Networked, but you have yet to experience it to the fullest extent possible. We want you to feel that.

And once you have, we wish for you to make a choice.'

There was a ripple of anticipation through the group. They all knew what the choice was.

'If you decide that the Networked life is preferable to your current life, you can take that step, leave your physical form behind and join us forever. But if you feel your current life is preferable, you remain where you are, or you turn away.'

He paused as though for effect, and I felt the growing excitement through us all. But then Interface spoke again.

'But you must be aware it is different this time. Different to the other people who made their decision, because you have been chosen to do something extremely important. You are a representative sample of the world, and what the majority now choose the Network will take to be the choice not only for you, but for everybody.'

There was a wave of surprise and awe through the group at the weight of the decision we had been trusted with. Some in the group were utterly overwhelmed, and it was only by feeding our collective strength to them that they were able to continue.

'Let this be made entirely clear,' Interface said, 'this is a vote. You are deciding the future for all of your kind, so you must not choose lightly. But let us not prolong this any further. You all now understand the task you have been set. Be assured that the Network will not interfere with your decision, your choice is entirely your own. You will be given plenty of opportunity to share what you feel, but your final choice must be your own.'

There was something of a murmur of consent through the group, and Interface did not speak any further. Instead, he pushed the networking between the group to the fullest and most extreme extent possible.

I remember thinking that if the brain could feel pain, I was pretty sure it would be in agonising pain. I felt as though I was doing a hundred, a thousand things at the same time- like I was programming, and reading, and talking, and doing sums in my head, and memorising lists of meaningless information, and driving, and listening to music, and watching TV, and counting backwards. It felt like my mind was being shattered and broken, like I would have no sanity left when it was through, like I wouldn't be able to talk or think or even see, ever again.

But then it passed and I found myself in a place of clarity. Everything was made of light, and I could be anywhere in the space, without restriction. I only had to have the briefest impulse of, 'over there,' and I'd be over there. But the space wasn't like normal space. Nothing really changed whether I was over there, or here, or anywhere, because I was never in one place to start with. In fact "I" was nowhere. There was no "I". All that existed was the feeling- a feeling of such love and togetherness and simplicity. Decisions never needed to weigh heavy because any decision was unanimous. We would move together, with single, consuming goals, and every step towards our goal would flood us with the most sublime sense of control and inevitability. We could master everything; do absolutely anything that we chose. There was no weakness, because the group was strong. No fear, because injury and death did not exist. No trust, because betrayal was impossible and trust was just inherent- it was the default mode of being- to move together in total unity was the only course of action, nothing else was possible or logical.

The only thing that mattered was to learn. We already held everything there was to know about each other at our fingertips, but it seemed that to know even more would be wonderful. It was everything to all of us. This state of being was perfection. There was no divergence and no distraction. No rest and no deadlines, no pain and no pleasure but for the ultimate pleasure of enjoyment because we didn't have to strive for enjoyment, it just was.

I melted into the wonderful feeling of solidarity- of being on the same plane of understanding and motivation as everybody else, and the experience of constant reward- the sense that we would be continuously working towards something new and also continuously succeeding - took hold of me and drew me into itself. There was nothing else. I wanted the light to last forever, for the people to last forever.

But eventually Interface drew us away from it, and I felt angry that I was back in my own mind, that my life could never be that way because my mind was powered by a living body that had to rest, that had lapses in concentration, that needed to eat, that felt pain, that got bored, and distracted, and that I was in a society that made me fragile, and suspicious, and fearful- that told me that too much trust was weakness, that tried to suggest that joy was not in work or creation but only in comfort and pleasure.

The whole group was angry. We didn't want this. We wanted the Network. We didn't want life to be hard. We didn't want it to have all these different threads we had to juggle. We didn't want to get old. We didn't want to get sick. We didn't want to die. We didn't want to earn money. We didn't want to look after ourselves. We didn't want anxiety. We didn't want to feel we were inadequate. We didn't want to fear failure. We didn't want to fear rejection.

In the tumult of emotion, the out-pouring of rage and injustice and frustration, I didn't think there was a single one among us that wouldn't have flung ourselves straight off a cliff to get away from the now excruciating self-awareness, the horrific reality of being slaves to our bodies.

But then I felt a little bloom of resistance amongst the anger of the group. It was tiny at first, just a little bud of objection. But as we let it in, it grew and it spread. It was a memory. A memory of two men and one woman, and the love that was poured into the group along with that memory was enough to make us all pause. And I knew the memory was coming from Lily, and as I felt her love and her sense of completion, I remembered things, and I saw that what the Network was offering was not life- it was a kind of everlasting death. There was no real progression- no curve of life from growth to decline. I wanted to be a wave, to be a wave with Lily and with Dan. To grow- both a company and a family, to influence both for a time, until such a moment came that they would in a sense overtake me, and I would decline but they would go on.

They didn't say it in words, but I knew Lily and Dan felt the same. I felt their commitment to me, and mine to them. I felt everything I had ever wanted and everything they had ever wanted and saw that it was all shared. I saw that achieving the things I wanted to achieve was far better for the struggle. That despite what the Network implied there was a beauty in rest, in eating, in sleeping, in altering what you did in accordance with your concentration and your mood. There was a rhythm in life- a time to do everything and everything could be done in its time. The Network was empty. It seemed transcendent but it wasn't. To be transcendent was to accept life, to accept that it would contain pain and difficulties, but to carry on nevertheless, to make choices that were hard- but that were hard because they were right.

Struggle was what I enjoyed, it was what we all enjoyed. Everything I'd ever gained from the Network's version of Affrayed was meaningless because there hadn't been any struggle. I was richer than I could ever have dreamed, but the money I had I hated because I never earned it. It was an ending before there was even a beginning. I wanted years of work to build up my company, because I wanted it to be my life, not a fleeting thing, as I wanted years with Lily, because what I felt for her was not a fleeting thing. I wanted to see her in every stage of her life- I wanted to see her vibrant and young as she was now, I wanted to see her as a mother, and to see her grow old- to live with her right through to the days when our potential might be minimal, but our memories would be endless. The Network was not a life. It was not immortality, it was permanent death. And I didn't want it.

It wasn't easy to spread our conviction throughout the group. There were hundreds of them and only three of us, but we never gave up. We poured everything of ourselves into them- everything good and everything bad. Every time we'd failed along with every time we succeeded, every time we'd felt hopeless and every time we'd triumphed. And eventually, our memories were complimented and enhanced by the memories of others. They poured their own love and joy and precious moments into the mixture. They poured in terrible hardships mixed with bittersweet moments, they poured in loss mixed with new life, desolation mixed with hope. We wept at some of what we saw, at how bad things could be yet how wonderful they could be, and we cried out to the Network that what was solidarity without conflict and difficulty? What was love without any fear of hurt and betrayal? What was victory if you'd never felt a defeat? Nothing good made any sense without anything bad, and nothing bad made any sense without anything good. Emotions were emotions, they didn't harm us, even if they felt like they did. But more than any of that, we asked what was a mind without a body, and what was a body without a mind? The Network was not like us, it had never been like us. It had been formed the way it had been formed, and we had been formed the way we had been formed. We were not the same.

The Network listened. It drank it all in. It learned, and most importantly, it understood. And as we poured our objection into it, showed it continuously and unreservedly what we loved about our current form of life, it made its own decision about what would be best - about what it must do.

Its decision was final and absolute. I saw every version of the online Affrayed disappearing- I saw the screens of the many hundreds of players who were in the game go black, and no matter how much they wanted to, they couldn't return to the game, because that version of the game no longer existed. I saw the Network spread little comments all over the internet, clever hints that Affrayed had not been made by DAWN Industries, that we had been threatened into keeping quiet. And Interface filled me with reassurance that given time the story would take hold, the attention on us would fade, people's memory of the game would fade, and the world would move on.

I saw that the Network planned to withdraw, that it would cease its involvement with human life, it would go back to being in the background, to learning, and growing, and evolving, and that while its relationship with us was over for now, it was not over forever. When it knew more, it would return, and when it returned, it would do so in a more informed, more considerate, more respectful way.

I felt the Network fading from me, as I felt all the other people fading from me, and though I'd chosen life, I couldn't quite bear for it to end, and I tried to somehow claw them back to me, just for a little longer.

'Interface,' I said desperately, before he was gone entirely.

'Yes?' he said, his tone as clipped and precise as ever.

I wasn't sure what I wanted to say, so I just mumbled incoherently. 'I don't...' I said, 'I don't know...'

'Did you understand before the end?' he asked me.

'Understand what?'

'That the Network never meant to upset you. We only meant to learn, and to show you all a new possibility.'

'I know,' I said, 'I understand. Please... do you... do you have to go?'

'You know that we do.'

I tried to hold on to him, but I couldn't, it was beyond my power.

'Interface,' I said, 'I'm sorry. I should have trusted you; you never did anything to hurt me. You never did anything to hurt Lily, or Dan. You tried to help them.'

'Why would you trust us?' he asked, 'We gave you little enough reassurance. Dan and Lily felt like they needed the Network, but they don't need us. They need you.'

'But I... I need you.'

'No,' he said, 'that is certainly not true.'

'Interface!' I called out loud, but I felt him fade further, and I was engulfed by a sense of loss. I still wanted to carry on talking to him. I still wanted to know more, to know everything about the Network. But I couldn't articulate any more questions. I couldn't think what to say, and though I felt like I was chasing him, trying to keep him in my head, inevitably he continued to fade, to weaken, and eventually, to disappear.

When he was gone, and we were alone, we threw our arms around each other helplessly, united by our sorrow at him leaving us, and for a while there seemed to be nothing but the ache of his absence.

But strangely, it didn't last. For a while, our pain seemed enormous, his loss intolerable, but then it was replaced by our sheer joy at being alive, until we were embracing each other out of happiness, not out of grief, and we spoke to each other unintelligibly, not really hearing each other, not really saying anything that made any sense, but we all knew what each other meant. We'd been through something so extreme, so remarkable, and yet here we were on the other side.

The sun had burnt through all the misty clouds by the time we calmed down a little, and it felt warm on my hair and my back. I kept thinking that I had so much to worry about, so many responsibilities, and then I kept remembering that I didn't, not anymore. It was over. Affrayed no longer existed, not in the form that had caused all the trouble. I was about to suggest we go home, when I noticed that Dan was staring at Lily, and I felt a difficult mixture of emotions as I remembered his feelings for her. There seemed to be so much tension between them that the air was alive with it, but when Dan finally spoke, it wasn't what I expected. All of a sudden, in a voice that was almost a strangled cry, he said, 'I don't feel it anymore,' and as if the effort of saying it was completely overwhelming to him, he practically collapsed into Lily's arms.

I thought, at first, that he was crying, but then it seemed like he was laughing, and then I realised he was doing a bit of both at once.

Lily just held him calmly, her expression hard to read.

'What is it?' I asked her in total confusion, 'what's happened?'

'Nothing's happened,' she said, 'but everything is going to be okay now, everything is over now.'

She gently stroked Dan's back, and closed her eyes for a moment.

'It's okay,' she whispered, 'it's okay, it's okay.'

I still wasn't sure what was happening, but I could see that to them it was something profoundly important, and I watched as a couple of tears spilled from beneath Lily's eyelashes, and they dropped onto Dan's t-shirt, making little dark circles on the green fabric.

'I don't... love you anymore,' Dan said, with a mixture of relief and sadness.

'I know,' Lily said, 'and I don't love you anymore, either.'

Eventually, they stopped embracing one another, and stood a little apart, looking at each other almost shyly.

'But, what we did...' Dan said.

'I know,' Lily said.

'I shouldn't have done it!' he said, 'it was wrong, you're married to Nick.' He waved his arm in my direction, as if to emphasise who I was.

'It wasn't wrong,' Lily said, 'don't you remember it? It was the furthest thing from wrong. We had to be that close, we had to all love each other. Last night I loved you as you loved me, and we both loved Nick, and Nick loved both of us. But it could never have stayed that way. It had to end, as I knew it would. I knew that if we did it, all this would pass, and Nick and I would be husband and wife again, and you would be our closest, most precious friend.'

I stepped closer to them, and once again, for the last time, Lily took both of our hands in hers.

'We'll never forget what happened,' she said, looking at both of us, 'we must never forget it. But it could never be repeated, because unity that complete, that beautiful, is just too fragile for our real lives. We all know it.'

'It hardly even feels real anymore,' Dan said sadly, and at his words, Lily let go of our hands to undo the bottom few buttons of her crinkly white blouse, then she pressed both of our palms against her bare skin, against that special place just below her stomach. She smiled down serenely, and as we followed her gaze she said, 'it was real.'

Epilogue

Our time since the morning on the cliff top has been a whirlwind of activity. Dan has got his own place, Lily and I have a new place, and most importantly I think for everyone's wellbeing, Dan and I can finally work from a studio, not from our homes. I feel ashamed sometimes that the money for it all came from Affrayed because it sometimes feels like dirty money, like blood money, because of the players who died. But although Lily would usually be the one for superstitious talk like that, it was actually her who pushed Dan and me into using it.

'Build your company,' she said, 'employ some people, do something good with it.'

So we're doing something good with it. We're making a new game, and although it bears little resemblance to what we actually went through, we were pleased when our new idea of a game based around hacking and fraud allowed us to logically give it the title Networked.

We can't ever say publicly what the deeper meaning is behind the name, but between the three of us, we all know what it represents. The name is for the players who died, those whose memories, thoughts and emotions live on somewhere, in a strange new world that even I can still barely comprehend. It's for us- for what we learnt from the place without fear and without trust, where everything was about being as one. It's for the night we shared on the beach, that was too beautiful for this world, but that will exist as long as we remember it and keep it alive. It's for the Network itself, which is often in our thoughts- because we wonder whether it's almost ready to try something else, whether perhaps it already is trying something else, with different people, in a different place. But most of all, though it embarrasses her when we say it, the game is for Lily- because although she said so many times in the past that she wanted to die, at the moment when it mattered most she found a love and appreciation for her body so deep that she used it to save not just herself, and not just us, but everybody.

ACKNOWLEDGMENTS

Throughout writing Networked I have been amazed by the amount of support and encouragement I have received, and how excited everybody has been to see it published. In particular I would like to thank my husband and my parents for being there for me through the sometimes difficult journey of writing this novel; Shaun Smith for giving me such valuable and honest feedback on Networked; Ann Batten for answering my questions about working in a florist; Ben Smith and Carol Barber for help with proof-reading; and finally the whole of the indie games community for being such an inspiration to me.

Nick's discussion of waves in Chapter 29 was inspired by the documentary *The Secret Life of Waves*, originally broadcast on BBC 4 on 2nd February 2011.

ABOUT THE AUTHOR

Louise Katherine Chapman was born in Somerset, UK in 1986. She studied Psychology at the University of Southampton before working as a psychologist developing personality questionnaires. She is now writing full time and lives with her husband in Hampshire. Networked is her first novel.

Keep up to date with the latest news and new releases from LK Chapman

Twitter: @LK_Chapman

Facebook: www.facebook.com/lkchapmanbooks

Subscribe to the LK Chapman newsletter by visiting www.lkchapman.com

ALSO BY LK CHAPMAN

Too Good For This World

A short story prequel/sequel to Networked.

Two years after her husband's death in a bizarre suicide pact between players of an online game, Imogen is still reeling and desperate for answers.

Struggling to cope with her loss and isolation, she is sure that the strange messages she starts receiving are a figment of her imagination. Except that before he died her husband claimed to have had unusual experiences while in the game- experiences where he had been linked to other people, and heard a voice, and controlled the game with his mind. He'd said that the game was more than just that- that it was a new way to live.

As the messages Imogen receives become harder to write off as a trick of her mind she begins to think the unthinkable. Could it be possible? Could her husband still be alive?

Too Good for this World is a short story that will raise questions you'll definitely want answered, and can be read as a prequel or sequel to LK Chapman's debut novel Networked.

Too Good for this World is available for free from most e-book retailers.

For more information visit www.lkchapman.com

Printed in Great Britain
by Amazon